Mothers

Mothers

a novel

JAX PETERS LOWELL

AN AUTHORS GUILD BACKINPRINT.COM EDITION

iUniverse LLC
Bloomington

MOTHERS

AN AUTHORS GUILD BACKINPRINT.COM EDITION

iUniverse books may be ordered through booksellers or by contacting:

iUniverse LLC
1663 Liberty Drive
Bloomington, IN 47403
www.iuniverse.com
1-800-Authors (1-800-288-4677)

Originally published by St. Martin's Press

ISBN: 978-0-5952-9857-0 (sc)
ISBN: 978-1-4917-3213-7 (e)

Printed in the United States of America.

iUniverse rev. date: 04/18/2014

For John

We shall not cease from exploration
And the end of all our exploring
Will be to arrive where we started
And know the place for the first time.

T. S. Eliot
—Four Quartets

AUTHOR'S NOTE

Twenty years ago, *Mothers* was a fictional depiction of what lay in store for two women who wanted to have a child of their own in New York City in the sixties and seventies. There were no books like *Heather Has Two Mommies* and children of such unions suffered greatly. The acronym LGBT did not exist, nor did the concept of same-sex marriage. Simply having sex with a person of the same gender was a crime and the basic rights lesbian and gay parents enjoy today were part of an unimaginable future.

The world of Claire and Theo and their son Willy, may seem quaint in light of the great strides made by the LGBT community in recent years, perhaps even implausible to millennials who take such things for granted. But make no mistake, *Mothers* is a cautionary tale. This commemorative edition enters an America where women's social and reproductive freedoms, once a settled matter, are again up for debate and, in many states, under assault. If I have learned anything, it's that rights are never settled, and should not be considered inviolate. I have only to look at the friends who inspired this story for this lesson. Together for twenty-five years, parents of two wonderful adults, they are just now, and only after a Supreme Court Decision, legally married in California.

Books are not matters easily settled, either. It's rare for a writer to edit a published manuscript. I have taken this occasion, not to alter the story or to change its voice, but to gently smooth over the inevitable excesses of a first timer.

1

Claire never planned on falling in love with Theo, or with anyone for that matter, but that's exactly what happened at the cheese counter at Fraser-Morris one gorgeous fall afternoon. "That's how life is," she said. "One minute you're happily going in one direction, well maybe not so happily, but at least seeing clearly what's ahead and then wham—you're on a hairpin turn veering off over a cliff."

It wasn't as though Claire hadn't given romance her best shot. She joked that *The Dating Game* was considering her for a lifetime achievement award; she never could refuse her mother and Aunt Fitzie who fixed her up with an endless supply of sons from their wide circle of prominent friends, luncheon committee acquaintances, and eager would-be mothers-in-law.

"Anyone with a pulse," Claire liked to say. According to her exaggerated calculations, she went on thousands of blind dates with boys who never seemed to grow up and leave the rambling Park Avenue and West End Avenue apartments of their privileged childhoods and who, by the tender age of twenty, were already ruined by the belief that an expensive dinner and a ride home in the family limo gave them the right to an after-dinner grope.

Long before Theo, in the odd-job years after film school she often double-dated with her best friends, Jessica and Baxter, who had just fallen in love. Inseparable, they would nibble burgers and drink Bloody Marys in the hip new places that were blooming all over New York with Peter Max posters, asparagus ferns, and fashionable flower children who came as close to the revolution as their trust funds would allow. But usually before the waiter arrived with the menus, something told her things would go no further, and most nights, Albert or Charlie or Jeffrey or Gus made their good nights, leaving the three friends to their nightcaps and the lazy talk of people who are comfortable with one another. Watching Jessica and Baxter tumble into a taxi and home to bed always made her sad. It wasn't envy, really. She adored them both; it was just that way down at the bottom of her feelings the sight of them, so in love, made the hole insider her a little bit bigger.

One summer, she took a half share in a beach house in Quogue, which entitled her to a damp room over the windy dunes every other weekend. There she met a nice man named Alan, but after two dates, he threw her over for someone named Helen who had a full share and an apartment closer to his in the city. He told Claire Helen was more "geographically appropriate."

"Can you beat that?" she told me. "Dating a girl because she's convenient! Supermarkets are convenient. Dry cleaners are convenient. Love is never convenient. You go out of your way for love. For love, you should be willing to go anywhere . . . to Brooklyn, if necessary!"

When she was being silly, Claire said she was attracted to Theo because as a child she refused to take ballet lessons at the Wills School of Social Dancing, a decision that left her with a flat-out kind of walk she referred to as "the galumph," and never could resist a good dancer. In more serious moments, she said it was really her brother Roland, who had died in a car crash at the age of nineteen and whose spirit had taken up residence in her body, who had chosen Theo for her. But she was always quick to add that this was long before she was comfortable with the whole idea.

The Hirsh family was more than well off, which made it even harder for Claire to find true love. Money has a way of generating its own heat, and she never could spot a fortune hunter before he broke her heart, so after a while, she just gave up on dating and borrowed other people's boyfriends the way other people shared umbrellas. Always chummy, always a pal, never a threat, Claire was everyone's friend and no one's love.

Until Theo.

They met on one of those rare and stunning autumn days that hooks people on New York as irrevocably as any drug. Claire described it as the kind of day that fills a person with the arrogance of living in this shimmering place full of interesting people and abrupt changes in circumstance. As she walked through the leafy Village streets toward an uptown cab, she felt every bit as full of possibility as that dazzling afternoon. She was heading toward a dream that was finally coming true, and the power of that simple fact washed everything in a light even more golden than the glorious afternoon before her. She'd spent years photographing weddings and bar mitzvahs and christenings and shooting public-relations events and not being able to sell her heart's work; then one day the owner of the Light Gallery simply looked up from his light box, where Claire's slides were scattered like Scrabble pieces, and asked if she would be interested in their giving her a show.

"Just like that," she'd said, snapping her fingers. "After years of drudgery and dreaming, at the age of thirty-three, a little long in the tooth to be considered wunderkind, I became an overnight sensation."

But even as she walked toward the future she had pictured for so long, excited, confident, and a little bit scared, she sensed something dangerous in the crisp breath of that day, and it hinted everything would change.

Claire had always wanted to be a photographer: not a fashion photographer like so many of her college friends who ran to see *Blow Up* and pursued glamour with every conscious thought. She wanted to be someone who could see into the souls of people by capturing that split second when all of human experience is written in one ordinary face, the "decisive moment," as Cartier-Bresson called it. She burned to become the next Stieglitz, Berenice Abbot, the Margaret Bourke-White of her generation.

It started the day Aunt Fitzie took her to the Jewish Museum to see W. Eugene Smith's photo essay on war. Claire experienced a transcendent power in the eyes of a young Marine, his face greased against an invisible enemy, one arm holding the lifeless body of a comrade, the other raised in a fist clenched with hatred for his buddy's killer, tears carving gullies of sorrow in the fierce blackness of his cheek. A young man and his dead friend leaned against a tree and in that moment of howling loss, a shutter clicked and a photograph recorded all that we need to know about war. A thin, shy girl stood in a cavernous room resonating with the power of that picture, and Claire's dream was born.

"Claire was not the same girl after that," said Fitzie, who never tired of telling the story. "I'll never forget how afterwards she blinked into the sun just like a shutter opening and closing. 'Aunt Fitzie,' she said,

'I'm going to see like that someday.' I knew it right then and there, my little Claire was going to be famous."

Soon after, Claire bought a battered Leica from a man in a gloomy secondhand store on lower Broadway who told her it had once been used to photograph Paul Robeson. Every click brought her closer to that crazy afternoon when she walked through Greenwich Village saying *"One-woman show one-woman show one-woman show"* over and over like a mantra.

"Meshugge," Mrs. Stein would have said, shaking her faded curls at the antics of young people today. The Rabbi, what would he make of it? He'd want to put a *"baruch"* on the pictures, bless them, so they would sell for "the nice girl with the camera."

Claire thought of the long winter she had spent with these people, taking the subway every day, hurtling to the tip of Manhattan, then inching along Brooklyn's spine, coming up into cold air tinged with salt and the sound of gulls swooping in and out of the great hulking skeleton of a roller coaster. How they welcomed her to this strange place haunted by the shrill laughter of its youth, these old Jews who sat on its shore against a backdrop of rusted clowns, condemned rides, and toothache-sweet cotton candy.

She had photographed rows and rows of them, wizened men and gnarled grandmas on faded beach chairs studying the ocean as if a lost relative might suddenly appear from across the years. They kept the vigil day after day in all weather, as though watching the horizon and the deep water that changed from inviting blue to cold black was the only guarantee against a return of the terror that had so brutally stolen their innocence. Claire believed one of them would sound the alarm if anything evil washed up, something far worse than the used condoms and needles that now littered a beach that once held the power to heal overheated souls from the suffocating Lower East Side tenements who came to breathe fresh salt air and to walk on its powdery sand before going back to the sweatshops.

After a while, they trusted her and looked forward to her visits. They spoke of ordinary things, children and grandchildren long gone to subdivisions on Long Island, people who came to visit one Sunday a month, dutiful children who politely listened to their talk of aches and pains, sons and daughters who lived beyond the cabbage and the old linoleum of their parents' lives.

They spoke to Claire of things that were never whispered in their own families, of sisters and brothers, mothers and fathers, husbands and wives torn from them without mercy, gone to the death camps. They told her stories that made the drugs and the violence and the muggers lurking in the doorways of their decaying neighborhood seem almost innocent.

At first they preened for Claire's Leica, the women smoothed thin, dyed hair, touched lipstick to mouths frayed at the edges like old sweaters. The men stood a little straighter, and ran arthritic fingers along invisible crease lines of pants softened by sitting. After a while, the camera was just another sound in their lives, punctuating their conversations with the tall blond woman who wanted to hear their stories, the well-mannered girl who showed them respect.

Lost in their memories and their clicking mah-jongg tiles, these were her beloved Coney Island people, dark as raisins, looking out from her pictures in silent tribute to the restorative powers of sun and salt air. Claire worked on the show all summer and now, as her subjects took their places on the gallery walls, wiser as a group, and oddly victorious over something they could not have vanquished in the separate struggles of their lives, she hoped they would approve.

She entered "F-M," as her mother called this Madison Avenue outpost of first-pressed Tuscan oils, imported truffles, pâté, porcini mushrooms, and endless varieties of caviar and foie gras, foods her Coney Island friends had rarely seen, much less have afforded, and could not help thinking they would no more understand the slouching affectation and the ritual wasting of expensive food that attends an opening night than they would the workings of the Vatican.

Drifting up and down the aisles, propelled by a dream close enough to touch, Claire looked more apparitional than real; a tall, slim, serious-looking woman dressed in black with long pale hair. In the light pouring in from the front window, a fine cobweb traced eyes of silver-gray and fanned out over porcelain skin, leaving it looking cracked and in need of a good watering. The result was a face that wasn't young or old, attractive or homely, remote or accessible, but rather one that found its beauty among its contradictions.

"I'd like to order some cheeses and pâtés, for an opening party at the Light Gallery," Claire said to the freckled redhead behind a counter piled high with cheeses of every imaginable variety, some so ripe Claire had to restrain herself from dipping a finger into a particularly runny Camembert. "Maybe some triple-crème Brie and Pont-l'Eveque?"

"What kind of show is it?" the woman asked, wiping well-manicured hands on an apron so smudged with food, it could have been a Jackson Pollack canvas.

"Photographs, actually," Claire answered, a little surprised by the question.

"Yes, I know the gallery," the woman said. "I live downtown. I meant what *kind* of show is it? What's the concept? Who's the artist?" she asked.

"Me," Claire replied.

The counter person smiled. And waited.

"I call it *Coney Island*. Old folks sitting in the sun, Russian bulls charging into the ocean in February, the immigrant thing, Nazi-camp survivors, Puerto Ricans and blacks moving into the neighborhood, one group living in distrust and begrudging respect of the other, that sort of thing . . . ."

I must be practicing for the opening, Claire thought, surprised at her own candor, so out of character. She had just given a synopsis of her work to a perfect or maybe not-so-perfect stranger. But the woman's sincerity was unmistakable, bread knife tapping the air as she listened, head on fire in springy Lucille Ball curls.

Still, Claire was embarrassed. "What's this got to do with cheese?"

"It's got everything to do with cheese," she said. "You asked for Brie and Pont-l'Eveque. Jews in Coney Island don't eat Brie and Pont-l'Eveque. People who go to gallery openings eat Brie and Pont-l'Eveque."

"So?" Where was this going, Claire wondered.

"So, you want something Middle European like Liederkranz, Bruder Basil, or Havarti with caraway seeds, with a nice black bread or sour rye."

Before Claire could get in another word, she started again.

"People should experience art on every level," the woman declared with a little thump of her knife. "Why not serve what your subjects would eat? Herring would be nice, with pickled beets, maybe some borscht or Dr. Brown's instead of that ghastly white wine everybody pretends to drink at those things."

She's a little nuts, Claire thought, but she couldn't help being mesmerized by this person who talked about food as though it were the love of her life. There was something wonderful about bringing such passion to one's work, something really compelling.

"Art can't be appreciated on an empty stomach." The woman's green eyes blazed with the conviction of one who believes beyond all else in the rightness of what she is saying. She paused only long enough to offer Claire a sliver of Bruder Basil. "Or worse, on one that's full of the wrong food."

"Think Proust's madeleines, Colette's blanquette de veau, Dickens's gruel. Food gives art its impact on the senses. For a Coney Island show, hot dogs, at least!"

"I never thought of it that way," said Claire. "You are absolutely right. Let's do platters of hot dogs, with a nice spicy Dijon, maybe some matzo balls and borscht with sour cream."

She dug in her bag for the details. "It should be delivered to Light Gallery, 79 Perry Street. Tuesday at six-thirty. We've sent out a hundred and fifty invitations—"

The woman's frown was as sudden as a power failure. "I couldn't possibly."

"Why not?" asked a stunned Claire.

"We don't do hot dogs here."

Claire felt lightheaded. "What's your name?" she asked.

"Theo."

"Mine's Claire. Would you mind if I took your picture?"

I GREW UP with that wonderful shot of Theo hanging in the foyer—face flushed, hair flaming against her food-splattered apron, behind the cheese counter at Fraser-Morris. One hand holds a little piece of cheese, and in the other is a bread knife, pointing straight at the camera.

Claire never tired of telling me how the two of them ended up driving out to Nathan's Coney Island for hot dogs for the show, dropping in on the Rabbi and Mr. Kimsky, laughing in the syrupy light, moving toward something neither of them would have predicted, two new friends, one blond, one redheaded, both resisting the attraction for all they were worth as the radio blared, "Baby, It's You" into that glorious, unending day.

Claire and Theo. My mothers.

I see them even now, so young and innocent of the life they chose, and yet willing to take it on, not so defiantly as the flashing eyes, wide, crooked grins, hands on hips, thumbs hooked into the same bell-bottoms I see again on the narrow hips of a new generation would have you believe. They look determined, I think, not to let anyone know they were afraid.

I hold these images—some real, some imagined, everything filtered through my own enormous need to remember—up to the mirror of my own broad face, framed in ginger, sprayed with the buckshot of Theo's freckles, her roundness augmented into manly bulk with a tendency to soften in the name of good food, a face that has seen more than it should in its thirty years and wears a summer coat of sun block in honor of Claire's tendency to burn. In the gathering moments preceding the flash of their combined tempers, the eyes that normally wear the benign indolence of wet moss, gaze back at me in a color that can only be described as cold steel.

My name is William Roland Bouvier-Hirsh. William for my maternal great-grandfather, Roland for my poor lost uncle, Bouvier for the Cajun side of Theo, and Hirsh for the Fifth Avenue side of Claire. But everyone calls me Willy, except my grandmother who always called me *Williamdear*, even after that no longer seemed appropriate. There is no question I'm their son, from the tactile joy I derive from my solitary hours stirring and chopping and tasting in a hopelessly overstocked kitchen worthy of Theo's gifts, to the compulsion I feel to examine and record what I see in the language I have substituted for Claire's ever-present roll of film.

They are with me in every impulse, every reflex, every twitch of memory and muscle, and in the idiosyncrasies acquired through the slow unwinding of my own experience. I feel their presence in the time-softened exaggerations of their friends and in the faces of the people I love. They are reflected in the wide-open heart of my wife, Annie, who celebrates those parts of me most like them, who calls me her "woman's man" with real affection. Their names are written in the unfamiliar tug I feel for the two perfect creatures of my own design before me now.

One baby is blond and pale, serious, even in sleep. Fluttering images have already begun their dance behind a veil of golden lashes, brushing infant skin with dreams far older. She considers all faces that come within her tiny range with the practiced eye of a seer. I sense she's taken her first picture of me and I wonder what she'll leave in, what part of me she'll crop out.

The other reaches for imaginary colors and wears the spark of a bonfire in the making. Her first questions live in her toes and in her fingers, opening and closing around the steady stream of magic that moves around her, that only she can see. Her milky breath stirs the angel who perches on a small boneless shoulder and the ghosts who sit on mine.

Our pediatrician says they're just as strong as you and me, but when Annie is sleeping and I tiptoe along the cold parquet toward their cribs and the amber puddle of the light we have left on in the nursery, the sight of them fills me with awe. Clumsy with love, I'm afraid to touch them with my large man's hands. They slumber through the early-morning scrape of the garbage cans on sidewalks swept clean of danger and the hot blood of the night before, and I imagine I can see their dreams, both fragile and fierce, issuing forth into the gray wash of morning to wait patiently for their owners to reclaim them. My girls are all fat legs and arms curling like new pieces of paper, stretching in the unfamiliar space, blissfully ignorant of what is to come. They are twin spirals of life filling the room with their small determination, and I am amazed at having a part in this.

My tiny muses. As I work, writing as I often do in the quiet of the day reserved for housekeepers, retirees, shut-ins, and second-story men, I see their perfection in the stops and starts, words and phrases, then whole sentences that darken pages scribbled on deadline for strangers who live in my world, but do not share its history. Lately, I race to the end of these obligations and by the time the messenger I have hired to carry my articles to the magazine arrives in a burst from the revolving door, I am already lost in another story. I am luxuriating in the words I will use to explain their lives to them, words not counted in characters and in lines and chunks of copy neatly surrounding a sidebar, but words that will carry the voices of their history and mine as tenderly and as truthfully as I can manage.

I watch my babies, round and shining like spoons on a well-set table, moving to the rhythms of our voices, the light, the memory of a warm amniotic pulse and the beating heart of the clock we have placed near their cradles to ease the sense of loss that has not yet left their muscles. I know I must tell them where they began, why their own hearts might break more easily than others, why one is rooted to the earth, why the other sees faces in the clouds.

I was too young to know, and if I had not been, I nevertheless couldn't know all there was to understand about my mothers. How could I pretend to grasp what they did not? Much of what I will tell my daughters is stitched together, suspended in time—truth, memory, regret, bits and pieces. Sentences, whispers, words hurriedly poured into a phone, laughter, conversations overheard and imagined, snapshots and stories outlined in the great, silent longing of children. Still, I knew more in the curve of a cheek, the pressure of a touch, the cadences of our kitchen, the dark heaviness of a sigh long after the lights were turned off, than most who take the fact of their parents for granted.

I don't know where imagination ends and fact takes hold, but I do know I must urge my girls never to waste precious time looking for this useless place. I'll tell them it's not enough to know what happened, but how it changed us all forever. Annie says I must tell them the truth, but I know no one can ever do that. She worries about my tendency to color things.

"It will get you in serious trouble some day," she says and I gently tease her. "I'm paid to do this."

"Fiction is for liars, not journalists," she replies, "and you are a damn good one."

"Liar or journalist?" I ask.

She beams. I imagine I, too, am one of her children, a large unmanageable boy who loves to rattle pots and make a mess in her tidy kitchen. "Both," she answers.

"But isn't belief in what *could* have happened, what *might* have happened, truth enough? Isn't imagining just knowing without seeing?"

My wife is able to disagree with her whole body, but there is no energy for that today. Her wide beautiful mouth curves down only slightly in its corners. "How could you know these things?" she says. "You were only a child."

"I think we're born knowing everything," I say, sounding like Ram Dass, the Great Karmac, and Claire combined. "If we do it right, we spend the rest of our lives finding out just how much that is." I feel myself color at this, but I stubbornly believe it. I think too many people spend their lives avoiding, denying, afraid of what they know, of what they feel. I want my girls to look inside themselves, not to others, for their strength.

Annie has heard all this before. Today, she slips into the nursery, as she often does after she turns toward the warm rut my bulk has made in our bed and knows I am up. They are hungry and she is drowsy and content. She smiles at what I am saying, but I'm never sure whether she is agreeing with me, or indulging me, or just using the sound of my voice to lull herself back to sleep. She takes the twins from their cradles, fills surprisingly strong arms with them, looks over her shoulder at me as though I am an older child who has been asked to watch his young siblings, and I imagine she is relieved they have not been drowned or suffocated while she slumbered; now a real grown-up is in charge again. I wince at this thought, and feel the special envy new fathers reserve for their wives, remembering I was warned of this by someone who wanted so much to create miracles, but could only play a small part. In the weak light of this morning, I see no part is ever that small.

Claire made me promise I would always go out of my way for someone I truly loved, even though we both knew I was too young to know what that could mean, what price it could exact. I can only tell my girls what happened and hope they will begin to understand and trust their own lives to fill in the rest. If I do this right, who knows? Someday they may go as far as Brooklyn for me.

2

Theo left her little walkup on Barrow Street and moved into Claire's rent-controlled apartment on Central Park West, a soaring space filled with light and Claire's collection of antique toys and ancient cameras, to which Theo added her prized *batterie de cuisine*, vintage clothes, and tribal jewelry. They lived in the greedy symbiosis of new lovers, arising sleepy-eyed from their bed to run all the way to the Thalia for a midnight show of *Casablanca, Sunset Boulevard*, anything Bergman, brazenly stealing kisses in darkened doorways, one never tiring of learning the geography of the other in the purple, pink, and copper bath of sunset over the distant water towers and terraces of the East Side. They avoided friends until their fragile bond grew skin enough for what lay outside their apartment door.

They wore each other's clothes as if to become the other. Tiny Theo in Claire's black suede baseball jacket, which came down to her knees and lost its severity in the bubble of flame above its collar. Claire, up to her elbows in bangles, trader beads, ivory, and silver as if to claim her lover's music as her own. Theo cooked at all hours as though what was happening between them needed constant stirring. She fired the big kitchen with its black-and-white tiled floor, wide leaded-glass windows and sweeping view of the park out of the dormancy of an occasional cup of coffee and Mary Hirsh's leftovers into the simmering heart of their happiness. They ate couscous, baked Alaska and moussaka in bed. For Claire, whose idea of a feast was a bowl of Jiffy Pop and a pint of Rocky Road, life with Theo was like living inside a really good cookbook, written by someone who understands that food really *is* love. Claire was sure Theo was the person she had waited for all her life, and the one her mother had dreaded.

"I have to tell my parents," Claire told Theo when she was positive it was love, that it was serious enough for that.

"No, you don't," said Theo.

"I do," Claire insisted.

"Why?" asked Theo.

"Because it's dishonest not to."

"The truth can be very cruel, Claire. Why not just let them come to it themselves? They will, you know."

"I can't. I'd be living a lie."

"It isn't important to me that you tell them." Theo said, seeing what was ahead.

"I know. But it is to me."

"When?" Theo asked.

Claire tried to make light of her terror.

"I guess you don't just wake up one morning and say, 'It's a gorgeous day, not too cold, not too windy, I think I'll walk over to Fifth Avenue and tell my mother I'm a lesbian."

And so, on a day she hadn't known had arrived until it announced itself as the right one, just as the moment you choose to plunge into cold water does not give a clue until it's upon you, Claire sat in the resounding silence of her mother's dining room, on the Fifth Avenue side of Central Park, taking small bites of the English muffin the Hirsh's housekeeper, Lucy, had spread with strawberry jam and served to mother and daughter on a polished corner of the long, graceful table. Bereft of candlelight, and lacking conversation lubricated by good wine, the surface that was as familiar to Claire as the thumb print she always managed to leave on its gleaming face, showed its age. It was too early in the day for a table that entertained so often. It seemed already empty of her reflection.

"We could eat in the kitchen," Claire had offered, trying to buy some time. *Maybe she won't hate me if I tell her in the kitchen, where daughters can tell their mothers anything and mothers are supposed to understand completely and without judgment.*

Lucy set Claire's cup and saucer and plate on a placemat and stood over her, one hand on a bony hip, the other still holding the towel she had been using to dry the Hirsh breakfast dishes when Buddy announced Claire was on her way up.

"Where you been, darlin' girl? You're gettin' thin."

Lucy had worked for Mary Hirsh for as long as Claire could remember and had as much right to know as her mother.

"Come over this weekend and I'll make you a pecan pie, fatten you up a little."

Claire made a face and blew out her cheeks.

"Can't you see I'm huge? As it is, I have to lie down to close my jeans. It's just these shoes that make me look skinny." Claire lifted one thick platform sole up in the air, but anyone could see she didn't have her heart in it.

"You're gonna break an ankle in those things," said Lucy playing along.

"Thank you, Lucy," said Mrs. Hirsh, dismissing her in the way women who have lived with servants all their lives do, marking out the shifting borders of privacy and privilege in the tone of her voice.

Mary Hirsh pretended not to see Lucy's disappointment and turned to Claire. "This is fine, sweetheart; your father and I breakfast here every morning."

Claire thought of Barnaby. *Never around when you need him, is he?* She thought of Theo waiting for her at the apartment, what she'd said: "If you do this, you can't take it back."

Her mother's knife picked at the English muffin like a scab.

I can't take this back.

"I'm in love, Mother."

"Darling, that's wonderful!"

She looks so happy, Claire thought. All those years of fixing me up with the sons of every friend who ever reproduced. All those weak-chinned replicas of the founders of So-and-So & Sons, Blither, Dither, Mather and Schwartz, and Feinberg et Fils, all those mothers hoping for a good match, a fancy reception on the St. Regis Roof.

"Do we know him, dear?"

"No, you don't, actually," said Claire, hearing the last easy words she would ever say to her mother tumble out and disappear forever. "It's not a him. It's a her."

Her mouth was moving, but her brain was saying, *It's too late now. I've said it. I've killed her. I may as well bury her.*

"Mother, she's wonderful. I know this must be very difficult for you right now, but once you get to know her, you'll see why I love her so much." Claire could feel herself spinning out of control, prattling, but she couldn't help it. While she was talking, something in her stately, silver-haired mother was locking shut, and nothing Claire could say was going to stop it.

Why don't you shut up and let her talk? But I need to make her understand.

"Her name is Theo Bouvier. We met at Fraser-Morris when I did the food for the Coney Island show. She's beautiful and kind. She's a chef. She's moved in with me. I love her."

"Are you telling me you have become a lesbian?" said Mary finally. She pronounced the word carefully and with a precision that would have sounded brave if Claire hadn't known her mother better. Something twitched in the corner of Mary's eye. Claire shivered in the warm room.

"No. Well, yes. I mean, it's not something you become, like a lawyer or a house painter." Claire knew this was no time for humor.

"I see no point in continuing this conversation," said Mary

"Mother, please don't do this. Can't we talk about it?" Claire pleaded.

Lucy, who'd been listening at the kitchen door, rushed in to pick up their plates in time to hear Mary Hirsh say to her daughter, "You'd better leave."

There were no shouts, no threats, no recriminations, none of the maternal angst Claire imagined such a confession would arouse. It was worse. The apartment door simply closed, and the Hirsh elevator carried Claire away from the sight of Lucy's shock and the sound of her mother's tears.

Afterward Claire told Theo, "It was as though I'd blown out the sun."

"Is that all she said?" Theo asked.

"No, she said she had plans for lunch."

* * *

AFTERWARD, whenever the subject of Theo was raised, my grandmother closed her eyes and released a sound of martyred despair. Claire and Theo nicknamed her *Mary, Queen of Sighs* to inject a little levity into the heaviness of her silence and all it meant. Mary loved Claire in her own way, and perhaps more deeply than even she herself knew. After all, there had to be something of Mary in the obvious gifts Claire brought to the camera, that unswerving eye. Claire took every opportunity to draw mother-and-daughter comparisons, but my grandmother; a product of her generation, kept her distance, hoping the infatuation would pass.

On the rare occasions when they met—after Theo, Mary never dropped in on Claire and gave as much notice as she could, even though it was only a brisk walk across the park to her own rooms on Seventy-second and Fifth to ours at Seventy-second and Central Park West—she was never rude to Theo and was gracious to a fault. She simply ignored Theo's presence in her daughter's life as anything but a close friend. No matter how often Claire brought up the subject of their relationship, Mary Hirsh closed it with the finality of a coffin lid.

Claire didn't know many people in her position, and the few she did know had been disowned, abandoned, disinherited, and made to feel unclean by their shocked and disappointed parents. Most had cut all ties and drifted in a world of their own creation; some left the city, others clung to its most remote corners. This was 1963 after all.

As the Age of Aquarius dawned on New York, Claire photographed its clownish manners and strident rebellion and understood that even the new freedom that strutted itself at Freak Fountain and behind the velvet ropes of Shepherd's and Killer Joe's had its own rules. Peace, love, drugs, promiscuity, and protest were fine as long as there was at least one of each sex participating.

Claire continued to push the issue. In her angrier moments, she reminded her mother that if Theo had been a man, any number of flaws would have been overlooked in the name of marrying her daughter off. In desperation, she raised the subject of her mother's own mixed marriage; in *her* day, it was shocking for an Irish Catholic girl to marry a Jewish boy, even if he was from Philadelphia.

My grandmother never took the bait. She simply assured Claire that she loved her very much, even though she found her personal life impossible to accept. We never really knew what my grandfather thought until much later, and by that time no one cared. Like so many men of his generation, he let his wife speak for him on domestic matters. If he held an opposing view, he never let on. He knew better. Barnaby Hirsh was an old-fashioned man, raised with the understanding that his role was to make money and provide for his family, not to venture onto the soft ground of his feelings. That was where women walked, and it was where his son Roland lived, and Barnaby had buried that part of himself with the boy.

Claire's younger brother, Peter, attempted to chisel away at the wall Barnaby had erected in honor of his firstborn and at the solid weight of his mother's private heart. He tried to be both boys, attempting to succeed where Claire had failed, but he was almost ten years younger than the receding image of Roland, an afterthought who had no taste for his father's well-heeled footsteps, or for the inevitable comparisons that left him hollow.

Peter took the only route a self-respecting, misunderstood young man could at that time. He moved into a railroad flat near Hudson Street with a free spirit named Molly who grew small pots of marijuana in the few slivers of light that managed to penetrate their long tunnel of an apartment. He took up poetry with a vengeance not seen since Dylan Thomas drank himself to death at the White Horse tavern down the street. By the time Claire dropped the L-bomb, Peter and Molly had become almost respectable, with a toddler named Charlotte, and Harry on the way.

Brought up by people who believed the only crime was being dull, Theo had a tough time understanding the tension between Claire and my grandmother Doris and Roy Bouvier—Roy always like to say he was a distant cousin of Jackie Kennedy's, but not distant enough for her—raised Theo's siblings in a permissive, live-and-let-live atmosphere. They believed rules imposed on children before they had a chance to develop their own instincts created neurotics and criminals.

It wasn't unusual to see young Theo, the baby in this boisterous family of seven, toddling around the garden in absolutely nothing at all but freckles and red curls, digging up "yum-yums for dinnie," and Doris, serving it up on her good Green Stamps china. The first time Claire and Theo flew out to the Bouvier trailer in Broken Arrow, Oklahoma, Doris proudly told Claire she knew Theo was destined to be a great chef the day she found her cooking a cactus in her new Revere Ware pot. "What's a few spiny things," drawled Doris showing Claire the pitted old saucepan, "if it helps put the first woman in the White House kitchen!"

Theo's brother Buster expressed an interest in Buddhism at the age of twelve, so Roy shaves his head in their tiny stall shower, and

Doris sewed him his own little saffron robe. Years later, when Roy Junior decided to enter the priesthood, all the Bouviers went to mass at St. Elmo's on the tribal land and Theo's sister Desi, a self-described shaman, did a special dance for the occasion. By the time Theo's oldest brother, Duncan, decided he would be happier as a middle-aged woman, Buster had forsaken Buddhism and was on to macrobiotics. The only ordinary Bouvier was Caroline, who moved to Arizona, married a partner in the stuffiest law firm she could find, played tennis, organized barbecues, joined the country club, and visited Doris and Ray only when guilt got the best of her. The boys called her *Miss Goody Tucson* but Doris defended her daughter's right to be average, saying, "Bourgeois is just another form of self-expression."

The night Theo told her mother what Claire meant to her, Doris looked long into her daughter's eyes and seeing the truth in them, said, "I guess if you can't love your own kind, who can you love?

Claire adored Theo's crazy family of kissers and huggers, but Theo reminded her that it was just as hard growing up with the Bouvier freedom as it must have been with the Hirsh convention.

"There's not much a thirteen-year-old can do to shock two old Bolsheviks who personally knew Louise Bryant and John Reed and just casually mention in passing that you'd look great as a bleached blonde. Or that if you're going to smoke dope, you ought to let them know so they can get you some good reefer from a jazz guy they know who might be passing through." This was the childhood that drove her out the door, and finally, all the way to New York.

Theo liked to say that while most people came to Greenwich Village to be wild and as far away from home as possible, she came to be average. But, as Claire liked to point out, there was no fear of that.

Everything about Theo was lush, fragrant, and a little flamboyant. She wore fuchsia and melon and fire engine red, colors no other redhead would dare. Her skirts dusted the floor, and her kimonos held untold secrets in the sleeves. When she laughed, it bubbled up from somewhere deep inside her and set her jade and silver bracelets jangling.

When Claire tired of Theo's grass-is-greener approach to the Hirsh family standoff, Claire headed to Serendipity with Suzie, her agent and partner in ice cream since their days at Bryn Mawr, where as roommates, they personally raised the average freshman weight gain from five pounds to a whopping fifteen. Claire used to say Grandma was responsible for at least ten pounds the year she fell in love with Theo.

As was their custom, they got down to business while they waited for their splurge.

"She's your mommy and you want her to approve of you," counseled Suzie, who also served as big sister, confessor, and proof that heterosexuality isn't as healthy as everyone thinks it is. Suzie had been married five times if you counted Duane, the boy she eloped with after her high-school junior prom and kept it a secret until the mail-order annulment arrived the same day as her SAT scores.

"This isn't a lesbian issue," said Suzie, tucking into a hot fudge sundae. "What we're talking about here is the universal need for maternal acceptance."

"Of course it's a lesbian issue," Claire argued. "My mother can't accept me because I love Theo. She's put terms on her love for me."

"And you expect her to put aside everything she believes, and acknowledge your life without reservation and judgment just because you're her daughter and it's your due?"

"Yes, I do."

"Claire, sweetie, you've just put your tormented little finger on why every psychiatrist in New York can afford to go to Europe for the entire month of August!"

Claire dug into her own gooey concoction. "For someone who dates all the wrong people, you're pretty smart."

"Did I ever tell you what my mother said after Brian and I broke up and I mentioned I was going to Fire Island for the summer?"

"No," said Claire, surprised that she had managed to miss one of the Byzantine twists and turns in Suzie's love life.

"I'll never forget it," said Suzie. "I said, 'Ma, I'm thinking of renting a house in Ocean Beach, maybe meet somebody new, somebody nice, somebody heterosexual . . . .'"

"You didn't," said Claire, shocked.

"No, I didn't say 'heterosexual,'" said Suzie, swiveling in her chair to face two women at the next table who were learning over and listening so hard, they were in danger of tipping over. "I just wanted to give those two something to take home to Westport."

"God, Suze! You're impossible."

"I know. That's why you love me. Anyway, my mother looked me square in the eye and said, 'all the men out there are divorced.' So I said, 'yeah, Ma, so?' And Claire, you won't believe what she said next." At this Suzie paused and took a long, dramatic drag of her Nat Sherman.

"She said, 'Suzanne Elizabeth, you don't want to associate with people like that

"People like what? You're divorced."

"My point exactly," said Suzie, grinding out the vile-smelling black cigarette Claire tolerated because she knew Suzie couldn't seem to function without it.

"I said, 'People like who, Ma? I'm divorced, too, remember?' 'That's different,' said my mother."

"That's denial," said Claire.

"No, my sweet dumbbell, that's Mother Denial. It's bigger than the iceberg that hit the *Titanic*—and hell couldn't melt it.

"In the end, it's what's keeping your mother from accepting Theo and will, by virtue of this same perverted Mother Logic, allow her to make an exception of you. Trust me. One day she will wake up and decide other people are lesbians, not her daughter. So if her daughter isn't a lesbian Theo can't be one either. And everyone will live somewhat happily ever after."

Suzie leaned over and took Claire's hand, suddenly a lot sadder than her cowboy fringe and ropes of pearls would suggest. "I envy you two. You have something I've been looking for all my life. Sooner or later your mother will see it and come around. Give her a chance."

Claire wanted to believe Suzie was right, and gave my grandmother every opportunity to prove it, but in the meantime, Theo worked on the Hirsh household the only way she knew how—through their stomachs.

She left Fraser-Morris not long after she met Claire, and opened her own catering business in a little storefront on Seventy-fourth and Second. She and Claire cooked up the name, The Latest Dish, and Claire shot menu covers, business cards, and price stickers, along with an ad for the neighborhood flyer, all with the logo of a sensuous and bright red mouth caught in a satisfied smile, a crisp white napkin dabbing at its corner.

From this modest bunker of mouthwatering delights, Theo lobbed great platters of lemon chicken and lasagna and Swedish noodles with caraway seeds, one of Mary's favorites, at the fortress that was 920 Fifth. Buddy, the Hirsh doorman, told her he started drooling the minute he saw her turn the corner, always careful to add in a brogue that went all the way to Dublin, "And I don't mean any disrespect by that, miss.". Theo fought unfairly with strudel, and Grandpa's favorite lemon cheesecake, and death by chocolate, a dessert that could make even the Rosenbergs talk, but she always took care never to seem too familiar, signing the distinctive card "Bon appetit! Claire."

While Theo cooked, Claire worked hard, trying to make the most of her new celebrity. She'd sold most of the Coney Island series and this paid for a trip to Greece, with enough left over to begin saving for the weekend house they talked of owning one day.

"Claire Hirsh has unlocked the last ghetto with a gimlet eye," one critic wrote. And she had captured a world: Mr. Kimsky playing chess in the park with a shadow; the reflection of Temple Bar El's Star of David in Mrs. Klein's rhinestone cat's-eye glasses as she watched a gang of toughs saunter down a windswept boardwalk; the Russian frozen in the tender act of buttoning Mrs. Goldstein's coat, hands like plates of meat, eyes sick with love; the Crazy One, lost to everyone including herself, Mrs. Levkowitz' bony fingers clutching the frayed sleeve of a sweater reduced by time to the color of milky tea and offering a leathery arm turned out like a ballerina's leg, no face, no eyes, no hair, no name—only numbers fading into the soft flesh inside her wrist.

Mrs. Levkowitz told Claire she couldn't cry until she saw the face of a young American soldier who stepped over the barbed wire and held her hand until she could be taken to the field hospital. "Only then did I allow myself to feel what had happened to me."

Claire loved Mr. Brodsky, a dapper little man from Warsaw, who sat on a faded deck chair, watching for U-boats in Brooklyn, and bragging about his response to the young fellow from the Coast Guard who tried to get him to evacuate one leaden afternoon when the radio warned of a hurricane heading for New York's barrier beaches.

"You really should go," Claire had urged him before rushing home herself.

Mr. Brodsky's English was still as terrible as the day he stepped into the great hall on Ellis Island. "I vas in Dachau," he said, "You vant I should run away from a little vind?"

In late March, the year before my mothers met, when the sting of the wind carried the unmistakable smell of spring, a man with numbers tattooed on his arm summoned the courage to ask Claire if she would take his picture and put it in the newspaper, hoping his sister was still alive to see it.

Now the critics rhapsodized. Collectors paid a helfty sum for Claire's beloved friends in their expensive frames, good track lighting trained on every grainy pore. Important conversation flowed around them, smug talk of Photography as Investment, while trays of triple-crème Brie and pears were passed under their noses.

For her part, Claire was deemed to be in a position to judge things—Right and Wrong, Good and Evil, Moral and Immoral, Boring and Interesting. She had been launched, adjudged a serious artist compared to Cunningham and Capa. Just before I was born, her Harlem heroin addicts and the forgotten residents of the city's charity wards earned her a Guggenheim, which, thanks to Aunt Suzie and her refusal to allow Claire's head to swell, I believed was an illegal pitch in softball.

Claire had always been loyal to those who believed in her, and celebrity did not change this. People who were not in a financial position to buy art, who had loved her work when she was unknown, left small amounts of money at the front desk with notes asking her to hold a favorite print, as a sort of cultural layaway. Which she was always happy to do. A young, aspiring, filmmaker bought Mrs. Levkowitz in this way and kept in touch with Claire. He told her he was moved by the eloquence of the cropping, her decision to leave out what he imagined to be a crooked smile, suitcases full of life under the eyes, a plastic poodle pinned to her collar, all the things that said, 'Look at me! I am not a number!' Later, when he became a household name, he credited Claire with creating the early stirrings of an idea for a film about the Holocaust that would be his masterpiece.

As Theo chopped, sautéed, boned, pounded, broiled, poached and chiffonaded her way to her own growing celebrity, Claire focused on hers in a darkroom under the stairs that would someday lead to my sleeping loft.

When I was a small boy, I believed they were both made of light and magic. I remember watching Claire disappearing into that tiny room with its eerie light, rushing out, with a photo held aloft for Theo's approval. I remember counting Theo's freckles while she whipped soufflés into clouds, and let me lick our blue spongeware bowls of every bit of chocolate. I remember paging through the big scrapbooks of Claire's notices and Theo's restaurant reviews and Suzie telling me "kudos" were small chewy candies given to players who hit "Guggenheims."

Even now, it's difficult to imagine why two such accomplished, ascendant, and thoroughly original creatures would voluntarily disrupt their lives for a baby, especially an enormous, drooling, moonfaced one like me, but to my eternal amazement, every bubble and squeak, gurgle and goo took front seat to critics, collectors, and customers—food, photography, or otherwise. I accepted their devotion as my due. Today I see how truly extraordinary this was. When she was sure I was old enough to understand, it was Theo who told me how I came to be born.

3

Claire ran out of estrogen at the age of thirty-five, which Theo explained, was the stuff necessary to make the eggs that make babies. Claire's heart pounded for no apparent reason and she picked fights with Theo, who seemed young and fertile for spite. She cried for hours on end and, on the rare night she didn't battle insomnia, soaking sweats woke her up. Theo infused herbs for sleep-inducing tea, boned up on hot-flash remedies and kept Claire company as she sat on the porcelain lip of the bathtub making low, heaving sounds that broke Theo's heart.

"How can you love someone who's drying up?" Claire would sniffle into Theo's breast.

"You don't drop someone you love just because they're a little sweaty," Theo would say, leading her back to bed where she would stroke her back and murmur softly until Claire finally fell asleep. "I really wanted to have a child someday," Claire whispered into the pillow one especially difficult night, but for everyone else, she put up a brave front.

"Who needs to ruin real silk when you can 'shvitz' in something washable?" Claire wisecracked to Suzie and to Jessica, who followed the details of her symptoms with morbid fascination.

"Why make jokes?" Theo asked. "They're your friends; why don't you tell them how you really feel?"

"Would you really like to know how miserable you're going to be in twenty years? Anyway, they depend on me to be funny." Theo was not convinced.

In public, Claire carried a fan, hoping the affectation of a carefully rehearsed snap would divert attention away from the sudden drenchings, which almost always struck when she was saying something clever or important, leaving her face slick, her clothes sodden, and her mood dark. Claire's one vanity was her hair, a delicate shade of blonde that took hours to achieve, but not even her colorist, could reverse the dulling march of receding hormones. Coarse white hairs rose up in her part. Every morning she plucked a few more and finally took to wrapping her head in two feet of gypsy silk.

Despite what Claire called her depressing and premature slide into cronehood, she cheerfully took the vitamins Theo laid out every morning—E and B6 for the black moods, and C for water retention. She drank papaya juice for digestion and swallowed a foul-smelling powder called *fo ti* and drank ginseng tea, which the herbalist on West End Avenue said couldn't hurt and might even help with the hot flashes. Weather permitting, Claire played tennis in the park and jogged around the reservoir for her bones, and when it rained, she ran around the tiny indoor track at the Y. She worried about losing calcium and the threat of osteoporosis hung over her like bad air. She weighed the risks of the new estrogen-replacement therapy that was causing much talk and new fears.

"Well, at least I won't get breast cancer," Claire said, looking up from the pamphlet the doctor had given her and patting her flat chest in the self-deprecating way Theo hated. "You need breasts for that."

Claire's gynecologist, Lydia Collins, did not escape her patient's short temper. Claire called her smug because she kept photographs of her own babies on her desk where, she said, "unfortunates like myself can see and have their hearts ripped out." When Dr. Collins confirmed premature menopause after several soggy months of symptoms, erratic periods, and blood tests that measure hormone levels, Theo said Claire began to see her life as a biological time bomb. She started acting a little crazy, and it showed in her work.

I remember a photograph of what appeared to be a poached egg in a bird's-eye-maple frame. I couldn't understand why anyone would want to hang a picture of a poached egg in their front hall until Theo explained it to me.

At three o'clock in the morning, while cleaning the apartment under the influence of the most horrible bout of PMS Theo had ever seen, Claire found an old diaphragm in the cubbyhole behind her closet. She had saved it along with her turquoise felt poodle skirt, a pair of ballet slippers said to have been worn by Pavlova, and a Davy Crockett hat that was home to a family of extremely fat moths.

Theo, alert to sudden fluctuations in Claire's moods, pulled on her robe and watched her rummage around the kitchen muttering about the stories the old thing could tell.

Claire emptied the refrigerator, unwrapping and rewrapping leftovers, and making a terrible mess, until she found a couple of congealing slices of corned beef from one of her *duty dinners* at the Hirshes'. She warmed the beef in the oven to perk up the color, toasted an English muffin, and handed half to Theo, who wasn't even conscious enough to know she wasn't hungry. Claire centered the other half on one of their good cobalt-blue plates, plopped the diaphragm on top, and then whipped up what turned out to be a pretty decent hollandaise for someone who couldn't cook. She topped the whole thing off with a sliver of olive meant to pass as a slice of truffle, and, babbling about the injustice of running out of eggs at the tender age of thirty-five, snipped a bit of the asparagus fern, placed it on the plate, and photographed the whole thing. Then she collapsed into bed and before she fell asleep, told Theo she was calling it *Eggs Derelict*.

More and more of this strange preoccupation with fertility began to creep into Claire's work. The haunting images with which she had developed her loyal and paying following were being replaced by what can only be described as a kind of neonatal perspective.

She photographed a woman teetering on swollen feet on the Fifth Avenue bus, forced to stand in what looked to be her ninth month. A man sat in the background, eyes narrowed as if to say, "You wanted to work like a man; well then, stand like one."

Claire's Leica recorded twins in strollers, triplets in custom-made carriages and identical sweaters, which made them look like human three-packs of paper towels. She snapped toddlers waddling along the promenade in Brooklyn Heights and pampered tots in English prams, their distinctive schooners sailed by stern nannies in starched white.

In grisly contrast, Claire rode up to 125th Street and found mothers in too-tight leather jackets whose unborn children kicked and fought and competed with a vein for attention and almost always lost out. She carried crisp new twenties to pay these women to allow her to take their pictures, hoping they would use the money to buy food. Seeing the speedballs glittering in their eyes, she knew better.

No one was safe from Claire and her determination to document her own hunger to breed. It seemed to Theo that Claire just aimed right into New York's reproductive organs and clicked. She mentioned this to Suzie over one of the lunches she had fallen into the habit of having with Claire's oldest friend whenever she, too, needed to talk.

"I suspect even the most revolting fact of urban life, the discovery of a new generation of roaches hatched overnight behind the stove, would somehow strike Claire as tender," Theo told Suzie on one such occasion.

"If that weren't so damn true, it would be funny," said an uncharacteristically somber Suzie, clearly distressed at this grotesque development in Claire's career. "It wouldn't be so bad if Diane Arbus hadn't beaten her to it."

"Things are getting a little tense at home," Theo told Suzie.

When a Madison Avenue gallery offered to mount a show of Claire's oddest body of work yet—a series of babies' behinds she called *A Sitting*—instead of enjoying the obvious victory, Claire brooded for weeks over whether she should have held out for La Mama, which, in its own infancy, offered gallery space from time to time.

"It would have been so right, Theo," Claire moaned after an argument with the gallery manager, who called her work "reproductive art" in the brochure.

"And what would we have served, *formula?*" asked Theo a little too sharply. "No, better still, you could breast-feed the guests and save all those dirty dishes."

Not all the critics were unkind, but the show did not sell out. One snide reporter in suspenders and a bow tie wrote, "One enters the sweeping space and gets the distinct feeling of strolling around inside a giant pair of rubber pants." Another writer, a little more familiar with Claire's earlier work, showed compassion and compared what she called Claire's "nursery period" to Picasso's Blue.

"How ironic. If I *had* a period, I'd have a nursery, wouldn't I?" Claire said ruefully. "Can you believe people have the nerve to show up at your party after writing drivel like that!" She and Suzie were greeting guests: Claire the nervous artist, Suzie the agent, wineglass in one French-manicured hand, a smoldering Nat Sherman in the other, eyes narrowed, mouth set in what Claire called her twenty percent smile.

"Claire, sweetheart, may I point out that Coca-Cola is probably not going to pay five thousand dollars for the privilege of hanging one of your baby bums in their lobby," said Suzie as she surveyed the crowd for possible buyers. "But Carter's or Gerber's, maybe!" Suzie could see the market potential in anything.

There were thirty-two bottoms in all—tiny black behinds that shone like wet licorice, some white as paper, others rosy as an English cheek. All the colors of the world hung around the room—yellow, tan, butterscotch, peach, brown, freckled, dimpled, dewy, sunburned, smooth, perfect little moons fat as cream. On the far wall, as though by virtue of its impossible size, it deserved more space than the others, hung the show's centerpiece, a preemie's bottom so small it could fit on the tip of a finger.

Theo stayed home that night, allowing my grandparents to "have the evening," as she put it. My mother had a real gift for knowing how other people felt, and understood that it would not be fair to put Claire under any more pressure by also having to endure the excruciatingly civilized tension between Theo and Mary and Barnaby Hirsh. She would wait at the apartment and fix a late supper for anyone Claire chose to invite home, and that would be her special gift.

Trailing an entourage, Claire arrived at the apartment around eleven. Baxter and Jess claimed they could stay for only an hour; otherwise they'd end up owing four years' tuition to the sitter who was watching Jennifer and Brooke, twin angels born that year. Suzie had several potential buyers in tow, who Theo suspected were potential dates more than anything else. Thad and Alan, Theo's old friends from Barrow Street, arrived with masses of baby's breath for "the muse" and behind them were two elderly Park Avenue matrons; Mrs. Peabody and Mrs. Babcock, who insisted on being called Emmelyn and Mildred and gushed at everything in the apartment. They were escorted by James, the gallery manager who'd called Claire's art "reproductive," but who was now chastened by many glasses of wine and the prospect of Peabody and Babcock's checkbooks.

In keeping with the show's theme, Theo charmed everyone with a buffet of nursery foods: a crusty meatloaf, baked macaroni with a combination of Cheddar, Gorgonzola, and Brie, pureed vegetables in hollowed tomatoes, and a heaping basket of chocolate brownies. The napkins were diapers, each fanning out from a pacifier. "Never used!" Theo assured her wary guests.

The door had barely closed on Suzie and her potential buyers when Claire embarked on one of those woozy conversations that can change the course of life forever.

An exhausted Theo had just slipped a pillow behind her head and melted into their overstuffed sofa, dangling one shoe on her toe, when Claire began.

"Every thirty seconds, people are having babies they don't want. Every time I pick up a newspaper, another baby is found in a garbage can or beaten senseless or stuffed into a pillowcase and left on the Cross-Bronx Expressway. Women are out there burning bras and demanding the right to have a say over what happens to their bodies. 'Get on the pill,' they say, 'choose your own fate,' but what about me? I have no say. I can't choose. I've run out of choices. What's reproductive freedom, if you can't reproduce?" Tears were coursing down Claire's cheeks, her delicate skin turning a mottled red.

Theo leaned over and enfolded Claire in a hug. "It's late, sweetie, you've had a tough night. Why don't you go to bed, while I clean up."

Claire's voice was a hoarse whisper. "Do you think we could have a baby?"

"What?"

"I said, let's have a baby."

Now Theo was wide awake, retreat moving into her muscles.

"I don't think we can do that, Claire. We're women, remember?"

"What I really mean is, do you think you could have a baby and we could raise it together?"

Theo sprang from the sofa as if it were on fire and stormed into the kitchen, one perilously high heel off, and the other still on. She began to hack away at a brownie.

Claire followed. "Can't we talk about this, Theo?"

"Oh, sure. Nice party, let's have a baby."

"I'm sorry, honey. It really was a nice party," said Claire, suddenly contrite.

"About a day late and a dollar short," Theo shot back, her brows knitted into a solid line. "Do have you any idea what a responsibility a baby is? You can't just put it in a camera bag or make a nest for it in a bureau drawer or put it down for a nap in your fur coat. And just when the light is perfect for your series on *Carhops, a Disappearing Breed*, it will not wait for you to get the perfect shot of a bubble hairdo, it will spit up on your shoes."

Claire stood in the doorway watching usually serene Theo tear plastic wrap in short ugly bursts, her heart seizing up at the ferocity of her words.

"Aren't you overreacting a little?"

"Overreacting? May I remind you that we are lesbians, Claire—gorgeous, lovable, and smart, but lesbians nevertheless. Do you want your child to hear the bad names the world calls women like us? Butch? Dyke? Fill in the blanks, Claire!"

"Theo, stop it!" Claire shouted.

At this, Theo paused, dropped the knife, pulled off her earrings, and rubbed the deep lines they had carved in her lobes. Claire reached over to rub her neck, but thunderheads gathering in the green eyes said this was not the time.

Theo tried reason. "It's one thing to live in New York surrounded by permissive, liberal friends and another to raise a child in the real world. Your own parents haven't been able to make peace with us, and they love you more than life itself. Isn't this hard enough?"

Suddenly exhausted, Theo collapsed like an old sofa whose springs had suddenly given out. She looked a little dazed as the mess she had been making of the brownies came into focus. But she took none of it back.

As always, Claire tried to cover her hurt feelings with humor.

"Well, you don't have to be so polite about it, Theo, you can say what you really feel."

"Does everything have to be funny with you?"

"Everything is funny because if it isn't, the pain will swallow me whole," said Claire, laying her cheek on the cold tile of the countertop. "If I could, I'd have a baby right now, but I can't. And you can. You can, Theo."

"Let's talk about it tomorrow, Theo said as she turned out the lights and gave Claire a chaste kiss. "It's been a long day."

They didn't talk about it the next day or the day after that or the one after that. In fact, after that night in the kitchen, when each had said more than she intended, they carefully avoided the subject.

Claire still used her camera to express the "baby thing," as Theo diplomatically put it, and in spite of a dwindling number of deposits left at the lobby desk, the Leica would not be stilled. In the downstairs darkroom, ever-increasing numbers of babies were born out of ghastly-smelling developing fluid and whisked up to dry, still damp, like so many diapers on the line of her growing disappointment.

One gloomy Sunday afternoon with a dull rain beating on the huge studio windows, Theo looked up from the *Times* crossword puzzle and picked up one of the contact sheets Claire had laid out on the floor, where she was organizing her next show. Very slowly, eyes hard as glass, Theo said: "You know Claire, they've never been able to pigeonhole you as a feminist artist, but it's beginning to look as though your view of the world extends no farther than your own vagina. That's a little narrow, don't you think? Where are those riveting images, those universal, non-gender-dependent works of art you once created?" Theo waved the contact sheet like a summons, her cruelty deliberate, out of character, cutting.

"Speaking of female stereotypes, why don't you go bake something," Claire lamely shot back. The sting of Theo's words followed her out of the room and into the darkroom, where she sat on an apple crate and wept until Theo went to bed.

Doors slammed and words dangled in the air in the Bouvier-Hirsh household. Always, there were apologies, but they began to sound the same, balm applied to a scab that wouldn't heal, the residue of what could not be taken back building up like toxins in drinking water. A tense truce settled over them, but the atmosphere in the apartment was thick with their separateness, all that was unsaid.

Theo closed the shop for a few weeks in February and went home to Broken Arrow, "to do some thinking," she had said. Claire spent more time with Peter in the old apartment he and Molly were quickly outgrowing, and with Jessica and Baxter, whose lives seemed to be as solid and as permanent as the walls of the brownstone they were bringing back to life with oddities from their travels and the giddy music of their two small girls, Jennifer and Brooke. Claire went to Coney Island for a long-overdue visit with her old friends. Mrs. Levkowitz patted her face and said, "If he loves you, he'll come around eventually."

This was the winter of 1963. Dark, silent, unusually cold.

In March, the days began to soften and so did Theo and Claire. Slowly, almost imperceptibly, they were swept into the rhythm of forgiveness that comes when love loses its innocence and concessions must be made if it is to endure.

Claire was shooting new work on babies with Down's syndrome, who in those days bore the terrible scar of the word "mongoloid" and were hidden in the deepest corners of places like Creedmore and Willowbrook. This was photo journalism and it had all the signs of the earlier and more powerful images. Theo's catering business was quickly becoming a hit. *Gourmet*'s editor-in-chief wrote the magazine's review; "Theo Bouvier's 'Latest Dish' is the word on everyone's lips." There was talk of a cookbook and a line of products.

Theo came home flushed from the stove and full of tales of near-disasters in her tiny shop's kitchen. She carried shopping bags brimming with divine-smelling leftovers. The apartment simmered in the constant heat of creation. Theo's mistakes, as well as her triumphs, found their way to the red-lacquered Parsons table. They ate a chocolate mousse Theo had chilled without whipped cream to cut its sweetness. They devoured headless brioche, nibbled muffins that had spilled over their tins, lopsided cakes that couldn't be used, and chocolate cookies that fell apart in mouthwatering chunks. Claire had resumed the habit of leaving her darkroom in time to help Theo close the store and walk back home through the gathering dusk of that endless, melting spring.

"Good God, Theo, what have you done?" said Claire one warm evening in early May, rolling her eyes at the corn tortillas Theo had layered with chilies, grilled chicken, avocado, salsa, and sour cream. "Is the world ready for this?"

"I call it Mexican lasagna," said Theo, sliding the casserole into the oven. "I'm thinking of doing it with corn muffins and a green salad for the Friedlander brunch. Taste test starts in about twenty minutes."

Claire set the table near the window overlooking the street lamps coming on in the park. Theo changed out of her food-spattered work clothes and when she sat down to their Mexican feast, Claire placed a frosty margarita next to her plate. Claire couldn't help thinking how happy Theo looked, sitting there in a voluminous white poet shirt, happily licking the salt off the rim of her glass. A young Shakespeare relaxing after a hard day on a sonnet.

"You really are good at what you do, you know," said Claire, taking Theo's hand in hers between bites.

"You are too," said Theo, turning Claire's hand over in hers for a quick kiss that tasted of lime and cilantro. "Ready for dessert?"

"What did you have in mind?" said Claire, too full to do anything but watch Theo clear the table. "How you can cook and eat like this every day and not get fat?" groaned Claire, tugging at her jeans.

"Large clothes," shouted Theo back into the dining room as she reached up into the cupboard for two taxicab-yellow dessert plates. Three huge strawberries and a scoop of raspberry sorbet went on each one, then a large dollop of what looked like apricot purée.

"Finally something dietetic for a change." Claire said when Theo slid the plate in front of her. Then, licking fruit sauce off the handle of her spoon: "This is fabulous. What is it?"

"Claire, I've been doing some serious thinking," said Theo, her tone suddenly grave.

"About what?" asked Claire, trying to ignore the alarm bell going off at Theo's abrupt change of mood.

"I thought we'd try," said Theo.

A warning was now reaching up to squeeze Claire's heart.

"Try what?"

"It's baby food," said Theo slowly, letting the words sink in. "I figured since we're going to have so much of it around, we ought to get used to the taste."

4

For most people, the search for the perfect mate is an arduous process that takes many years, sometimes as long as a lifetime. We all have an Aunt Suzie for whom even that much time isn't enough. Just as an apparently ideal candidate moves into sight, some quality which he or she does not possess—insight, sensitivity, courage, a good sense of humor, a love of small animals, concern for the environment—surfaces in another person, leaving the current object of desire pale and disqualified by comparison, and the whole game of getting-to-know-you starts over.

The subtle unraveling of character, as each trait conspires to sum up the whole, can be as painful as slowly peeling an onion from the wrong end, which any cook will tell you involves a good deal of crying. All too often, the end result is disillusionment, broken engagements, divorce, and inevitably, a return to square one, leaving the seeker older, wiser and better equipped to handle the next round.

Claire and Theo did not have that kind of time. Even though, at thirty-four, Theo had enough eggs to last as long as it took to find me a father, plus some to spare for my sister (a thought she would keep to herself until the right moment), she envisioned the process in terms of months, not years. Once she decided she really wanted a child—not for Claire, but for herself and all that she could bring to its creation—she rose to the idea with every ounce of energy she had.

Claire did not say how much the idea of Theo with a man troubled her, even though such an encounter couldn't be described as making love exactly, more like coupling for a good cause. The thought chilled her. She remembered how she felt when she watched Jessica and Baxter tumble into a cab and home to bed, their heads together in the back window as they waved good night. She thought of Suzie telling her about Brian and the woman she'd found with him in their bed, how defeated she'd looked. And her dead brother. Roland: Would he have had children? Would they have been close? She missed him even more now.

Claire remembered the night she and Theo played true confession, and she admitted she'd once gone out with a guy she met on the Third Avenue bus, who turned out to be a fry man in a fish house somewhere around Wall Street and who never quite managed to get the smell off his hands. So, too, she admitted she'd dated one of the family chauffeurs, but didn't find him quite so appealing out of uniform. When the laughter died down and it was her turn, Theo said she'd been married once.

"I was very young and it didn't last." Theo said, sounding far away. "I'm sure I did it to prove something to Doris and Roy, but I can't imagine what. David was his name."

Theo claimed the marriage was, in many ways, the beginning of her attraction to women; she laughed about poor David dragging the legacy of that into the bedroom all his life, but Claire was acutely aware of the fact that Theo was still very much the object of male attention whenever they went out. Claire hated herself for thinking it: *If only she weren't so beautiful.*

I suppose way down at the bottom of her own insecurity, Claire was afraid Theo would leave her. To make matters worse, the man they were looking for was no ordinary person—he had to be perfect—which brought Claire closer to her terror. *What if Theo has our child and I lose them both?*

It was she who wanted to have a baby, not Theo. How could she admit to something as petty as jealousy? She chalked it up to cold feet.

Theo knew. One morning, when Claire's glum look gave her away, Theo followed her into the darkroom, kissed her tenderly on the back of the neck, and said, "You know, I'm not sure I can carry this off, either. I think I'll feel like some tramp in a sleazy motel."

They avoided talking about how it would happen; instead, they talked about who. For weeks, they assessed every man they knew and ones they didn't. They discussed character, looks, intelligence, predisposition to disease, moral fiber, and athletic prowess, artistic versus analytical leanings, the ability to plan versus spontaneity, fullness of hair, mental illness, and table manners.

Each evening as Theo was closing The Latest Dish, Claire sat at one of the tiny tables, Leica slung over one shoulder, nibbling at slivers of smoked bluefish or pâté while Theo wiped down burners, moved platters of chicken, Swedish meatballs, lobster, fat shrimp, and ham burnished with her secret marinade out of the display case and into the walk-in refrigerator. One night, as Theo lined up ingredients for the next morning's baking, assessing the dishes that would and would not hold, and made mental lists for her dawn foray to the wholesale market, they began to ponder the delicate question that carried them home each day.

"Well, you can't exactly sidle up to Baxter, let's assume he's a candidate, and say, 'Listen, Bax, we're considering you for the job of fathering our child, so, in twenty words or less, could you sum up your medical history? You know: heart disease, cancer, diabetes, phobias, allergies, baldness, hernia, insanity, the clap, that sort of thing," said Theo, securing the gate over the front door.

"'And by the way, Bax, photocopies of your degrees and scholarships, and the results of any neuro-psychological or intelligence-related tests you might have taken would be real helpful, too,'" Claire chimed in.

They entered the park and felt its lush green slow their steps.

Theo agreed. "We have to be pretty sure about our man before we pop—no pun intended—the big question. It would put a strain on a friendship if we had to reject someone we love just because bad genes or a sloppy past disqualified him from fatherhood."

It was a warm evening, and the tennis courts were full. They stopped to watch a fast doubles game, played by four trim men somewhere in their mid-fifties.

"Eye-to-hand coordination," Claire said, admiring a high-speed volley that split the quiet like gunfire. "You never notice it until it's too late then, twenty years and thousands of dollars later, the kid's still taking cha-cha lessons."

Theo was watching a couple who had been playing singles and noticed the man congratulating the woman for a game well played. She listened hard for the patronizing words men often use to cover defeat, watched for the gestures that would belittle the woman's performance, but heard no such thing, "C'mon," he said, toweling off his sweaty face. "O'Neal's. I'm buying."

"I don't know whether it's learned behavior or genetic," Theo said, watching them zip their racquets into bags and swing them in the direction of well-earned refreshment, "but I think it's critical for our candidate to like women. I mean *really* like them, not just long enough to get them into the sack."

Claire laughed. "You mean a man who understands why a woman caught in the grip of PMS is beautiful even when she's ripping his face off."

"Precisely. A man who can feel the pain of water retention and feel puffy, too!"

"No allergies, either," said Claire. "I can't stand children who sniffle."

"Agreed," said Theo resuming her strolling. "What about baldness? If we have a boy, I wouldn't want him to grow up bald."

"Well, it wouldn't be so attractive for our daughter to grow up looking like Zero Mostel, either. Anyway, I think the baldness gene is on the mother's side, so no matter what we have, it'll be your fault."

"I don't feel strongly about whether the donor's a vegetarian, do you?" asked Theo suddenly serious about her favorite subject. "That should be a conscious decision later on, don't you think?

"We could ask *him*," said Claire, eyeing an attractive, well-muscled guy in gym shorts loping toward them on the path.

Theo grabbed Claire's arm and missed. "Don't you dare!"

Just as the man passed, Claire grinned maniacally, did an exaggerated backwards twirl, and fell into step with him.

"You, sir." He struggled to hear her over a loud argument between a German shepherd and a feisty poodle. "Yes, you. You look like a healthy fellow, could you lend us your, ah, equipment for a day or two?"

The man slowed down and touched his ears, pointed to the barking dogs, and strained to hear what Claire was saying.

"Certainly. We understand," Claire said, grandstanding for Theo's benefit. "You would require a deposit and some identification—a driver's license, or a Bloomingdale's charge, perhaps."

The jogger came to a full stop and stood directly in front of Claire. He raised his palms, as if to say, "Okay, you've got my attention. You've ruined my run. What?"

"I *said*," said Claire, pointing to his shorts and drawing out every word for Theo who was now red to the roots with embarrassment, "Do you know where we could get similar sporting equipment?"

His eyes narrowed as if to squeeze some deeper meaning out of what he had just been asked, knowing he was being made a fool of, but not quite sure how. A number of responses formed in his face but did not materialize. He wiped his face with his shirt, shook his head and muttered something about everybody being nuts in this city.

"Don't you think a well-developed butt is an asset?" Claire said as they watched him trot away.

Theo groaned, but couldn't help laughing at Claire's nerve.

"If you like the sensation of being followed around by a basketball," she snorted, wiping mascara tears from her cheek.

Across the street from their building, a midnight blue Rolls was stopped at the light. In back, a distinguished silver-haired man read a newspaper. "Do you think the ability to amass great wealth is passed on by the father or by the mother?" Claire asked Theo, who nodded as though she might have been wondering the same thing.

As the light turned green, a pretty brown woman in a mini-dress and nosebleed-high platform shoes fell into step with them, and Theo wondered whether ruling out "color" was racist or not. At the same moment, Claire said, "He's got to be white, don't you think? Life is going to be tough enough with lesbian-photographer-chef mothers without that hurdle, too."

When things got hard and I searched for reasons to feel special, I remembered their stories of how difficult it was to decide who would help them create me. Whenever I felt angry at them for making me live outside the world of fathers and sons, I thought about how much they wanted me and the pains they took to make sure I would be whole and healthy; that there would be few bad surprises and as many advantages in my life as possible.

The party was an elegant ruse designed to narrow the field without causing any suspicion among the candidates. On the pretext of creating a family tree of friends and of sharing personal histories, questions that would be considered rude under any other circumstances could be asked in the spirit of the evening. It was entirely Theo's idea.

The First Annual Hirsh-Bouvier Family Tree Trimming
An Evening of Forefathers, Foremothers,
Skeletons, Feuds, Family Secrets,
Ethnic Food, & Ancestral Dish
All in the relative comfort of
115 Central Park West, Apartment 6D
Saturday, August 23, at 8 o'clock
Come as you were!
RSVP 629-4955

The air was close on the night of the party, heavy and hot, and Theo pushed open our casement windows to let in whatever breeze had risen on the steamy darkness. She wore a long tiered skirt in honor of Doris, who was part Cherokee on her father's side—which was why, she told Theo, she was always comfortable raising a family in a trailer. "It made me feel as though I could pull up stakes and move on with the seasons like my ancestors. Never did, but I like to think I could have if the feeling came over me." The skirt was caught at the waist with the silver and turquoise conchas Doris had given her when she moved to New York. "There's no sky in Greenwich Village," she had said, giving Theo the talismans that held all the stories running in her tribal blood. "That's why I left."

A small silver crucifix flashed at Theo's throat for the Bouvier side of the family. It had once belonged to her aunt Aimée Cassard, who claimed to be a direct descendant of Captain Jean Lafitte, and was as unpredictable as any pirate. Roy's people were Huguenots who fled persecution by French Catholics and scattered, some to Germany, others to South America and Haiiti; a handful all the way to America, burying themselves in the deep bayous of Louisiana. The Bouviers were clannish people who had their reasons to be suspicious of outsiders, people who are still a little wild. One of them left a wife and children, and a thriving New Orleans medical practice to fight in the Mexican War of Independence. They called him El Rojo, not merely for the flaming crop of red hair Theo and I inherited, but for his fierce and rather undoctorly ability to spill Spanish blood.

That night, the beveled glass of our French doors stood open like arms full of diamonds, and from behind them Claire watched Theo move about the room. Hurricane candles flickered on the long refectory table that would be the scene of one of her famous suppers and small votives bathed the oversized coffee table and the wide windowsills overlooking the park in warm light. Theo folded napkins, squinting as an artist would to ensure their symmetry, and arranged bowls of salty almonds, and lacquered trays of chèvre, salmon mousse, and vitello tonnato, her jewelry tinkling in the sultry air. Claire, overcome with love and desire, couldn't help thinking no matter what Theo wore, it merged with her violent coloring and became spectacular. Claire watched Theo fuss over the tables and flowers artfully placed around the room and she was filled with wonder that this woman who would soon bear the weight of their child had planned this evening with the cunning of a spider. She thought of their visit to Broken Arrow and how Doris had craned her neck over the row of cacti crowding the narrow trailer sill. "Look at that sky," Theo's mother had said, "always rushing off somewhere. Sometimes I'd like to know where it's going." Roy took a quiet pleasure in his wife's restlessness and she prayed Theo was not entirely her parents' daughter.

"The family trees are ingenious," said Claire, sweeping into the room in her own combination of Celtic and Jewish roots, a silver Claddagh pin caught at the throat of a black Irish-linen blouse, a black-and-white shawl to signify her Semitic side draped around one hip of a light summer skirt, her pale-blond hair drawn up off her neck, the Leica, as always, in the black camera bag within arm's reach.

"All the better to snoop on our friends!" said Theo, gathering stray rose petals that had drifted onto the table, leaving some where they fell to reflect in the crystal bowl above them.

"They'll forgive us when they find out why."

Claire gave a wicked smile. "Only if we tell them."

Theo had drawn family trees for everyone to fill out, funny little stylized apple trees, miniature cherry, weeping willows, cedars, sycamores, redwoods, black oaks, cypresses, eucalyptus, and the gnarled baobab. Each bore the name of a special guest; when everyone was gathered, Theo would say the information contained on each would be collected to inform the special friendship tree she would create and send out as a memento of the party and of each guest's unique place in this family of their own design.

They chose him that night. Or at least that's what I believed. I imagined they phoned and asked to meet him for coffee or invited him over for dinner. Alone. After the first awkward conversation, which probably included incredulity, suspicion, and the dawning realization that they were serious, they talked about it many more times. I can't imagine him agreeing to something like that right away, or even understanding it fully, not in the way we take the idea of sperm donors, artificial insemination, and in-vitro fertilization for granted now.

It was just fatherhood then, plain and simple, no fancy words for it, no cold legalese blurring what was in the blood, no lawful and binding contracts telling the parties what they could and could not expect from the agreement, what rights they were signing away. Custody and visitation, alimony and child support had no bearing on those early conversations. These were fighting words reserved for legally married couples,

At the time, I'm sure my mothers didn't consider themselves advanced or even brave, just hungry for something they couldn't have, and I think once he understood that Claire and Theo intended to have a child whether he agreed to have a part in it or not, my father relented. Maybe he had his own reasons, too, beyond his affection for them and their absolute faith in him.

For years, I would not ask his name. I believed it was better not to know the answer, which would lead to more questions and inevitably, to disappointment. I kept my suspicions to myself. When I did finally learn who he was, I understood much more, but I imagined him for far longer than I knew him, and that's how I see him still—young and handsome, and in shadow, one of a group of young people raising their glasses in a basement restaurant that is small, and dark and full of itself like so many on narrow crooked streets like Carmine, Waverly, and MacDougal. Or maybe they are outdoors, slouching toward the shaft of sun that has penetrated the cool shade of the avenue and has pooled on the sidewalk around their chairs. They are celebrating their pact and wondering if any of the passersby have such grand plans. My mothers are suddenly shy in his presence; their eyes glitter with wine. The woman with him is proud of what he is doing, but more afraid than she will let on, caught up in the spirit of the moment. They refill their glasses; this helps them avoid the conversational shallows that might lead to any discussion of the darker side of their decision, and they do not look back.

A FEW WEEKS LATER, on what should have been another warm afternoon in a long succession of steamy Indian-summer days, Claire found herself shivering in a Checker cab inching uptown on Eighth Avenue, which was a solid wall of traffic. A front of brisk Canadian air was blowing off the river and making for one of the most unseasonably cold October days in memory. She begged the driver to turn on the heater.

Dr. Collins had advised them that if they were determined to persist in such a risky enterprise as do-it-yourself artificial insemination, there wasn't much she could do to stop them (actually there was much she could do in 1964 when such things were illegal, but her only request was that they not compromise her by asking for her participation). But she did say it might work better if they kept the specimen as warm as possible and used it within two hours of ejaculation. "I wouldn't vouch for its motility after that," she had said, drawing the visit to a close.

Claire imagined tiny sperm teeth chattering in the jar next to her. "I *said*, do you think we could have some heat back here? I'm freezing."

The dazed hippie behind the wheel swiveled around, said something unintelligible, and pulled on the joint he had going in the ashtray.

Claire felt another blast of arctic air. "Could you at least close the window?"

The driver sounded like someone who's blown up too many balloons.

"You want a hit?" he asked, sucking up all the warmth that was left in the cab.

"No. I don't want a hit. I want heat. H-e-a-t and for you to go faster."

"Please don't die," she begged the thick wool sock on the cracked leather seat beside her. "We're almost there."

Two bleary eyes stared at her in the rearview mirror as she squeezed the sock under her arm and feigned shivering. "You coming down from a real bummer, ain't you?" said the driver, putting the cab in neutral and throwing his arm over the seat.

She had wanted to be part of this in some small way, and delivering "the goods" was as close as she could get. "Neither rain, nor snow, nor dark of night . . ." she had promised when she left for her errand that morning.

It was more than a bit awkward at "Chickpoint Charlie," as Claire, in a manic effort to cover her nervousness. had dubbed my father's apartment. It was in the black-and-white art deco tiled bathroom where she had powdered her nose, taken a million pees, a bath or two and once, after having multiple balloon glasses of wine, placed her cheek on that cool surface and slept until she was discovered and put her to bed under the familiar duvet cover, that my father was now trying to think about anything but the empty jar in his hand.

She'd needed some breathing room when she and Theo were suffering their "winter of discontent" and she had come here to sleep fitfully in their tiny guest room. They had served her coffee and croissants and tangy French yogurt on a tray that held a framed photograph of Theo and Claire smiling into the sun of a happier day.

Now she felt like an intruder as the makings of her son were being ejaculated into an empty jar of baby-food peaches.

"We wanted to get apricots," said his wife, motioning Claire into the kitchen, "but the A&P was out."

Claire had forgotten she'd told them about the night Theo announced her change of heart with baby food. Now she smiled at this kindness. "As long as it's sterilized, it doesn't matter what flavor."

"Would you like something to drink? Juice, iced coffee, tea?" My father's wife wiped the counter for the third time.

"No thanks." Claire thought: *Somebody ought to be recording this.* "Is it getting cold in here?"

"It's always warmer in the bathroom," she said, still hovering. "No cross-ventilation."

"I hope he's doing those visualization exercises I taught him," said Claire, staring at a spot above the stove. "I think it's important to see a healthy, whole person right from the beginning, don't you?"

"I'm sure he's visualizing something," she said, smiling at the thought of her dear and generous husband behind the bathroom door. "I just hope it's me."

Three hours later, Claire and the stoner rolled to a stop on Central Park West, and even though she sprinted through the lobby and up the stairs, where an edgy Theo waited to do her part, she knew she was carrying duds.

"I don't think the boys are in the mood today. Between the traffic and a damn gale blowing right on them, they're a full hour past swimming time, not to mention the stress of having to drive with a cabbie who is so high, he thinks neutral is a political position, these guys are way past their use-by date. I think they've lost that lovin' feeling, if you know what I mean."

"You know, I could just go with you next time," said an exasperated Theo. "I'm sure they'd let us do it there."

"That's not very romantic."

"Neither is dead sperm in a tennis sock."

Most people wonder what they'd be like with a different father, but I used to wonder what I would have been like if one hardy individual from that first chilly batch had, with its last shudder, managed to swim past the dead and dying bodies of his comrades and do the job. I could have been soft in the head, missing fingers, or at very least, one of those people who can't take the heat and faint at barbecues. Natural selection probably would have taken care of the result, but that would have caused too much grief; and, who knows, after a miscarriage, they might have called the whole thing off. Of course, I might have been fearless, the little sperm that could. Or maybe I'd have been stronger and more persistent, not so easily hurt, a little better at knowing the blind spots in the road and seeing around them.

Claire was prepared the next time. Leaving nothing to chance, she rented a bicycle with a basket, packed it with her warmest cashmere sweater, clipped her bell-bottoms and headed downtown. It was sixty-five degrees. The weather was on our side.

"Stork-o-Gram for Theo Bouvier!" Claire sang as she burst through the door less than an hour after the donor "did his thing," as she tactfully put it.

Claire presented Theo with a rose and the leftover Valentine's Day heart she'd managed to find in the marked-down section of D'Agostino's, then she followed Theo into the bedroom, where the sterilized instrument of my conception was wrapped in a freshly laundered and lint-free linen towel.

This part was entirely Claire's idea, discovered in the library, where she had spent hours poring over almanacs and farm journals and horse-breeding books and fat dusty tomes on animal husbandry to find out how prize stallions and bulls and Irish setters managed to sire whole families out of state. "People have been doing this for years," she told Theo. "Well, not exactly *people*."

"You realize I'm never going to feel the same way about Thanksgiving again," said Theo, unwrapping the bulb baster while Claire clutched the small jar still wrapped in her sweater.

"Be careful now—there's only a tiny bit in here," said Claire.

"Isn't it supposed to be cloudy?" said Theo, staring at the scant teaspoon of liquid at the bottom of the jar.

"It's okay. Dr. Collins says it turns clear after twenty minutes or so."

"Well, I guess that's not something you notice when you do it the other way, is it?" said Theo, eyeing the jar on the edge of the dresser. The baster was in her hand. She gripped the bulb and gave it a good squeeze, then let out a yelp.

"Claire, it's gone!"

Theo had just sucked the sperm right into the bulb.

She pulled off the rubber ball and peered into it. "It's got to be somewhere."

Then she felt the drop. "Oh, my God, I just got our child in my eye."

"Stay there. Don't move!" ordered Claire and Theo felt the Leica's flash go off in her good eye.

"Claire, do you mind!"

Theo staggered a little, still off balance from the flash. She squinted at the baster with one eye, considered the physics of the problem, and realized if she was going to make good use of the last bit of semen that managed, miraculously, to cling to the inside of the bulb, some acrobatics would be required. Determined that what went up would not, in this case, come back down, she sat on the floor and opened her robe.

"This reminds me of my first tampon," said Claire. "My mother couldn't get the words out, so she just said, 'Why don't you run along to your room and install this.'" She was on the floor next to Theo, whose legs were on the bed to keep her from falling over from an extremely precarious head-and-shoulder stand.

"'Insert,' 'push,' 'stick up,' or even 'shove' might have been a better choice of words," said Theo into her own chest.

"I read the instructions six times," said Claire, trying to distract Theo and keep her from toppling, "then I took the paper off and stuck the whole thing in, applicator and all."

"You didn't." Theo was starting to shake.

"I did, and it hurt like hell. I kept it up there for two hours until I finally couldn't stand it and told my mother the thing wasn't exactly as comfortable as she had promised."

"Claire, that's really dumb."

"No dumber than getting sperm in your eye."

Theo looked dangerously close to exploding. "How long do I have to stay like this?"

"I don't know. A little longer." Claire hoped there was enough natural light to record this special moment.

"Could we at least lower the lights, maybe put on some romantic music?" said Theo. She was trying hard to be a sport in spite of all the blood rushing into her head.

5

Theodora Bouvier and Claire Hirsh
announce the arrival of their son,
William Roland Bouvier-Hirsh,
10 pounds, 2 ounces, on June 8, 1965.
To share their joy with those less fortunate,
the mothers request that gifts of toys and clothing be donated to
the Elizabeth Blackwell Shelter for Children
in New York City

If my birth announcement had been widely distributed, it would have surely caused a scandal and perhaps even a criminal investigation, which may well have resulted in my permanent residence in a foster home. But it was sent only to family and trusted friends who understood the precarious nature of its admission, people for whom it was, or should have been, second nature to protect my mothers' privacy, as well as their joy, from the censure of strangers. It bore Theo's beautiful script and a photograph of a fat-faced cherub in a tiny sweatshirt that hung in a place of honor in our growing hall gallery.

If it were not for my untimely arrival on a rainy Tuesday night in that exceptionally wet spring, Grandma Hirsh might never have made peace with my mothers; but, as I know now, the deepest feelings live beyond the clear boundaries of right and wrong, should and shouldn't, yes and no, and the unspoken terms of social behavior. Nothing happens without a good reason, and new life gives everyone an excuse to start over.

Claire had been shooting a new series and was eager to finish before "B Day," after which she could not be away from home even for a few hours. The concept, she liked to say, looked at life as a repetitive disorder. She was fascinated by the self-destructive, and often fatal things people did to avoid the reality and the adversity of their lives. As Theo made arrangements with another chef to keep the store open while she was recuperating, and suffered the last indignities of what turned out to be a very large pregnancy, Claire photographed hookers, hustlers, and heroin addicts on Times Square and in The Rambles on Central Park West. She shot drag balls up in Spanish Harlem, the contestants sweaty with nerves, showing the shadows of beards no amount of Pan-Cake could camouflage. There were ballroom dancers at Roseland drifting out of Brooklyn and the Bronx on an ocean of sequins, moustache wax, and tuxedos worn in the seat. Bingo nights in overheated church basements in Astoria and Flatbush resulted in rows of women hunching over dog-eared cards, squinting up through cigarette smoke, listening for the numbers that would set them free. They all had one thing in common, she told the monumentally uncomfortable Theo, who welcomed hearing anything that would still what she swore was the sound of her own skin stretching—a moth-like drive to batter themselves against the brick wall of their own circumstances.

Positive Theo would deliver no sooner than the fourth of July, and reassured of this daily by Dr. Collins, Claire flew to Las Vegas for a weekend of shooting. "Let's put it this way," Theo told Claire for the umpteenth time. "You have enough time to fly around the world and back before the baby comes."

The plan was to shoot the "grinders," as the casinos called them. These were retirees, drifters, grocery clerks, people who needed every penny they played and yet fed the nickel slots in what could only be described as a dreamlike state, mechanically pulling the levers until one arm grew larger than the other, in the vain hope that one day, they would hit the big one.

"Are you sure you'll be okay?" Claire asked twenty times while packing for the trip.

"It's fine," Theo assured her, icing a cake she was testing for the store. "I'll just sit here and eat this cake until you come back. Really. I'm okay," said Theo, handing Claire her camera bag.

They agreed Claire would finish up on Sunday morning, when only the truly addicted filled the casino floor. Then, having gotten the last of the photographs, she would hop a flight to Broken Arrow and spend a few days with the Bouviers, then fly on to New York with Doris and Roy midweek. Doris was elated at the prospect of Theo's first child and her newest grandchild. That the new mothers wanted them to help out filled her with a sentimentality Claire would not have predicted. Roy didn't say much, never did, but Claire saw his excitement in the suitcase already packed for New York when she arrived.

"She was an amazing baby, our Theo," Doris told Claire, passing seconds of the gumbo she had cooked all day in honor of Claire's visit. "She'd tie her diaper around her little shoulders like a cape and waddle and strut around like the Queen of the Nile. Everyone fell in love with her, Claire. It's no surprise you did."

After dinner, Roy stood up, nodded at the women, and headed for the BarcaLounger he had set up in the small yard behind the trailer to catch a breeze. "Give you girls a little time together," he said into the metal hatch they called their front door. Doris gave him a broad smile. "There's a little Jimmy Stewart in him, don't you think?"

As Roy settled in for a "sit," as he called the times he gave himself over to the evening and his own thoughts, Doris got up, waved away Claire's offer to clear the table, and went into the tiny bedroom, motioning Claire to follow. "Want to show you something, Mama."

Doris snapped open a cracked leather suitcase with reinforced corners. It bore the faded remnants of stickers from "iagra Fa" and the "rand Can." Inside were the neatly folded and labeled baby clothes of all the Bouvier children; one after another, she offered them to Claire, who fingered the soft flannel of Theo's tiny kimonos and diminutive undershirts, even softer now with age. She couldn't imagine Theo that small, especially now with the enormous belly that held their child.

"I know Theo would love to see them again, but I really don't think you need to bring these to New York," Claire said, trying to be diplomatic, knowing they already had more baby clothes than I'd ever have time to wear. Between them, they had cornered the market on coveralls, sleepers, jaunty caps, and tie-dyed T-shirts; what they hadn't bought themselves arrived daily in the arms of Suzie, Jess, Molly, Peter, Alan, Thad, and Bax, including a miniature pair of high-button shoes and a string of baby love beads.

"Wait till you see the nursery, Doris," Claire said, remembering the day she and Theo, Bax and Jess and Suzie put on their painting clothes—in Suzie's case something another woman might wear to the opera—and converted the loft she and Theo had been using as a library into the most perfect nursery a child could have. She went to her bag, got the photos, and fanned them out on Doris' black-and-pink chenille bedspread: Claire in bib overalls, a blob of sunflower yellow on her nose, a ballooning Theo in shorts and her chef's apron, Bax and Jessica always correct in white painter's caps, and Suzie in high heels, defiantly holding a paintbrush in one hand, her Nat Sherman in the other.

"We painted an Oklahoma night sky right over your grandbaby's bed," Claire told Doris. They'd worked till they dropped. Then Theo served them chili in Mexican pottery bowls set on the brightly splattered tarp she had thrown on the living room floor, and they all told stories of their own childhoods, or at least, the versions they preferred. When the nursery was finished, it looked more like a nest or a tree house than a real room, with a ceiling of star decals from the Hayden Planetarium, butter-yellow walls, a cradle of robin's-egg blue (later a real bed with a bright red quilt printed with Peanuts characters), and no door to keep their baby from being lulled to sleep by the steady hum of the adults downstairs.

"I used to weave little strips of colored fabric for Theo's wrists, so she could wear bracelets and learn her colors," said Doris wistfully, letting Claire's happy chatter wash over her, thinking of her darling girl about to become a mother.

Claire was touched by the gift of light and texture and form Doris had given her daughter, thinking how gracefully Theo had carried it from childhood into adulthood, how she used it to nurture everyone who came into her life, and now, in the time they had spent together and in the baby she had conceived because of her, had given it freely and with love. Claire smiled at the thought of the layers of amber and trade beads and silver and ivory Theo always wore up to her elbows. They were her grown-up versions of the baby bracelets Claire held now.

"You love her very much, don't you?" said Claire, overcome by the sight of a miniature anklet hung with a silver moon and a star. Doris, surrounded by her memories, eyes brimming with her own version of Theo, just nodded.

"Yes, I do," Claire said, just as the phone rang.

THEO WAS TRYING hard to remember everything she learned in Lamaze class. Alone in the empty apartment, she struggled to tamp down the panic. No pillow, no jokes, no Claire razzing the man who was helping his wife on the mat next to them.

"You must be a very good friend. Is her husband away?" he had asked Claire in between his wife's and Theo's rehearsed grunts.

"I'm no friend," Claire had deadpanned. "I'm the father."

No nervous laughter now. Now there was only pain. She dialed Dr. Collins first.

"How far apart are the contractions?" the doctor asked.

"They're coming every three minutes," Theo gasped, as a new one plowed into her like a truck.

Dr. Collins grabbed her bag and asked her family to keep dinner warm. "Get in a cab and meet me at Lenox Hill."

Theo hung onto the back of the front door, lifted the ancient intercom and panted into the receiver. "Andy, the baby's coming. Have a cab waiting for me when I get downstairs. Lenox Hill."

"Jesus, Mary, and Joseph," replied the stunned doorman.

"Jesus, Mary, and Joseph." Is that Doorman for "Right away, ma'am'? Another contraction hit. Why isn't Claire here?

What seemed like a second later, Andy was at the front door, blushing and brimming over with an odd kind of pride Theo could only figure had something to do with babies born in his building.

"I've got five of my own, Miss Bouvier, you're in goods hands now," Andy said. He had knocked once, as he was taught to do, but let himself into the apartment with the house key he had remembered to put in his pocket as he raced past the office, tapping the snoozing janitor and pointing to the door. "Watch the door, *amigo*. We've got an emergency up in 6D! And get a cab. *Ahora!*"

Theo was dialing again when he rushed in, surprised at seeing her on the phone. Another contraction kicked in and it took her breath away, but she waited for Lucy to summon Claire's mother. She could hear the housekeeper shouting, "We're havin' a baby!"

"Is there anything we can do, dear?" Mary said, sounding as though she might be talking to Barnaby's secretary or the young girl who shampooed her hair.

"No, not really," answered Theo, hanging on to the table in the grip of a contraction. "I'm on my way to Lenox Hill Hospital, and Claire and my mother and father are getting the next flight here. I just wanted you to know."

The next one knocked the breath out of her. She pointed to the red canvas bag on the floor under the hall table. The emergency kid kit had been packed and ready for weeks. As Andy slung it over his shoulder, Theo's swollen legs began to buckle, and he caught her with a muscled strength his doorman's coat had never revealed.

"Off to the hospital with you, miss!" Andy said this loudly, the way he shouted greetings to the tenants over the blare of traffic and jackhammers, not meaning anything by it, filling the empty sidewalk with words the wind blew back to him. Just then Theo remembered the instant camera Claire had tucked into a side pocket, summoned up the strength to reach around Andy for the bag and patted the place she wanted him to open.

"Claire would have wanted a picture of me on the way to the hospital," said a now-ashen Theo. As Andy nervously fiddled with the camera, Theo hung the bag around her neck, put one hand on the place that used to be a hip, held on to the doorknob for dear life and attempted to smile through the most violent contraction yet.

"Andy, hurry up!"

"Okay, Miss Bouvier. Give me a nice smile. Could you move a little to your left? No, *my* left."

"Andy!"

Apparently, my head was in the wrong place. That hasn't changed much over the years, but that night, my inability to be in the right place at the right time did not make it easy for Theo. "It hurt like hell," she told me years later when I asked about the scar that peeked out from the top of her bikini bottom. "If I'd been given a choice, my darling boy, I would have run like a cowardly dog,"

Theo was already prepped, breathing hard and terrified when Dr. Collins arrived. The tall, elegantly coifed woman holding her hand said in the clipped tone of someone who does not suffer delays: "Where have you been, Doctor? My grandchild is coming and my daughter-in-law is in great pain."

By the time Claire, Roy and Grandma Doris landed at Kennedy, threw their luggage into a cab, drove through the sleeping borough of Queens, and burst through the hospital doors, bleary-eyed and manic, I was sleeping peacefully in the nursery, a little red but clean and sweet-smelling after a grueling battle with a pair of forceps and an umbilical cord that had turned deadly. Theo, too, was sleeping off the epidural

Dr. Collins injected to dull the pain of the Caesarean that in one swift and merciful moment of oblivion made Lamaze out to be the monster he really was. Grandpa Barnaby was nodding off in a plastic chair in the fathers' waiting room, accompanied by a life-sized teddy bear with the F.A.O. Schwarz tag still around its neck; Baxter and Jess had arrived with cigars and champagne; Peter was in a pair of khakis and a pajama top; Thad and Alan had Suzie in tow. Grandma Hirsh sat wide awake, ramrod straight, Claire's automatic camera in her hand, ghastly-green hospital scrubs over a soft bouclé jacket that should have been worn to the Palm Court; not to witness the blood and curses of a woman in hard child birth.

Claire tiptoed into the room where Theo slept, a trace of a smile on her lips. A long tube stuck out of the back of her freckled hand and snaked up to an IV bottle. On the bedside stand were the small framed photographs Claire had tucked into the emergency bag to make things feel more like home, remembering how Theo had said, "I'm not moving in, I'm just going there to have a baby." Claire placed a single apricot rose and a tiny silver teething ring on the pillow next to Theo, and the pale red lashes fluttered and through slits of luminous green, a voice thicker than Theo's murmured, "He's beautiful."

When Claire saw me for the first time, taking in my toes, and counting my fingers, she gasped at the amount of carrot hair on my large, old man's head. Bracelets of fat encircled my wrists and padded my ankles. She gazed into eyes that could not be a cross between her own silver-gray and Theo's green, but miraculously were. Grandma Hirsh stood quietly by watching joy, amazement, and love gather in her daughter's face. After a while, she stepped up to the glass, and took Claire's hand.

They watched me for several minutes and then Grandma's arm moved up along Claire's shoulder, and Claire met it by turning her body in to Grandma's. They stood holding one another like this for a long time.

"Did you feel this way when you saw me?" Claire asked.

"I still do," said Grandma through tears of her own. "I love you very much, darling."

No one, not even the boisterously happy young father standing next to Claire, could make out her answer or hear her whisper "I never meant to hurt you," to the older woman at her side. Nor did the graceful cadences of my grandmother's voice disguise the pleading in her question.

"Are you going to call him Roland?"

I WAS TO BECOME the subject of many photographs in my young life—not the grinning arrangements found in most family albums, but stunning black-and-white compositions, beautifully matted in row upon row of blond museum frames. There I am in the requisite pony cart in Central Park, on the carousel with Aunt Suzie and one of her besotted companions none of us remembers, in a bright-colored sling on Theo's back, with Jessica and Baxter and the twins, and with Peter and Molly and a scarecrow at the farm they'd bought just after I was born. In one I'm surrounded by all the basketballs, volleyballs, baseballs, footballs, golf balls, and beach balls my grandpa Barnaby made sure found their way into my "real" boy's life, my own round baby face a new pink Spalding.

Most of these show an infant, and later a toddler who takes the warmth and cosseting of female flesh as his birthright and who might even be shocked to learn that others were raised by hard-muscled people who did not encourage the expression of feelings, the playing of make-believe, singing in bed, or the unabashed enjoyment of a softly pulsing breast.

But there is something else in these early photographs, taken from the other side of the nursery's viewing window. I am only a few hours old, wrapped to bursting in hospital swaddling I cannot see beyond the tip of my nose, much less smile for a camera.

Nevertheless, I am aiming a big, goofy, toothless grin directly at Claire and Grandma Hirsh, the two women who would determine so much about my future beyond that moment. All the baby books say an early smile like this is more likely a bubble of gas, and it would have been impossible for me to distinguish anything beyond shadows and blurry shapes at that point, and even if I could I would not have known what I was seeing—but I know better. And I like to think they did, too.

It's impossible, but whenever I see that photo I get the feeling that at the moment it was taken, I knew something had changed irrevocably, and that it had happened because of me.

6

My infancy was hard on Claire. Mountains of pre- and post-natal reading material described the natural phenomenon of bonding, including the period of abject misery visited on most fathers in the months when neither mother nor child seem to have any use for him. Claire was convinced she would be the first non-birth parent in the history of mammals to transcend this biological fact of life. After all, wasn't she the one who'd wanted me in the first place? Shouldn't I have known this and divided my time accordingly?

It was, she would tell me, the loneliest time of her life. She envied Theo her exalted position as my "natural" mother with an intensity that could have crossed the line to murder at the drop of a nursing bra—or at the very least, seriously damaged what had become an increasingly fragile bond between them. Claire had had no idea how much the sight of Theo as sleepy Madonna snuggling her child would hurt.

At four one morning, an exhausted Theo had just slipped back into bed after an hour of humming, murmuring, patting, walking, and gentle stroking, which had quieted me down, but did not put me to sleep. She was sufficiently worn down to have decided to let me nestle with her in the comfort of her own bed.

"He can't breathe. He can't breathe!" Claire screamed, eyes wide with alarm as she fought to close the space between a dream and the dim safety of the bedroom.

Theo shifted me to her other arm and reached over and massaged her back. "It's okay, honey. It's only a dream."

"I dreamed I puréed you and passed you off as crème brûlée for the Marmelstein brunch," murmured Claire, still reeling from the hands of her subconscious on her throat. She would later describe this as a "textbook rejection dream." Predictable, but no less terrible.

Theo smiled. "No wonder you're upset. You're in the wrong dream. I'm the one who has cooking dreams. You can't cook, remember?"

"You were emptying the refrigerator into a suitcase that had no bottom," said Claire, still very much in the dream's grip. "Everything disappeared into a lid lined with sharpened teeth. The more I begged, the more you laughed. You picked up the kitchen table with one hand and threw that in too, then you dragged Willy out of his crib and put him in and sat on the whole thing because the suitcase was bulging and wouldn't close."

Instinct told Theo this was not the time to analyze, but to respond only to the dream. Claire was swimming too close to the surface of her fears for truth.

"Was I good as crème brûlée?"

"Delicious," said Claire, who had regained enough equilibrium to notice my feet sticking out from the other side of Theo. "But not as good as this little one," she teased, biting my toes and flinging her resentment into the toothless gurgle of my laughter, not caring that Theo would have to quiet me down all over again.

Some mornings, lazy and protected from the world, Theo slid out of bed to whip up one of her wonderful breakfasts, leaving Claire and me to the noisy beginning of a bond that would eventually grow as deep between us as the blood between Theo and me. When she came back, loaded with muffins and coffee, floating in her big silk kimono printed all over with the palm trees I came to imagine swaying to life and dropping coconuts in the perfumed darkness of her closet, the tension was gone and we were a family again.

Some days we stayed in bed for hours, slipping in and out of sleep, tumbling back into play, eating berries dusted with sugar, a jumble of arms and legs, large and small. One morning Claire set the timer and hopped back into bed for a portrait that gave her and Theo the look of two lionesses, one tawny, one fiery red, alert to any danger that might overtake the tiny cub wobbling between them on big clumsy paws, ready to take aim at anything that might shatter the happiness shining out from that photograph.

"People do terrible things in the grip of postpartum depression, Willy Wonka, and I suppose Claire was the first woman to suffer *post* without ever actually having experienced *partum*," Theo explained when I became a father myself and was convinced my sweet-natured

Annie had been spirited away in the middle of the night and replaced by a vicious wolf-mother."

You're just jealous," she said and Annie's being held hostage by her hormones, that's all. Don't worry, she'll come around just like I did."

For her part, Theo was kind to Claire; she instinctively understood the isolation she felt standing helplessly by, forsaken for the powerful magic of nourishment.

She studiously avoided the smugness of new mothers, that pained, mysterious, superior look that says, "I have suffered, I have lost my figure, but I have done something far more important than anything you could possibly imagine, more than you could ever do."

Maybe it was the tenderness Theo felt for her own father, left stranded in the maternal wake of Doris, who marshaled her ducklings and dispensed what he could not to the Bouvier brood. Or maybe it was simply the look on Claire's face when I nestled at Theo's breast, snug and content with the idea that while I couldn't exactly crawl back inside, I would always be as close as a button's breadth to mother love and my next meal.

I cried if Theo so much as left the room. I wailed when she returned to the shop for a few hours a day, and when I heard the familiar sound of her key in the door I grabbed the soft red curls that matched my own, smelled her mixture of milk and carnations and warm skin as she picked me up. Like every infant who knows his mother has not left him forever, I vibrated with happiness and relief.

Claire winced her way through these first few months. Once, as Theo stole a few hours at the shop to work on a new menu, she tried to give me her own skinny nipple, which left me howling and even hungrier for Theo.

"Helloooo! Is anybody home?" Theo called into the strangely quiet apartment. "Where is everybody?" She called again and felt her step quicken, the rolling sensation of fear, then a strange lightness in her legs at the sight of Claire, eyes closed and tightly coiled in the rocking chair in the nursery.

"I tried to nurse him," Claire said, grimacing at the rising wail that greeted the reappearance of nourishment.

Theo, still clutching the Latest Dish bag she had brought home, chest slamming with relief, didn't know whether to laugh or cry.

"What happened?"

"It hurt like hell is what happened. We're both a little cranky from the experience. I can't speak for Willy, but I, for one, feel a little foolish."

I think Claire really believed nature would make an exception of her. The realization that our enlightened notion of family had affected nothing in the grand biological scheme exhausted her. To the unseen hand that had drawn this ancient pattern, designed the pull of the moon and duplicated it in perfect symmetry in every single cell, we were just an odd little family of fish swimming in the wrong direction, slapping and flailing against what always was and always would be. Claire believed the universe had chided her for her overblown sense of self-importance. It humbled her with the sight of tiny fingers walking contours already familiar from a floating dream, eyes blind to everything but the shape and smell of mother love, food, shelter, safety, and a dry diaper.

She watched Theo unbutton her blouse and settle in to nurse her frustrated child and realized then nature didn't give a rap how much she yearned to switch places with Theo and told her so in the perfect cupid's-bow mouth of a little boy seeking his mother.

It seems ironic now that it was really Claire who prepared me for the shock and the resentment I felt at my own uselessness in the wake of my babies' urgent need for no one but Annie; that it was she who reached into the future to teach me this lesson in fatherhood through Theo's telling.

Apart from my impossible clinging to Theo, especially around feeding times, Theo and Claire shared everything equally, carving up their time with me as carefully as they would a rich pudding, every minute fairly dispensed and blissfully savored, along with those not so sweet, neatly divided.

They put a sign on the front door that read, "Shhh, Baby Sleeping! Do Not Ring Bell!" Theo, a born juggler, was able to see friends, cook, grow a business, and care for a baby, a lover, and a home simultaneously. Claire wouldn't even answer the phone during her time with me. Mind you, this was before voice mail and computers, so instead, she phoned Pearl, the operator at our answering service, and instructed her to give the following message to anyone who called: *Claire would love to talk to you, but knowing how much you hate to be interrupted by His Nibs, you'd probably rather she call you back during his nap which will be in about seven minutes.* Claire actually alerted the service to the approximate time of my nap every day.

Tina, Pearl's nighttime counterpart, knew all our friends, and loved to straighten out snarled dinner dates and movie plans, once told Jessica who had called to confirm the time of a lunch set for the following day that I had a little colic, nothing to worry about, but that she should probably go ahead and start serving without Claire.

"I'm telling you, honey," Tina told Jessica, "with Theo doing that party way up on Riverside and Claire on her own, it's gonna be a while before she gets that baby and herself dressed and settled down, then all the way to you."

They agreed that whoever wheeled the carriage into the park would say, if asked, that she was the mother, which more than confused the women lining the benches up and down the paths around the sailboat pond and under the pigeon-splattered gaze of Hans Christian Andersen. Claire enjoyed watching suspicion and envy move among them as they took in my miniature heavyweight status and eyed the lean length of her in the skinniest clothes she could find for these parades around the park.

On one of our outings, she smiled into the collective narrowing of eyes and sat down on a sunny bench. "I don't know what all the fuss is about. "I had a very easy time." Then, winking at my bracelets of fat, "It's amazing how fast twenty pounds comes off.

"They're still trying to figure out how I lost all that baby fat," she told Theo, who patted her still zaftig behind and said, "Let's hope I don't run into the same group."

Theo knew it was Claire's jealousy talking, but laughed with her anyway, and never let on that during my infancy, Claire seemed to be another child going through a difficult stage. Theo loved her even more for her vulnerability, for trusting her enough to let it show.

I attended my first formal brunch at Cafe des Artiste at three months and one of Claire's slide shows at the Hunter College auditorium at four. I slept undisturbed through the mimosas and the asparagus frittatas, right up to the blueberry cobblers and cappuccino, snoozing in the sling Theo had designed for such occasions. But I'm told the shadows of Claire's photographs cast on the ceiling, and the amplified sound of her lecture scared me. Somewhere between slides of wild dogs in Sao Paolo and Mrs. Levkowitz' numbers, I pierced the pin drop hush with the youthful protest of someone who has not yet learned to suffer the pretensions of the art world in respectful silence.

When I was six months old we dropped in on Grandma Doris and Grandpa Roy in Broken Arrow. This required I take my first plane ride, something I did not enjoy due to the new and painful sensation of popping in my delicate ears, which could not be relieved with a yawn no matter how much Claire opened and closed her mouth to get me to mimic her. My grandparents had not seen me since that first night at Lenox Hill, where they slept on hard hospital chairs while waiting for a proper introduction. The two hectic weeks that followed could hardly be considered a visit. Until my arrival in Broken Arrow, they had been content to follow my progress via a steady flow of gray manila envelopes marked "Photographs! Do Not Bend!"

Alternative lifestyles, same-sex unions, relationship-defining contracts, palimony, galimony, life partners, pre- and post-nuptual agreements—these were concepts my mothers helped pioneer, but they would have hated the numbing, politically correct jargon that makes so much that is out of the ordinary, exotic, and self-expressive seem colorless today. Acknowledgment of their relationship in anything more than the criminal sense in 1965 was unheard of. But that was also the time when bearded hippies and achingly young girls with flowers in their hair were celebrating anything they pleased in meadows and on mountaintops and in the communes that were springing up around a definition of peace, love, and anti-war sentiment. Claire and Theo watched with great interest from the distance of their situation. They, too, wanted to celebrate their own version of counterculture.

They decided to get married.

A few days before we left for Broken Arrow, Claire went to Cartier and bought matching rings of six connected bands of pink, yellow, and white gold, and hid them in her cosmetic bag to surprise Theo. My uncle the Reverend Roy, Junior arranged the ceremony and in the spirit of the times, dubbed it, "A Happening of God, Peace, Love, and Family Unity." It was held on the tribal land, which was the only place that would allow it, and it got him in plenty of hot water with the church management, which didn't stop him from telling them he'd "do it again tomorrow."

Baxter and Jess, Suzie, and my "uncles" Thad and Alan, flew out to surprise them. Uncle Peter came without Aunt Molly because they had decided my cousin Charlotte, who was only four, was too small to be left alone with a sitter for more than a few hours at a time.

"Are they coming?" Claire had asked him in a private moment before the ceremony.

Peter shuffled a bit and said, "Her arthritis has been kicking up lately, and you know Dad doesn't go anywhere without Mother."

"Arthritis doesn't keep her off those damn committees of hers, and she moves all right when one of her friends throws a charity ball."

"You know she loves Willy," said Peter, caught between loyalty and a lie.

He's still trying to get something from them, still trying not to take a side, hoping they'll wake up and love him as much as Roland, Claire thought. But he had come all this way to be at her wedding, and he looked tired. She had the decency not to pursue it.

Getting married is never without its complications, but back then there were more than a few hurdles for Theo and Claire, not the least of which was the fact that their union was recognized by no one except our little family. Given the absence of Mary and Barnaby Hirsh, even that approval was not unanimous. To further complicate matters, those were the years when people who gave birth or threatened to do so before saying "I do" bore the stigma of being "easy." But even marrying for the sake of a child held the implication that, however unsuitable the person was, one married a member of the opposite sex. My presence in the stroller they wheeled straight down the middle of an old sweat lodge they had transformed into a chapel put an interesting twist on the problem.

Claire, Theo, and I all wore white. "Otherwise, we'll just fight over who gets to be the bride," Claire decided. Suzie, who could manage only the basic guitar chords, gave *Amazing Grace* a college try. During the vows, Uncle Roy asked Claire and Theo if they would follow the requirement given by Jesus to the woman in the Gospel of St. John and simply "love one another." This was Suzie's cue to plunge into a lurching rendition of "Both Sides Now," which drowned out their answers, my wailed agreement, and the sentimental sniffling of all gathered.

Afterward, everybody piled into cars and went back to the Bee-Line for one of Grandma Doris's barbecue suppers.

Even though we've got our backs to the camera, the shot of Claire and Theo standing before Uncle Father Roy, who is asking them if they will love and honor and cherish each other and me forever while I listen and play with their rings from the carriage between them is the one I love the most.

When I showed it to Annie in the months preceding our own wedding, she grinned wickedly. "I knew your mothers weren't exactly traditional, but I didn't realize they *had* to get married."

I am told that somewhere around the two-year mark, I began to call Theo Mama and Claire Mommy. Claire used to joke that I called her Moma for the Museum of Modern Art, but I think she made it up to make me sound smarter.

Most Sundays Theo cooked a big potluck dinner and opened our apartment to as many members of our extended family as were in town and hungry. Everyone knew they could change their minds and drop by even if they'd said they wouldn't; Theo always managed to coax something wonderful out of our big kitchen and produce another place for stragglers, strays and friends of friends.

Of all my memories of Theo, this is how I remember her the happiest, beaming as the people she loved most enjoyed her food. Closing her eyes and nodding at their compliments, she would refill plates, touch shoulders as she passed chairs, inserting a comment here and there, telling a joke, finishing a sentence for Claire before moving on. This is how I see her—orchestrating, encouraging, appreciating, welcoming, and urging newcomers back, pressing gifts of food along with her kisses good-bye.

Happily deluded into the notion that the world was filled with good-smelling foods, loving hands, and doting aunts and uncles, I learned that love has its own language, its own smell, a taste that leaves an indelible mark on the memory.

On one such languorous afternoon in late fall, everyone was admiring a rocker Theo and Claire had discovered during a weekend visit to the farm Uncle Peter and Aunt Molly had just leased in the sleepy Long Island village of South Neck.

Baxter gave it a long and appraising look and said it looked like the work of Gustave Stickley. "If it is, there should be a brass tag somewhere underneath that says, "Craftsman Workshops, Eastwood, New York," but even if there isn't, luv, it's a nice example of the early

Crafts movement." Bax always encouraged enjoyment over investment, even in the acquisition of the far older and more valuable antiques and architectural oddities he found in remote corners of the world and sold in his antique shop, a series of connecting front parlors in a row of ancient mews houses on MacDougal Street.

Uncle Bax said "luv" the way a Cockney says "guv"; the ghost of his London childhood lingered in his broad A's and in the faintly aristocratic way his cigarette floated between long slender fingers as though someone else had put it there to surprise him. Baxter had just taken off his suede moccasins, touched the edges of his Sergeant Pepper handlebar mustache and assumed his own lanky version of a half-lotus, and was about to inspect the chair's oak underside when Peter and Molly arrived.

"Stickley, hell. More like 'Stick it to the city slickers' to me," said Peter in his exaggerated country-bumpkin voice. "I'm learning those farm boys don't give away too many bargains."

"Oh, here he is now, the Fifth Avenue hayseed," Claire teased.

"Well," Peter said, eyeing his sister and beaming an appraising smile at Theo's billowing sleeves. "You two don't exactly have 'local' written all over you."

"I'm sure there isn't much call for floor-length batik and toe rings on a potato farm," said Jessica from inside her shining black curtain of bobbed hair. She had been enjoying the exchange from the vantage point of her favorite chair, in front of the huge windows. The light was dropping fast. Against that backdrop, coiled among the cushions, she looked more like a figure from a twenties bas-relief than a young woman living in the Age of Aquarius.

When Aunt Jessica wasn't teaching the twins Italian or how to recognize the dressmaker details that define the difference between couture and ready-to-wear, she entertained her friends with stories, many of which featured her boss, a plug ugly fashion editor who made ridiculous pronouncements like *Never wear dancing shoes on the street!* and *A good suit can be worn inside out!* She loved to say the editor did this so people wouldn't notice her resemblance to J. Edgar Hoover. In between redecorating their English country house-cum brownstone on West Twelfth Street, which was always being photographed for interior design books, Jess wrote gloppy stuff about clothes in fashion magazines and was often away in a place called Location.

She drifted away from things, Aunt Jess, preferring the world of imagination to the mundane, albeit elegant, one she and Uncle Bax inhabited. Fabrics like chiffon, charmeuse, and cashmere were not *worn*, according to Jessica. They *floated*, *clung*, and *poured* like thick cream from the masterful hands of Hubert, Oscar, and Yves, whoever they were.

I loved to watch her work. As the blank white pages filled up with words, her lips moved constantly in an imaginary conversation. She smoked an imaginary cigarette in a silver cigarette holder. Her hands gestured extravagantly, as if gathering her power from the air. Theo showed me the neat printed columns signed Jessica McClain Baxter, for which, Claire said, Jess was paid "tons of money."

Claire never took pictures for Aunt Jess's magazine because she said it taught people to value the wrong things, and this was the source of tension between them. But not that day. That day, Jess sat next to my grandmother, who was never comfortable at our house but adored "that darling girl with the English husband."

Molly's hands flew into action before she got as far as the living room, and that Sunday was no exception. She offered me a set of antique blocks found in an old trunk in the farm's attic; gave several pots of her black-currant jam to Theo, who had promised to try it out in the store; and handed Claire some old photographs from the same trunk—all this before she was halfway across the living room. As usual, Peter followed close behind, waiting to peel away the coat he knew she would only get half off before it became entangled in her enthusiasm.

"You really must stop showing up empty-handed," said Jessica. She was faintly dismissive of Molly, but never mean to Claire's unsophisticated midwestern sister-in-law. She didn't understand Molly's disregard for fashion, her peasant's enjoyment of simple country pleasures, or her refusal to compete with her fast-talking New York family.

"Somebody's got to listen," Molly would say when Suzie and Jess and Claire were all laughing and talking, interrupting and stepping all over each other's lines in their manic version of conversation. "How else would any of you know what you've been talking about?"

Peter had finally given up living in Roland's shadow, rejecting the life Barnaby had so desperately wanted him to embrace, along with the muggers he was convinced waited for him on every street corner now that he was a father with responsibilities. Molly hated the idea of raising Charlotte and my two-year-old cousin Harry in the cramped apartment they'd once loved with the superiority of city dwellers. "They'll wither," Molly had said, always finding her words in the garden she loved. Tired of the infrequent writing jobs and irregular paychecks, Peter was trying his hand at growing potatoes and corn, running South Neck's small newspaper, and raising a family in relative peace and quiet with a minimum of summer people, who for the most part preferred the trendier Hamptons.

He and Molly had come alone that day, having left my cousins with Molly's parents, who were visiting from Ohio and thrilled at the prospect of having their grandchildren all to themselves for the day as were Peter and Molly at the idea of one of Theo's "afternoons."

"I love country on weekends," Jessica said in answer to Molly's gushing descriptions of the farm and their decision to move, "but really, isn't this taking things a little too far?"

"Why don't we all make ourselves a plate of something?" said Theo lest someone fall from the high wire that always seemed to stretch a little tighter when Mary Hirsh was present. "Thinnest first," she announced, looking directly at Jessica and Mary.

Apropos of nothing, which is the way she started most conversations, Jessica said, "Do you remember how you told us about Theo, Claire?" Jessica never waited for an answer.

"Bax and I were in Nevis or St. Martin or somewhere," she said, settling into her story. "I was doing swimsuits, which were awful in 'sixty-three, those tiny crocheted things that got soggy and fell off when wet, leaving absolutely nothing to the imagination. Bax was working too, scouting the island for good examples of the Dutch colonial period, anything that hadn't gone completely off in that insufferable heat, and I think he was having lunch in a mill or a plantation or a castle, I can't recall. It was a ruin, anyway, and the owners were anxious to sell off their collection. It was just before Christmas. No, actually, it might have been the day after, Boxing Day as Baxter calls it," she said, imitating her husband's clipped English accent. She sounded like the italics in her magazine.

"Sweetheart, you're drifting," Baxter said encouragingly from across the room.

Jessica smiled sweetly at the man who knew her too well.

"The plan was to stay on for a little holiday when one of those awful 'dear friends' Christmas letters arrived at the hotel from guess who?" Jessica tipped her head, shivering the curtain of silky black hair, which closed dramatically over one large almond eye.

"It wasn't an awful letter," said Claire, feigning hurt.

"Of course, it was, but you're a famous photographer and, as such, not expected to write compelling letters.

"Well, there it was," continued Jessica, "buried somewhere between the weather in New York and how many cigarettes Suzie smoked at the Coney Island show: 'I've fallen in love with someone named Theo and he's a she!'"

The lining of my grandmother's pale pink suit rustled softly as she shifted in her chair.

Peter shook his head at Molly, who slid a furtive glance at her mother-in-law.

"Well, I did what any best friend would do under the circumstances. I wrote an immediate reply."

"Opening with 'Oh my God, have you told your mother?'" said Claire, forgetting her mother's presence.

"No, it was 'Darling Claire, colon, Oh my God, have you told your mother?'"

In the kitchen, Theo shook her head and prayed Mary Hirsh had a strong heart, but Claire and Jessica were beyond noticing or caring. This was their ritual, a story they would repeat until they both believed their friendship had not been diminished by this drastic development in Claire's life.

"You weren't exactly sure how you'd fare either, asking if I would think you and Baxter boring heterosexuals, now that I was a lesbian, which of course, you had to type in all caps."

"I suppose it was a little silly to feel threatened by Theo of all people." Jessica continued, interjecting another "Oh my God, have you told your mother?" which brought up Grandma Hirsh's color. Claire, giddy from laughing, came up for air. "Do you remember how you signed off?"

"I think the complimentary close was entirely appropriate given the circumstances," said Jessica: "'Well, good-bye, you old dyke!'" This drew fresh laughter from Thad and Alan who had arrived mid-story.

"Are you all right, Mother?" Peter asked as Mary passed his chair.

"Fine, dear. I'm just going to see if Theo needs help in the kitchen."

At our house, no one needed to be called to dinner twice. After a while, Theo stood near the French doors and smiled, which was the signal to rise and move toward our red Parson's table set with Molly's homemade bread, a baked ham cut into a perfect pink spiral accompanied by a piquant mustard and horseradish sauce, bubbling Lyonnaise potatoes, and a large tureen of smoky lentil and andouille sausage soup. As people drifted out of the living room toward the fragrant, homey food, Jessica linked arms with Claire and, making sure Mary was out of the room, paused just long enough to let the moment settle. She tilted her head in Claire's direction and winked. "I guess we can all be grateful she didn't send pictures."

On her way to the kitchen my grandmother wandered into the foyer, which still held the sweetness of the armload of freesias and tea roses Thad and Alan had handed to Claire along with their coats, covering their generosity with a lie about not wanting to leave them to die unsold.

Uncle Thad, a soft-spoken chef, and Uncle Alan, a lover of exotic flowers, were Theo's friends from the Barrow Street years when they all met for coffee every Wednesday afternoon and the occasional dinner in Theo's floor-through with its huge, old-fashioned kitchen and working fireplace across from the stove, which made it the most coveted and most welcoming apartment in New York. They had banded together while they were still new in the city with its strange customs and hard lessons for people who didn't yet know the ropes.

Mary thought about these young people she did not understand, and she looked up at the letter from Jess that Claire had framed along with the rest of the mementos and photographs that lined the wall. Between the lines of its dashed-off spontaneity and brutal honesty, on pale blue paper spotted with something that might have been sun lotion near the clubby hotel crest, it revealed much about love and trust and taboo and perhaps more than Jessica intended about its author's fear of being left behind in her friend's new life.

Listening to the voices rise and fall in the living room, shifting to other topics with the arrival of fresh faces, Mary wondered what was best—showing the world such bare-faced reaction or allowing the passage of time to temper one's response. Biding one's time was Mary's way, waiting it out and letting the rigors of life decide. And in the end, perhaps, finding no need to comment at all.

When she slipped back into the room, the talk had turned to the time, when just after my first birthday, Theo had closed the store, Claire had loaded her camera, and they parked me with Baxter and Jess to take what they called their second honeymoon trip to Paris, where they stayed at a place on the Left Bank called L'Hôtel.

"Our cab driver had a small dog in the front seat that stood on its hind legs and stared over the seat at us every time its owner said, '*Quelle hôtel, mesdames?*' Each time the man repeated the question, the dog barked and growled more menacingly," said Theo, bending over to refill Baxter's plate, while he fiddled with the new chair.

"The cab driver closed his eyes and made the *puh* sound Parisians always make when they think you're crazy. Well, we finally found it and it was a lovely trip, but when we got home and went straight to you-know-who's from the airport to collect our darling boy," Theo said, ruffling Baxter's hair, "Jess answered the door with a face full of chalky white powder. She looked like some bizarre Kabuki player and, of course, she couldn't imagine why we were staring at her."

"I thought she was trying on some new look for the magazine," said Claire, jumping into the space she always found in Theo's conversation to make it her own. "Or making pancakes," said Theo, deftly jumping back.

"Well, I certainly didn't know what all the fuss was about," said Jessica. "It was just baby powder. I invented it with the twins. Whenever a baby bottom needed changing, I'd dust a bit on my face first. I, for one, would rather smell powder than poo," she said, pointing to my fat diapered bottom as I waddled by.

"That's my girl," said Bax.

"All this talk makes me think of Fitzie," said my grandmother, thinking of the sister who was always trying to make a match for Claire and who had passed away suddenly, a few months before I was born. She'd gone to Bergdorf's for her weekly styling and while she stood at the salon's elegant desk to pay, her heart seized and she died in the ambulance on the way to Lenox Hill.

"Poor Aunt Fitzie would never have dreamed of dying before her comb-out," said Claire of the aunt who had left a gaping hole in her own life. Fitzie never abandoned her and dropped in on Claire and Theo, when it was not the correct thing to do in the Hirsh family.

When the fading Sunday afternoon light drew its magic around sleeping children and wistful adults, softening the edges of their memories, it wasn't unusual to hear Grandma Hirsh and Claire tell stories about their beloved Fitzie, who herself had never married and who was, in many ways, the real mother of the family.

Sometimes, they laughed so hard they snorted, remembering the time Fitzie, whose real name was Margaret, decided to give little Claire a home permanent, then locked herself out of the apartment while the developing solution turned Claire's fine blond hair into something resembling felt. At other times they fell into a reverential silence, as when they talked of the man named Fitzpatrick who promised to love her forever a week before he was killed on that terrible day at Pearl Harbor.

Grandma always said the stories were for me, so I would know our family history and my aunt Fitzie's place in it, but I suspected this was her own way of grieving, of keeping her little sister alive a little longer, or maybe of holding on to something she and Claire could be comfortable sharing.

There was no such reflection that day. The front door buzzed and Aunt Suzie swooped into the room with someone named Philippe.

"Everyone say *bon jour*," she announced, then, abandoning the poor fellow to the others, made a beeline for me. "Hello, *mon petit cuteness*, my adorable boy," she said, swallowing me up in a flash of rhinestones and the unlikely swoosh of taffeta and leather. To my utter delight, she never failed to take off her hat or her pearls or whatever shiny object she happened to be wearing and hand it right over to me, as though everything about her was merely a prop for my pleasure. That day, I happily munched a felt flower from her hat, slowly chewing every bit and smiling a mouthful of purple petals for Claire, who immortalized the moment in a photograph she called "Late Blooming Flower Child."

Suzie's friends pretended to blend in with the family but followed her every move the way inmates watch the guards, never overtly enough to draw attention, but always aware of the other's position. They usually ended up talking with Barnaby, who said very little, content to watch his wife's reactions, measuring the distance he needed to keep from his own feelings about those Sundays.

I grew up believing I was the natural heart of these people, who hadn't really known each other before I was born—and, in Grandma and Grandpa Hirsh's case, hadn't wanted to. I carried my responsibility for their happiness on my tiny shoulders. I cooed in the awkward silences, and kept the conversation going with the antics of a small comedian doing pratfalls on fat legs. I screeched my pleasure at the slightest attention and, like every creature still small enough not to be misled by words that do not match intention and who operates purely on sensation, I always curled up with the one who needed me most.

On one of these Sundays, Thad came to dinner without Alan and everyone was unearthly still. I climbed into his lap and clung to his sweater and was the only person who could make him smile that day—and all the other days that followed, when he came to sit in the corner of our apartment just to hear our laughter and to be in the company of people who loved him unconditionally. No one asked to see the part of him broken by the endless round of meals served in teaspoons, the constant ministrations and indignities suffered by his beloved Alan, who could no longer open the dark shop and pick flowers for Theo and Claire and their boy.

I became his belief in the future simply because I was at the beginning of mine. I had no concept of death or of the cruel disease called Amyotrophic Lateral Sclerosis that was taking Alan away from us muscle by muscle. First to go were his strong arms, which could cut through bundles of thick stems from the wholesale market in a single slice; then his legs, which stood all day in the tiny shop, danced, ran, took great long strides all the way up from the Village to our apartment, and then forced him to sit in the humiliating lap of a chair. Finally, he could no longer speak or swallow and every labored breath brought him closer to the final gasp. Nor could I fathom the bitter irony of this illness's association with the great Lou Gehrig and the manly sport Alan had no idea how to play.

I had only the headlong interest in life enjoyed by those still close to its source. I did not fear the hand that held a warm cloth to Alan's crusted lips, pulled out thick ropes of mucous from lungs that could no longer cough and trembled in the face of his lover's harsh sentence, nor could I offer comment on how he was handling it. I simply gave him proof that life goes on, and he gave me the security of thinking all families were thus.

There would be many Sundays filled with the reassuring jingle of Theo's bracelets, the click of Claire's camera and always, the easy laughter, loving arms, and soft laps of friends and family, each one unique as a snowflake in its particular cacophony of footsteps, doors opening and closing, a choreography of laughter and voices rising and falling on fragrant gusts from the kitchen.

The advancing light of each of those afternoons moved as though an unseen hand ushered the memory of it into a kind of emotional bank account, toting up a balance against the inevitable rainy day when I would first hear the word "dyke," a word I would always remember as not spoken, but spat, like something viscous and foul caught in the throat.

7

If Claire and Theo's life together was complicated, I never noticed. If the world received them with less than open arms, and judged them harshly for their decision to live openly as a family, that was not my concern. I was the child and like all children, I squeezed all experience through the fine sieve of my own needs. But I was not blind to the choices made on my behalf.

Although it did not come as nataurally to her as it did to Theo, Claire tempered her artist's life and its implicit creative and personal freedom in the name of motherhood. Instead of rushing down to Washington to chronicle the sprawling protest of Freedom City, shooting the mounted police ringing the Monument, and scattering protesters like jackrabbits, or bearing witness to the explosion of rage in Harlem and Newark and Detroit, she changed diapers. She cheerfully attended school conferences and doctor and orthodontist appointments, walked me to school when I wouldn't ride the bus, and imposed the time constraints of family on the compelling images she continued to coax out of the bath of her darkroom. There are photographs that prove her dedication to mothering, compositions taken just as carefully as the ones she and Suzie discussed in important whispers during my nap. There was Theo wheeling my carriage, Claire and me at the bus stop, taken by the driver, my every bruise, scrape, bump, smile, Christmas, Passover and pout dutifully noted—"First tooth!" "Today kindergarten, tomorrow Columbia!" There is one called "Willy's first diaper;" she actually photographed it before flushing its contents and throwing the diaper into the service bag.

Everything stopped when I arrived home from school with graded tests, pictures drawn in art class, Pilgrim hats made of kraft paper, crudely drawn maps full of bits of cotton from the tops of medicine bottles, matted clumps of grass, gluey slivers of wood. My appearance trumped even the hollow-eyed madness of putting a show together, phone ringing off the hook, dozens of conferences with Suzie, who paced the apartment smoking the awful black cigarettes Theo tried to outlaw in the name of my developing lungs.

"When Baxter does it, it's elegant; when I do it, it's air pollution," Suzie complained once such afternoon, filling our living room with her peculiar brand of fog while Claire pored over contact sheets. "I'll give you a lollipop if you don't tell Theo," she said, ruffling my hair. I never told, and even though I never smoked myself, I still love the bitter smell of Suzie's cigarettes.

When she heard me come in, Claire dropped the grease pencil and the loupe she used to examine the tiny squares on each page of the stack in front of her and slid down the hall in her socks. "What wonderful things have you been up to today?" she would sing, planting kisses on my eyelids, ears, inside my collar and only pretending to scoop me up, because I was now too heavy for the real thing. Then she would fold her legs lotus-style on our deep pillows, pat her lap, and invite me to present the day's accomplishments. She took my doodles seriously and critiqued them as carefully as she did the efforts of the eager photography students who gathered in our apartment in steadily increasing numbers.

"Why did you choose green for the sky?" she asked, gazing thoughtfully into my second-grade splatter.

"Because when I stand on my head, the grass is where the sky should be." I answered with the absolute confidence of one who has not yet learned the boundaries of scientific possibility.

"Don't ever forget that, Willy Wonder," Claire said. "Anybody can see, but only special people can draw what they feel."

I showed her a paper marked with a big red F, scrawled across the top like an incision, shame reddening cheeks as I waited for what I was sure would be her profound disappointment.

"Great! Wonderful! That's my baby!" Claire exclaimed, thrusting my composition at Suzie. "Any fool can see what happened here. Willy's teacher has no imagination."

"Are we going to have another artist in the family?" said Suzie, grabbing for the place under my arms I loved and hated to be tickled.

"You'd better grow up fast, otherwise you're going to have the world's oldest agent."

It never occurred to me that there might be issues on the table more serious than my childish efforts. Nor could I imagine waiting in a silent apartment with a sitter for my parents to come home the way many of my classmates did.

Theo's burgeoning business had not yet grown into the mail order and cookbook empire it would become. Claire's decision to work closer to home, combined with Theo's un-businesslike refusal to keep the shop open on Sundays even though that meant doing brunches far into Saturday night because we needed one day a week together as a family, were the facts of my life. Like all children who see, but choose to ignore the small cracks that become the deep fissures that will one day sunder their parents, I felt no guilt pressing on my shoulder.

When I was old enough to walk four avenues over to the store, I did not think it at all unusual for Theo to rush out from behind the counter or the kitchen to greet me, nod appreciatively at a painting or read a composition aloud to all gathered, her voice full of praise and quivering pride. I often found my art-work tacked to the menu board that announced the daily specials, and once I got a round of applause from customers for my Mothers' Day poem, which described my life as doubly blessed, a reaction that was all the more surprising for the lack of attention, beyond the odd snicker, it had received at school.

It wasn't until I was a man myself and aware of my own sexual needs that I saw how much in life competes with that pleasure and began to wonder how my mothers found the time for the lurid and unnatural acts they were accused of. When my own children were born, I saw firsthand how little room there is for love and what a cruel joke society plays when it marks people for life according to how they might have conducted themselves in the unbearably short season of passion before life presses in and bed becomes a place to be dead for a few hours. As a child, and especially as a curious young boy with dangerously little to go on in the way of carnal knowledge, I assumed Theo and Claire made love in a dark, mysterious way I could not imagine and could not hear, even though I tried my best to listen over the creak and rattle of our sleeping apartment.

It never occurred to me that they collapsed after a grueling day in a small kitchen, and in a foul-smelling darkroom, exhausted by errands, and the endless details of a household that includes a growing boy. Not until I did the very same thing, grateful for the sound of Annie's gentle snoring, did I realize that sleep could be as irresistible as sex once was.

I didn't know their relationship, because of its outsider status, needed the special nourishment of time alone and time spent with people with whom careful presentation was not a requirement. Nor did I think they could ever be prey to the problems that beset the mothers and fathers of my schoolmates, mainly because I saw them as heroines who had declared their love to the world and having done that, could only be loved back. I suppose this is the fantasy in which every child lives, and in spite of my growing distance from the other kids, the disapproving looks from their parents and the increasing uneasiness of the truce between my grandmother and Claire, I held on to it for as long as I could. Seeing our parents as human is the real terror of the world we are about to enter. Like every child before me, I dragged my feet.

Most of my weekends were spent rutting around the spongey ground of Uncle Peter and Aunt Molly's farm with cousin Harry and Bartie and Blisset, their eternally muddy black Labs. So, too, did I have countless overnights at Jess and Baxter's brownstone with its secret back staircase, ballroom-sized pantry full of old bottles and foreign-looking tins, and a musty attic that came as close as a boy could imagine to living in a haunted house. The idea that any of this might have been arranged for anything other than my exclusive pleasure was inconceivable.

How could I have known that it was highly unusual, if not entirely unheard of, for little boys to regularly attend their parents' friends' soirees, especially those held in one of the most beautiful old houses in Greenwich Village? All I knew was that I never tired of sitting at the top of the long curving stairs, where Jennifer and Brooke and I were allowed to observe the festivities. I loved following my mothers in the room below carving separate paths in the swirling party.

On night, I observed the proceedings with particular concentration. Theo touched shoulders, arms; cheeks as she talked with people, smiling broadly. She always seemed to be moving, eyes, head, hands, nodding as she said, *How wonderful to see you . . . Aren't you sweet for saying that . . . Of course, we've love to . . . Claire is around here somewhere . . .*

I watched Claire, standing in her favorite spot, just to the left of the blazing fire Baxter had set in the carved hearth, the drink she pretended to sip balanced above her on the wide mantel. She looked uncomfortable when approached by a man sporting a velvet jacket and mutton chop whiskers that reached his chin. "I saw your show at the Witkin," he told her. "Bravo, my dear, bravo." He tried his best to draw her out, but after a few moments, he moved on to someone more receptive, while she kept a quiet distance from the small knots of people flirting with conversation, tall and cool and unapproachable, slightly above it all as only shy people can be.

Two more attempts were made before Jessica took matters in hand.

"Claire darling," Jessica said, echoing Brooke's perfect imitation of her mother rescuing mine, "Have you met Fernando? He's doing wonderful things with flatware!" I pretended to enjoy the twins' incessant giggling at the guests, but from my hideout at the top of the stairs I watched carefully that night, missing nothing, believing that sooner or later, the distance would tell me something being close never could. I figured if I watched long enough when they weren't looking, I would understand why other people didn't like them. Even though I wasn't exactly sure what a lesbian was, I was convinced I'd know it when they did it.

Angel, the fat kid from Buenos Aires in my second-grade class, said lesbians hated men, but liked to wear their clothes. I saw Theo give Uncle Baxter a hug and a big kiss on the lips, and when she whooshed by in tangerine taffeta that grazed her ankles and I heard a guest say, "You look fabulous! Where did you find that gorgeous skirt?" I knew Angel couldn't have been right.

A tall woman with silver bracelets, masses of white hair, and sunken cheeks, asked Theo how she managed "to cook all that gorgeous food and not get fat?" Upstairs, I laughed, knowing how much she hated that question, inevitable when someone discovered she was the owner of The Latest Dish. Theo really believed she was fat, no matter what Claire said to the contrary.

"Wonderful pâté, don't you think?" Theo said, ignoring the question and winking in Jess's direction as she picked up a bite-sized square of toast. "I don't know where she finds the time."

Everyone loved Theo and flirted shamelessly with her: I think she enjoyed it immensely. That night, one of Baxter's friends smiled at her and she smiled back. Claire looked pained and distant as she watched the man approach Theo, the tiny lines around her mouth becoming more pronounced as she clung to the edge of the room, determined not to let anyone see her discomfort. Seeing Claire's jealousy, something flattened in my stomach, like being on the bottom of a roller coaster just before it starts climbing.

Theo saw it, too, and moved in Claire's direction, but just as she got there, a large woman Baxter had introduced as "the new Dr. Spock" steamed over, interrupting them. "I understand you are raising a son together."

"We are," Claire said warily.

"How are you handling the absence of a father?" the woman asked. "Is he someone you know?"

As Claire fumbled for her composure, Theo jumped in. "If you don't mind," she said, "when my son asks that question, I'd rather not have to say I told a rude stranger first." As they walked out of my line of sight, I heard Claire ask, "Why did you say *my* son, Theo? He's *our* son." They were gone before I heard the answer.

Angel, who sometimes called lesbians dykes, said they *did stuff* that was against the law, but he didn't know exactly what. Later that night, when I could barely keep my eyes open and rested my head on the banister, after all the other guests had left, Uncle Bax put on a Van Morrison album and Theo and Claire and Aunt Jess and Aunt Suzie held hands and danced with each other to *Brown-Eyed Girl*, while he pretended to play the drums on the back of a chair. Suzie's date sang along and watched her with sad eyes that said he wouldn't last long, much less require a trip to Brooklyn. I couldn't imagine anyone calling the police because of that.

There were no such revelations in South Neck. There was only cousin Harry and I and the slam bang of small boys egging one another on with an energy unknown to anyone over the age of twelve. There was Charlotte, who despised us with the loathing of older sisters. Aunt Molly and Uncle Peter lived calmly in the eye of this storm and did not believe in over thinking the actions of their brood.

I loved the farm's open pastures, the smell of earth, the stereophonic creak of the front and back porches, and the apparent disregard for our safety on the parts of these gentle grown-ups as we skidded around the property in the company of galloping dogs, pausing long enough to race Peter's Jeep up the driveway at lunchtime and at supper-time. I loved the freedom out there, no elevator, no lobby, no doorman between me and the wind and sun, no shoes to keep the sand from between my toes. But it was out there that I learned about boundaries, necessary to people who lived out in the open for all their neighbors to see.

Of all the crazy things about the place, I remember the fence the most. It rolled up the hill behind the house, past the barn where owls nested in the rafters and dust motes hung on needles of light that pierced its rickety slats, ghosts of dairy cows lowing in the dark empty stalls. The fence followed the slippery sound of a brook down alongside Aunt Molly's potting shed, where she spent most afternoons up to her elbows in dirt, teasing tender shoots out of their small pots and gently transplanting the more mature seedlings into loamy soil that felt good on her gardener's hands.

The pickets rolled past the pool and grazed the back of the old bomb shelter Uncle Peter had converted into a writing studio. There he said a different sort of war was raging, between himself and the old Smith-Corona, which did not give up its secrets easily. Later, when I too tried my hand at writing and struggled to find the right way to say something so everyone would understand, not to show off for the few people who were willing to work at my meaning, I remembered Uncle Peter saying when everyone in the small town of South Neck slapped their foreheads and said, "Right!" he knew he'd done his job.

The fence wasn't imposing or impenetrable like the ones you see around prisons or zoos. It had no signs that warned "Keep Out!" or "Beware of Dogs!" even though Bartie and Blisset, who always peed with delight at first sight me, would tear the limbs off anyone who tried to sneak behind its enveloping whiteness. It was about as standoffish as it got in the farming community I liked to think of as my second home and where I believed my presence had more to do with my love of the place than with my mothers' need for privacy.

Theo usually closed the store for several weeks in August, when we'd go somewhere special like Martha's Vineyard, or Maine, or one year, the Grand Canyon with a stop in Broken Arrow to visit Grandma Doris and Grandpa Roy. July was my month at the farm. Most Friday nights during my stay, Claire and Theo would arrive tired and stiff after a long night in traffic on the Long Island Expressway just so they could be there when I woke up. When the store was too busy for Theo to get away, Claire would make the trip alone, even though she hated to drive.

No matter how late, I listened for the car door to slam, the crunch of footsteps on gravel and Bartie and Blisset thumping out their greeting on the legs of chairs. Then the screen door would slap, Molly and Peter would kiss them hello, and everyone tiptoed into the kitchen, where they thought Harry and I couldn't hear them from our summer beds on the sleeping porch.

"Guess who's here," Uncle Peter would tease me in the morning as Claire and Theo hid in plain slight behind him. No matter how often they did this, I always pretended to be surprised to see them. As I got older, this got sillier, but it was our ritual, our family greeting. Molly would cluck about "the cobbler's daughter" and dispense her "energy cocktail"—tomato juice, brewer's yeast, and a banana—to a tired-looking Theo, as we told the stories we'd saved up all week.

If you squinted through the slats in Uncle Peter's fence, you could see everything on the other side, the way you can tell if Christmas lights are balanced before you decorate the rest of the tree. As we drove past the farm on the rutted lane that ran alongside it, down the hill to the front gate, I imagined we got a glimpse of our own lives the way strangers saw it, flashing like the faces of people you'll never know in the windows of a speeding train—Claire and I fiddling with a camera while Harry and Blisset posed with Bartie in Aunt Molly's gardening hat. Theo ringing the triangle on the porch, shouting "Chow time!" in the direction of a squirming pup tent. Two stacks of inner tubes with heads and feet. City kid and country cousin discovering the grass is greener wherever they're together.

I imagined being watched by a big man with kind eyes and hair that might have been four-alarm red before the sun baked it to brick. One brown bicep caressed the side of a Ford pickup loaded with lobster pots, the other gently held the road with one finger hooked into the steering wheel. He turned his head at the edge of our fence just in time to see a face as familiar as his own on the other side, thinking he, too, had imagined it.

Park Road, a one-lane blacktop that ran past the front gate, was the only town road considered important enough for the South Neck public works department to paint every year with a fresh dotted line after winter and the town plow ruined it. The mailbox bore no number but simply said *Sound View Farm* in the same neat script as on the jeep's driver-side door, only a little bigger so the postman could see it. His name was William Milowski, but Harry and I called him Whistlin' Bill because he never delivered a letter without a song or a pocketful of biscuits for all the dogs on his route. We always knew he was coming because of the racket they made the minute they heard Bill in his Estate Wagon whisling while he inched along the road's shoulder. Below the mailbox, where only a car making a U-turn could see it, a small sign on a stake barely two feet tall bore the words, *Private Drive*, which was all that was necessary out there to let people know where you stood with respect to unexpected company.

I think what I loved most about the fence, which stood a discreet distance behind this quiet declaration of family privacy, was that it always held its ground politely without ever having to get ugly and lose its loopy up-and-down grace. I know it was just my imagination, but I always got the feeling that its gate swung open a little wider for me.

While Uncle Peter's neighbors believed in fencing off their land, they rarely locked their doors, and every now and then, when Harry and I got back from the beach, we'd find a pie or a jar of homemade apple butter or a bunch of lilacs twisted in tinfoil waiting for us on the kitchen table. There was never a note, but we always figured out who'd left the treat. As Aunt Molly said, "People tell you an awful lot about themselves in the presents they give."

If someone left an anonymous gift on our doorstep in the city, we'd eye it suspiciously and buzz down to Andy for a description of the caller. If someone looked directly at you on Central Park West and did not avert their eyes, you'd look around for a cop if you were smart. Baxter and Jess and Suzie and sometimes Grandpa and Grandma Hirsh teased Molly and Peter about their decision to forgo sophistication for South Neck. I didn't see the big deal. My mothers were about as sophisticated as it got, and as I was to discover, not everyone liked them.

I loved the way South Neck people looked right at you and said *how do*, period, no question mark. When we were old enough, Harry and I liked to strut down Main Street past the Beehive, where the high school kids came to drink root beer floats and dance to the jukebox in the back. We gagged on the pack of Camels we'd pilfered for the occasion, and tried to pass for freshmen instead of the nerdy eighth-graders we were.

On rainy days, Harry and I watched summer people stand in line at Saugatuck Farm for the privilege of paying too much for the fresh peach and strawberry-rhubarb pies Aunt Molly gave away for the pleasure of it. We'd tip our invisible hats to Mrs. Henrietta Ott, the last survivor of the old whaling families who built the big white clapboard houses on Main Street. They looked like birthday cakes to us, with their turrets and gingerbread and gazebos out back, widow's walks up top, where sailors and sea captains' wives watched for months and sometimes years for the ships that would bring their husbands home with fresh supplies of candle oil, ivory, and silk, bits of scrimshaw tinkered during the long months at sea. Sometimes all that came back was a respectful ship's officer delivering news of a death at sea, or maybe a letter penned in a quiet moment before the sea turned hellish. It was hard to believe the gnarled old woman in tennis shoes who smiled back at Harry and me remembered all that *Moby-Dick* stuff.

A little farther on, we'd run into one of the Roses who sold my uncle the farm and who still owned practically every acre from Main Street down to the bluffs where neat rows of potatoes and broccoli fell away to wheeling gulls and whitecaps on the choppy sound below. I liked to nod my head and close my eyes in acknowledgment the way I'd see them do at the 7-Eleven when one pickup pulls out and another takes its place in the dusty lot.

If Uncle Peter's neighbors in South Neck knew my mothers were lesbians, they didn't say much for or against. In fact, they didn't say anything, period. I was Peter's sister Claire's boy, Charlotte and Harry Hirsh's cousin, their neighbor Molly's nephew, and that's all they needed to know. They couldn't have been nicer to Theo, asking her about table settings and new recipes. They were curious about what city people ate at their parties in the good-natured way I mistakenly took for acceptance.

The fence around my uncle's farm didn't teach me to keep my distance—I already knew how to do that—but it showed me that you don't have to be unfriendly or slam a door to have a little privacy. It stood in plain sight, unlike the one deep inside of people the kind you never know is there until, when you least expect it to, it slams shut, catching you hard.

8

There were no picture books entitled *Heather Has Two Mommies* or *Daddy's Roommate in 1972*. No one had written *Gloria Goes to Gay Pride*. There was just Claire or Theo, anger spilling over the sides of the small school chairs from which they lodged endless complaints. And there was my seven-year-old belief in the benign nature of the world; the fact that my mere presence in it conferred immediate acceptance, love, friendship, and understanding.

With each taunt, another of these illusions lay at my feet, glittering like so many shards of glass on the asphalt of the McCall School yard. It was on this sunless, fenced-in lot where conformity equaled acceptance, that boys like me learned to defend budding manhood with pounding hearts and angry fists and all differences were pummeled into the sameness mistaken for strength. At any age, a boy with two mothers is a threat, an aberration to be dealt with harshly. In the second grade, he may as well wear a bull's eye on his back.

Dyke. A word whispered behind my back, flung at me at recess, a fighting word. The taunting was ceaseless and cruel.

One day, just as the final bell signaled the rush for the exits, Theo swooped into my classroom to demand an explanation of how I came to know this word, not part of any civilized curriculum.

"Maybe you'd like to tell me why my son has a black eye?"

"It would have been so much better, uh, Mrs . . . . Miss Hirsh . . . if you and your uh, . . . had agreed to present a more conventional relationship—well, I mean, for Willy's sake. You know how boys can be in the formative years," my teacher Mrs. Langelotti.

"No, I don't, actually, and perhaps you'd define 'conventional' for me," snapped Theo, eyes blazing with fury, humiliation, and hurt enough for both of us. "I seem to be having trouble understanding."

Sleet battered the classroom's tall windows while we waited for my teacher's reply. The radiator knocked.

"Well, I just meant you could have told him something that would have been more acceptable here at school." said Mrs. Langelotti from behind a scarred old desk containing the ghosts of all the teachers who had ever intimidated a roomful of school children. Theo pictured her casting about for the one small victim who did not know the answer to the question dangling in the air, her search punctuated by the lowering of heads and the sound of feet shuffling under desks. In the edgy silence of the universal mantra—*Don't pick me, don't pick me*—Theo knew a teacher's cruelty always landed on the one who least expected it, who least deserved it.

I waited at a safe distance, the pain in my eye receding in the wake of this fresh embarrassment. It was three-thirty, but I listened hard for the sound of a witness who might be lingering on the empty linoleum outside classroom's frosted glass door.

My teacher saw my mother sitting in the small chair next to her, and I think she understood Theo's shining anger could not be avoided, that she was not safe behind that desk or her authority. Did Mrs. Langellotti realize she had pushed her purse between them and kept it there the whole time as if it could protect her, not only from what my mother had to say, but also from what my mother was?

"Are you suggesting we should have drawn straws to see which one of us would pretend she was his maiden aunt?" Theo asked. "Or maybe you think we should have told him we were roommates; then, when he saw us kissing and hugging, or barged in on us in bed, he could see our relationship as something dirty, something he could spend his whole life trying to hide. Or maybe he could develop a really sick attitude toward women and grow up to be a rapist or a mass murderer. Is that what you mean by 'more acceptable?' Perhaps you should think about what's right for Willy instead of what's comfortable for you. You have no idea how dangerous you are, Mrs. Langelotti."

Theo drew out the "Mrs." as though it were something obscene.

"Do you understand that I pay this snooty private school a ridiculous amount of money for tuition so that *it* can pay *you* to teach my son his lessons and to keep him out of harm's way until he's old enough to make his own decisions about what's bad or good, right or wrong? Do you understand, Mrs. Langelotti, that your personal bias toward me or toward my partner has no place in your classroom?"

My teacher was very still behind her big teacher's desk.

"Good," said Theo, arising her chair like an heiress from a priceless antique. "See that you remember it. And see to it you keep those little savages from hurting my son again."

I stood as close to the door as I dared and Theo softened at the sight of me. "Come on Willy," she said, her voice suddenly too warm, too loving, too full of her lack of regard for the judgments of others; every muscle struggling to contain her rage. Then so Mrs. Langelotti could hear. "Your *other* mother is going to meet us somewhere special."

"Miss Bouvier . . ."

Theo turned and stared hard.

"I *am* thinking about what's right for Willy."

"That's *my* job," said Theo, slamming the door and sending up a cloud of chalk dust which left a silky film on the two stick figures I had dressed in the bright Crayola skirts when we were asked to draw our family portraits, and which now wore a wad of bubble gum and the word *dyke* scrawled across my mothers' names in a mean shade of magenta.

Later that evening, while I was looking for a picture of a cow to paste on Argentina, it started.

"It was bound to happen," said Claire.

"Knowing that doesn't make it any better," snapped Theo.

Claire, looked up from her contact sheets, grease pencil in one hand, loupe in the other. "I know."

All evening Theo had tried to concentrate on the Museum party. It was her biggest, most visible catering assignment yet. If she could carry it off, she would have all the "ladies who lunch" eating out of her hand. As she stirred and chopped, and brushed glaze on a test duck that would be lacquered as richly as a Fifth Avenue living room and go in my lunchbox the next day, Theo tasted a bit of the sauce from the back of her hand and chucked. "What irony. A caterer whose success rests entirely on people who never eat!"

But just as this small amusement released a bit of the day's tension, the events came rushing back. No amount of cooking could cancel the bitter aftertaste of that. Langelotti's pinched face rose before her and she marched into the living room again. Talking was the only thing that helped. Talking to Claire.

"You should have heard that officious bitch, telling me we should have made up a story for Willy. Practically telling me we've ruined him, her damn purse sitting open between us like Harridan's Wall," huffed Theo.

"Hadrian's Wall," corrected Claire, without looking up.

"My version is more accurate. God, I hate stupid, intolerant people who pick on little kids because they don't have enough guts to pick on people who can fight back."

Without waiting for Claire's response, Theo stomped back into the kitchen, only to return in less than a minute.

"The nerve of her, calling you my 'friend.'"

"I am your friend, sweetie. I'm your best friend."

Claire reached for Theo as she paced close to her chair, but missed.

"Don't be simple, Claire. And don't try to calm me down. I'm really furious."

"Okay."

It was still going on when I brushed my teeth and kissed them good night.

Whenever Theo got really mad, which was almost never, she cooked, even at three o'clock in the morning. She became uncharacteristically clumsy, which is why Claire got up and followed her into the kitchen several times that night to make sure she was chopping only the food and not her fingers. This little problem of Theo's could be a real liability for someone in her line of work; once, when some junkie attempted to hold up the store, the anger that had replaced Theo's initial terror engulfed her so completely, she cut off the tip of her pinkie.

Curled in my Peanuts quilt, acutely aware of the fact that I was the reason for all the trouble, I floated above their voices under the painted clouds of my sleeping loft, listening to the sounds below me, sharp and crackling like bursts of gunfire, then receding as I strained to follow their muffled words into the kitchen.

Theo stood in the kitchen doorway watching Claire work, completely absorbed in the images around her. *They're all strangers. Just damn strangers.*

"Maybe she's right," said Theo. "Maybe this is the part that gets harder on us, so it can be easier on him."

"What do you mean?" asked Claire, bracing for wherever this was going next.

"You should have seen him standing there today, Claire. He wanted to disappear. He wanted *me* to disappear."

"Don't be ridiculous, he worships you. You're his mother," said Claire, surprised by the bite of this unalterable fact.

Theo moved across the room to rest on the arm of Claire's chair, the pastry brush still in hand, forgotten for the moment. "I know. That's the point. He doesn't love us because we're lesbians and we're doing this swell thing and aren't we just a couple of rebellious modern women. He loves us because we're his mothers. End of story."

"But we are, sweetie," said Claire.

"What?"

"Lesbians. We're lesbians, Theo."

"Do you have any idea how selfish we've been?"

"No," said Claire, uncurling her legs and rearranging herself in the chair, as if finding her balance would keep her from being knocked over by this, 'but I have a feeling you're going to tell me."

"We've been so busy demanding our rights as parents, shoving our lives in everybody's faces, forcing people to accept us, we're forgetting Willy's feelings. He's just a little boy and I think we ought to start biting our tongues with his teachers and thinking about how we can make it easier, not worse, for him, don't you?"

Something angry and raw appeared in Claire's face, but Theo continued.

"Honey, I know how it is to be different, to have crazy parents who live in a broken-down trailer, talk to trees, and sing labor songs, to wish you were just like the other kids."

Theo had spent her anger in great heaving gulps and in the physical exertion of cooking and now the sight of a solitary tear rolling down Claire's cheek filled her with an uncomfortable mixture of guilt and tenderness. She gently wiped it away. "Don't you think we should give him the chance to choose us, the way we chose him?"

Claire pushed Theo's hand away. "I'm not going to pretend to be your roommate or your old-maid cousin, if that's what you mean." She felt Theo pushing her out of the picture; the faces in the photographs on the floor looking up at her were witnesses.

"It's not going to stop at Willy's teacher or some classroom bullies, Claire. It's going to get worse."

"It is not. All kids go through this in some way or another, especially boys. They tortured my brother at this age, and my parents were not only rich, they were as conventional as it gets." She was tired of Theo's determination to make this more than it was, and turned back to her work.

"This isn't art, Claire. This is life. You can't crop out what you don't like," Theo said just before she slammed the kitchen door.

PEOPLE with a small amount of power over others are dangerous. This is especially true at free clinics, unemployment offices, military installations, and, of course, in schools, where a certain kind of sadism lives just under the surface of things. The knowing of a child is such that whenever his parents take on a teacher, he understands he will be made to pay, as I knew I inevitably would. It happened in small ways, in the nuance of her questions, in the bright light of an afternoon I would never see coming. But that day, listening to Theo cutting my teacher off at the knees, I could only think: You don't want to mess with my mother.

I'm sure Mrs. Langelotti would have denied she was making me pay for her discomfort at my unusual family situation. Still, she picked on me with a vengeance usually reserved for people who are more equally matched. She started the day after Theo's visit.

"Did everyone have fun during winter vacation?"

"Yes, Ms. Langelotti!"

"Will someone tell us what they did?" She canned the room, looking away from me, lulling me into thinking she would call on someone else, waiting until the very last second . . .

"Willy, how about you?"

I was too young to know how to tell a story without mentioning the key characters, how to invent a version that was more acceptable. I learned to do that much later. That day, I stood on wobbly legs and looked into the smug faces of my classmates, and the mean eyes of the one who defaced my picture, and told them about New Year's Eve, how Theo taught us to wrap little balls of dough around a list of things we didn't like anymore and wished would go away, and to throw them into the fireplace.

"I told them how my mothers let me have a sip of champagne and stay up with them to throw another little pile of dough into the fire at midnight with all the things we wanted Baby New Year to bring. "In the morning our living room smelled like a loaf of bread," I said.

Somebody giggled. Mrs. Langelotti said, "Be polite, girls!"

Nobody heard me say, "We drove out to Uncle Peter and aunt Molly's the next day and my cousin Harry and I played in the barn until dinner or that we had a picnic on the front porch so we could watch the snow," because they were twisting in their chairs, smirking at one another. They didn't notice that I left out the part about wishing Claire would go to sleep and turn into a real father, or how I balled up my dough and wished it with all my might I could live with Harry and Charlotte and pretend I was their brother.

Every time I mentioned my mothers and I heard more snickering, each time a little more brazen and Mrs. Langelotti said nothing to stop it. I heard the tapping of paper on wood as notes were being passed; they sounded like mice scurrying in the thick walls of my bedroom at the farm. As I hurried to tell about the snowman we built so I could sit back down on the tip of my spine and appear smaller than the big carrot-haired kid with a swollen eye I was, my face burned.

Just before recess that same morning, as everyone got ready to tear down the stairs to the cafeteria, Mrs. Langelotti, "Don't forget to remind your parents that tomorrow is Parents' Day; they can come early and watch you in class." She saved her zinger for last.

Willy," she said, "that means your mothers, too."

She delivered this parting shot with impeccable timing, and then turned her back for a moment, allowing a spitball to land on my collar, along with the threat of renewed hostility on the battlefield that was recess. I would have run away if it had not been for Carl.

He was small for his age, dark and solemn, all eyes, like a drawing in a picture book. He swayed a little when Mrs. Langelotti introduced him to the class and he didn't seem to mind that he was the focus of all the attention. He didn't smile and he peered out from under black lashes that kept us from seeing he was really looking at a point in the middle of our foreheads, a technique I would later borrow to calm my nervousness in front of large groups.

"This is Carl Jacoby from Chicago," she announced with one hand clamped on his shoulder. Did she think he was going to run away? Or faint? I wondered, but didn't really care. They had forgotten about me for the moment.

"What do we say, class?"

Thirty angelic faces gave no sign of their capacity for cruelty.

"Welcome, Carl!"

The sleet had given way to a cold so chilling the drawings taped to the big casement windows were stiff with frost. The schoolyard was dangerously slick, determined unsafe for children by the headmaster who almost fell when testing it before the lunch bell. We filed down to the dark cafeteria, where no matter what was being cooked, nothing ever tasted the way it did at home. Down there, all food became one big lunch smell; even pizza and hot dogs took on the same stale odor of the steam table. Outside, we were free to eat lunch in relative anonymity and Theo always packed something wonderful—homemade pizza, hand-ground peanut butter, French raspberry jam, a cup of thick soup in a thermos—and I enjoyed it unmolested. But inside, people who did not buy cafeteria food were sissies.

I didn't see Carl Jacoby standing behind me as I slipped my lunch into the trash outside the noisy lunchroom.

"What are you doing?" he asked.

"Nothing," I said, emptying my paper sack.

"Could I have your banana before you throw it away?"

I handed him the banana and continued to dispose of my lunch, careful to keep my distance from the can's foul smell.

"Cool bag," he said, eyeing the red lips of Theo's *Latest Dish* logo.

"My mother's store."

"Wow." Carl said, his mouth full of banana.

I wondered why he was still standing there, why he hadn't joined the noisy group now pushing through the cafeteria's swinging doors.

I've got two mothers," I said, warning him off.

"I've got a grandmother," he said hopefully.

"Where are your parents?" I asked.

"Dead."

"Yeah?"

"They were in a plane crash, and after the funeral I had to move here to live with my grandmother. She said they shouldn't have been sitting on the wing, but I don't think it was their fault," Carl explained, his eyes darkening at the memory.

"Are you an orphan?" I asked.

Carl shrugged.

"Maybe I could borrow one of your mothers some time," he said.

WARY OF EACH OTHER at first, Carl and I spent the next few weeks tiptoeing around the edges of our lives, filling in a little more as our trust in each other grew. I began to dream of lost parents in picture frames, people who sit in shining perfection on the lids of grand pianos in dark apartment buildings with cool tiled lobbies and doormen who treat schoolboys like gentlemen.

I dreamed of people who died in grisly plane wrecks, strapped to fiery wings, or in the backs of ambulances, their red lights and sirens screaming "Move, move, move, move over, now!" behind the cars of the living, people on their way to work, to the movies, to the beach.

I was haunted by parents forever frozen in heavy silver—a strong-jawed dad, a pretty mom, a smiling boy between them, reaching up to hold their hands.

Carl's grandmother had a parakeet named Jimmy who slid down a slippery rubber mat into the kitchen sink, chirping "Jimmy's bath, Jimmy's bath" as he showered under the tap and performed other equally amazing feats for an old lady with skin that rustled like the tissue paper in Bergdorf boxes, a woman who doted on her lonely grandson from Chicago.

I wanted to be the boy who lowered his eyes when the teacher announced Parents' Day, looked wistfully out the window when the other boys talked about father and son weekends at sleep-away camp, the one the other kids drew back, telling him their dads said it was okay for him to come along with them, who accepted their gift without eagerness, as his due.

I dreamed of playing shortstop in the Junior Little League without having to endure Claire and Theo flipping a coin to see who would pinch-hit in the father-and-son game because Uncle Peter lived too far away or Uncle Bax was in Bermuda or Burundi or somewhere buying stuff for his store and Uncle Thad didn't know how and Grandpa Barnaby's knees were too old to slide into home plate.

In my dream, Claire did not win the toss (or lose it, depending on how you looked at the matter). She wasn't out there slipping on the grass, acting like she was my father, while all the real fathers laughed at her behind her back and Theo sat in the stands, hollering her head off, taking us out for pizza afterward. In my dream, Claire and I weren't dirty and depressed and we weren't the only family not invited to go to the Flick and have banana splits.

Dead parents can't embarrass you.

I suppose that's why Carl Jacoby and I became best friends.

9

So many photographs. Acid-free, double-matted in frames of museum-quality bird's-eye maple. Rows of them line the long corridor of our lives. They lead the visitor from our hall buzzer and peephole thick with paint to the faded and slightly tipsy-looking wooden figure of Jiggs, who hands us our mail, keeps our keys and sunglasses on a tray glued to his gloved mitts, and longs for Maggie, who was not cut out for such work.

These pictures illuminate the path from our front door in clean pools of light from invisible ceiling tracks; they instruct honored guests, the newcomers alike, and ushes them up to the French doors that separate carefully chosen illusion from the plain truth of the family living beyond its beveled-glass panes.

I called it the *Great Wall of Normalcy*, a crash course in Claire and Theo and me that is a prerequisite to settling in one of the overstuffed couches, chairs, hassocks, poufs, and pillows dotting our large sunny living room. One after another, the photos speak: "See, we are just like you. Our knees get skinned. We graduate. We marry. We mourn. We have a son and he is the food Theo hungers for in her search for the perfect recipe. He is the truth Claire seeks in Mr. Kimsky's battered leather bag of a face, in the heartbeat before the eye registers the camera and the soul goes into hiding Our photographs say, "Park your assumptions at the door." They warn, "We are not responsible for baggage left unattended." And that means that invisible trunk you're dragging around, the one so full of 'should's and 'mustn't's and and rights and wrongs and judgments handed down from the beginning, that you can't lift it. The one you have to sit on to keep closed, but it always bursts open eventually. That one. That's the one that's not welcome here."

For Grandma Doris and Roy, Suzie, Jess, Baxter, Thad, Uncle Peter and Aunt Molly, people who already knew us and loved us, and especially for Grandma Hirsh, who gave us as much begrudging affection as someone of her generation and social standing could manage, but was very quick to point out that love should never be construed as approval, our wall was a reminder that life is not as racy as imagination will lead you to believe and children quickly grow where there was once only enough room for rebellion.

Our wall says, "We are just like you. Only different."

Our pictures are the gauntlets we throw down. Make no mistake. They are a test.

If the evidence can be believed, my progression from grinning Buddha to small boy to wary teenager to man, to artist, to husband, to healer of wounds was measured in smiles, party hats, and ponies, never far from my mothers' steadying hands.

My mothers are guarded in these pictures, two women squinting into the future with questions knitted into their eyebrows. They see disappointment—mine? theirs?—lurking in every stranger's smile, and this shows in tight lines around the mouth, in the proud thrust of a chin. They gamely push their faces into the camera as if to say, "We are young, we are beautiful, we own the world." Something in their eyes says they don't believe it.

My mothers primp and mug and wrap themselves around friends and family the way protesters lock on to street lamps when it's time for the police to drive up in the van and drag them away. Theo sweeps a stray lock away from Claire's forehead and, in the seconds before the click, proves the eye is not always quicker than the hand. They say *fromage* instead of *cheese* and it's why they always seem to be pouting.

I am a fat, freckled child in a snowsuit, a thatch of orange hovering over me like the fiery tongue of a Zippo lighter, a small flame in a huddled knot of mourners. It was taken the day we all climbed into long black cars and drove over the Queensboro Bridge to say good-bye to Alan in Calvary Cemetery, a place I will always remember as an endless field of loose teeth. I'm holding Aunt Jessica's hand, and I remember how it shook inside her soft kid gloves. As I watched, but didn't really understand the ritual of death, my own hands curled into fists, always ready, even then, to throw the first punch.

I am the boy who towers over Theo at twelve, the young man in a mortarboard who pretends not to see maternal pride beaming in the third row. I am the groom weeping for joy as Annie floats toward me on the arm of her father, Harry at my side buoying me up like a strong wind. I am the reason Theo sits so proudly in the pew reserved for parents, her pale skin ashy with fatigue despite her obvious happiness.

Among our family pictures, there are people I do not know, grinning into the years before I was born. There is what looks to be an all-female soccer team in front of the Parthenon, with Claire and Theo down in front wearing shorts and sneakers and sunglasses, the Leica dangling between them. Claire's blond hair is ironed flat, parted in the middle; Theo's a fiery Afro. Their arms are around each other and their smiles hint of having begun to invent the details of the story they would tell me one day.

"When we arrived in Patmos," Theo would begin, "the old women in black crossed themselves at the sight of us. They thought all our husbands were dead and we were traveling together to get over our grief. So they sent all the men in the village to the taverna to dance with us and by the time they found out we were a planeload of lesbians on vacation, they were stuck . . ."

"They already liked us!" said Claire, supplying the well-loved punch line.

There are other images not on the wall. These live in the sepia light of my memory. Two women slow-dancing in the kitchen with the radio on. A tumble of red and blond hair on a pillow. Theo sleeping in the crook of Claire's arm. Claire's pale skin mottled and swollen in grief. Theo boning a chicken with the strength of a Bedouin. The hard sound of ice thrown into a glass. The long, graceful fingers of an artist turning the pages of a bedtime story, the short stubby ones of a chef, wearing every new cut, burn and scrape like a Purple Heart. Two platinum wedding bands woven together; inseparable. Claire reads *Robinson Crusoe*, Theo *Black Beauty*. One cries for the horse, the other laughs at the idea of a servant in a place with no dust bunnies. A chapter a night for Mr. Baby. Quiet laughter. Voices in the dark.

I loved to watch Claire's images floating in the sink and coming to life as she plucked them out of the basin with her tongs, always at the perfect moment of creation, giving a little whistle when she was pleased, the sound of a tire with a slow leak when she was not. When she worked her face was taut as bone, the white-blond hair caught up in a comb to keep the thick curtain of it from closing over her photographs, lower lip pushed out in concentration in the Martian light of the darkroom where I was always a welcome, if not bumbling, assistant. I wanted to be one of those pictures, able to touch the place in her that could weep for joy as she lifted them out of their bath and proudly carried them to Aunt Suzie.

Flashes of things darker and more disturbing. The set of a jaw. Muffled voices. The strangled sound of disappointment. An elderly woman in a bright pink raincoat who came to blow out the sun.

CARL JACOBY lived in the magic kingdom of Tudor City, and it was the scene of our blood brotherhood for one giddy year. Set high above the FDR Drive like a turreted medieval town, it was as close to suburbia as two city kids could get. In summer, it was our cool, ivy-covered lair and in winter a silent grey fort buffeted by icy blasts off the river we imagined was our private moat.

Like Gramercy Park, its rich relative a mile farther downtown, this warren of buildings, stone paths, and steep steps, built in 1928 for working-class New Yorkers, had its own commons, with bright green grass that bore no relation to the dun clumps that pass for lawns in most other parts of town. It nestled between the buildings and was enclosed by a high wrought-iron fence with curved bars on top just like the bear cages in Central Park. Inside were trees and benches, monkey bars and seesaws, swings and secret paths that were soft under our bare feet. We saw it as our private jungle. Carl had his own key and wore it on a chain under his shirt, hidden away from the greedy eyes of older boys who would mug a kid for less.

On Saturdays and Sundays and sometimes on school holidays, when Carl's grandmother allowed him to visit me, making sure his bus money was safely tied in a clean white handkerchief, we played *Where's Papa?* in the park. The best places for this were at the zoo or the carousel or the Wollman Rink, where divorced fathers and their pretty girlfriends spent the weekend with his kids. "They have to," said Zachary Rifken, a weasely-looking kid in our class whose own parents had been divorced twice each, which left him with eight guilty grown-ups, all of whom wanted to buy him stuff.

These Saturday and Sunday families were easy to spot because the fathers looked tense, and the girlfriends smiled too much to be real mothers, and the kids were always overdressed and sullen, wishing they were somewhere else, especially when the father made it a point to hold the girlfriend's hand. Aunt Suzie told us when parents fight, the court always gives the children to the mother, even if she doesn't deserve them. The court gave Carl to his grandmother. Later, I asked Claire what the court would do in my case, but she said, "don't worry, my sweet boy, that will never happen to you."

Our game was simple: Carl and I looked for faces in the crowd and whoever picked the person who most resembled his father or, in my case, the one who looked like me, won.

Some days we made our own fun in Mrs. Jacoby's gloomy apartment. Bookends with energy to burn, we bobbed at either end of the cut-velvet sofa in the sunken living room where plastic runners protected the rug and doilies and antimacassars lay on every surface. I loved the Jacoby apartment with its smell of lemon oil and clove and the sharp tang of birdseed for Jimmy the parakeet.

Carl's parents peered out from silver frames carefully arranged on a piano nobody ever played. We called it The Runway because that's where they were headed when Carl last saw them last, waving good-bye from tiny airplane windows as their plane taxied away from the windy gate.

"Onetwothreefourfivesixseveneightnineten!"

A steady rain poured shadows on the wallpaper as I skidded on Mrs. J's freshly waxed parquet, breathlessly looking for a hiding place before Carl came up for air and raced after me. Jimmy came in low, dive-bombing the coffee table, a bright blue warplane packed with steaming white death pellets, aiming for my hair and screaming "Hello! Hello!" I crouched under the dining room table, swallowing hard to cover the sound of my pounding heart. Mrs. Jacoby shuffled by, her feet puffy and shining in carpet slippers, She had no idea I was there. Maybe Carl would miss me, too. An overhang of musty lace kept my secret, screening the light like the dark confessional at St. Pat's Grandma Hirsh insisted we visit one Saturday on the way home from Rockefeller Center. *Bless me, Father, for I have two mothers. I have two and Carl has none.*

Sometimes we played stagecoach on Mrs. Jacoby's vanity table. Pushing aside dusty bottles of Ma Griffe, and Shalimar and a man's tortoiseshell brush-and-comb set, we sat on the glass-topped surface, resting our feet in the small depression with secret drawers I imagined, held love letters from Mr. Jacoby, who had disappeared into the merchant marine the week Carl's father was born. We pretended the small boudoir chair was our team of black stallions carrying us through dangerous Apache territory with our pouches full of gold and mail for the settlers. I am part Cherokee on Grandma Doris's side, so if we were attacked, and we always were, I would say, "I am Willy Two Squaws," and the war party would let us pass.

Afterwards we did our homework in Carl's room until the Latest Dish van picked me up and delivered me to the shop, where I helped Theo clean up and nibbled cookies until Claire arrived and we'd all walk home through the park. When Claire was away taking pictures and Theo was cooking for a big party, I was allowed to stay for Mrs. Jacoby's sauerbraten with gingersnap gravy and potato pancakes or an A&P pot pie, which we never had at home.

When Carl came to our house, Theo let us pick our dinner from anything in the store and Carl always ate a fudge brownie while deliberating, which we all swore never to tell his grandmother. While Theo cleaned up, Carl and I waited on the stragglers who begged her to stay open one more minute, which she always did because she couldn't stand the face of a hungry person.

It was April and we had just come in from mucking around in the fort. School had let out early and we waited in Carl's room to be called to lunch.

"Do you miss them?" I asked, thinking about Carl's parents sitting on the wing.

"I miss them on Saturdays," Carl said.

"How come?"

"My dad didn't go to the office or talk on the phone that day," Carl explained from the other side of his Wild West bedspread.

Claire and Theo had no such rule. Were they really parents?

"My grandmother says some kids just have mothers and some just have fathers and some have to spend a little time with each one because they live in different houses and some are dead like mine, but I think she said you had to have one of each to have parents."

I DON'T REMEMBER whose idea it was, only that we were too restless for homework and it was a day that seemed too far from our third-grade exams. It was also a Wednesday, the day Mrs. Jacoby put on her wool coat and took her good leather bag out of its dust cover, and got on the crosstown bus to Lord & Taylor, where she had tea with her friends. On these days, she allowed us to play in the apartment alone. We decided to hold the séance on the baby grand piano, because it was black and the dining room table wasn't spooky enough.

We found the emergency candles in a kitchen drawer and I contributed the pilot's wings I got from a trip to Broken Arrow. Carl laid down the ratty piece of flannel from his old baby blanket he always kept in his pocket, so they'd recognize them.

"I feel funny calling them Edgar and Marilyn," he said, working up his nerve.

"If you don't," I reasoned with perfect nine-year old logic, "how are all the other dead people going to know who you want?"

After draping rosary beads around our necks because we'd heard you could accidentally wake up the devil if you didn't, we dragged Mrs. Jacoby's kitchen stools into the living room and sat at opposite sides of the piano, fingers touching, lights out. As the candles flickered and hissed in a draft from the window, we urged the photographs to come to life. Just for a minute. Just to make Carl feel better.

"Eeeedgar. Marrrrrrilyn. This is your son Carllllll and his friend Willeeeee. Where arrrrre youuuuuuu?" We elongated our syllables, hurling them into eerie tunnels we assumed only the dead could hear.

We heard something shift in the shadowy corners of the living room and the hairs on our arms and on the backs of our necks stood away from flesh. There was a creaking sound, the air was suddenly cooler and we felt something, a presence.

We called again—"Eeeeeeedgar. Marrrrrrilyn. Speeeaaak to us"— pretending we weren't scared stiff.

In the gloom, we didn't see what the dripping wax was doing to the glossy surface of the piano Carl's father had played every Saturday morning for his teacher, Mr. Gilchrist. Nor dd we hear Mrs. Jacoby's key in the lock. We didn't see her until we felt the first blows. "Leave them alone. Let them rest. My poor Edgar!" she screamed, throwing down her shopping bags, blowing out the candles, rubbing at the wax with her coat sleeve, and hitting us, all at the same time. "Look at your father's piano!"

I did not identify the heat that rose to my face that day as shame until many years later when I saw Mrs. Jacoby's look in someone else's eyes and I recognized its familiar flush. That look went down to the core of things. It said, "you are not like us, and here is proof."

"You made my Carl do this," she said.

Shame is a cumulative thing. If you feel it enough, you believe it.

CLAIRE HAD JUST come home from a shoot in Atlantic City and was showering off the casino muck, as she jokingly called the grime that rises up from the rug and attaches itself to money that is prayed over, spat on, and moved hand to hand. Theo and I were in the park playing tennis. Actually, Theo was playing and I was clumsily learning to return her serve. Andy had seen Claire go up, so he let the intercom buzz while Claire found a towel and her terry robe, and squeezed a rubber band around her hair, which was dripping uncomfortably down her back.

Cursing her timing, she mopped up her wet footprints and she went for the intercom.

"There's a Mrs. Jacoby to see you, ma'am," Andy said, sounding the deeply resonant tone he affected in the presence of strangers.

"Give me two minutes, then send her up, will you, Andy?"

When Claire opened the door, Carl's grandmother was wearing the most awful pink raincoat she had ever seen. She looked like a wrinkled bottle of Pepto-Bismol.

"I won't be long," said Mrs. Jacoby, refusing the hanger Claire offered.

"Please, come in and sit down. Willy adores your grandson, Mrs. Jacoby. Theo and I are so grateful—"

"My son was a good boy."

"I'm sure he was, Mrs. Jacoby. I'm so sorry. It must be difficult for you. I lost someone. A brother. My parents . . ."

My parents, what? Claire thought. *I don't know what my parents felt. They never told me. Here I am pretending I know how this woman feels.*

". . . miss him."

"My son and daughter-in-law were not modern," Mrs. Jacoby said, flatly ignoring Claire's small talk.

"I'm sure they were wonderful parents," replied Claire, giving herself time to grasp the woman's point.

"I can't afford private school on my pension, but I send Carl to McCall to keep him away from the undesirable element." Here Mrs. Jacoby paused and Claire rushed to fill the silence that swirled around it.

"You can't be too careful in New York. That's why we send Willy there, too."

"I'm an old-fashioned woman, Miss Hirsh," said Mrs. Jacoby, gathering her purpose around her, "and I would rather have my son dead than live the way you do. Willy is a nice boy. I don't know how you could raise him in such an evil household."

Claire struggled for air. It's one thing to know you are in the presence of an enemy, quite another when someone you've trusted with your child, throws a punch into your solar plexus.

"My personal life is none of your business, Mrs. Jacoby," Claire said, feeling her throat close.

"My business is Carl. It's better Willy doesn't see him anymore."

"Carl and Willy are best friends! Think whatever you like of Theo and me, but don't make the kids pay for it."

"Your son tried to call my son and daughter-in-law back from the dead this afternoon. You can live any way you want, but I'm not going to let him turn my grandson into a godless queer."

She was gone before the corrosive lump in Claire's sternum turned to tears.

When Theo and I got back from tennis, noisy and sweaty and eager to give Claire the blow-by-blow, the shower was running, and it kept running for a long time. Claire sat through dinner looking scalded, as though she had scrubbed her skin with steel wool. She wore a blank smile, the kind you paste on when you come in second and the camera records tears as brightness around the eyes. She nodded vacantly when Theo said, "Say hello to the future USA Open champion, and she barely noticed when Theo boasted she'd sold out her Tuscan salad with bruschetta before noon.

All the while, my small-boy mind was still wondering why Edgar and Marilyn didn't hear the phone ring when Carl and I called. Maybe we had the wrong area code, like when we forgot to dial 516 for Uncle Peter.

"What do people do in heaven?" I asked.

"I like to think your uncle Alan is making corsages for the angels," said Theo, looking sideways at Claire.

I wasn't satisfied.

"If somebody calls you up there, can you hear it and come back and visit?"

Theo considered my question.

"Well honey, I think being in heaven means you know everything that's going on, even if we can't see you or hear you. It's not like being in a place, exactly. You can't get phone calls, but I think you know when people you love think about you."

"How?"

"It's like blowing out your birthday candles and making a wish. If you really concentrate and see what you wish for on the little TV screen behind your eyes, it will come true. If you do that when you want to talk to someone in heaven, they'll hear you,"

"Like a dream?"

"Yes, just like."

"Will they answer?"

"I think so. But only you will hear it." Theo smiled and tapped her chest as she said this, as if remembering something she had forgotten, something wonderful.

Claire made a strangled sound and dropped her fork. She pushed away her plate and slid her chair back with such force, the legs scraped the kitchen floor.

"Think it was something we said?" Theo lamely joked, as Claire stalked out of the room.

"Maybe she misses Uncle Roland," I ventured.

"Maybe," said Theo, staring at the kitchen door, which was still swinging with Claire's shove.

I heard them talking long into that night. The bedroom door slammed, a toilet flushed, water ran, and the light in the kitchen went on again just before dawn. I couldn't make out what they were saying, but the heaviness of their footsteps on the bare floors, and the unfamiliar smell of a cigarette burning, told me this had something to do with me.

Grandma Hirsh had once said I made enough noise to wake the dead, but I didn't see the harm. How could it be hard to go back to sleep in heaven?

10

The day after Mrs. Jacoby came to our apartment, Claire refused to get up. A steady rain slashed our tall windows and in the gloom, a fine mist clung to the outlines of budding trees in the park below. The clock radio clicked on at six-thirty, right in the middle of Imus who was saying something about flooding on the East River Drive. As she did every morning, Theo wound up Tweety Bird, our mechanical canary, and held up its cage at the foot of my stairs to wake me with its tinny song. Then she ground the coffee beans, started the pot brewing, and padded back into the bedroom to start her shower and rouse Claire, who had kicked the radio across the room.

"C'mon, kiddo, there's art to be made," Theo said, giving Claire's behind a gentle swat. Claire pulled the blanket over her head and wouldn't budge. She tried tickling Claire's feet and luring her into the kitchen with the promise of a poached egg. No response. Then she leaned over the lump that was Claire, rubbed her back and whispered something, but it did no good. Claire just burrowed deeper into the duvet.

The phone rang.

"C'mon Claire. That's Suzie calling to remind you you're going to Brassaï today. Remember him? Photographer, Paris, the twenties, cafés with mirrors?"

"I'm not getting it," called Theo as she headed for the kitchen.

A pale foot slithered out from under the covers and kicked the phone across the room in mid-ring.

"That's really mean, Claire," Theo hollered over a blast of peanuts in the grinder. "She got up early for you."

Suzie was an insomniac, which was why she never phoned before noon.

The phone rang again.

"I'm still not answering it," said Theo, moving down the hall toward their bedroom, straightening pictures as she went.

"Claire, for God's sake, answer the phone."

"It's still ringing, Claire," said Theo, slipping into her kitchen clogs and buttoning the starched white shirt she wore instead of a chef's jacket.

"Please, Theo, please . . ."

Claire jabbed wildly at the phone as the answering service picked up. "Bouvier-Hirsh household," said the operator.

Theo relented and picked up the phone as Suzie was leaving a message.

"Hello, Suze."

Claire covered her head with her pillow. "Tell her I have the flu."

"Claire has asked me to tell you she has the flu," said Theo, staring down at Claire, who glowered at her. Theo hated to lie because it only put off the moment you had to tell the truth and, by that time, whatever it was was always worse.

"Tell her we're going to Madame Romaine's for omelets after," said Suzie, "something full of Stilton and pears."

Theo stood over Claire as she talked to Suzie, frowning down at her while smiling with her voice, the way she did when she called school to say I was running a slight fever and thought it best I stay home.

"Suzie says you're going to Madame Romaine's after . . ."

Claire peeked out and shook her head.

"Tell her I didn't get to sleep until four," pleaded Suzie, annoyance and worry in her voice.

"I don't think that's going to work this morning. She's upset about something that happened yesterday. Go back to sleep, she'll call you later."

Theo and I ate our cereal and English muffins and tried to pretend everything was okay, but whenever one of us wasn't watching, the other would slide a look toward the kitchen door and listen for the familiar slap of bare feet on cold tile. When I stood at the door for our family hug, Theo said, "Mommy is feeling sad today, sport."

My slicker was making my school blazer bunch up where I couldn't reach. Theo, seeing me struggle, slid her hand up the back to pull it down for me, but she didn't give me a quick tickle, which is what she always did. That was how I knew it wasn't just Claire who was feeling sad.

"She's mad at Carl's grandma for being so mean to you," Theo explained.

Claire waited until we were gone and tidied up the dishes that had fallen to Theo's breakfast whirlwind. She picked up my toys and put them back into the old sea chest Uncle Bax had refinished for me. Making my bed, she smoothed my sheets over and over as though they needed consoling, not she.

Claire considered the easy comfort of our home, once her solitary haven, meticulous in its carefully composed clutter, now rumpled and alive with the push and shove of a family. It seemed as if someone had broken in during the night and gone through our things with a stranger's dirty hands. *Everything looks exactly as it did yesterday, but nothing is, or ever will be, the same.* As she retrieved the slipper I'd left under the kitchen table, she saw the red circle around Friday and Theo's enthusiastic scrawl on the big weekly planner pinned to the back of the open pantry door. *Peter's this weekend with Carl and Willy!*

Claire stared at it for a long time before she called her mother.

"I'M NOT ALLOWED to talk to you anymore."

Carl stood on the sidewalk outside our red brick school building. It was still raining and the sidewalk was slippery as parents rushed the building with golf umbrellas, briefcases, and children in blue blazers, a telltale pajama leg peeking out from under a soggy raincoat here and there. Vehicles double- and triple-parked, discharging my schoolmates into the expensive hush of East Seventy-Fourth Street, which if not for the howling mob surrounding the vacant lot we called a schoolyard would have been just another row of consulates, mansions, and maisonettes between Park and Madison. The Latest Dish was only three and a half blocks away and, as was her custom, Theo dropped me off in the van on her way to the store. I waited for Carl's bus so I could say I was sorry for bothering Edgar and Marilyn in heaven, which was how Theo explained the problem to me.

"Carl's grandmother is just getting used to them being in heaven," she explained as we turned off Madison and double-parked. "She was angry because if they heard you and came back, she'd have to say good-bye and feel sad all over again. Can you understand that?"

"I guess."

I didn't understand. I knew if Grandma Hirsh saw Roland again, she'd be happy. I know because when I asked her what he looked like, she showed me the photographs and the baby book she kept in a rosewood box in the bottom drawer of her armoire. "I would give anything to see him again," she said, "even for a moment."

I edged closer to Carl, who held an umbrella open for both of us. "I didn't mean to wake up your mom and dad,"

"My grandmother says having two mothers is against the law," he said solemnly.

I was aware of heat building up inside my slicker; the white button-down shirt Theo had ironed that morning was beginning to stick to my skin.

"She says they do stuff with other women and don't believe in God."

I wondered if the police would arrest me, too.

Carl shifted uncomfortably and looked beyond me to a group of boys disappearing into the front door. "My grandmother says your mothers aren't real parents."

Tears stung the undersides of my eyelids and I squeezed as hard as I could to keep them from spilling over. I moved closer to Carl. Something hot moved up from my shirt to my head and down into my hands and I heard myself shout, "I hate your grandmother and I hate you and my mothers do *so* believe in God and you can't come with us to my uncle Peter's farm on Friday . . ." The rest was lost in the buzzing in my ears and the blood pumping into my arms.

Carl was crying when somebody's father pulled me off him. Rain was running bright red down the front of my slicker like the poster paints in Mrs. Flynn's art class.

Not far away, in the store's cramped kitchen, Theo was cutting butter into pie dough. As she dipped the knife in and out of the jar of ice water, working the floured board with absentminded skill, she imagined Mrs. Jacoby's frayed mouth hissing the words "godless queer, godless queer" over and over again. She didn't realize she was bleeding until she saw the same stain repeated on every pie shell on her work table and the water reddened a deeper shade with every pass of the knife.

CLAIRE HATED TO DRIVE, especially all the way out to South Neck on a Friday night, but Theo's stitched hand was wrapped in a big white glove of gauze and she'd taken some Percodan for the pain. This forced Claire to get behind the wheel of our broken-down VW Beetle, which neither of them had the heart to sell. Grandma and Grandpa Hirsh kept it in their building's lot for us. By the time we'd cabbed over to the East Side, rung the night bell, walked down the steep hill into the garage, and packed the car, it was late. Later still when we got to the farm. Aunt Molly gently steered a groggy Theo, who had fallen asleep before we hit the Long Island Expressway, into the guest room.

Claire stayed up with Peter long after Molly settled me into Harry's small room under the eaves. At the kitchen table, lit by a pale moon and and the small lamp that teetered on the ledge of an ancient hutch, they shared a brandy. In the prayerful sweep of their arms, the way their bodies leaned in and yet held something back; their long, narrow faces, all angles and seriousness, suspended in a halo of blond, they were brother and sister down to the bone. They spoke of the history that ran in their blood, and of things that did not include me, or Theo, or Molly or Charlotte or Harry or the slumbering beasts that rested large sorrowful heads on their feet.

Peter entered the silence, broken only by the occasional thump of a tail and the knocking of a gust rising up from the Sound.

"Why did you call her?"

Claire felt a cold nose on her foot. "I should know better by now."

"What did she say?" asked Peter, not because he really wanted to know; he'd heard it all before, but because he knew Claire needed to talk.

"Dad answered the phone and I, fool that I am, thought he would actually have an opinion, some fatherly advice."

"Did he?"

"Are you kidding? He said what he always says. 'Let me get your mother.'"

Peter had his own thoughts about Barnaby, but kept them to himself.

"Then she got on the phone with that her-royal-highness-will-see-you-now voice she always uses when, God forbid, any of us need to talk. And, of course, the minute she says that, it's Dad's clue to slump deeper into his chair and pretend he's napping. For once, I'd really like to know what Barnaby thinks, if he has any balls at all."

Peter sipped his brandy and waited for Claire to get around to it.

"Why can't she, just for once, take my side? Why can't she say, 'Dammit, you're my daughter and I don't care if you're a lesbian, that woman was out of line.' No. She has to throw salt in the wound and say, 'How did you expect the poor woman to react, dear?'"

"Because she can't, Sis. Why is it so important that she bless everything you do? She loves you. She adores Willy. She'd give her life for him—"

"No," Claire interrupted, "she'd give *my* life for him."

"In her own repressed way, she loves Theo, too," said Peter. "She just can't pretend she approves. You know that."

Claire ran a finger around the brandy bottle's wax seal and edged it closer to her glass, then tilted its neck toward Peter, who covered his snifter with his palm.

"And what do you know, little brother? Do you know that no matter what you do, they will never notice you, no matter how you twist yourself inside out for them, try to understand their pain and to forgive their silence? Your little newspaper could win a damn Pulitzer and you would not be any different in dad's eyes because you're not Roland?"

Peter bowed his head, but Claire could not stop herself from releasing the anger she'd been holding all day.

"You explain them and defend them, but she's still going to say, 'We lost our son,' with you standing right there.

"Yeah, I do, but thank you for pointing it out," said Peter coldly. "I also know that inflicting pain on somebody else when you're feeling it yourself seems to be a trait not restricted to our parents."

"Well, you know the Hirsh family motto, 'No kindness goes unpunished,'" said Claire, taking her brother's hand in what he understood was as close to an apology as she would give.

"Claire replenished the amber liquid until it swirled dangerously close to the rim of her glass. "I poured out my heart to her, Petey. I told her how Willy was ripped away from his best friend because of a stupid, superstitious old woman. What could this innocent little boy do to hurt her, get queer germs on her precious piano? I told her about the look on Willy's face when Theo told him he couldn't go to Carl's anymore and how he wanted to call and apologize for bothering the dead trying to get some sleep in heaven."

"You know, I sometimes think she's sorry it wasn't me."

"C'mon Claire, you know better than that," Peter said. "She's sees him in you, that's all."

Claire tried to hold back the tears all day. She tried to work in the darkroom, but the images in the pan swam. When the school called to tell her I had beaten up a boy half my size, and when Theo phoned from Lenox Hill's emergency room to say she had severed some nerves in her hand, and even when her own hands shook on the steering wheel because she forgot to take the detour that would avoid the little clump of trees just beyond the peach orchard where it took three hours for police to pry a blond teenage boy from behind the wheel of what once was a Chevy Impala convertible, she did not cry. She held the wheel tighter and hardened herself against the memory of watching them pull a blanket over Roland's face, a face so like her own, of watching her father lock shut, his grief becoming something that fed on silence and ink from behind the curtain of *The Wall Street Journal*.

Here in her brother's kitchen, where she could say anything and still be loved, she let the tears come.

"I'm so afraid," said Claire between sobs.

"Afraid of what, honey?"

"Afraid I'll screw it up. Afraid Willy will hate me for giving him this life. Afraid Theo will get sick of me and take him with her. Afraid I'll be alone, one of those sad, interesting woman in trousers with a strong face and a tragic past. Somebody who pretended she was a mother once."

Touched by the trust that prompted her to show him her fear, Peter reached over to cup his sister's wet cheek.

"I love him too, you know," he said.

"I know you do, Petey," said Claire, blowing her nose.

Peter thought about how Claire informed her photographs with a kind of emotional baffle, how her images jumped from the wall to say hello with one hand and pushed you away with the other. He wondered if she knew how appealing she was, how lovable and how impossible to leave when she let this show, not just in her work, but in herself. He wondered why she who was so good at looking, could not see the wound in their mother.

"I asked her to tell me how to be a good mother."

"What did she say?"

"She said I should have thought of that when I went to bed with Theo. She told me I was lucky the woman didn't have me arrested."

"You know," said Peter, thinking of the chill that had settled over their parents after Roland's death, and how he wondered what he had done to cause it, "I don't think kids are ever too young for the truth. You'd be surprised what they can handle if given the opportunity. I think a good mother would do that. And you know what?" he asked, taking her hand.

"What?"

"You're a very good mother. And Theo adores you."

Claire gave a reluctant smile.

"Why don't you tell her what you're afraid of and trust her with it?"

THEO DID NOT wake up when Claire stepped softly into the guest room, undressed, and slid under Aunt Molly's blue-and-white star quilt. Careful to stay clear of the bulky bandage lying awkwardly on the sheet, she touched Theo's bare shoulder with just enough pressure to cause her to sigh deeply, and roll over to let Claire snuggle at her back. Claire turned her face toward the pillow and into the warm curve of Theo's neck and raced the advancing light to sleep.

11

In the dream, he is a big man. His hair is a warm reddish-brown, long and curly, my own hair with the flame turned down. His words start somewhere deep inside him and rumble up to a wide, generous mouth, creased by what I imagine is an easy laugh. Deep bass notes hang in the air long after they are spoken. I try to make him speak to me, but he's too tall and can't see me at his side. I tap the hard muscle of his thigh, but he doesn't know I'm there. I call up to him, but he can't hear me. He's holding Theo's hand and she's smiling. Claire is sitting on a bed full of potato chips and offers the bag to Theo, but she refuses it, putting her hands in her pockets when Claire insists. Claire begins to cry and Carl comes out from under the covers and wraps his thin arms around her neck. He calls her Mommy, but she pushes him away and chases Theo and the man with silver-gray eyes. I run after them. Just as they see me, I wake up.

"I'm gonna pee. Wanna come?"

"No thanks, I've already had one."

It was a Saturday afternoon, a few weeks before classes let out for the summer, and I was spending the day with Uncle Baxter, one of the last before my month at the farm. We were eating bologna sandwiches on disgusting white bread, the kind you can use to hang wallpaper if you run out of glue. Aunt Jessica was in the dining room arranging the table for one of her "little suppers," as she called the parties she gave when they weren't on location in London or in Morocco or any of the other places named on the collection of postcards in my dresser drawer. On these occasions, Uncle Baxter held forth on the provenance of his latest find and Aunt Jess stirred new people into the evening as easily as the exotic spices she carried home in bits of colored tissue paper and knotted handkerchiefs for the dishes she gamely tried, but never quite carried off the way Theo could.

That night, they were having something called a *tagine*, but that afternoon Uncle Baxter decided to provide me with some perspective on what manly men eat for lunch on Saturdays when there are no women around. "Next you'll be taking him to a poker game," Jessica sniffed.

She was amassing a small army of silver candlesticks in the center of a glass table set on a pair of richly veined black marble pedestals that had once held up a mirror in J. P. Morgan's bedroom. Alongside it, sat a church pew unearthed in a dusty attic down near St. Ives, the same summer they found my antique rocking horse and a cache of royal livery buttons—onyx for Claire and silver greyhounds for Theo. The Gothic pew, with its pocket for prayer books and the hymn sheets now held placemats and napkins and table runners. Its seat, polished smooth by centuries of devout behinds was buried under a pile of fat cushions in an inky-blue toile depicting Napoleon's victory over what looked to me like a flock of geese.

Aunt Jess shook her silky black bob from somewhere inside one of the enormous gilt mirrors cantilevered on each end of the room. "Willy Nilly," she said, 'I'm amazed you survived all that bathroom business. I remember your mommy being so scared you'd never see a penis and grow up thinking you were some kind of defective girl, she made Uncle Bax drag you into the loo every time he had to tinkle."

"Poodles tinkle, Jess love. Real men pee," said Uncle Bax, brushing the crumbs off his handlebar mustache and curling up the edges, so I could see the funny face he was making for me.

"As you wish," said the huge almond eyes in the mirror.

Aunt Jessica was the kind of person who couldn't say "pee" if her life depended on it. I couldn't imagine her peeling off her underpants, sitting and talking to me or to Theo in the next room in the absentminded way Claire left the bathroom door open without missing a word in the conversation.

The mood was not so lighthearted when Theo and I arrived at Jess and Baxter's. The day started out uneventfully, all three of us walking through the park to Fifth Avenue, idly chatting about Aunt Molly's peach chutney for the store, Uncle Peter's latest editorial on land-hungry developers, Suzie's newest adventure in dating—the owner of a discothèque boasting a tank of live snakes and scorpions—Harry's case of poison ivy and how we would have to remember to pack calamine lotion for my vacation.

We talked about how much Baxter and Jess would miss me when I was at the farm, and what he and I would do that day while Theo worked on a new menu and Claire walked over to St. Mark's Place, where she was documenting an unlikely truce between Hell's Angels and hippies. It was easy family talk and it carried us through the muddy, rain-slicked park, which was beginning to show signs of an early summer. We covered everything except why this was a Saturday that would not be spent with Carl and why a morning like this might turn ugly for no reason an eight-year-old could see.

We stepped onto Fifth Avenue and found ourselves nose to nose with Grandma's doorman, who was banishing a pile of leaves to the gutter.

"Hi, Buddy," we all sang.

"So your father don't slip," said Buddy, touching his cap to Claire as we marched past the building, returning his salute in unison.

"How's the grand lad?"

I smiled from beneath my Grange cap, which I hadn't taken off since Uncle Peter had explained it was what real farmers wore on their tractors.

"Buzz up a hug up to Barnaby," Theo called over her shoulder.

Two very thin women in short plaid skirts and Capezio flats walked by, wheeling identical blue strollers.

"Did you know twinsets cause cancer in laboratory rats?" said Claire, smirking at them.

Theo stiffened, not sure what might be next. I felt my own muscles follow suit.

"For your information, I could have had a pre-war, park view, twinset kind of life, too," Claire said. Her voice had acquired an edge since Mrs. Jacoby's visit.

Theo was about to say something but thought better of it. I wondered if she was going to remind Claire that she could not have had me by herself because she was not my birth mother, but only my "family mother," as they explained when I was too little to know any better and asked if they both carried me in their stomachs. The moment passed.

"I could be picking up Willy from Brearley—I'd call him Wills, of course—or planning a benefit for the preservation of crown molding," Claire continued, oblivious to the color rising in Theo. "Claire Hirsh of the Manhattan and Long Island Hirshes has nuptials held against her will and will heretofore be Mrs. Spunky Danforth, Three Sticks. Jess would write something ridiculous about what everyone was wearing."

"That's mean, Claire. Jess is your best friend. Why can't you appreciate that she loves beautiful things and has a gift for describing them, instead of picking on her for not being a serious artist. Art is made in different ways by different people," Theo said, quickening her pace as if to outdistance Claire's dangerous mood.

"It's *fashion*, for God's sake," said Claire.

"Just like that big, black, ridiculously expensive Italian bag you simply must have for your precious Leica and spare rolls of film," Theo shot back.

"You're not exactly the butch-haircut-and-Birkenstocks type yourself, darling," Claire said evenly. I understood these things were not pretty because I had learned early to understand sarcasm, Claire's favorite way of fighting.

Earlier that winter, Claire shot a group of elderly women in alligator shoes scurrying along under their ankle-length fur coats. Theo laughed and we made a game of spotting more—popping out of the Met, swarming out of the boutiques and little restaurants that line the side streets between Park and Lexington. Extra points were given for matching hats and handbags.

One day Claire slipped the Leica out of her bag and pretended to shoot us grinning at her from inside our mufflers. Her real subject was a woman standing near a fire hydrant waiting for what looked like a rat on the end of a rhinestone leash to relieve itself. Both wore mink coats.

"I wonder what Jess would say about this," Claire had said. We made a game of that, too, coming up with captions, and applauding Theo's winner—Does an animal have to die so you can dress to kill?

It was all in good fun. But not today. Today there was no laughter in Claire's eyes. I got the feeling I was going to get hit by a truck I'd never see coming.

"Why do you make fun of people who are different from you and expect the same people to respect the fact that you're a little different from them?" said Theo, crossing away from *A La Vieille Russie*, and taking a shortcut between horses and their hansom cabs, ignoring their irritated snorts. She stopped in front of the statue of Abundance in her fountain across from the Plaza.

"This is not about Jess, is it Claire?"

"No, it isn't," said Claire.

Theo held her ground. "What, then?"

"It's about your insistence on keeping our son in that damn snooty school with all those vain, shallow, and bigoted people. It's about us and how you're changing. It's about Willy and how he's going to have nothing but heartache if we don't get him out of there."

We watched Claire disappear into the crowd pressing against the windows at Tiffany's and Bergdorf's, Rizzoli and Charles Jourdan. It swallowed her up and she was gone.

It was only ten-thirty when Theo and I arrived downtown. Aunt Jess was working on one of her columns. She sat at her lipstick-red typewriter surrounded by clippings, sketches, photographs, hair clips, swatches of silk, tweed, herringbone, satin, suede, and a large basket full of scarves and bracelets. This particular morning, a lone shoe of aubergine velvet stood on top of a sweater of the same rich hue. As she worked, waves of Puccini crashed over her and when Theo, Uncle Baxter, and I passed her open door, she was typing with her eyes closed.

"Hi, Aunt Jess."

"Willy, darling!" She looked startled, as if surprised to find she was not in the atelier of some as-yet-undiscovered fashion genius. In her slightly breathless way, she blew us a kiss, then caressed the fabric and said to no one in particular, "Isn't it ironic that something as luxurious as cashmere could possibly contain the word 'mere'?"

Uncle Baxter raised a bushy eyebrow at his wife, who was, in his opinion, well on her way to becoming the world's youngest eccentric.

"Nothing short of stunning," he said. "You really should mention that to someone, darling."

Aunt Jess had a way of turning these minor revelations into compelling fashion copy that had readers rushing off to Saks or Bergdorf's or Bendel's. She was a genius at this.

We all knew better than to interrupt, but that morning an uncharacteristically tense Theo in need of a talk entered Jess' office, while Uncle Bax did his best to entertain me.

BAXTER APPLIED a gentle pressure at my back, nudging me away from the study. "You want to walk in the park?"

"Nah, we just walked here," I said, remembering Theo's angry steps swallowing long blocks, lights turning green in her path, my own steps quickening in her wake, afraid to ask why Claire left us so suddenly.

"We could have an exciting round of you-know-what," Uncle Baxter suggested, seeing my mood was low.

Where's Papa? wasn't as much fun with Uncle Bax as it was with Carl, because I knew he was playing the game just for me. His father was lost, too, "somewhere off the coast of Bermuda," he'd said when I asked him if the elder Baxter ever came to America to visit. "Old Dad got hit by a cricket bat and died of a cerebral hemorrhage," Baxter had explained. "Mother remarried ten years later, a decent chap, but when the poor bloke looked up at the mantel and saw the silver art deco cocktail shaker with Dad's ashes—Dad loved his martinis, he did—all he could do was wonder what sort of container he'd end up in.

"He became so distraught at the idea of his remains in an egg coddler or a pickle jar or tucked in the toes of his patent-leather evening pumps, he suggested they take a cruise and give his predecessor a decent burial at sea. So one night in a full moon, they tossed my old dad right off the top deck."

"Was he a sailor?" I had asked.

"The funny thing is, he never liked the water. Didn't swim. Hated boats. But Mother's husband feels much better."

True or not, Baxter's stories had a way of shaking me out of the small tragedies that beset growing boys, so I soon learned not to ask too many questions or spoil the gift; but that day I sensed something going on. I noticed Theo let Jessica hug her for a long time before they moved into the study and Aunt Jess closed the door behind them.

"C'mon, let's go play store," said Uncle Bax, determined to amuse me.

Our Saturday custom was to have lunch, walk over to MacDougal and his shop, where he'd welcome the young couples who wandered in and out of the rooms, pretending they knew what they were looking at, pretending they could afford his prices. Baxter knew he really didn't have to open up for these people, because they rarely bought anything, but browsing was what they did on weekends after brunch and he couldn't disappoint them.

Back then, doing the galleries, flea markets, boutiques, and antique shops like Uncle Peter's was a kind of mating ritual on Saturdays in New York. Couples played at furnishing imaginary apartments. They seduced one another with their knowledge of the postmodernists, performance artists, and the new graffiti kings. They slouched in and out of the galleries, stood before my mother's own work, and in reverent tones discussed the deep emotional issues of the day. They used the word "resonate."

It was, as Uncle Baxter explained, courtship fueled by consumption, a way of saying we like the same things, we are safe with each other. As we walked to the store, Baxter and I made a game of spotting couples lounging in small cafés, sipping cappuccino and feeding each other little bites of cheesecake and cannoli, their eyes drinking each other in, the day's packages tumbling around them, discarded like so many articles of clothing and as Jessica might have put it, "melting into each other like good cashmere."

Uncle Baxter did not enjoy the browsers that day, nor did he flirt with the women and wink at the men and tell long, outrageous stories about the beautiful things in the store. He gamely offered the After Six mints he called digestives, kept in a tin on his massive Jacobean desk, even though he knew the browsers would leave with nothing of consequence—a modest silk dresser tassel that might turn up around a pretty neck, or one of the small Georgian silver frames he'd had reproduced in London.

Baxter told me no stories of his own crazy courtship of Jessica, not that morning. Instead, he focused on me as though for the first time, as if a hairline fracture had suddenly appeared and he was assessing the damage. This was the same squinty-eyed look I'd seen him give a flawed ball and claw foot or a prized armchair, as he tried to figure out how to reinforce it without destroying its lines,

I did not have much heart for people watching either. Sensing this, Uncle Baxter flipped over the "Closed" earlier than usual that day.

"Let's just putter for awhile," he said, tossing his keys into the ornate silver temple bowl on his desk.

We headed towards the back room for the ivory chessmen and seventeenth-century tournament board Uncle Baxter set up for us on a gate leg table near the window.

"Harry says Grandma Hirsh called last weekend and Uncle Peter got really mad and hung up on her." I said, trying to remember what Uncle Baxter said about each piece.

"You must have been pretty mad yourself, to pop Carl like that." There was a mixture of pride and maybe even a little amusement in this, as if he were seeing a new side of me, a side he liked.

"I guess."

Carl's face seemed small just before I punched him. Even smaller when he realized the blood spurting on his sweater was his own. I did not say how much I missed him.

"Can you keep a secret?"

"Sure," I nodded.

"Promise not to tell Jess or your moms."

"Okay."

"I think he deserved it," said Uncle Baxter, grinning his evil grin. "If somebody says something bad about you or your moms, it's okay to haul off and show 'em what you've got. That's what your old Bax thinks. I'm not telling you to solve everything that way, kiddo, but I think there's too damn many women in the family, telling us how to behave."

"Uncle Bax."

"Right here."

"Are they fighting because of me?"

"Nah," said Uncle Bax, unconvincingly.

"Are they going to get a divorce?"

"I wish I knew, sport."

12

I believe forgiveness given prematurely is its own form of punishment. When the hand is offered before the heart says it's time, judgment lurks behind every smile the way a speck of blood clings to the gap between tooth and gum and tells you there is something wrong beneath the toothpaste pink brightness. When forgiveness is coerced or offered for the wrong reasons, every incident adds to the pressure mounting in the spaces between words. Every gesture, every conversation, and glance carries an unbearable weight, until the force can no longer be contained and the explosion comes as a shock to everyone but the one who has never stopped raging in one-sided, long-suffering silence.

Claire said this is the moment the camera records when it sees the subject before its presence is noted, before the lip has had time to uncurl the grimace worn by people who are too quick to please, before the eyes brighten and mask malice, when a trick of light reveals the lie.

I've seen this myself with drunks when they feign sweet temper and spite rises up higher and higher out of each successive glass until the very thing they work so hard to hide strangles them in such a familiar way, its appearance is loudly celebrated in whiskey's coarse voice.

Forgiveness is never the dramatic end of things we've all seen on the big screen, the instant cleansing of hurts, but the only beginning of a slow rewinding of trust. Often it's a tactic when one sees the other is willing to risk a staggering loss rather than strike a compromise, forcing the issue into a manageable, yet pernicious, retreat. There the wound crusts over, infects, and feeds on every slight.

Theo told me some people eat, growing large with their disaffecton. Some slide into drugs or prayer, while others wear a perpetual look of pained sweetness while they wait for their moment.

I've seen this myself in school when a teacher made us apologize for words and deeds we were not yet ready to accept as cause for contrition, when we were forced to lose something of ourselves in the name of peace. We can only lie in wait, harboring thoughts of revenge while we play alongside our prey.

Real forgiveness is a lot like being tall. It sneaks up on you. You don't see it until you find yourself more sympathetic and generous to those against whom you harbor ill will. There is a general softening, small kindnesses add up and suddenly you realize no other course was ever an option. You no longer give too much to hide your guilt; the word "no" no longer holds the power to lay bare the coldness of your heart.

Claire was not the first person my grandmother pretended to forgive. She never forgave Roland for dying and Barnaby for shutting her out after his death. Baraby's was a silent grief that did not include her, and he kept to himself the empty place that had once been filled by my uncle, the flaxen-haired boy he named after his own father, the son who would inherit the Hirsh instinct for business and make him proud. That place was now occupied with other men who never spoke of their own disappointments, men who appeared promptly and in appropriate attire for their wives' cocktail parties and charity balls. Like Barnaby, they attended to their social responsibilities with silken charm, revealing nothing of themselves in the rapt interest they paid their dinner companions, first to the left, then to the right.

Mary suffered this loss because it wasn't in her nature or in her upbringing to do otherwise. It would never have occurred to her to examine her feelings, nor would she have known what to do with what she found. She could not simply ask her husband to share his grief, nor could she give him the kind of comfort he would never have solicited. Mary did not question Barnaby's distance because it covered the deeper wound of seeing Roland every time she looked at Claire. She did not grieve with her daughter, or try to understand the special loss that comes with the death of a twin, because she didn't know how. Mary hid behind her belief that adults who acknowledge the feelings of children are courting disaster. My grandmother assumed Claire would leave these feelings behind with her sophomoric crushes and the dreadful poetry she penned onto the thick pages of an artist's sketchbook.

In a family that understood such things, Claire showed all the signs of survivor's guilt and bore the full brunt of her parents' grief. She affected the tapping of Roland's fingers on a table, the wink that took the sting out of an unkind remark, and when these gestures were greeted not with understanding, but with stern reprimands, as though she had trodden on the velvet cord that sealed off his room, she retreated until the woman I knew as my mother was formed, not unlike the tree in California that grew despite a hole in its trunk you could drive a Greyhound bus through.

The cord that binds twins cannot be severed in life or in death. Claire had not lost a brother, but an important piece of herself. Pounds melted away from her naturally slim frame the year her Roland died. When I told my wife Annie the story of my mother's lost twin, it was she who made the connection between Claire's guilt about eating, her determination to take up less than her allotted space in the world, and her love for round, ripe Theo who would feed a parking meter if it stood at the table long enough. But that was years later, when many things were understood.

Roland came first after a hard night of labor that ripped Mary open and and caused her to curse Barnaby, who was waiting it out at his club. In those days, men of his generation and standing accepted cigars and brandy for their progeny, while exhausted wives were given a touch of rouge for the appraisal. Mary swore at the nurse who held cold cloths to her wrists and temples and murmured a constant stream of comfort as the reluctant Roland and, minutes later, his beet-faced sister, made their way into the world

When my grandmother looked at Claire and later at Theo and me, I believe she always saw that loss, never her gain.

OUT IN SOUTH NECK, Harry and I felt the late August chill in the earliness of dusk and in the growing distance we put between ourselves in preparation for the inevitable separation of the new school term; his a reunion classmates, mine a reminder of the one who had chosen not to be my friend. As we readied ourselves for this annual separation, something hard was forming around my mothers.

They no longer fought with any passion. Their disagreements seemed to have lost the energy they once had—and with it, perhaps, the belief that enough conviction could really change anything. There were no more stormy scenes on Fifth Avenue, no more tearful reconciliations at the urging of friends. Forgiveness came too easily and on its heels, signs of a deeper loss—a slight incline of the head, resignation in the droop of a shoulder, a door that closed too softly.

They became wary of each other, as though one false word might destroy their carefully constructed truce. They avoided pet names like *honey* and *sweetie, boovie* and *bug,* once spoken in laughter and ease, filling the house with their mischief and me with a sense of peace. They did not speak of Mrs. Jacoby and Carl and instead focused on how we should present ourselves to the world, what kind of school I should attend. In the guise of what was best for me, the fault lines cracked and the rift grew wider.

Claire wanted us to make friends with other mothers in similar circumstances and to move away, if necessary, where there were no Mrs. Jacobys and Mrs. Langelottis and neighbors who warned their sons away from us.

Theo had begun to make new friends who would provide a more "balanced" view of the world, than Claire was willing to provide.

"Can't you just pretend we're a traditional family?" I heard Theo say one night. "I know what I am and what you mean to me. If it means Willy is accepted by his teachers and the kids in school, why do you be so damaned militant?"

Their voices became shrill, and I pulled the pillow over my head to block out the sound of Theo hissing, "I am his birth mother and I will do whatever is right for *him*—not *us,* not *you, him!*" The strangled sound of Claire sobbing and Theo slamming their bedroom door became the discordant music of nighttime.

After that, I tried to stay out of their way as much as possible.

One of Theo's friends, Lulu Clark, began to spend more time at our house.

"Please call me Lulu," she'd said when Theo had looked down at the name tag that read MRS. CARTER LEIGH CLARK, JR., "Everyone does." Lulu had been filling her time with charity work to staunch the deep gash recently inflicted by her husband's decision to leave her for his young legal assistant. "I don't know which he found more attractive,"

Lulu had said over the small steaks and oysters Theo had provided to capture the taste of Victorian New York's tables, "her legs or her family lineage."

Theo noted the thin line of bitterness around Lulu's mouth, heard the betrayal in her voice, but when she found out Lulu had a son, Drew, in the fourth grade at Goodwin, she decided to invite her to lunch at the store.

I suspect Theo liked Lulu mostly for her ignorance of our family situation, but I also think she felt a sisterly sense of pride in the halting and often perilous progress Lulu was making in her attempt to remake her life and replace her errant husband with someone equally *comfortable*. It amused Theo that no one in Lulu's crowd ever used the word rich except to describe the nouveau riche, like that Skull couple who were buying up all the pop art that year. It was all "deeply shallow," as Jessica liked to say, but Theo had her reasons.

"Ever wonder why there's no such thing as the *Senior* League?" said Claire coldly. "Because they couldn't call themselves Lulu and Dodo and Missy and Muffin, that's why. What does she call Drew-Poo?"

Open hostilities resumed one night when a sleepy and apologetic Lulu called close to midnight to say she was sending me home in a cab after I had refused to sleep in one of the pup tents that had mushroomed on the Clark living room floor for the Carnegie Hill version of sleep-away camp for Drew and a pack of howling boys from Goodwin.

"I don't know why he went down to the lobby in his pajamas like that, but I suspect the other boys were bragging about their dads—all that father-and-son business that is so important at this age," Lulu told Theo as Claire rushed to dress so she could go down to our lobby to wait for me.

"Yes, he really misses his father," said Theo—as softly as she could, but not softly enough for Claire to miss it.

"You're a brave boy," Mrs. Carter Leigh Clark, Jr., said, trailing a good six inches of nightgown under a hastily donned trench coat, as I hurried to get away from the snickers that caused the Aber-crombie & Fitch pup tents to jiggle in the dark.

I did not cry until after the Clark's doorman gave the cabbie our address and I sat in stale-smelling darkness as we plunged through the sleeping park.

Claire was on the sidewalk when I got home. Upstairs they both fussed over me and Theo said Drew was being mean because he missed his father and Claire explained that the other boys followed his lead because sometimes people do cruel things in groups to prove they belong. They put up a good front, but I felt their anger at my back pushing me up the stairs to my loft, out of its way.

After getting me settled, still feeling the sting of Theo's lie, Claire tried once more. "Why don't we move to Berkeley or Amherst or somewhere like-minded people are raising children away from all this?"

"Great," snapped Theo. "Let's live in some hippie town full of tie-dyed tee shirts, vegetarians, and lesbians who can't bring up their children in the real world. You could photograph people's auras and I could open a Tofu Take-Out, maybe adjust chakras in my spare time. Instead of saving for college, we could squirrel away two or three million dollars for the thirty or forty years of analysis Willy will need after a childhood like that."

"Stop making fun of me," Claire warned.

"I'm not making fun of you. I am simply trying to point out in terms you can understand that we will damage Willy by not showing him all the differences and letting him choose his own path."

"Well, he chose his own path tonight, didn't he?" Claire shot back. "Straight down to the lobby in his pajamas. Those kids showed him the door, Theo. Your Lulu and her son and his friends called Willy names. Did they call us dykes to his face or just whisper it behind his back?"

"Can't we go underground for a little while?"

"Underground? Where is that, Theo? Is that where you get to be the mother and I get to be his aunt and Willy doesn't know who's who anymore?"

"What's the harm, Claire?" I wondered about that, too. There wasn't much to recommend life above ground either.

Theo continued to see Lulu and other women like her. Some had husbands, houses in the Hamptons and lives full of charity work; others had full-time jobs and like Theo, businesses of their own. But they all had one thing in common—boys my age.

I never let on that I preferred spending my time with Harry and Baxter, and Uncle Peter and with my new friend, Mr. Luis de Jesus

Cosmopoulos, whom she did not know, whom nobody had ever met, except Uncle Bax, and even he hadn't realized he had.

One chilly afternoon in October, the phone rang and it was Lulu.

"Where is your mother?" she asked.

"Which one?" I asked, loyal to Claire.

"Well, Theo, of course."

Theo had a habit of smiling before she picked up the phone, the way people bounce a tennis ball a few times before serving. Lulu had invited us to Vermont for the weekend with her new beau, as she coyly referred to the divorced father with whom she was sharing several homes and multiple children.

"Theo, be a sport and don't come on Saturday night. It's going to be couples only and—well, you know what happens when a single woman shows up. Why don't you and Willy drive up for the day on Sunday and we'll have a nice lunch, maybe even have some snow."

"You know what's really funny?" Theo said when she realized I was standing in the kitchen doorway listening. She was still smiling, even though there wasn't much reason to.

I shook my head.

"Claire isn't even here to say 'I told you so.'"

Like all children who live under the sentence of their parents' problems, I constantly nudged them closer to their shared history. I pointed to our wall and encouraged reminiscing. "Tell me *Lesbians on Vacation*," I begged. I tapped the photo of Theo at the Fraser-Morris cheese counter and asked to hear about the day I already knew by heart. I held their hands, but they would allow no blurring of the lines they had drawn.

WHEN SHE WAS HOME, Claire spent more time in her darkroom and when she was not, in the Village with people she claimed were "more progressive," and "understood the artistic nature." "People," Claire informed Theo every chance she got, "who did not believe mothers and lesbians were at opposite ends of the planet."

Most nights, Theo was asleep when Claire tiptoed into the apartment. I wanted to know where she went, but I was afraid to ask. One Saturday after we'd been at Jessica and Baxter's, Claire said,

"What do you say, want to meet my friend Ruth?" "Sure," I said, feeling vaguely disloyal to Theo.

Claire and Ruth talked for hours that afternoon, poring over photographs, reading aloud, eating oranges and drinking tea and honey in thick mugs. They sat on a weathered leather sofa that creaked every time one of them shifted position or punctuated the conversation with a loud thump on its arms. After giving me a big hug and a plate of cookies all to myself, Ruth let me exlore her book-strewn apartment, which seemed exotic after Claire and Theo's controlled clutter. A fat Siamese purring loudly sat in my lap as I ate my cookies and looked at the books Ruth pulled from the shelves for me. She chain-smoked and wore thick glasses that enlarged her eyes. I didn't want to, but I liked her.

After her evenings at Ruth's—during which, I imagined, other women like Ruth gathered around the living room, their conversation multiplying the intensity I witnessed that day—Claire would head straight for my loft and sit on the edge of my bed. She'd peer at me for a long time, her pale eyes glittering from the lateness of the hour and more wine than she was used to.

One night, as I pretended to be asleep, she whispered, "What shall I do, darling boy?" There was sadness in her voice; the smell of tobacco and something mossy clung to her clothes. I don't know why I didn't open my eyes and hug her that night. The fact that I didn't haunts me still. She might have explained, told me something that would have changed everything, but I suspect I sensed she was communing with the idea of me and not the flesh-and-blood, stocky, red-haired reality. Maybe I was afraid to break the spell. Or maybe, if I woke up and spoke, I would have been easier to leave.

Theo used to say that taking pictures is a way of not participating, of staying out of the fray. It was better, she said, to dig right in and get your hands dirty, and even if life disappointed you, you could say you tried to affect its course. She said it was why she ended up a chef, because you could rearrange the elements, concoct something of your own invention, cut the bitterness with something sweet, add and subtract and know the second the experiment passed your lips whether you'd succeeded or not. If you fell on your face, you always had the next meal as an opportunity to try again. She said this with no malice or accusation, as she had many times before, but with the deep sadness of knowing she was powerless to change what informs another's actions, even someone she loved.

It was the week before Christmas and Theo had barely climbed out from under the pile of orders for pumpkin, mince, and sweet potato pies. This was the time of year Theo brought her work home, her concession to "making the numbers," which, she explained, meant doing a whole year's work in two weeks and being at home with us at the same time. Our red Parsons table groaned under the weight of other people's holiday dinners, brunches, cocktail parties, and office mixers. There were gift baskets in the making, platters of marzipan, pfeffernüsse, truffles, and swarthy gingerbread men waiting for buttons, mustaches, and other distinguishing characteristics. When it was time for our own dinner, we simply cleared a space for ourselves and ate around the life-like cookies as though they were friends of the family.

Most years, Theo did this work happily, humming carols and letting me lick bowls of chocolate ganache, brownie batter, and cookie dough. Claire and I were her trusted assistants, tasting the results and inviting the pounds to add up.

Never trust a cook who cannot lick his own fingers.

"Who said that?" she'd ask.

"Brillat-Savarin!" I'd answer without hesitation, sounding like an idiot savant.

No such coziness this particular night. Theo was bone tired and looked too thin, which was unusual for this time of year, given her penchant for sampling. Freezing rain needled our windows, and Theo worked with grim determination. In the overhead light of our kitchen, there were hollows in her cheeks, where last year at this time—before Mrs. Jacoby came into our lives—there had been apples. Shadows carved half-moons under her eyes, setting off the sharp edge of a collarbone I couldn't remember ever having seen before. She moved like someone begging for sleep.

I made a place for myself at the table and made a halfhearted pass at my homework. We were very much alike, Theo and I, in that we labored better in chaos than in the solitude Claire preferred. Many years later, I found the manic buzz of a newsroom just the inspiration I needed for the noisy pursuit of journalism, but on this particular night there was no comfort in the clatter around me.

Theo worked silently and so did I. Afraid to interrupt her, and even more uncomfortable at the idea of being in another room with Claire, I tripped over verb tenses to get to the sense of *Emilio y Los Detectives* for Spanish class as sleet clawed at our reflections in the windows.

Theo looked up but did not speak when Claire walked in, rubbing the darkroom out of her eyes.

"If anybody cares, it looks like I got some interesting stuff today."

Theo shook her head into the sink where she was rinsing out a muffin tin, but did not turn around.

Claire sat down next to me. I looked up and smiled. "I do," I said.

"Has Emilio solved any cases yet or are they saving it for when you have a bigger vocabulary?"

"It's kind of boring," I said, seizing the opportunity to close the book.

"They should put pictures in those books," Claire said, looking at Theo's back, which stiffened slightly.

"That way, you could imagine what's happening before you actually learn the words."

"Or you could decide what you want to happen and use the pictures to make your point," Theo said coldly. Then to me: "Got your favorite stuffing coming up, with a fresh cranberry sauce and roast chicken. Make a little dinner room on that table and I'm sure I could find some fudge brownies around here somewhere." She was working hard to smooth the sharp edge in her voice for me, and not quite succeeding.

"C'mon, Theo, give it a rest," said Claire. "We're all tired. Let's just have dinner."

Theo arranged our plates at the stove and carried them to the table. When she sat down, she looked at Claire for a long time. Her voice seemed to ache with sadness, "I think taking pictures is a great way to avoid participating in life."

I stiffened, sensing this accelerate into another one of the "discussions," which had ruined more than one meal and was why Claire preferried to have me to herself during the day when Theo was at the store.

At Theo's opening salvo, I felt my food balling up in a knot at the bottom of my stomach, where it stayed, resistant to the forces of digestion for many hours. Claire held her fork in the air for what seemed like five minutes, then she got up slowly, lifted her chair in to the table, taking care not to let it scrape. She removed her plate, napkin, and cutlery, transferred her dinner into the open containers from which Theo had just served it, put it back in refrigerator, and kissed me on the top of my head. "I'm not very hungry tonight," she said, touching Theo's shoulder as she left the room. A few minutes later, we heard the sound of the shower, and some time after that, the front door closing behind her.

It would be many hours before we realized she was not coming back.

13

Theo and I didn't pay much attention to Claire's leaving. After a silent meal, Theo went back to her baking, I to my homework, and each of us to our private thoughts about what was happening to our family. When Claire did not return late that night or the next day or the day after that, Theo fought her rising panic with calls to their friends.

"Don't worry, sweetheart, she'll be back. She has to sulk awhile," said Suzie, who was more concerned than she let on.

"No, I haven't called the police," Theo told Jessica, who had just heard from Suzie. "Yes, I've tried the gallery . . . yes . . . and Thad . . . Peter and Molly aren't home . . . . Yes, I'll keep trying."

"We went to see somebody named Ruth who had a cat," I offered.

"I already called her, Willy. She says she hasn't seen Claire for a few days."

Theo took a long breath and dialed Mary Hirsh.

"We're having a rough patch, some problems," Theo began. "We had an argument the other night and I thought, well . . . I thought she might be with you, to cool off, think things over a bit."

Claire's mother offered nothing.

"If you know where she is, Mrs. Hirsh, please tell me. I'm beginning to get worried," Theo pleaded, knowing she had said all she could. In the cold silence that followed, the evidence that my grandmother's "forgiveness" had been premature came down like a sentence.

"You know, Theo, we've discussed this situation with our son and we really must do the best thing for our grandson."

"You don't need to worry, Claire and I can work this out ourselves," said Theo, shrugging off Mary's tone of voice and the chill it gave her. "I just need to know where Claire is right now," said Theo.

"I think it *is* necessary, dear," Mary continued, ignoring Theo's question. "We really can't allow this situation to continue—"

"What *situation*? What do you mean 'best thing for Willy'? What's Peter got to do with it?" Theo's hand began to shake.

"Raising a young boy in a household like yours is unhealthy, Theo. I can't sit quietly by and allow my grandson to be pushed and pulled about in that sort of environment. Your lifestyle is a form of child abuse and our attorney is appalled that Willy's grandfather and I have let this continue for as long as we have."

"Your attorney! Mrs. Hirsh, Willy may be your grandson, but Claire and I are his mothers and this is his home—"

"And may I also say, dear, that raising Willy in a household like yours is against the law; that any agency interested in the welfare of children would remove him immediately."

Just before Theo hung up, Mary said, "Did you really think we would allow this?"

Mary's tone terrified Theo more than her words. Theo thought about that night over nine years ago when I was born, when Mary had held Theo's hand and rolled her own tweed jacket into a ball to support her head. Had she been planning this all along?

There's a photograph of my grandmother sitting stiffly on the ground in a pale pink linen suit which would have been more at home at a garden party than at an impromptu picnic in Central Park. The spirit of that day is long gone—the sudden burst of enthusiasm for Jessica's romantic idea of transporting our Sunday dinner to the public lawn just beyond our windows, Claire laughing with her whole body as she skidded around the table packing our wicker hamper, with plates and all the food Theo had just set out. Theo winding daisies into everyone's hair, including Uncle Peter's long blond wisps and my fiery mop, Uncle Baxter rummaging in the closet for Peter's old football, a bottle of wine in each pocket, Suzie slipping into an old pair of Claire's sneakers, Barnaby shaking his head at the silliness of "this new generation." Thad hoisting me up on his shoulders for the grand march into the park, Harry forgetting his sulk at Aunt Molly's refusal to let him eat the tops of the miniature cupcakes Theo had baked for

Jennifer and Brooke's dolls, all of us singing our family version of Arlo Guthrie's song, "You can get anything that you want / At Theo's restaurant."

All of this is lost to the viewer now. All that remains is my grandmother sitting on a tattered Indian bedspread, her crocodile pumps parked neatly on the ground next to her, heel lined up with heel as though they might be waiting for her in the closet; not on the scruffy lawn of Sheep Meadow. There is too much brightness around her eyes. At first glance, she seems to be working hard to appear oblivious to the imminent threat of grass stains on her expensive suit, but it's the people around her that threaten her far more. Time has washed this photograph of all but its secret, and I wonder what warnings live in other pictures, what other signs I've missed.

I know my grandmother loved us very much, but even a child I could see she came alive whenever my mothers hit a difficult stretch. Even before "the troubles," as my grandmother's Irish doorman called our bad times, the slightest display of temper or disagreement seemed to cheer her up. It would have been so much easier for her if Theo and Claire broke up.

Some say the heart already knows how things will turn out, but the brain keeps it from telling anybody. I suppose I always knew my grandma Hirsh had never forgiven us, because I mentioned it to Mr. Cosmopoulos the first time we met.

I MET HIM just before Claire left for good. It was a few days after Thanksgiving, and I was walking back to school after lunch at The Latest Dish. Theo thought it best that I be given permission to do this, in order to avoid any further unpleasantness with Carl and the sizable following he had attracted in the wake of the "incident" the previous term, which had given him instant celebrity status. I couldn't bear to see proof that the most important friendship in my young life had been forgotten in little more than a summer vacation, so I went to the store, where Theo wound a clean apron around her waist, nibbled at the edges of a bagel, and sat with me as long as she could between customers.

That frantic noon, we counted a record ten times that she had to jump up to wait on a customer before we decided I'd be late and she'd better wrap the rest of my meal to eat on the way back to school.

A heavy voice filled with gravel rolled up behind me. "Hey mister, what's that you're eating?"

"Moussah-something," I said, eyeing the man warily.

"Looks like moussaka to me," he said. "My mother used to make that when I was a kid in Crete. You Greek?"

"I dunno. Maybe," I said, holding my lunch close to me in case he made a move.

"You gotta be somethin'."

I thought about the costume party my mothers had the year before I was born. I knew it had something to do with my birth, but I couldn't remember exactly what except that everyone talked about their family trees and what countries their parents and grandparents had come from, so my mothers could pick my father, but I forgot what they had said about ours. I knew Jewish and Protestant were religions; not where you're from.

"We're lesbians," I said, thrusting out my chin for the inevitable sneer.

"So you *are* Greek! I knew it!"

I was confused. People called my mothers many things, usually in a low whisper spoken from one side of the mouth in that deliberate way meant to leave you wondering whether you had actually heard or had only imagined what was said. But no one ever called them Greeks. I wasn't sure if I should hit him or run.

"Lesbos, mister. If you're a lesbian, you're from Lesbos. Coupla islands down from Crete, which means we're practically neighbors. Nice place. Clean. Not like here." As he spoke, he swept the pavement before him with a disgusted look. A rookie cop with a boy's neck that had not yet grown into the stiff blue collar of his patrolman's serge was absently writing tickets for the line of cars illegally parked along Third Avenue and ignoring the pleas of the owners, who dashed out of restaurants ahead of him, napkins still tucked into their well-pressed business suits. Looking up from the tedium of his summons book, he narrowed his eyes at us. I didn't recognize it then—I had no reason to on the relatively vagrant-free streets of the mid-seventies—but it was a look that said, "Ain't you a long way from the Bowery?"

Just then, the man said something funny, something I didn't understand, which sounded like "teeny tie my shoe," but I was afraid to ask him what it meant. Maybe it was his name. Or maybe it was a nonsense word and he was crazy like Leon, who lived in one of the efficiency apartments over the store and often paced the sidewalk in front of mom's window trying to decide what to buy before going in. Leon rubbed his head, rolled his tongue, and moved his eyes constantly, never looking directly at anyone, even when Theo gave him extra cookies.

This man was odd, all right, and even from my taller-than-average fourth-grade perspective, he looked at least seven feet tall. But I wasn't afraid of him. I couldn't tell you why. I just knew it. Leon always gave me the feeling he was capable of hurting someone, but not this man. He just looked lived-in.

His hands were the biggest I'd ever seen. They hung at his sides like giant slabs of bacon, red over the knuckles where the wind had chapped them and pale between the fingers where the weather could not penetrate. If it were not for the fact that he kept them still, they might have seemed dangerous. I think he knew they could scare people if he used them too much.

Hair the color of octopus ink grew wild and as long as tentacles where the rubber band lost its grip on a thick ponytail; dark ropes coiled around sharp cheekbones. A proud aquiline nose hinted more at Diego Rivera than at Zorba the Greek. Red suspenders held up a pair of faded jeans as soft and loose as a pair of Grandpa Barnaby's pajamas. I suppose what intrigued me most was the fact that he called me mister, even though I was a kid.

He said it again. "Teeny tie my shoe."

"I guess they didn't teach you any Greek. I asked you your name, mister." The gold in his front tooth glinted in the hard winter sun as he waited for my answer.

I was still guarding the foam cup that held my rapidly congealing lunch. "Willy. Willy Bouvier-Hirsh."

"Mine's Mr. Luis de Jesus Cosmopoulos," he said with a crisp salute. "I know what you're thinking. Strange name. Everybody says so." He settled against a parked car the way a storyteller finds a comfortable position in an easy chair before leaning forward to cast his net.

"My father met my mother the first and only time he ever left Crete," said Mr. Cosmopoulos, folding his big hands over a pear-shaped stomach that pushed his suspenders to the breaking point.

"He'd always wanted to see the Andes, saved up for years, and she was waiting for him right behind the front desk when he checked into his hotel in Lima. That's spelled like 'lima bean,' but pronounced 'Leemah.'" He barely paused for breath before plunging back into his story. "Her name was Maria Teresa and she was the most beautiful girl he had ever seen. Part Castilian Spanish from some Conquistador way back and the rest pure Peruvian Inca." He was careful to pronounce the "th" sound in place of the "s" in "Castilian."

"Married her right on the spot. Well, a week later, anyway, after he talked her into it. By the time they got back to Crete, I was kickin' hard to get my start in the world and neither of my grandparents ever spoke to my father again. Can you imagine livin' in a fishing village no bigger than spit and never talking to your own flesh and blood when they passed you on the street? My grandmother wore black just like my father was dead. You know the word 'stoic'?"

I shook my head no.

"Well, that's the Greek way, mister. You could threaten to jump off a twenty-story bilding and they'd just look at you. They named me Luis for my *abuelo*. That's Spanish for 'grandpop.'"

He wrote the word "*abuelo*" in the dust on the car's fender and next to it he wrote "*niño*," with something he called a tilde over the second "n." He said, "*Neenyo*, that's what I was when all this happened, a boy, just like you," and suddenly his eyes went blank, the muscles in his face slackened, and he stared at me for a minute, seeing nothing.

I was a little frightened, but I moved closer. "Mr. Cosmopoulos? Are you okay?"

"Nah, I get a little lost sometimes," he said, pulling on his ponytail as though pulling himself back to his place in the story. His eyes brightened again, as if someone had switched on a lamp, and he continued.

"They named me Luis for my maternal grandfather, that means my mother's father, and *Hay Seuss*, that's how you say 'Jesus' in Spanish, for the savior who saved my father from marrying some moon-faced Cretan girl my grandparents would have picked out for him, and I can tell you they had no taste in women. Yessir, Mr. Bouvier-Hirsh. They named him for the good Lord who had the decency to drop him right on top of those Andes mountains where his bride and my mother, God rest her soul, was waiting for him to show up. Ain't that something? What about you?"

He talked as though he were running a race. I was tired just listening.

"That's my mother's store" was all I could muster, pointing to the red neon lips UncleBax said once belonged to a famous speakeasy, I could make out the outlines of Theo's arms disappearing into the cases, and handing a white box over the counter to someone. Later, when I understood such things, I could describe what I felt at that moment as the first stab of separation, the understanding I was experiencing something wholly my own while my mother went about her business. I can't say this was altogether pleasant, and yet I felt an odd exhilaration.

"Some lucky one you are, mister," said Mr. Cosmopoulos, pursing his lips and whistling appreciatively. "I love her cannelloni with mozzarella, tomatoes and pesto. I take some home to Shorty every now and then. I wrap it in tin foil real good and it tastes like it just came out of the oven." He brought a huge paw to his lips and kissed his fingers. His eyes shone like black olives in oil.

"Shorty would tell you he prefers your mother's puttanesca sauce. He says it's got just the right amount of heat and an authentic sense of immediacy. And I don't have to tell you why I'm an enchilada and moussaka man, what with my background and all, but those cannelloni . . . maybe there's a little Italian in me after all!" I guessed Mr. Cosmopoulos ate the way he spoke, with gusto.

"When food is that good, you'd be surprised how far word of mouth travels!" This last remark struck him as very funny. His booming laugh seemed to come up from the toes of his thick brown wingtips, which had soles like running boards. "A regular underground sensation!" he snorted, these last words rocking him back into his private joke. "You're one lucky kid, with a mother who can cook like that. So Theo Bouvier is your mother."

"I've got two."

"Does the other one cook?"

"No. Claire takes pictures."

"What kind of pictures? Wedding, bar mitzvahs?"

I tried hard to think of a way to describe Claire's photographs.

"They gave her a Guggenheim" was what I finally came up with.

"No kidding," he said, looking impressed.

"She takes pictures of strangers when they're not looking. Some people leave money with our doorman until they can take them home, but most of the time she sells them in a gallery after they're criticized."

"Whaddaya say about that! Sounds real specialized. That's the ticket today. Everybody's a specialist. Not too much room for generalists like myself." He seemed pleased that I had confirmed something he felt deeply.

"So where you from?" he asked, changing the subject abruptly.

"Central Park West, but I go to school over on Seventy-fourth and Madison and my grandmother Hirsh lives on Seventy-second and Fifth and well, there's Mom's store. I guess we're from New York."

"I'd say you are. So what do your grandma and grandpop think of this two mothers business?"

"Grandma Doris and Grandpa Roy always say, 'As long as you're happy, that's what counts,' and my grandpa Barnaby doesn't say much. But I don't think my grandmother Hirsh likes it, even though she pretends she does."

I didn't tell him that my moms weren't as happy as they used to be because saying it would have made it true. I didn't tell him that we went to Grandma H.'s apartment for Thanksgiving, even though Theo didn't want to go and everybody was on edge, or that I overheard her saying I was Claire's boy and that Theo was Claire's "friend."

"Sounds like you got yourself a grandma like mine, one of the Furies in a black dress and a personality to match, huh, mister?" He peered down at me with eyes that seemed to grow darker and more luminous, eyes that saw through me all the way down to my secrets.

"Grandma Hirsh says black is too somber, and is appropriate only for funerals," I said, summoning my regal grandmother in her matronly pumps, pearls, and pale woolen suits with linings that rustled silk against silk, the faint smell of lilies of the valley lingering wherever she sat.

"Aunt Jessica says she's a tweed-and-Chanel-Number-5 person."

"Who's Aunt Jessica?" he asked, keeping an eye on the policeman who was walking around a battered Chevy with an expired inspection sticker.

"She's not really my aunt, she's Claire's best friend. She tells women how to dress in her fashion magazine, and Mom says she's a glorified clothes hanger, but I think she's neat."

Mr. Cosmopoulos ignored my answer to his last question, his gaze still moving off over my head. I followed it, but could see only the wide avenue, people rushing along the sidewalk, heads down, eyes hard against the onslaught of horns, sirens, jackhammers, wary of any hint of trouble in the faces of strangers.

"You know, sometimes I think it's easier when you can see what you're up against, don't ya think?"

I wasn't quite sure why I agreed, but I nodded at this and we stood on the sidewalk like two old friends who understood each other perfectly.

EACH TIME WE MET, I learned something else about my new friend. He worked odd jobs and told me all about the newspaper business, how trees are ground into pulp for only one day's use; that he was about to make a killing in the new recycling industry. He lived in what sounded like a cramped apartment on Madison in the twenties with a man named Shorty, who had a bad temper and couldn't keep a job long because, he said, "people didn't understand perfectionists anymore."

Usually, I ran into him near the store, leaning up against a parked car. I'd run in and get us both lunch, which sometimes he didn't eat, taking care to keep the soot out of the wrapper. "Shorty's going to love this," he'd say, "I'll save it for him." After a while, I remembered to get enough for all three of us.

Once, when I asked Theo to ladle out more chili than even a kid my size could eat, I told her I wanted extra for a friend, and she filled the container with the generosity of a mother delighted to know her son was finally becoming popular. I didn't really lie; I just let her think I'd made friends with someone from school. After that, it was easier to surprise Mr. Cosmopoulos with beef stroganoff and lamb curry taped and wrapped tightly to take home to Shorty.

Some days, he was waiting for me near the hole in the fence near the McCall schoolyard. "Hey mister, what'd you learn today? Anything worth knowing?"

I'm not sure why I didn't tell anybody about him. I meant to, but I never got around to it. I guess I wanted to keep him to myself a little longer, or maybe I just wanted something no one could fight over.

One cold Saturday afternoon, Uncle Bax and I were walking over to the antique store and spotted Mr. Cosmopoulos sitting on a bench in Sheridan Square.

"Well, well, if it isn't Mr. Bouvier-Hirsh," he said, bowing and sweeping his huge arm to where his waist once might have been. "And who's this gentleman accompanying you on this fine day?"

I introduced Uncle Bax, who smiled politely but withheld his hand the way he did when a difficult customer took too much of his time and bought something trivial. I couldn't see his mouth under the handlebar mustache, which was just as well because I knew there was mistrust around the edges.

Mr. Cosmopoulos sensed my discomfort immediately. "Can't sit here all day," he said. "Transferred to the downtown office for a coupla days."

"Where do you work, Mr. Cosmopoulos?" Uncle Baxter asked.

"Nowhere if I don't get there fast!" boomed Mr. Cosmopoulos over his shoulder.

No one had ever brushed Baxter off so quickly.

I waited for him for a long time the day after we found out Claire had left us and Theo cried all afternoon after talking to Grandma Hirsh.

I walked over to the store at lunchtime, even though Theo had not opened it that day, and I stood near the hole in the fence long after the last bus pulled up to the curb. I walked slowly home through the park, but Mr. Cosmopoulos did not pop out of a clump of trees, nor did he materialize on any of the benches I passed along the way. If he had, I would not have known how to explain. I guess that's why he didn't show up again until I was able to say the word "divorced."

14

As word of Claire's disappearance snaked up and down aisles of fruity-smelling school desks, radiators clanging and hissing the news in the shorthand of that particular jungle, hostility toward me began to cool. The irony of my situation was that I was now getting along better at school. While there was no sudden flurry of invitations, or overtures of friendship; Carl Jacoby did all he could to prevent that, wary looks replaced outright scorn, and curiosity won out as the other boys found it impossible to resist my new status as a divorced kid. I had become normal in their eyes and they offered advice on custody, dating, stepsisters and stepbrothers, and the useful art of pitting one parent against the other.

One boy, called Rabbit because his mean eyes were always pink around the edges, shared the secret of how he started a bidding war for his affection.

"Just before Thanksgiving," he bragged, "I told my mother dad and his new girlfriend were taking me to Aspen for school recess, so she'd have enough time to plan on taking me somewhere better."

"Where'd you go?" I asked.

"Barbados," he said with a smirk. "When we got back, I told her how much dad and Glynis—that's his dumb girlfriend's name—were looking forward to taking me to Aspen and teaching me to ski, and guess what she did?"

I couldn't imagine.

"She waited until he bought the tickets, then beat him to the punch. Mom and I and her boyfriend Eduardo flew to Aspen for Christmas."

"Then dad had to come up with something even better for spring break. We're going to a dude ranch where I get my own personal horse," said Rabbit to collective eye rolling. "Now mom's saying we'll rent a farmhouse in the South of France this summer, so I can practice my French with her new boyfriend, Jean-Claude."

"You're lucky," I said, confused at Rabbit's bored tone. I would have done anything to spend that much time with Claire or Theo. I was more than a little jealous.

"Yeah," he said. "It's okay."

I was curious about the parents who took Rabbit on such wonderful trips, but I never saw them. Some mornings, a Bentley driven by an elderly chauffeur deposited Rabbit on the sidewalk without a word of encouragement or farewell. On others, a Lincoln Town Car squealed to a stop with seconds to spare before the first bell.

I didn't care if being divorced meant I could go to Aspen and on all those vacations and in fact, I didn't really know what Aspen was, even though I pretended I did. I just wanted Claire to come home and things to be the way they were. But I didn't mention this to Rabbit or to the other kids in class. They'd forgotten they didn't like me, and were having fun teaching me how to be one of them.

When I told Mr. Cosmopoulos Claire didn't love us anymore, he said, "You know, mister, sometimes people are so afraid of getting left, they leave just to get it over with. Doesn't hurt so much that way."

I wasn't completely sure what he meant by this, but I had a good idea. After I gave Carl a nosebleed, people looked at me differently and said I had a bad temper. I could see where things were going, that's all, and I liked the feeling of throwing the first punch. This strategy didn't win me any friends, but at least people thought twice about picking on me.

We stopped going out to the farm. Whenever Uncle Peter called, Theo spoke to him in a clipped tone. Sometimes she hung up, her green eyes cold, twin blotches of color rising high over the dusting of freckles that fooled people into thinking she wasn't as dangerous as she could be.

I missed Harry. We tried to keep in touch, but it wasn't the same. Our conversations were stilted by an overblown sense of loyalty to our parents. This and the painfully short attention span of young boys, whose lives can change entirely within a few weeks, conspired to lengthen the distance between the farm and the apartment. We drifted.

Afraid of my grandmother's threats of legal action, Theo no longer felt comfortable using the garage in the Hirsh's building, so there were no more late-night cab rides through the park. She began to park our car in the side streets around Central Park West and when Andy's voice came over the intercom—"Better hurry Miss Bouvier, they're writing tickets down here!"—Theo ran down the hall in her slippers, nightgown billowing out from under her coat, and moved our Bug to safer ground.

We jumped when the phone rang, every artery pumping with hope that it was Claire. We scanned mail addressed to her. Suzie called to say Claire had sent some film for safekeeping. The envelope was post marked Chicago, but no return address. They talked softly for a while and I heard Theo say, "I just miss her is all."

While Claire was gone, I developed the jump in my right eye that has appeared all my life to tell me I am under a great deal of stress just in case I am not aware of it. In those days I didn't know what stress was, only that it wasn't normal to feel something queasy in the bottom of your stomach from the minute you got out of bed in the morning until you closed your eyes at night.

I found it comforting to spend as much time as I could with Mr. Cosmopoulos, who knew how I felt even though I hadn't told him. I looked for him in our special place, just around the corner from The Latest Dish, a few feet into a quiet side street where we could sit undisturbed on the stoop of a brownstone, but not so far into it that the view of the avenue and its busy sidewalks was obstructed.

"You never know who's going to sneak up on you," said Mr. C. Situated thus, we shared the lunch Theo provided and I was always cheered at the sight of his red suspenders and the lightbulb that went on in his eyes when he saw me. I took care to watch out for him in the Village, too, and not to run into him on my Saturdays with Uncle Baxter, who asked me how I knew "a weirdo like that." I suspect the dislike was mutual.

When I told Mr. C. Grandma Hirsh didn't like Theo anymore, he answered with stories of Greece and his own parents and about a magic bean the doctors took out of his head that left him out of work and a little confused.

"Gave me second sight," he said, tapping the left side of his head, "but one day it went soft, just like a bad lentil."

I especially liked the stories about his own son, who was grown up and living somewhere in New Jersey, and I never tired of hearing that he was just like me when he was a boy. I imagined what it must have been like to grow up with him. Whenever I asked if I could meet his son, Mr. Cosmopoulos drifted away. "That boy's busier than a one-armed paper-hanger," he'd say. "He's got a pretty little wife, big job down on Wall Street, and a boy just like you." When I asked if he could meet us one day for lunch, Mr. C. pretended he didn't hear me, but that didn't stop me from asking.

"It's amazing what I see in the recycling business," he said, changing the subject. "I'm telling you, mister, the stuff people throw away. Not even broken. No, sir, nobody wants to fix anything anymore. Too much work. Easier to get something new."

Mr. C. saw everything on the street. Once he saw a purse-snatching that happened so fast he was the only witness. Another time a blind couple kissed good-bye, and her overhead one say, "See you later."

I watched for these things, too, but was always too late. He told me most people don't even know what's happening right under their noses. "Don't just look, mister, learn how to *see!*"

I often thought he looked elsewhere when he talked because he was watching out for me. Claire stared into the faces of her photographs as she talked to me in her darkroom; only the occasional pressure of her hand on my shoulder let me know she was listening.

Mr. C. said his wife didn't love him after he came home from the hospital because he couldn't remember her name. After the bandages came off, and new hair grew over the stitches he called his "Frankenstein's zipper," she moved away and took their son with her. There was a problem getting his old job back because even though he tried very hard to remember what it was he did there, he couldn't. The judge said if he didn't want to support his son, he couldn't see him either. I learned he named his son Angel because when he was born he looked exactly like one of Raphael's cherubim, but when Angel grew up; he changed it to Gabriel, preferring the abbreviated "Gabe" for its solid American ring. Mr. Cosmopoulos's seemed sad when he told me this, but brightened again at the thought that at least his son had chosen an angel's name, and a very important angel's at that, for his alias.

"Then she got married again and I laid low for a while," he announced one bright snowy afternoon, "and one thing led to another. I figured I'd let the boy get to know his step-pop without worryin' about what I think."

I waited for him to get back from "his travels," as he called those moments went the lights went out in his head. I wondered if Claire would get married again, too.

"Maybe that's what Claire is doing," he said out of the blue that bitter afternoon in late January.

"What?" I asked.

"Laying low, of course."

That was the same day he said he'd take me home to meet Shorty.

I FORGAVE Claire for leaving long before I understood why. To me, she was a modern-day Joan of Arc, above the law, larger than life. She used her camera, our lives, and even the fact of our lesbianism—for years I believed in the power of that word to define me as well as my mothers—as a good documentarian would. I felt protective of her, more like the parent than the child. I, too, felt we had a responsibility to tell the truth, even if it meant being ostracized, which at the ripe old age of nine, I pronounced "Osterized."

I believed if Theo loved Claire as much as I did, if she had taken her more seriously, hadn't fought with her so much, she would have stayed. If I had been better—not held that séance, not bloodied Carl's nose; pretended I was happier—she would not have left, and I would not have had to consider the drastic steps I was ultimately forced to take. I could not have said this at the time, but I believed Claire was a gift we had insufficiently appreciated and thus had been taken away.

One night I heard Theo talking with Suzie. "My work is appreciated in small bodily rumbles and requests for seconds, then it's gone. Hers is collected, praised on the public altar and she earns enough to support us without me. Not only that, she wins Guggenheim into the bargain. I'd make my neuroses art, too, if it paid off like that!"

Suzie held Theo's hand in her own, rings glittering in the brittle winter sun of our living room. "Don't you know she'd trade places with you in a minute? You've made something she can't. This is about trust, Theo. This is about allowing her to be the mother, too."

Theo drew her hand away. "You know where she is, don't you?"

"I wish I did," Aunt Suzie said.

One afternoon on Twelfth Street, Jessica said to Theo, "You know I love Claire dearly, but I've always felt she was biting off a bit more than she could chew. It's so much better to understand one's own devils before rushing off to record someone else's, don't you think?"

"You're just mad at her," I shouted, "because she won't take pictures of ladies in fur coats and dumb clothes for your stupid magazine!" I ran down the stairs and slammed out the front door before anyone, especially the twins, saw my bottom lip quiver with a baby's need to cry.

Uncle Baxter, shoeless and shivering, came out after me.

"She'll be back before you know it," he said, sitting down next to me on the cold stoop.

Uncle Peter called every day until Theo finally agreed to drive the hundred miles out to the farm. I listened to him tell her how my grandparents had shut Claire out after Roland's death, how they rejoiced when Peter was born, and how they lost interest when Peter did not measure up.

"She didn't have a chance, Theo," said Peter. "It's not that she doesn't love you—she does; she just expects to be hurt. Every second of her childhood reinforced that, every time she was compared to Roland and found lacking. I think what she does is get out before she gets thrown out."

"All I wanted was the best for Willy. She's got to understand that," said Theo, letting her guard down a little.

"She's got to, but she doesn't. She thinks that by rejecting the idea of being so open about your relationship, you're rejecting her. In a way, she's your child, too, and you're choosing the boy over her all over again."

"So what am I supposed to do, find her a good therapist, and let her whine about her childhood for ten or twelve years while our son grows up fighting everybody who doesn't like his parents?"

"Isn't that what kids do anyway?"

"Whose side are you on, Peter?"

"There are no sides, Theo."

"Yes, there are. There always are."

On the way home Theo explained. "Your uncle Peter says she's afraid we won't love her anymore, so she's pretending not to love us anymore, but she really does."

Uncle Thad spent an hour every Wednesday at three o'clock with a hippie turned psychotherapist, who wore long flowered silk dresses and brown orthopedic shoes. They sat on the floor of her loft in the Flower District, where she encouraged him to cry, writhe, and relive his birth trauma in order to unlock his primal pain. She urged him to beat a yellow vinyl pillow with a baseball bat and imagine he was beating his father. He was, in the jargon of the decade, "into his anger," and had his own version of why Claire had left.

"When Alan died, I thought my life was over, too, but I realized the grief I was feeling wasn't new. It was abandonment, the agony of separation. You know," he said, "if we understand it, pain can become an old friend warning us of danger. But if we don't look at it and try to run away from it, as I suspect Claire is doing, it runs us."

Thad thought Theo should see Dr. Yvonne for a while. "Why not feed yourself for a change, instead of everybody in New York.

"You know what I think . . ."

"Thinking is what gets us in trouble, Theo. Feeling is what we need to do more of."

"I think you go for the flowers. I think on a hot day with the windows open and all those truckloads of freesias and freshly cut roses all over the street and Dr. Yvonne in one of her flowered numbers, that place must smell exactly like being with Alan."

Thad gave Theo a wistful smile. "And I came here to help *you*."

Theo swallowed her pride and called the Hirsh household again, hoping Barnaby would answer the phone, but my grandmother, indifferent to her suffering, said, "We all have to make choices, dear, and I think Claire has made hers."

Theo and I were the prisoners of our friends' opinions. Everyone had a version of why Claire left. No one had heard from her, but they all said she loved us and would come home when she was ready. I listened politely, but it had been over a month and Claire was beginning to feel as dead as Alan when the coffin lid came down like a falling piano.

I turned to Mr. Kimsky, who gave me my first lessons on the power of imagination. As my mother's favorite photograph, he presided over breakfast, lunch, and dinner, wearing his brown-and-yellow plaid shirt buttoned straight up to a long, old-fashioned collar that squeezed the skin of his neck into a turkey wattle. One wiry hair, having somehow escaped his razor, sprang from his Adam's apple and reached for the lapel of a shiny double-breasted suit worn with the cocky dash of a man who knows he's too short. On the surface, it was a simple photograph of someone who got dressed up to play chess on the boardwalk, his dark eyes hooded in concentration and noonday glare, owlish glasses riding on the tip of a large and intelligent beak, his opponent an unseen shadow across from him, lost in the edges of the photograph.

He was much more to me. If I lost a shoe or a button, I'd look up and ask him where it was and see it lying on my closet floor. I invented a history for him. He was my long-lost grandfather, my own father's father, who was himself a victim of amnesia and couldn't remember his own name, much less the fact that he had a son on the West Side. I imagined he was hit by a bus just as he was about to leave his grimy walkup in Coney Island and move in with us. He was my uncle Roland, and on other days, my father, who had slipped into the body of an old man, come to hang on our wall and watch over me.

The implausibility of these biographies grew in proportion to my need to escape the facts of mine. I believed when the right moment arrived, Mr. Kimsky would tell me where Claire was.

While I found the picture of Mr. Kimsky mostly comforting, the shadow across the checkerboard terrified me. I hated its dark hold over my friend, the way it hovered over him like an oily stain, and I believed if I crept into the dining room in the middle of the night and suddenly turned on the lights, it would be sitting there, ugly and evil, mocking me for cowering behind the kitchen door in my flannel pajamas.

Claire once said a good photograph can foreshadow the future. I think that's why I was so afraid of that shadow. It was the future I was up against.

I didn't understand what was happening, but I sensed, as children always do, it was serious. No one warned me of the rumblings from the apartment across the park, the lies that were being told about Theo or of the swift and imminent change about to occur, but the minute I saw the nervous young woman from Social Services in our front hall sitting on the edge of Claire's prized Thonet hall bench, I knew she was there to take me away.

She wasn't sitting exactly, for that would have implied some commitment to comfort, some softening of the spine. No, I remember more of a crouch. It struck me she seemed both predator and prey as she waited for Theo and me, her hands folded quietly over the sheaf of official-looking papers in her lap, thick legs that did not often hurry crossed at the ankle.

As though to trick the observer into thinking she was not interested in us, but merely in doing her job, her body remained still while her eyes took everything in. She missed nothing. At one point, she studied a picture of Claire on the cover of *Aperture*, Theo in *New York*'s "Best Bets," and one of Claire with me, arms draped around the shoulder of a strong, silent, and extraordinarily lifelike sculpture of a cowboy on a bench in front of a trading post in Arizona, the perfect American family if you didn't look too closely. She lingered on the framed letter Jessica sent when Claire gathered the courage to tell her she was a lesbian, but didn't seem to find it as funny as everyone else in our family did. Nor did she smile when she came to the photograph I loved best: Claire and Theo, both in white, exchanging their vows with me right there between them, a fat Cupid playing with their rings.

I had no idea there had been a hearing Theo lost, or that she had known this day was coming. How could she have warned me without saying what my grandmother accused her of? Instead, she prayed for a miracle that never came. She prayed Claire would come home and save us.

Department of Social Services, Child Welfare Division. Seal of the City of New York. I saw the stamp, surrounded by a circle of raised bumps as she took in our collection of mismatched silver candlesticks, the open box of chocolates someone had sent us, letters that came for Claire stacked neatly for her return. A bag of groceries wore the slowly darkening stain of something melting inside, dropped on the hall table, forgotten in the suddenness of that afternoon. She carried a fat briefcase, bulging I believed, with evidence against us. It was parked at her feet like a cab with its meter running. She looked everywhere but into my mother's eyes.

The memory of that particular day is more physical than anything else, a tearing sensation I believed capable of leaving bruises. I understand why the expression *broken heart* is so apt. Something did break inside of me that afternoon. I suspect it was the snapping of trust; it was the first time I saw cruelty in people claiming to love you.

Many years later, Annie would tap quietly and insistently on the door that closed that February afternoon and I wonder sometimes if, in the beginning, before I loved her, I opened it because I was won over by the fact that she simply would not go away.

The afternoon Social Services came, I did what anyone would do under the circumstances. I slowed down the action. In the way that cars drift into each other and seem to kiss before crumpling, Theo moved as in a dream, gathering my things, stopping to refold a pajama leg, tucking an extra sweater into my duffel bag, dragging the entire length of her arm across her eyes, as though to wipe away the sight of her loss. She drew me close; fear and sweat under her familiar scent of vanilla and oranges clung to her cold, sticky back I hung on to her and we moved from room to room as though we were one person. When she finally spoke, she swayed a bit and I was afraid she'd fall.

"You're going to have to stay at your grandma's for a while, sweetheart," Theo said in a thick voice I had never heard before, even the night Claire left without eating her dinner.

"Why?" I demanded.

"Grandma doesn't think I can take care of you by myself."

"Why won't Claire come back and tell her you can?" I asked in a high squeaky voice that didn't sound like mine either.

"I don't know, baby."

"Why do I have to go?"

"You have to go because Grandma went to court and asked the judge for a letter that says you have to and if we ignore it, they'll arrest me."

"For what?" What could she have done for them to take me away?

"It won't be for long. I promise," she said, holding my head in her hands, staring at me with a crazy, swollen face willing what she was saying to be true.

We both wanted to believe that if Claire had been there, she would not have let her mother do this terrible thing, but this thought remained unspoken as if to voice it would subject it to scrutiny it might not be able to stand up to.

I ran into the foyer shouting and punching at the air until my fists found the woman from Social Services. "Get off Claire's bench! Go away!" I screamed at her for making my mother cry.

"Hey! Hey! No need for that, son," said a voice that did not seem to belong to the object of my anger.

I didn't see the cop standing just outside the door, a ruddy-faced man with a cruel smile. He caught me mid-punch, lifting me up by my elbows and away from the frightened woman, who was nervously paddling backward toward our open front door.

"Usually, it's the parents getting violent in these cases, but this one's a real fighter," he said, winking at the social worker with a mocking, sadistic laugh that told me he enjoyed what he was doing. The woman ignored him, gathered up her coat and briefcase, and headed for the elevator, past our neighbors who were standing silently in the hall, their faces a mixture of curiosity, shock, and something else I couldn't exactly describe—only that it made me keep my eyes on the mosaic tiles outside our door.

Theo was at my side in an instant. "Put my son down this minute, or I'll have you arrested, you goddamn pig."

"Don't be damning me, miss. It'll be you who's arrested," said the cop, raising his voice for the people in the hallway, "and damned in hell for the mockery you've made of this poor lad."

He towered over Theo, the leather of his holster creaking with an ominous sound as his fingers closed around a thick club hanging from a clip on his belt, but the moment passed and just as suddenly as the unseen hand had turned down the volume, it was back, deafening and pounding in my ears. It was the first time I can remember wanting to kill someone. I could taste his blood in my mouth, but I was only a boy, powerless to protect his mother.

Theo raced after us, parting the elevator doors like Atlas holding up the world; she handed me the antibiotic the doctor had ordered for my ear infection. She kissed me one more time before they pushed her hands away and all I could see was her face disappearing in the diamond pane on the elevator door, saying something I couldn't hear and to which the mean-faced cop answered, "Tell it to the judge."

In the lobby, Andy was waiting with a crisp salute and a breezy "Don't you worry, Mr. Willy, your mom will get you back home with us before dinner." I don't think it was my imagination that once I was safely through, Andy allowed our heavy leaded-glass front door to close within inches of the policeman's face.

The sunlight was blinding; it hurt my eyes to take in the brightness surrounding the police car waiting at the curb. The woman was talking to me, doing her best to sound soothing, but I squeezed myself into the corner of the backseat, as far away from her as I could get. As we rode through the park, a younger officer with a weasel's face slid open the grill and asked if I wanted him to put on the lights and the siren.

"You play with them," I said, twisting around to see if the cab I saw Theo wildly hailing was still behind us.

"Guess they don't teach you manners where you live," he said, turning around and giving the curves through Central Park his full attention.

If I had been paying attention, I would have seen this coming. I would have heard the whispers that stopped when I walked into a room. I would have understood the concern that tightened Uncle Baxter's jaw the day he took me to his shop so Theo and Aunt Jessica could talk, and if I had turned around quickly as we left the house that day, I would have seen an uncharacteristically muffled Aunt Jess standing at the window watching us turn the corner. Even the twins, who always treated me with the superiority of older girls, had seemed over solicitous; they'd even stopped speaking French in my presence, their preferred method of exclusion. If I had thought about it, I would have realized Grandma and Grandpa Hirsh hadn't visited once since Claire disappeared.

THEO SAT in the Hirshes' lobby all night after they took me away. Every hour, the buzzer sounded upstairs and Buddy said in the most proper Irish-doorman voice he could muster: "Miz Hirsh, Miz Bouvier is here to see the grand lad."

In that marble echo chamber, I could hear Theo coaching him: "*Son*, Buddy. I'm here to see my *son*." Each time Buddy went through the motions that could have cost him his job, I saw Barnaby's jaw stiffen at the jolt of the buzzer and felt my grandmother's cold disregard for my mother a few floors below.

They put me to bed in the room that had once belonged to my uncle Roland, which smelled of camphor and plastic and stood in the doorway like ghosts until I pretended to fall asleep. Around midnight, after making what Grandpa Barnaby called a scene in the staid hush of their building, Theo finally went home.

I did not know it then, but she left only after the police were summoned and informed her that if she did not go quietly, she would have to spend the rest of the night in jail. When I woke up and stumbled out of the unfamiliar bed and onto the thick carpet that cushioned my cries of alarm, Grandma told me that Theo had given up and realized it was better for me to be with people who could raise me properly; but the next day, when Barnaby insisted that I should be allowed to talk to her, Theo said that was a lie.

"I love you, honey," she said, with as much pain in her voice as I have ever heard. "I would never let Grandma take you away from me; not as long as I live. And I don't think Claire would want that, either." I know she was trying hard not to alarm me with her rage, but I was as scared as I have ever been since.

"I want to come home," I wailed.

"I hope you die!" I screamed, almost knocking my elegant and now despised grandmother off her well-shod feet. I barreled down the corridor, past Grandpa Barnaby with his half-glasses on the tip of his nose, nearly tripped Lucy who carried an armload of freshly ironed sheets, and slammed Roland's bedroom door.

In the room that held my uncle's secrets for over thirty years, I gave some preliminary thought to an idea I could not articulate at the time, but that Theo alluded to in defending her decision to decamp the night before, something that would sustain me often in the course of my lifetime: the idea of losing a few battles in order to win a war.

15

My grandmother's apartment smelled of money. It whispered its presence in yards of cream silk damask framing postcard views of the sailboat pond, the reservoir, the Met's hulking conservatory and fell into large, extravagant puddles on the Aubusson below. It formed an invisible barrier, like the many-layered apricot glaze on the living room walls, and the Philadelphia sideboard made for William Penn, gleaming with restorers' wax. My grandmother's apartment was no place for a rambunctious boy. There was something else besides money in that atmosphere of pine needles, cedar closets, and mink coats. Something faintly medicinal, like the sharp smell that lies at the dark bottom of a pile of rotting leaves.

Meals involved cutlery we didn't bother with at home. These were served by Lucy, who lived in the only room I felt welcome. When Claire was small, Lucy left her family in Jamaica and came to live with Grandma. She fussed over me as though I were the King of England, or the son she'd left left behind when she fled her father's Catholic wrath. After Roland died, it was Lucy who was able to staunch Claire's grief with her sense of mischief and real affection. I think she sometimes confused me with Roland.

"Don't fight with that trout. "Lucy's got sometin' in the kitchen for you!" she'd say, easily slipping back into the competition she and her employer had waged for the Hirsh children's affection for nearly forty years. I could listen to her lilting voice for hours. No one I knew spoke like that except Bob Marley, whose music made Claire happy enough to dance around the living room in her socks. But even Lucy's attempts on my behalf were in vain.

"William dear," my grandmother said, ignoring my grim determination to starve in the enemy camp, "give that trout a try for

Grandma. We wouldn't want you to grow up afraid of new things, would we?"

The fish that I had been taught to eat with a surgeon's skill and a chef's instinct for bones lay untouched, its spine intact. Eating it seemed like capitulation, but it did remind me of a happier evening at my grandparents' table.

"Trout! That was whitefish in my book," a slightly tipsy Theo had said the second we were in the cab and out of Buddy's earshot. "Only your mother could ask a good cook to take a perfectly nice fish and push it to the brink of edibility. Didn't you love the way she called the brisket *boeuf en daube?*"

"She doesn't even know she's doing it," Theo with an evil giggle. "It's subconscience."

"Subconscious," said Claire, correcting her.

"You've got to give it to Lucy. When Roland and I were kids and found out there was a Jamaica, Queens, we decided Lucy had been raised raised by New York Jews and taught to cook kosher."

Well, I can't imagine your mother serving fungi and jerk chicken." said Theo, sputtering at the idea of such a ridiculous idea. I couldn't imagine what fungi was, but I knew I didn't want any.

By the time we crossed the park, Grandma's dinner was forgotten and Theo, flush from Grandpa's wine, warmed to one of her favorite culinary theories.

"Isn't it interesting that the lower down people are socioeconomically, the more highly flavored and interesting their food? You'd think it would be the other way around."

Claire helped Theo out of the cab while I held the door, bowing from the waist. Between pronouncements she gave us extravagant, blustery hugs. Giggling, we burst into the lobby.

Andy greeted us with mock disapproval and an exaggerated sweep of the door.

"And what have the Bouvier-Hirshes been up to tonight?"

"Grandma's," I said.

"Brisket?" he deadpanned, which started us going all over again.

All of that changed. There was no one to laugh with on the way home because I couldn't go home, only to school and back in the company of Lucy.

"Don't know what she's doing fooling with nature like dat." Lucy said, smoldering with disapproval. She muttered darkly all the way to McCall, vaguely embarrassed by the white uniform peeking out from under her coat, her skinny legs unaccustomed to hurrying encased in chalky white stockings, wary as she approached Seventy-fourth Street.

Every morning my fantasy was the same. The Latest Dish van with its bright red lips along the side would screech to a stop. My mother, all in black, in night goggles and grease paint, would jump out and spirit me off, leaving Lucy wondering whether to give chase or cheer.

"You got two mothers who love you and that's more than most," Lucy would say as we walked along. She told me how she used to take Claire and Roland to the park in their navy-blue pram, how he liked his sister right beside him, how protective he was of her, even as a baby. I wonder if my presence in the Hirsh household brought back the shock of Roland's death, toppled something that had taken my grandmother many years to construct.

Lucy had her status as an employee to fall back on, when things got crazy, and I felt her retreat. Afternoons, Grandpa went to his club, or to his study at the far end of the apartment, as far away as he could get from us without actually leaving. I'd follow him into its crisp, leathery interior to ask about Roland or why I didn't see Uncle Peter anymore or why Grandma always called Theo "Claire's friend" and wouldn't call her my mother.

"Your grandma would do anything for you," was all he'd say before raising his newspaper, which was my unspoken dismissal.

Once he said: "Your grandmother was never the same after Roland." But he never finished, leaving me to wonder what she was like before.

At home we never ate supper at the same time because of the demands the store placed on Theo and Claire's erratic work schedule. But at the Hirshs', clocks could be set by the prompt arrival of meals. And just as we sat down, the phone rang; it was always Theo, demanding to speak with me. Lucy brought the phone to the table, where I was expected to talk to my mother as though no one was listening.

"I love you, Mama," I'd say as Grandma's fork hovered over her plate, suspended in the act of eavesdropping.

"I love you, too, sweet baby, and I miss you so much. Honey, I know they're listening, but just say yes or no, okay?"

"Okay."

"Have you seen Mommy?"

"No."

"Has she called?"

I squirmed in my chair, feeling trapped. "No."

"Uncle Peter?"

"Uh-uh."

Grandpa stared at his plate, trying to give me a little privacy.

"If he comes over, will you tell me what he and Grandma talk about?"

"Okay."

"Do you know I'm going to get you home as quickly as I can?"

"Yes."

"Will you ask Mommy to call me when you see her?"

"Yes."

The throaty sound of Theo struggling to keep the tears out of her voice. "I love you."

"Me, too."

Grandpa tried. "Mary, excuse the boy, for God's sake."

"Families shouldn't keep secrets from one another," she'd say, her expression fixed and unbending.

GRANDMA SPENT the mornings at her desk, where she answered mail and ordered floral arrangements from a shop on Madison Avenue. I asked her why she didn't ask Thad to send flowers for her. After Alan died, he'd kept the shop open and she always praised the French tulips he'd brought to our Sunday afternoons.

"William dear, Peter is your uncle and poor Roland was your uncle, but Thad is *not* your uncle. He is a homosexual and he is not a member of your family. Do you understand?"

I didn't. I hated her.

Most days, the apartment felt hollow, the small sound of Lucy's key in the lock amplifying its emptiness. No Suzie, no Claire, no students looking up from their photographs to see their mentor transform from master teacher to mother fussing over the details of her son's day, no celebrity treatment at the store. Just Lucy trying her best to keep me amused. That my busy grandmother believed it was healthier for a servant to raise a child than his own mothers, was a bitter irony.

Whenever I could, I waited for Lucy to turn on the small TV she kept on the kitchen counter, and when she was sufficiently preoccupied by one of her show, I'd slide the Hirsh telephone out of its cradle and call Theo at the store, each digit on the rotary dial a bomb going off in my ears, the ringing drawing her closer and closer, my panic rising until I heard her say, "The Latest Dish." But this was not enough to ease the unbearable silence of that apartment.

This was not the exquisite quiet of the darkroom, where I felt closest to Claire, or the afternoon lull that amplified the scrape of my chair on Theo's tile floor, one of her apple muffins easing the wait for dinner, the day's drawing hanging on the shop's menu board for all to see.

Even when the tension and the separateness built up around my mothers, they had tried to rise above their problems for me. Often they succeeded, not letting the growing distance between them intrude. There were times I believed I was the only person in the world who could hold them together. Now Claire was gone and no one knew where she was; not even Grandma, which Theo never believed no matter how hard I tried to convince her.

Theo was not allowed to see me until the hearing and judge's final decision, which was three weeks away.

I begged Lucy to take me to see my mother. "Grandma won't find out."

"I can't, you know that, precious."

But one day, when we were well past the school and the danger of being seen, I sat down on the sidewalk and threw a tantrum, refusing to stop until Lucy agreed to take me to see Theo. At the shop, Lucy pretended not to see Theo's grateful tears and, refusing her offer of food, stood guard at the door. She said she was looking out for my grandmother, but I knew she was giving us time alone. Theo felt my arms and legs and head for damage, while I insisted there was none, and she asked questions I didn't understand, questions intended to give her some clue as to Hirsh's next move.

She was delighted to hear that Judge Bailey, who had signed the papers, was the same Judge Bailey who had dined with us at Grandma's earlier in the week. When I asked why Claire wouldn't just come over and tell her mother to let me come home, Theo's eyes narrowed. She was firm in her belief that Claire and Uncle Peter were behind this somehow.

Lucy didn't take me to the store again. When I asked her why, she said, "It near tore my heart seeing you two say good-bye."

The school was instructed to make sure I stayed in for lunch because Grandma was worried Theo would kidnap me. Even though I assured my teacher only strangers could kidnap people, not their mothers, she would not relent. I dined in the schoolyard on all but the most bitterly cold days.

One afternoon, moments after the teacher stepped inside to warm up and the older boys who doubled as schoolyard monitors busied themselves shooting hoops, Mr. Cosmopoulos appeared, to cheer me up with stories about Shorty and their friends and neighbors downtown.

"Thelma had one of her parties and Shorty wouldn't go, so she walked right in and pulled him out of bed. Can you imagine the nerve of that?" said Mr. C. "She said, 'What's the matter, isn't a formal invitation enough for you?' She's got his number, old Thelma!"

One day he slipped me a portion of my mother's own moussaka through the hole in the fence. He knew without my telling him that this was as close to being home as I could get, having the warmth of my mother inside of me.

Before moving to my grandparents', I couldn't wait for the final bell, but now I prefered the school's overheated rooms and the clang and rattle of its radiators. banging like Marley's ghost. I no longer despised the battered desk with their pencil shavings and spitballs, the rotting-apple smell. I took a perverse pleasure in my celebrity as the object of a custody battle, a dubious status Rabbit had personally conferred on me, explaining to everyone in my class, including myself, that this was indeed what was going on. Anything was better than the slow, ticking of my grandmother's apartment.

I trace my enjoyment of ironing, for which Annie is forever grateful, to those days. I kept Lucy company while she pressed my grandfather's shirts like a master plasterer, applying a blast of starch only in the places that showed, leaving others soft on the skin. I watched her come down on a cuff and stay there until it could hold its own against any weather condition and, with the lightest hand, gently press the iron to my grandmother's silk blouses and slips, linen sheets and pillowcases, folding as she went, her talk punctuated by the hiss of steam. Hers was a freshly laundered world, a place where any stain could be removed, any wrinkle smoothed away.

Waiting for my life to right itself, I wondered where my father was, what he thought about my grandmother stealing me from Theo. If he knew where Claire was. I thought about the judge who signed that piece of paper while he ate lamb chops at my grandparents table and the serious harm father would inflict on him. For the first time, the conviction that he would appear and set everything right wobbled like the childish illusion it was.

16

I F I looked hard, I could make out our tall windows in the line of
Gothic spires, stone gargoyles, and gabled roofs etched along the
western edge of the park. On bleak winter mornings, a smudge of weak
sunlight glanced off the panes directly under ornamental busts that
kept the sleek art deco silhouette of our building from disappearing
into an envelope of mist. When I was small and lost my bearings on
the vast rolling green of the Sheep Meadow, I had only to look up and
see the sleek carved heads and hooded eyes of home. Now, from my
deep sill on the East Side, these guardians seemed poised to dive into
the dull March sky and swim to me like two giant mermaids from the
Jazz Age.

Theo seemed miles away, a faint glow in the swirling leaden soup. I
imagined her padding listlessly around the kitchen, the bright kimono
slipping off a shoulder, its magic sleeves forgotten in the ache of
knowing I was just across the park and as lost to her as she was to me.
I could see her starting the coffee, alone in the big apartment, missing
Claire and missing me. She stared into her cup with no heart for the
day, and felt loss in the explosion of a teaspoon in the cavernous empty
sink.

I thought about home constantly. Everything in my dead uncle's
room had been dusted, polished, aired, and wiped clean of any traces
of its former occupant; it no longer comforted, but enclosed, like the
circumstances that had trapped me. I looked for the toy soldiers I
had played with during my earlier visits, for the neat stack of books—
Jack London, *A Tale of Two Cities*, the Encyclopaedia Britannica—his
collection of wooden tennis racquets, and the yellowed photograph,
framed in silver, of Roland and Claire, sitting in a pony cart drawn by
the same creature on whose back I was sure I had bumped around the

rutted track of the children's zoo. But everything was gone, replaced by the meager assortment of belongings Theo packed for me the day I was taken away. I believed if I had been free to touch his things, I might have known what to do, but now there was no surface that held his thoughts. I wondered if he had run into Edgar and Marilyn Jacoby, still strapped to their seats, wild-eyed and dazed from their plummet to earth.

My grandparents' apartment building, which had always been bright and safe and mine to enter and leave at will, had become a fortress. The welcoming *whoosh* of its elevator groaning under the weight of people heavy with packages, chill, and news of the outside, creaked with warning and the heavy drag of chains. The richly polished hush of its hallways, once full of soft voices, the secret click of locks, keys palmed in soft gloves and other mysterious signs, now gave off the dark smell of a prison out of which there was no exit. I think that was the hardest of all, seeing the cold edge of my grandmother's orders to block all possible escape routes in the watchful eyes of the staff, especially Buddy and Lucy, who didn't conceal their sympathy for my plight.

"She just want her boy back is all, that poor dead child and she don't care who she hurts to get him," Lucy said into the cloud of steam over her ironing board.

"Theo is your real mother, and your grandma is tryin' to get you away from her before the court decides Claire's got no rights being a lesbian and all. Nothin' to do with you, precious. The girls had a big fight and broke up and your grandma's afraid she's gonna lose you just like she lost poor Roland. Understan, dahlin'?" Lucy leaned hard on one of Barnaby's cuffs as she said this, though pressing the truth into the cloth itself. I didn't understand. Claire was my real mother, too. I didn't see how making me live here would bring Uncle Roland back.

Even though he was under orders not to, Buddy told me when Theo came to the lobby to ask him to phone the Hirsh apartment and announce her intention to see me. "Your mother was here last night, lad. Sat here for two hours, she did, trying to get up to see you." The words slid from one side of his mouth and twisted in my direction while he kept the other side perfectly still, eyes front, on the door, all business, as though only half of him was disobeying orders. "She misses you, lad, don't you ever forget that." Whenever he opemed the door, he sang out his greeting extra loud: "Good morning, ma'am! And a fine day it is, sir!" proclaiming his innocence to those who might report our conversation to my grandmother.

After supper, I waited for Barnaby to nod in my direction and say, "I'm sure you've got better things to do than to sit here with your old grandpa and grandma," Then taking care not to scuff the legs, of the stiff-backed Queen Anne chair that had become my place at the long table Lucy set for three, I went to my room.

One night, Grandma followed me and sat on the edge of the bed while I brushed my teeth in Roland's bathroom. "You know I love you, don't you?" she said, examining a corner of the bedspread as though secrets were contained in its cotton batting.

I kept silent because I didn't know that at all.

"I know this is terribly difficult for you, William dear, but some day, when you're older, you'll understand why I had to do it," she said, patting the edge of my blanket, inviting me to hop in. "A long time ago I lost my own little boy, your uncle Roland, and even though I love your mommy Claire and Theo, too, in my own way, I want to make sure you grow up like other boys, go to the right school, enter a profession, get married and have children of your own."

She didn't look at me when she said this, but across the room, at a point beyond this moment. The thin skin on the backs of her hands sounded like crepe paper as she drew one hand over the other, then let one flutter up to her pearls, which encircled a neck that rose, stiff and patrician, out of a pale cashmere sweater. It reminded me of the seashells, baked bone white, lining the path to the tiny Bouvier trailer, where I imagined Doris and Roy plotted to fly to New York and talk sense into this grandmother who claimed to love me.

"Theo says when I get married, she'll bake the tallest wedding cake in the world and Claire promised to take pictures for Aunt Jessica's magazine," I said hopefully. They made these promises the day I asked them who I would marry and I laughed at their suggestions—Jennifer, yuk, Brooke, double yuk, maybe goggle-eyed Georgine Feinberg who cornered me in the laundry room and planted a slobbery kiss on my four-year-old cheek. Did my Grandma know they, too, hoped I would find someone nice when I grew up? Would I go to hell for wishing she would die that night, so I could slip past the ambulance driver and the medics and poor shocked Barnaby in the confusion. Neighbors in their bathrobes would gather in the hall and shake their heads at the distraught little boy following his grandmother's lifeless body out the door.

"If you love me, you'll let me go home," I told her, full of the need to pound something, grateful for the pillow, remembering how upset everybody got when I couldn't stop pummeling Carl.

"I *do* love you, William dear, that's why I can't," she said, then left the room, leaving behind a cloud of perfume that drifted down onto my bed and settled into the folds of my pajamas. This was the smell, along with the slippery sound of silk-lined clothes; I would forever associate with deception. I wanted my grandfather to make her see how cruel she was, but something in Barnaby's eyes told me he had long since given in to the strength of my grandmother's will and could be counted on only to growl occasionally, like an old dog who dreams of blood, but has no teeth for the fight.

"Why can't I go home, Grandpa?"

"You've got to bide your time with your grandma," he told me.

When I could no longer hear the sqeak of shoe leather on the Persian rug that rolled past my bedroom, I tiptoed out of bed and over to the pale window, where I sat for hours on Roland's sill, dreaming of escape. Some nights, when the moon floated over the trees, it seemed to beckon me. The bare arms of trees moved against the black semicircle of night, and came alive in the dark gusts that gave them voice. I imagined running through the sleeping park, past the rider less carousel horses and the ghost skaters on the pond carving sharp circles in the black ice. I would be careful not to trip over the bundles of rags huddled in the deepest hollows, exhaling foul breath into dreams of soft beds and real blankets. I would avoid the sharp knives glinting in the bushes, ready to ambush a boy out at night. The trees would grab at my bleeding ankles as I became entangled in the sharp brambles that lay at their roots. But I would keep running until I got home.

I would have tried if it were not for the fear Theo drive me back herself. I couldn't have stood that. I longed for the Theo who shamed Mrs. Langelotti taking her disapproval out on me, the Theo who called Mrs. Jacoby and said *she* was the one not welcome in *our* home. I didn't want the Theo who lied about losing my father to something tragic, who stopped using the word "lesbian," until finally Claire left us forever.

I wanted to be someone my mother broke rules for, no matter the consequences. The Theo I dreamed of broke down the richly paneled Hirsh door, and gun blazing, demanded that my terrified grandparents hand me over or else. She and I would disappear into the night, and laugh at her audacity from the safety of Baxter and Jessica's attic.

I wanted no part of the Theo who could be controlled by a law, even if the penalty was prison term. Maybe that's why, when I finally got my opportunity, I headed in the opposite direction.

LUCY'S EYES GLITTERED with the fight her body was waging against the new strain of flu circulating in New York that year. The virus was so lethal the Health Department had set up makeshift clinics all over the city, where people were encouraged to get free shots.

"I'll tell you why they call it the swine flu," Lucy said, drawing the shawl collar of her robe over her puny chest to cushion a cough phlegmy and deep, "because you feel lower than a pig in a sty."

She spoke in a thin, conspiratorial wheeze. "I trust you'll get to school today without telling your grandma old Lucy is too sick to take you." I was sure she'd hear my heart clanging under my pajamas, but she shuffled back to the kitchen, like one of her tales of the living dead who stalked the abandoned sugar plantations of Jamaica.

I remember warm slippers on cold tile, a feverish Lucy spooning oatmeal into my bowl. As I slid into my place at the kitchen worktable, she set my cereal before me and pushed the milk pitcher and sugar bowl in my direction. I was afraid she would see right through me, but she just stared into a mug of strong Caribbean coffee laced with something more fortifying than cream. Lucy saw nothing but her misery.

As was her custom, my grandmother slept until those who were not so fortunate were safely off the street. She avoided the commuters huddled in their coats, who rode in from Queens and the upper reaches of Manhattan and issued forth, up urine-splashed subway stairs and into the dazzle of her Fifth Avenue.

The last time I dressed in the dark was to ride the subway with Claire. She fingered the metal skin of the Leica as it lay in her leather satchel waiting for the right moment to photograph people who tunneled to work under the river, racing the sun to the day. Corona, Bayside, Astoria, Beechurst. I remember soot-streaked windows in houses built before the elevated tracks brought strangers to within inches of their thin curtains. We were close enough to see last night's dishes in the sink and inside the car hurtling between stations, and plunging underground for the final sprint under the river, the smell of hair tonic, cologne, and sour breath.

We were stiff from standing most of the way, "strap hanging," Claire called it. Propelled upward in the crush, we found ourselves face to face with Buddy, who, from seven-thirty to nine every morning, including the extra quarter-hour that held potential for stragglers, stood guard over my lightly snoring grandparents, asleep twelve stories above the crowded pavement, with the fierceness and the single-mindedness of a Doberman. We sipped coffee with Mary until, as my grandmother liked to say, "the streets were respectable again."

Buddy and José, a shy man from Bogotá who came on at midnight and was hoping to assume Buddy's exalted position when the senior doorman retired, were the only people with a key to the building. Not even my grandmother or the cardinal's sister, who lived in a series of musty rooms next door, had one. When residents or guests arrived, Buddy simply let them in; if he wasn't on the door, it was correctly assumed to be locked, and the visitor waited. Only the uninitiated would disturb the elegant hush and press the bell. Everyone knew Buddy's absence meant a delivery person was being escorted up the back elevator to one of the service doors behind each apartment, where one of the building's housekeepers would greet him cordially and accept the parcel with no idle chat or undue delay.

Barnaby once bragged to Uncle Baxter that this minor inconvenience resulted in zero burglaries the year it was instituted and that at the co-op board meeting all objections had been voted down, including those of his own wife, who was appalled at the idea of having to wait on a public street even if that street was Fifth Avenue.

After breakfast, I dressed quietly, and filled my duffel with sweaters, underwear and pajamas, and a well-thumbed photograph of Claire and Theo and me, the same one Theo slipped in the bag the afternoon of my arrest, which, contrary to patient explanations of the difference between temporary child custody and police custody, I believed for years was the case. I was careful to leave a pair of socks draped over the edge of an open drawer and my comb on the broad rim of the sink along with an uncapped tube of toothpaste. My grammar lay open on the small desk at the foot of Uncle Roland's bed. This, I hoped, would give me at least until four o'clock afternoon before suspicion turned to alarm when I didn't turn up after school.

I took the photograph, not just because I wanted it with me, but because all Grandma had was a picture of an eighteen-month-old baby peering out from a heavy, velvet-backed silver frame. It was childish, but I believed it would be harder for them to draw a Wanted poster without a recent photo.

The bag was heavier than I remembered, but I swallowed the sound of my own effort as I padded down the long hall past my grandparents' separate bedrooms, past the Manet in its place of honor over the English sideboard.

The rope of my grandmother's voice uncoiled at my back, hit its mark, and pulled tight.

"William dear, aren't you forgetting something?"

"Late for school," I said, fear crouching in my chest.

"Aren't we forgetting something?" The sound of her dressing gown rearranging itself, the sweet stale morning smell of her as she smiled and lowered a cheek for my dutiful peck. I put the duffel down and met the swaying pouch of her face halfway, planting what I hoped was a kiss as half-hearted as the ones yesterday and the day before that, hoping I would not give myself away by trying too hard.

She looked over my head in the direction of our housekeeper's room, while I prayed Lucy wouldn't suddenly explode this lie with the terrible racking cough I had heard earlier.

"Where's Lucy, darling?"

"Waiting in the hall. Bye, Grandma."

She eyed my lumpy luggage. "Why don't we take a taxi down to Mark Cross this afternoon and buy you a proper school bag?"

"Sure," I said, barely breathing.

First there was the long gangplank of polished parquetry on either side of the Tabriz runner, and the cedar closets holding Grandpa's British warmer and Grandma's mink coat. Now the Empire table, masses of tulips lolling on broken necks, a silver shell holding keys, a flyer from Bergdorf's and a small rug upon which simple desert people once prayed.

Six more steps. Five. The smooth click of the lock. Three. A door closing on well-oiled hinges, the sound of my grandmother's velvet slippers walking away from her last chance to keep me from my mothers.

The elevator door opened on an empty lobby. An open can of Brasso and a soft cloth left discreetly behind the bench. At the door, Mr. Cowperthwaite in baggy sweats and his soft-eyed beagle waiting in the lee of the snapping canopy. Buddy was delivering something. My heart raced as I walked as quickly and as nonchalantly as I could toward the bright light pouring into the gloom.

"Glad you came along, son," beet-faced Mr. Cowperthwaite said, slipping in out of the chill. "It's cold out there. I hope you're bundled up."

"Yes, sir," I said to my left shoulder as I braced for the gust that blew me around the corner toward Madison Avenue and downtown.

17

Grandma Doris was making cactus tea in an ancient pitted kettle that blew its whistle with the urgency of a much younger utensil. Everything in the Bouvier household seemed afflicted with this leaping energy; people and objects moved as though stung, except Roy, who presided over the poltergeist from his green leatherette BarcaLounger in the salon, as Doris called the living room. It was no wider than a hallway, but back in the twenties she had read about Gertrude Stein and Alice B. Toklas and other patrons of the arts who had opened their Paris apartments and country houses to disheveled, poor, often drunk but always brilliant bands of painters, writers, sculptors, musicians and that these spontaneous gatherings were called salons.

In Broken Arrow, Doris Bouvier was known as an arts patron of sorts, and even more as a refuge and mother confessor to rebels, runaways, clairvoyants, religious fanatics, and all manner of oddballs who were not exactly well received in this conservative and solidly Protestant town on the edge of the plain built by people who risked everything in the great land rush. Their descendants never took another chance, even if it meant ordering the same thing for lunch every day of their lives.

"I can't understand how you can put everything you own in the back of a gut-jolting prairie schooner, have your babies in the freezing cold back of the wagon while the wind or worse howls for your scalp, risk dysentery, and sudden death, then give rise to generations of people who are afraid of herbal tea and a little chanting. If you ask me, these folks lost more than their spokes on the way out here," Doris liked to say, shaking her head at the narrowness of her neighbors.

The old Bee-Line, shaped like a silver bullet, with neat rows of rivets marching along its seams, front door hatch hung with a spirit pouch, and a collapsible clothesline out back, flapping with Roy's three-to-a-pack plaid shirts, stood in shining tribute to Doris Bouvier's sense of the eclectic. An herb garden eked out of the hardscrabble yard contained rosemary, thyme, sweet basil, and chives, as well as strange medicinal things like mugwort, comfey root, and belladonna. Doris mixed people with the same flair and you never knew who might turn up at her red and white Formica kitchen table. Once, when I was too small to understand but big enough to be curious, Claire and Theo dropped in on Doris and Roy unannounced and sent an entire family of Salvadoran refugees scrambling to the top bunk in the spare room.

The kettle hissed and rattled on a tiny burner. Doris banged cupboard doors, stretching fleshy arms into dark corners looking for the "I Love Grandma" mug we sent one Mother's Day, and another decorated with daisies and peace signs that announced her determination to suffer "No Nukes." More rattling. Cutlery. Plates. A plastic bear filled with organic elder blossom honey. Boxes of cookies encased in plastic and twist-tied against the bugs that crawled in out of the Oklahoma dirt.

"Damn ants," Doris said to the flat ground rolling away from the porthole over her sink in shimmering waves toward a horizon straight and sharp enough to shave a man's face. She fashioned a cardboard gangplank out of the back of a cookie box, then hit the front door with a well-padded hip, and placed the dazed ant on the front step. "Too cold out there. He'll be back," she said, letting the door slap shut. She cracked two ginseng capsules into the tea and finally came to rest alongside a plate piled high with Mallomars.

Doris peered at her visitor from under a mop of straw-colored hair so white at the roots, she could have been wearing a tennis headband. Eyes the color of pine needles fixed on her guest. "Does she know you're here?"

"No." Claire shook her head without looking up from her tea. She hadn't planned on coming here and now she didn't know what to say. Doris and Roy lived too far away to see the small changes that added up to the stranger who had once been Theo. It seemed like a good idea to ask these people who adored their grandson for help, but now the trailer felt hot and claustrophobic. Even Doris and Roy seemed smaller and a little seedier than they had on Claire's last visit, when she didn't see them quite so clearly, having observed them only through the filter of her feelings for their daughter.

"Theo has changed," Claire began, sensing the need to start somewhere outside herself.

"Everyone does, sooner or later, darlin'," said Doris, waiting for the rest of the story, which, in her experience, never had much to do with how it began. Was Claire in cahoots with Mary Hirsh, as Theo had suspected?

Doris remembered the tumble of Theo's tearful words. "How could Claire do this. He's our son. *My* son."

Claire took her time, as Doris knew she would. "Theo was an independent and I loved her for that," said Claire, sipping her tea. "She saw life differently; it wasn't just about sex." At this, Claire colored a bit, remembering where she was. "After Willy, the Theo I knew started to disappear, a little at a time, until she was someone I didn't know."

"What happened, honey?"

"I guess it's what didn't happen. She never lied about us, you know, about our relationship. Even when my mom refused to acknowledge her existence, she never stopped encouraging me to just keep saying the truth until it became easier to hear. She used to send food to soften my parents up and when I was really down about it, she'd tell me it could be worse. 'Her daughter may be a lesbian, but at least she's eating right,' and I'd laugh in spite of myself." Claire looked lost. "I don't know, Doris, I just don't know."

"Yes, you do, we all know everything there is to know, we just have a hard time seeing it is all," said Doris. She had plenty of time to wait for Claire to get around to it.

"When Willy was born, we told everyone we trusted we were his parents and damn anybody who thought less of us. I felt more a part of a family than I ever have. Half mother, half father, happy. Then he started school, and we both knew it wasn't going to be easy, but I didn't think Theo would turn on me and side with people who punished our son just because lesbians made them uncomfortable."

"Are you sure she was siding with them?"

"She went out of her way to make new friends with all those Upper East Side phonies from Miss Porter's and the Junior League who wouldn't know a lesbian if they fell over one. Then she let them think she had a dead husband somewhere, so their kids who all just happened to be Willy's age would play with him and he could have normal friends." What would you call it?

Claire was still reeling from the shock of overhearing Theo's conversation with Lulu Clark.

"Do you think she meant Mrs. Jacoby was right, or that Mrs. Jacoby was an example of the reactions Willy would face if you two didn't try to keep things secret?" Doris had her own thoughts about not correcting other people's perceptions of you, letting them think whatever was easier for everybody concerned.

"Do you know, one of them actually asked me if Theo would mind if she invited an interesting man to accidentally drop by while she and Willy were visiting for the weekend? What was I? Her roommate? What was I supposed to say? 'Sure, fix her up. I'm just her husband.'"

Doris could see humiliation, more than anger, in Claire.

"You know, I've always been a wanderer, never stuck with anything, stayed with anyone, loved something long enough to claim it. I borrowed people, wore them for a while, then returned them like library books, a little ashamed of myself, but not enough to stop doing it. I guess I never wanted to wait around for things to be different from the way they started, or for them to be over."

"Until Roy?" Claire asked.

"Nope. Until Theo. I could have left Roy anytime, and he knew it, told me it was what held him, the idea that I might up and disappear any time. Kept him on his toes, he said. Even as the babies came, I never felt my roots sink in; I figured one day I'd take off and write them postcards from the next place and Roy would raise them with the romantic version of their mother. But all that changed with Theo."

"Why Theo and not the others?"

"Because from the minute she was born, she was just like me, and I saw in her what I could never see in myself. She was and still is someone who is satisfied with the life she's dealt and doesn't bother herself about what's around the next bend. The part of me I was afraid of most had to be born in another person before I could love it."

"But she's not like other people, she's different," Claire insisted.

"I encouraged Theo to break the rules because I knew how easily she could be hurt by them. Down deep, she's a sweet girl whose crazy mama taught her being a little different is a great place to hide."

"Are you saying, deep down she's not really a lesbian?"

"No, sweetheart, I'm just sayin', deep down maybe she didn't mean it the way you took it. Maybe she was just being a mother, the mother she taught me to be."

Doris didn't say, but it had taken a long time getting used to it, the idea of her daughter with someone else's daughter. She never let on except to Roy. For the first time, she felt her years.

"She didn't even want Willy. I was the one who wanted a baby. I wanted a baby so bad, it almost ruined my career, all those sappy pictures of fetal development and fat Madonnas and everybody reproducing but me. But I didn't have any damn estrogen left and I begged her to have our beautiful boy and then, bit by bit, she started acting as though it were her idea and just threw me away like some dyke who embarrassed her in front of her friends. Is *that* being a mother, Doris—is it?" Claire's voice startled Roy, who was napping on the recliner.

"Most people don't really change at all," Doris said. "They just become what they really are and it takes the other person by surprise. Kind of like buying a house, then finding out the roof leaks. If you love the house, you'll stay and fix it."

Roy called out from the BarcaLounger "How are my gals doin'?"

"Just fine, sweetheart. You want some Mallomars in there?" Doris shouted back.

Roy Bouvier ambled into the narrow kitchen, palmed a handful of cookies, and touched his wife's shoulder with the tenderness of a bridegroom. Then he aimed a broad smile at the young woman he, too, had not come easily to thinking of as his daughter-in-law.

They watched him edge around the table like a cat measuring space with his whiskers. Claire pulled the cake off the back of her cookie with her fingers and took baby bites of gooey marshmallow. "How's our boy Roy?" she said.

Doris would be cross with him for getting to it so bluntly. She liked to draw people out, but Roy couldn't stand not knowing.

"I'd be better if I knew where my grandson was."

"What do you mean, where is your grandson? He's at home with Theo where he always is," said Claire.

"When did you last speak to Theo or Willy?" Roy asked, his face hard with disbelief.

Doris shot him a look that said, "Now you've done it, nobody tells the truth when they're cross-examined."

"A few weeks ago—I knew Theo would be at the store—I talked to Willy."

I had asked her why she left, when she'd come home. I told her I was sorry for making her leave, and promised to be better.

"It's not your fault," she'd said. "It's a problem your mama and I are having. I didn't leave *you*, Willy Wonka. I love you. I'll always love you even if Mama and I live in different houses."

"Am I divorced?" I had asked.

Now Claire regretted she had answered truthfully. "I don't know honey. Maybe."

She faced Doris and Roy.

"I've called from the road several times since, but Theo always answers the phone and I hang up because I don't know what to say that will change anything."

Claire didn't say "the road" was an apartment belonging to a pretty young woman named Dakota she had halfheartedly picked up at one of the many truck stops she was shooting along the way, believing her own ruse, looking for the truth about the lives of strangers so she could tell herself lies about her own—*I haven't really left. I'm just working on a show.*

"Lotta tattoos around here," she had said when she sat down at Dakota's counter and noticed bright red hair skinned back under an Orioles cap.

"Beats Miss Grundy hairnets," Dakota had said when Claire focused her camera on its peak and the face directly beneath it. Cat's eyes penciled out to the temples, downy young skin in the spots the Pan-Cake missed. This face had seen more than one brush with the bad side of people.

What is it about women behind counters? Claire had thought.

They drank coffee and talked about the men scattered around them. Dakota told Claire they reminded her of crumpled cigarettes, bleary and stale, stinking up the place from haulin' ass, downing too many reds, and living with the constant fear of eighteen wheels skidding off an icy road with ten tons behind them.

When Claire asked her if she ever got tired of slinging hash, and having her butt pinched, Dakota leaned over the counter and smiled deliciously. "I'm okay here. It's around my type that I get in trouble."

Later, in Dakota's tiny ground-floor apartment, they drank a rough wine that needed food neither was willing to make.

"What is this stuff?" said Claire, feeling the burn.

Dakota smiled sweetly and raised her jelly glass. "Road Kill Red."

It wasn't the first time Claire tried to exorcise Theo in this way, but soon the sharp edge of loss returned. When she saw Theo's face in Dakota's, pale and dusted with freckles in the morning light, it was time to move on. That's when she decided to make a run for Broken Arrow.

"Your mother got a damn court order, claiming abuse, probably from one of her fancy judge friends, and took him away from Theo. And now he's gone, Claire. We think you might know where he is," said Roy bluntly.

"My son is missing and you think I *kidnapped* him?"

"Roy doesn't mean to accuse, Claire. We just want to know why your mother has taken Willy away from Theo and where he is now.

Roy ignored his wife. "Do you know where he is?"

"No, I don't, and you're going to have to believe that!" Claire said, slamming her shin in her haste to get up from that table and away from her accusers.

"I guess we don't have much choice," Roy said.

Doris knew when Roy got that riled there was a good reason. May as well stand with him and fight his way. Claire squealed off in a rented black Camaro. Before she turned her back to the road, Doris wrote down the license-plate number.

THERE WAS A COUGH and the faint whistle of air in a windpipe before she heard the familiar "Hirsh Residence."

At any other time, Claire would have spent at least five minutes inquiring after Lucy's health. She would have asked what she was taking and why she was not in bed. But today she simply said, "Lucy, please ask my mother to come to the phone."

"What the hell have you done with Willy?" Claire shouted over the roar of traffic on the exit ramp over her head. She had driven too fast, as far as she could get from that stupid capsule Roy and Doris called home, and then pulled over at a foul-smelling phone booth in the middle of East Shit, Nowhere.

"Where are you dear? We've been worried sick." How infuriatingly genteel her mother became when cornered.

"You got a court order and took Willy away from his home. You said you suspected abuse. Abuse! I can't believe it. How could you do such a thing?

"I did it for you, darling, of course."

"For me? I didn't ask you to do such a horrible thing!" Claire shouted down the highway noise.

"Where are you?" Mary asked again. "This connection is dreadful."

"I'm on my way home. And you'd better have an explanation!"

With sudden clarity, she remembered the young bully in the butcher shop who threw sawdust in her face when she was four years old. She remembered how it clung to her hair and to her coat. "I'm going to hit you," she said, shaking her child's fist at him. She wanted to bloody that fat kid's nose, pummel him until he spat sawdust, but was powerless to lower her arm, which had frozen in mid-threat. Now she stood in the middle of the Oklahoma flats, realizing her own mother was that bully and she was letting her win. The empty dial tone pushed her out of the booth, back into her life. And mine.

18

Mr. Cosmopoulos said, "If you want to know how things stand between your folks, look at that picture you're carrying around in your duffel. It's all there, mister. The mouths are smiling, but the eyes are hard. Look at the distance between them. Are they touching? Or holding themselves apart? People break up long before they know it. Take a good look. You'll see it, mister."

I pretended not to hear him, but I did see what he meant. I thought of the wall of photographs at home and wondered why I'd never noticed how death, masquerading as the long afternoon light, cast Uncle Alan's face in shadow. Something in Uncle Baxter's sidelong look at Aunt Jess just before the click, her eyes gone flat and black, like a darkened stage where the players are hiding in plain sight, flashed a warning.

After dinner in South Neck, the Thanksgiving before last. The turkey carcass, a row of half-eaten pies, apple-sausage stuffing, mashed potatoes redolent of sage, its spoon lakes drained of gravy, sweet potatoes with marshmallows for the children's table congealing in Pyrex dishes. Molly and Theo and Claire wrapping platters, licking the last bits off their fingers. Harry and I racing up the back stairs to gape at Charlotte's boyfriend, an awkward South Neck senior who gave the impression of being strangled by his clothes as he nervously waited for my cousin.

The noisy and important business of boys. Peter on the fireplace bench, absently stirring the logs; Barnaby and Grandma Hirsh in opposing corners of the room; the room itself wrapped in its own thoughts, punctuated by the soft ticking of the silver mantel clock, fat crackle of applewood, gusts of laughter from the kitchen. The sudden tumble, coatless, to the porch, Grandma protesting the cold, Claire's camera on the tripod, timer ticking, giggles. *All together, one, two, three, hurry now, smile. C'mon, c'mon, c'mon . . . .*

Click. It's all there, frozen on the wall, just as Mr. Cosmopoulos said—the angry set of Claire's jaw, wide-open longing in Theo's eyes. Their hands rest on my shoulders, careful not to touch each other. Barnaby searches his youngest son's face, measuring him against the memory of another. Uncle Peter turns away and offers his hand to Molly, who stands apart from the group, feet planted on the top step, arms clamped firmly around Harry, her body language as clear as a sign that says *Keep Off*. Her fingers waggle across the empty space, for Charlotte, but she is already reaching for the boy whose name she will soon forget. The tightness around my grandmother's mouth tells us all we ever needed to know of her intentions.

Mr. C. said people are always watching for something that doesn't come, which keeps them from seeing what does. This made me think of the afternoon we hung Mr. Kimsky over our red dining room table. I had no idea this would be the last photograph of us together, the last time things felt normal. Theo and Claire, Suzie, Uncle Baxter, and me, smiling dumbly at the ticking timer and the tripod from which Claire had hung a sign that read *Fromage*. I had no idea how important it was until the morning I left and found myself wishing I had remembered to squeeze it into my bag with the one I had already packed. Of all the stories I told Mr. Cosmopoulos, the story of that day seems to hold the most clues. I was learning the lesson of secrets revealed not only in photographs, but in the details of a story chosen for the retelling.

Mr. Kimsky never sold. Aunt Suzie kept in touch with everyone who signed the gallery guest books or even casually considered the possibility of buying a print, and dutifully mailed announcements of new shows. She phoned important collectors like the director of Amnesty International, who had purchased the one Claire called "The Vigil," a quiet and powerful image of a woman in a frayed blue coat, red scarf knotted tightly under her chin, squinting out to sea. But after the first post-show rush, interest dropped off.

Uncle Baxter wondered aloud if people who bought Mr. Kimsky's friends and neighbors were art collectors or actually Holocaust victims themselves.

"To think," he said, "these poor devils were being gassed, while my schoolmates and I looked at the whole war as a school holiday. All we worried about was London's supply of Malteasers."

Aunt Suzie held forth on the tragicomic symbolism of Coney Island itself lurking beneath its rusting rides, its decrepit boardwalk, and seedy clown face.

Jessica had another theory. "This one didn't do as well as the others because it's so stark, no kitschy salt and pepper shakers like the ones on Mrs. Klein's windowsill, no painted ties or cat's-eye sunglasses studded with rhinestones. Mr. Kimsky is too serious."

"Why does your wife have to reduce art to fashion?" Claire asked with no animosity.

"It's her job," said Baxter. "Besides, she's very cute."

I watched them mark the wall, stand back, and envision the white space shimmering at the edges of Mr. Kimsky's brown-and-yellow plaid shirt, the hooded eyes, the beak of a nose, the sun burning out the chessmen, leaving only the shadow of his unseen opponent.

Claire stood on a chair and pounded a nail.

St. Kimsky of the dinner table.

Claire stood back, admiring her work. "Do you all know why this is my favorite. It's my favorite because it makes you work. It doesn't lead the witness. It's full of clues. Look there, see that tiny hair insinuating itself into the picture, like a cockroach that won't die?"

I looked closely at the lone hair that had escaped Mr. Kimsky's razor. It was barely visible, yet tenacious in its quest for his collar.

As Baxter made a lame joke about the whole-in-the-wall gang for my benefit.

"Honey, what's so funny?" Claire asked me.

"Nothing, Mom."

"Pay attention. This will be important some day."

"The thing about roaches," said Claire, still up on the chair, "is no matter what people do to them, they won't die."

"Mine leave little suicide notes, but they never do it," said Suzie agreed, launching into the losing battle her own building was waging.

"Willy, did you know roaches can live on nail clippings and squeeze themselves through electrical sockets to get out of a place that's been sprayed or freshly painted?" Claire continued.

A huge water bug once fell right out of a crack in the caulking around our tub. Theo said, "If he can afford the rent, he can stay."

"Isn't that the human spirit?" Claire said, "impossible to kill."

The vile greenish-black creature paddled furiously toward my soapy toes. Theo scooped the water behind it with an empty jam jar, and beat a hasty retreat to the incinerator.

"And the shadow of the other player," Claire continued. "Isn't that how we all get through life? We play against what we think might be life's next move. Look at Mr. Kimsky's eyes. We can't see them."

Baxter nodded his agreement. "They say it's impossible to look an animal in the eye and kill it."

Suddenly Theo was laughing at us in that way she had of pretending she was being funny while saying something mean. "Leading the witness? Life's next move? The human spirit as cockroach? Claire, this is your nine-year-old son, Willy, not the art critic for the *Times!*"

"Maybe Mr. Kimsky didn't sell because he doesn't look like anyone's uncle George, or there was no more room for another picture over the TV and the snack trays."

Then the kitchen door swung closed and Theo's offered us all hot cocoa.

Claire said nothing. Baxter and Suzie looked like children who'd been slapped. Before anyone could say a word, Theo took a last shot from the kitchen. "Suze, air conditioners and water heaters are installed. Pictures are hung. And I know you were smoking."

Cocoa was poured, a plate of blondies passed. Baxter told stories of Brooke and Jennifer on location with their distracted mother. Suzie pretended no one knew she was smoking behind the bathroom door. Claire said no more about the picture. But I knew the day was something to save for when I looked for reasons why things turned out the way they did.

After Baxter and Suzie left, Claire said, "Damn it, Theo, you come in and don't even have your coat off and you're at me already."

"You don't even listen to other ideas, Claire. You use that camera of yours to club people with your point of view, and God help anyone who disagrees with that withering, what-do-you-know-about-art-anyway look of yours."

Claire wheeled around. "And what about you? If a cement block sat on the table long enough, it would never occur to you to ask how it got there or what it might be trying to tell you, you'd just feed it. Maybe some things are not about eating, Theo, ever think of that? Maybe my art is about feeling connected."

"Connected to what?" Theo shot back. "The idea that no matter how intractable and ridiculous your position, there's a photograph to support it?"

I padded into the kitchen that night where Theo was sitting in a pool of light, blindly turning the pages of a cookbook.

"I don't want you to fight anymore."

"I know you don't, honey. I love her, too. We're very different, your mother and I, and we can't help it sometimes."

"You're both lesbians," I offered, looking for common ground.

She slipped an arm around my shoulder, and smiled in spite of herself. "If only it were that easy.

"Do you know why I cook, baby boy?"

I didn't.

"Because sometimes it's hard for me to say 'I love you.'"

"You say 'I love you' to me."

"You're easy."

She seemed so defeated that night; her tired faced sagged, shoulders down, feet apart and flat on the black-and-white tiles like someone who had taken a drug to quiet the nerves and killed the spirit instead.

I WALKED for a long time. A bitter wind pressed my chin into my collarbone and I began to shiver, not only from the cold, but from the tension of expecting to be caught and from the slow realization that Mr. Cosmopoulos might not come.

"Well, mister, looks like tomorrow's the day," he had said when I told him Lucy was so sick, she had barely made it to school. "If you don't make it, I'll give you a rain check."

After I turned the corner off Fifth Avenue, which seemed like miles away, but was only about a hundred yards, I walked east and crossed to the southeast corner of Madison, careful to avoid the greengrocer who always tossed me an apple when Lucy and I passed by. I turned right, watching for classmates and neighbors who might stop me and ask why I was going in the wrong direction.

I headed south, afraid to look back, trying to act as normal as I could. I quickened my pace without breaking into a run, imagining baying hounds on my scent and a red-faced policeman at my back. I did not draw an even breath until there were at least six blocks between Grandma's building and me. Down the humped spine of Madison Avenue, art galleries gave way to small apartment buildings and expensive boutiques and coffee shops where models huddled over black coffee and grapefruit sections in beautiful starvation. Somewhere in the sixties, I slowed down.

Drivers lounged against long black cars, their peaked caps tossed on front seats, smoking cigarettes and stamping out the chill as they waited for their employers to down the last piece of toast, pull on their coats, and promise to return at a decent hour to the brownstones and maisonettes in the quiet side streets. Hotel doormen whistled for taxis, while French, Italian, Japanese, and Farsi filled the cold morning. Snippets of an argument drifted over snapping awnings.

As I walked, the human swarm grew, the blare of traffic with it. Cabs, buses, town cars horns, speeding bicycles, all converged in a seething wave of noise. Every bus and subway stop fed long columns of workers into giant hives with names like IBM, Helmsley Spear and Graybar. Miniature tornadoes lifted my hair and reddened my face as I watched revolving doors usher people inside and swallow them whole. I rode the sharp edge of an increasingly nasty day.

I passed Schrafft's, where Theo took me for hot chocolate in thick pottery cups. My stomach rumbled at the sweet dark memory of cocoa and cream. I passed the gloomy Archdiocese building, black as a nun's habit. Grandpa Barnaby told me the old Cardinal lived there and used the money in the poor box to buy caviar.

From the tall shadows of Madison Avenue, I glimpsed the wide luxury of Fifth, the Plaza and the grand department stores where women with tinted hair knew my grandmother by name and wrote her tastes in red leather books. A pair of old lions guarded the Public Library at Forty-second Street.

I walked down Murray Hill to Altman's. A knot of shoppers waited for the doors to open and I realized it was almost ten; I'd been walking for over an hour and let the crowd carry me into the overheated building. To avoid the suspicious store detectives I imagined lurked behind every mannequin with a police sketch of me in hand, I trailed discreetly behind a red-haired woman who could have been my mother or an aunt. Together we marched through Handbags and Gloves, and by the time she got to Scarves, I was steps away from the main door on Fifth, nice and warm from the shortcut Claire taught me one rainy Saturday when we looked for an anniversary present for Jessica and Baxter.

I didn't see the bike. I just felt a rush of wind as it came so close to hitting me that it ripped the handle right off my duffel bag. A man in a topcoat and what I might have identified as a bowler hat, if I had known what such a hat was called, helped me to the sidewalk. I tried very hard not to cry.

"Are you okay?" he asked, patting the front of my jacket, and feeling for broken bones. "Do you want me to call somebody, a doctor maybe?" He held my sleeve and searched the street, then brightened as he spotted a blue uniform walking toward us. "Here comes a cop; you want me to call him, maybe you want to report a hit-and-run?"

I didn't. "I'm going to see my father," I said, pointing to the Empire State Building. "He works in that building over there."

I know he was watching me as I walked in.

I was EATING a hot dog at Nedick's on the corner of Thirty-fourth and Sixth when he finally came. I waited as long as I could on the corner of Fifth and Thirty-fourth; Mr. Cosmopoulos had whispered through the school fence that he'd meet me there at twelve o'clock sharp and take me the rest of the way to his place. But by three, the wind had bitten through my coat and I knew I had to keep moving. I had been to Macy's many times and remembered Mr. C.'s face had brightened when I mentioned this to him. I thought he might be there, so I walked along with the crowds on Thirty-fourth Street and entered huge store's maze of buildings. I badly needed to use a bathroom, and felt better after finding the "Lounge" with its high ceilings, marble floors and rows of old-fashioned stalls. I rode the oldest and slowest escalator I had ever seen, imagining it, too, shivered as its passengers put their cold feet on its creaky wooden back.

Back outside The World's Largest Department Store, Herald Square was strangely muffled. It had begun to snow. Big wet flakes flew over raised collars and the lowered heads tof people trying to get home early. Umbrellas had sprouted up everywhere, sprays of flowers, peek-a-boo vinyl, and cheap sidewalk models that snapped in the wind as soon as you paid your money There were no English umbrellas with monograms gilded collars like Grandpa Barnaby's. And no Mr. Cosmopoulos.

I felt a snow flake land on my cheek and melt into a tear, then another and another, coming faster now, soaking my hair. I slipped a cold hand inside my jacket, felt way down to the bottom of my school khakis and counted my lunch money. Two dollars. I hadn't planned on snow or Mr. C. coming so late. Was he coming at all? Had he forgotten? If it snows, do you still get a rain check?

I had already eaten the muffins I packed for Shorty, nibbled from my coat pocket as I walked along the street. Grandma told me never to eat in public, but I couldn't help it. I thought of Lucy fixing one of her snacks to tide me over until dinner; even the thought of something from the McCall cafeteria was appealing at that moment. No one was thinking about food back at Grandma's. By this time, they'd known for hours that I was gone. I felt a twinge of guilt for Lucy, shaken from her sickbed, and told it was all her fault, packing her bags in shame. Even if Mr. C. never came, I could never go back. I'd join a gang and live on the streets by my wits as I had seen on the six o'clock news.

The hot dog was still sizzling when the Nedick's man put it into a thick roll. I nodded yes when he pointed to the onions and again at the relish. He just smiled when he got around to the chili and the cheese. He filled up a large paper cup with pulpy orange juice and watched me try to find a place for the mustard.

"Where you been, mister?"

Familiar red suspenders peeked out from a stained parka, black ponytail curling under what looked like an old sock stiff with frost. The counterman eyed him suspiciously, ready to intervene, when I jumped from my stool and hugged Mr. Cosmopoulos.

"Been looking for you hours and you're sitting here, eating hot dogs. What happened?"

"Bike hit me."

"Lucky you had that bag."

"I guess."

He pulled his huge gloves over my trembling hands, and his stocking cap way down to my melting eyebrows. We walked along in silence into the swirling whiteness.

"So clean, snow. When God can't stand looking at how dirty we make things, he just sends down a coat of this stuff. Makes everything nice and quiet. Gives him a rest. Doesn't have to hear everybody bitching and moaning, if you'll excuse my French."

I hadn't heard him say anything in French, but I let it pass. I was just so glad he hadn't let me down; he could have said anything. We walked until the noise of workday New York at our backs. When I asked him why he was opening the manhole cover on Twenty-ninth Street, he said, "Didn't ever say I lived *on* Madison Avenue, did I?"

My fingers cramped on the cold metal bars but Mr. Cosmopolous, accustomed to holding on with one hand, guided my foot with the other. His voice spiraled up through the darkness. "Hold on, mister, these steps are slippery and doctors don't make house calls down here."

We stepped into the dark tunnel; my legs and arms were still wobbly from the climb. As my eyes became accustomed to the pitch-black, I saw we were moving toward a feeble light strung up on makeshift wires. In the broad apron of what might have been a subway tunnel there were two tattered chairs, a large shelf of books, maps, magazines, and newspapers, a mirror, some toiletries, and a cupboard neatly stocked with cans of soup, beans, and clean Latest Dish containers. There were three cots, one freshly made up with a new blanket and a pillow still in plastic.

"Home, sweet home!" Mr. C said, sweeping his arm across the entrance to what looked like a campsite.

A small man with the dense build of a boxer and a pronounced limp walked toward me. He wore a plaid shirt and round wire-framed glasses that had been mended with a little tape. He did not smile, nor did he frown.

"Meet Shorty!" Mr. Cosmopoulos bellowed.

"What took you so long?"

"Mr. Kimsky?" I said too softly for him to hear.

19

Shorty's resemblance to Mr. Kimsky was uncanny. He and Mr. C, and the motley band of souls who inhabited the dark corners of the abandoned tunnel, reinforced my belief in a parallel universe. I put my nine-year-old's faith in the elegant, if not scientific, idea that carbon copies of every one of us lived somewhere, millions of light-years away, on a green planet just like Earth with cities like New York and Chicago and Broken Arrow, Oklahoma, and Greenwich Village and South Neck. But *that* planet was way ahead of us. I was a senior in high school up there, S.A.T.'s behind me, an acceptance letter from Harvard in my pocket to show to all my friends. Up there, Grandma had given up and let me go home. Alan, Roland, and the Jacobys had not perished after all, but were merely victims of amnesia. Claire and Theo were together and happy again, and it was discovered that children with two mothers had, on average, higher I.Q. scores, better relationships, and a higher level of creativity than kids who had one of each. I suppose this was where I got whatever small shred of courage I possessed, believing in a world where my present was already history, where what was happening to me was no big deal, was old news somewhere else.

Is an older, handsome version of me running a touchdown to wild cheering, and the red flag of my father's hair in the row reserved for parents? Am I telling my own children a story about a boy who ran away to join the underground people while my pretty wife and their grandfather, his hair now burnished to copper and threaded with silver, chides me for frightening the children so close to bedtime. Was my parallel world under the sidewalk all this time?

If I am here, is the other Willy still above ground? Is he sitting at Grandma's table right now, politely waiting for Barnaby to excuse him, getting ready for bed in Roland's room, putting on the pajamas under the pillow, wondering what will happen if Theo doesn't win in court? Does *he* know I'm here?

Mr. Cosmopoulos had gone "upstairs," as he called the sidewalk above us, and I was sitting across from Shorty, who was tapping cocoa into a chipped enamel saucepan balanced on an electric coil. A black extension cord snaked up from this contraption and was clipped to a thick cable that ran along the grimy rock roof of the tunnel before it disappeared into the gloom farther down the line.

"Not like your mother's, but it'll have to do," Shorty said, using his shirttail to wipe a bent Horn & Hardart spoon, then peeled back scalded curls of milk skin. "Milk's easier to get than water down here."

"Is my picture in the paper yet?" I asked.

"Didn't want Luis to bring you here, you know. We got enough trouble without a kidnapping on our heads."

"You didn't kidnap me. I ran away."

"Tell that to the cops."

He limped over to me with a steaming mug. His face was not friendly, but his gesture was, and I was not as confused by this as I once might have been. My grandmother looked friendly enough, but was not. I hadn't thought about how my running away to visit Mr. Cosmopoulos might look to other people. I figured I'd stay with him until I figured out what to do. Now I worried about the trouble I might be causing. The cocoa was silky, and rich and, surprisingly, as good as Theo's.

I sneaked looks at Shorty as we drank.

"Do you play chess?" I asked.

"Do you?"

"Grandpa Barnaby was going to teach me, but I left before he got around to it."

"I might."

In the glare of the bare bulb that hung over the section Shorty called the parlor, I saw nicks in Shorty's face, as if someone had been chipping away at him.

He saw me look away and brushed a hand over his cheek.

"I fall down."

"Oh," I said, sorry I'd hurt his feelings.

A woman's voice, raspy from cigarettes, rose behind me. "Don't let him scare you, Red. His bark is much worse than his bite. Fact is, he's got no bite. Teeth are rotten. Aren't they, Mr. Shorty Pants?"

She moved into the circle of light. She wore grimy brown corduroy trousers and a pair of black high-topped sneakers. An old sweater that had been darned with bright thread and masking tape clung to her with its last button. A faded blue terrycloth-towel was fashioned into a turban and safety-pinned around her head, fringe of dirty blond hair sticking out. She dangled a battered purse in the crook of her left arm, palm up, forefinger leading, just the way my grandmother and her friends carried theirs when they went out to lunch.

"What's that?" she asked, peering into my cup.

"Cocoa," I said.

"Cocoa? Ha! I knew it! He doesn't know how to properly entertain a guest. Been down here too long." She arched one scraggly eyebrow right up to the frayed edge of her turban, ran a finger over the cardboard box that served as our table, and sniffed. "Where are your manners, sir? Not even a tablecloth!"

She stepped back to peer at me with an odd combination of approval and mistrust. "I will call you Monsieur Rouge. Everyone calls me Mrs. DeVries, and so you must, too. You'll come over to my pied-à-terre when you're settled in and we'll have a proper visit. I'll serve hors d'oeuvre, make a nice roast, and you'll tell me how my boy is doing in school. You will call first, though, won't you? Cornelia hasn't come in a while and I'll have to straighten up a bit. I'll let myself out, Shorty dear, don't get up."

Then she muttered something about expecting a package. We watched her pick her way back into the dark and toward a feeble light farther down the broken track. She moved like loose clothes in a suitcase.

"That's Thelma, said Shorty, tapping his temple. "Her elevator hasn't gone all the way to the top for years, if you know what I mean."

I didn't know what he meant, but even though she didn't look like any of the women I knew and she smelled strong, like Claire after she'd been running hard, I thought Mrs. DeVries was a lot friendlier than Shorty. I looked forward to going to her house for dinner.

Mr. C. returned with Chinese takeout and soon the milk crate was covered with cartons of sticky white rice, sweet and sour chicken, and ginger beef and pork in black bean sauce. Shorty dug around in a shoebox for chopsticks and little packets of soy sauce, hot mustard, and sweet plum sauce. I was too embarrassed to say I didn't know how to use the chopsticks my hosts provided.

After dinner, we sat and talked awhile. Then I followed Shorty and Mr. Cosmopoulos from the orange crate to the tattered chairs a few steps away. Claire always stayed behind in the kitchen to start the dishes—"You cook, I clean up," she always said—and Theo led their friends into our living room where coffee and chocolates waited on the low table surrounded by cushions. Mr. C. excused himself to tidy up and disappeared into a room I hadn't noticed before. That's when Shorty told me about the plate.

"Got a plate in his head, you know," Shorty began and I wondered how a dish could get inside a person's skull.

"Happened before I met him. Had a family, then one day, he just wandered off, couldn't remember who he was. Amnesia."

I thought, wouldn't it be great if Uncle Roland and Alan had that, too; that they weren't really dead.

"When they found him," Shorty continued, "he was in bad shape. Crazy. They took out a tumor the size of an orange, stitched him up with cat gut and Krazy Glue, and covered the hole with a metal plate. Down at St. Vincent's. Says he can tell when it's gonna snow, even down here."

I wondered if Mr. C. really did forget to meet me, if his plate told him to come get me out of the snow.

"Did his memory come back?" I asked.

"Most of it, but he forgets a lot. Goes blank. Forgot to tell me you were coming."

"Did they find him?"

"Who?"

"His family."

"He didn't want to be found and they didn't try real hard. Writes to his son, though. In Jersey somewhere. Pretends he's a traveling salesman. Kid thinks he lives in a fancy apartment on Madison Avenue. Doorman, another Greek, took a liking to Luis and saves the letters for him. Says he'll go see him when we move into a better place."

"How long have you lived here?"

"Since '59."

Shorty tilted his head in the direction of Mr. Cosmopoulos's heavy step. "I hear you're Greek, too."

"Not exactly," I answered.

Shorty got up and moved toward a commode hidden behind an artificial palm tree. Mr. C. sat down. A battered twelve-string guitar stood in a corner. Mr. C ran his hand over it the way parents touch their children in passing. A few notes scaled the grimy wall and fell.

"Shorty telling you about my plate?"

He curled his hand into a fist and knocked his left temple.

"It's right here. Go ahead, hit it."

I politely shook my head no as he kept on knocking.

"C'mon. It's hard as a rock."

Mr. Cosmopoulos told me Shorty had been in the Korean War and was shell-shocked, which meant he still saw pictures of the war in his head. No matter what he did, he couldn't make them go away.

"Got his leg blown off, trying to save one of his buddies," Mr. Cosmopoulos said. "They pinned a medal on him, put him in the Veterans Hospital on Welfare Island, then forgot about him. One day, he packed one shoe and the wooden leg and left."

Mr. C. drifted away and I waited for him to come back.

"He was in the bed next to mine in St. Vincent's free ward," he said after a time. That's for charity cases and if you don't make it there, they put you in Potter's Field and nobody comes to cry except the poor bastards who dig the holes in that godforsaken place.

"We were both in pretty bad shape. Shorty had a bad case of the DTs. You know what that is?"

I shook my head.

"That's delirium tremens, mister. Means the booze got you and won't let go, makes you shiver and sweat and think you've got bugs crawling all over you. You think you're gonna die, and some do."

A chill ran through me at the thought of roaches on my skin.

"Well, I wasn't any good to anybody either, talking nonsense, big bandage wrapped around my head. What a pair we were, the blind leading the blind, but we got along all right, and afterwards we helped each other out. Stayed in a coupla roomin' houses down on the Bowery. Gave us the creeps. Heard about some people going underground and decided to give it a try. Been together ever since. The world forgot him

188

and I forgot the world! Whaddaya think about that? Two peas in a pod!"

Mr. Cosmopoulos laughed at his joke.

I suppose telling secrets about someone you love is a form of getting new people to like them, protecting them, so they don't have to explain things themselves. Sometimes Claire would get up and wander out of the room when we had company. Theo would say, "She really wants to see you, but she's working on a show."

"If he likes you, he'll show you his Purple Heart," Mr. C. said.

I didn't realize how much damage the bike and the snow had done until it was time to unpack and settle in for the night. I pulled out soggy pajamas, stiff jeans, sodden underwear, a shredded book. My spare sweater was stained with toothpaste.

"Don't worry," Mr. Cosmopoulos said. "Tomorrow we'll wash everything at a place I know. Shorty'll iron them up. He's a real spit-and-polish man, aren't you, Shorty?"

"If I have to," came the muffled response.

Mr. Cosmopoulos felt inside my bag and lifted out the toothpaste tube slit side up to avoid wasting the rest of it.

"He doesn't like me, does he?" I whispered.

"Sure he does. It was Shorty's idea to invite you down here, give you a little break from your troubles."

"He said it was your idea and that people might think you kidnapped me."

"Nah. That's his way of not letting you see how soft he is."

"Are you and Shorty married like my moms?"

"I guess you could say that. Been together long enough to qualify. We don't have any fancy name for it, though. We just watch out for each other, make sure we got enough to eat, don't get sick or too lonely. Somebody to talk to, fight with. Nothin' sadder than not having anybody to pick a fight with."

A spiral of panic curled up from my knees.

"My picture!"

Mr. C. looked up from the piles he was making—stuff to fix, stuff to wash, stuff that's okay.

"Us. My moms and me. I put it right there."

He turned what was left of the front pocket of my bag inside out. "Where?"

The loss of that picture hit hard and unleashed something I had been holding back all day, maybe a lot longer than that. Everything came flooding back. Poor Lucy. Grandma. Buddy. Mr. Cowperthwaite and his dog. The unbearable tension of being terrified, yet willing my feet to move to the door. Shivering in the wind, long blocks, the hard faces of strangers hurrying past, the bike, its rider aiming at me, never looking back, the snow freezing my eyelashes and the gut-pounding fear that Mr. C. wouldn't come and I would starve or be killed by bands of muggers who slept on the streets and preyed on little kids like me.

I was shivering uncontrollably—not from cold, but from the long walk, dark descent to this place, a sudden slip, skin curling away from my knee, bubbles of blood rising to the surface, panic reaching for my throat, the sound of rats scurrying away from loose rock, Mrs. DeVries, Shorty. Claire gone. Theo gone. And now, all I had to remember them, gone too.

Mr. Cosmopoulos rubbed his big paw up and down my back.

"Let's fix up this bed," he said gently. "You've had a big day, mister.".

He opened the plastic cover on the new pillow, careful to keep it intact, and wrapped a soft flannel shirt around it for a case, tying the sleeves so it wouldn't slip. He opened the blanket next, again taking care with the wrapper, and I saw the big white streak in one corner. "That's nothing," he said, "just a bad dye lot. It'll keep you just as warm as one that's got all its color." There were no sheets, just more shirts sewn together, which he fussed over, smoothing and re-smoothing just like my mothers.

"You don't remember people because you carry their pictures," he said after I climbed into my one dry pair of pajamas and got in on the side he had turned down. "And you don't forget them because you don't have any."

I lay there listening to the distant rumbling of traffic overhead, something dripping somewhere, and the soft chords of "Malagueña" from the other side of the dark.

I fought sleep for a long time, trying to squeeze the lost photograph into my memory. A sunburned Theo wrapped in a pareo and Claire in shorts smiling on a dock, both listing a bit from their day on Uncle Peter's boat. I am closer to the ground than they, and have already found my land legs, a small anchor between them, hands extended as if to keep them from drifting away.

When the music faded and was replaced by soft snoring, the silly sidewalk rhyme that had been playing over and over in the back of my head became louder and louder. It was last thing I remember before exhaustion finally won out.

Don't step on the cracks!
You'll break your mothers' backs.
Make three wishes,
And break the devil's dishes.

20

In the following days, everything focused on food. What was simply taken out of the refrigerator, oven, or freezer, delivered from the pizza parlor, snipped from Theo's herb garden, stirred and prayed over by the superstitious Lucy, or blindly grabbed from the snack jar on the counter took enormous effort underground.

There was no other work beyond securing enough to eat. Every meal was a miracle, the direct result of Mr. Cosmopoulos's resourcefulness and Shorty's talent for merging disparate ingredients into something palatable, and more often than not, very good. A network of contacts "upstairs" abetted their efforts. Dimitri, a friendly ex-Marine who washed dishes at Fong's Szechuan Garden, had been responsible for my feast that first night. A newspaper dealer named Jimmy the Scoop, known to enjoy the bottle every now and again, donated his unsold papers to our cause and never failed to tuck a chocolate bar, a bag of peanuts, or a two-pack of cupcakes into the ink-stained bundles. Even my clean clothes were courtesy of Leroy at the coin-op who gave us slugs when the owner wasn't looking.

A backbreaking day spent scouring the sidewalks for small change netted some meat for a dish Shorty called Hamburger Hill, a mound of mostly beans and rice seasoned with something mysterious and hot. The pint of milk, dented can of orange juice reconstituted with a soda bottle full of the fire hydrant's best, the loaf of rye bread, and the eggs I enjoyed two at a time, their yolks unbroken and glistening on my chipped plate, cost Mr. C. a whole afternoon of delivering sale leaflets for the man who managed the D'Agostino's on the corner. Shorty rarely ventured out except for a checkup at the veterans' clinic or to the occasional "meeting," the announcement of which usually arrived on the heels of a foul mood and a run of sleepless nights of "ghost pain," in the general vicinity of where his leg should have been. He returned a little softer around the eyes, but the stairs were tough for him and he preferred their dark nest with the likes of Thelma and the shadowy Raul who spoke to no one but his cat, a punchy looking one-eared stray tabby named Valentino. He didn't seem to mind the constant rattle of the trains and the threat of flooding from the water mains that crisscrossed the walls, leaving it to the gregarious Mr. C. to venture out for supplies and who never accepted a cup of coffee without scooping up all the sugar, salt, pepper, mustard, ketchup, and jelly tubs his big hands could hold. It was his job to see to it the larder remained stocked.

I understood it was my job to accept these gifts without protesting the hardships faced on my behalf. I never questioned Mr. Cosmopoulos, who was far too proud and extravagant in every gesture; to admit the perils he faced securing my comfort. Nor did I ever confront Shorty, whose own style of giving was grumpy, begrudging and all the sweeter for it. I was the guest, and, as such, I was bound by unspoken rules. I accepted their hospitality and pulled it off with the ease only children can bring to such an endeavor.

My favorite thing to do was to go to Leroy's coin-op several blocks south of the "front porch"—which is what we called the old manhole over our tunnel. Mr. C. and I would share a Newsstand Jimmy chocolate bar while we waited for Shorty's plaid shirt, my flannel pajamas and Mr. C.'s baggy jeans to dry. I loved listening to buttons clacking against the sides of the dryer and watching pants legs stand up for a second, then collapse and tumble again. The clean smell of lint and detergent reminded me of bread baking. We pressed our things with our hands, folded them carefully, and held each garment up to our noses for a sweet whiff of the previous customer's fabric softener before we packed it all into my duffel.

It was in Leroy's, waiting for the big machine to stop, that I decided to ask Mr. C. if he and Shorty were bums like the men we'd seen sleeping on sidewalk when we walked down to the Bowery and he pointed out the hotel where he and Shorty once lived.

Mr. Cosmopoulos thought for a second, tugged on his ponytail a couple of times as though he were jump-starting a car, and said, "Let's see, are we bums? Well, mister, we've got a roof over our heads—such as it is, a little inconvenient and out of the way—and we earn every bit of food we eat and trade honest work for extras. Nobody's sleeping on a bench in our neighborhood and no winos. No crazies either, except Thelma, but she's harmless. And no drugs. Anybody tries that in our tunnel, out they go.

"So no," he said with a thumping finality, "Shorty and I are not bums, just down on our luck. In between things, you might say." And then quietly, as if to put a finer point on it. "No, not bums. A better word would be *independents*."

Outside the laundry, there was a pile of greasy blankets and newspapers in the doorway of an abandoned tenement. As we got closer we saw it was really a man, hunkered down against the sooty wind. His hair was long and matted, and under it was a face creased where dirt had hardened and fanned out in streaks. His skin was as deeply tanned as Aunt Suzie's when she returned from her winter vacation, but his eyes were bloodshot and crusted. A mixture of urine, sweat and excrement rose up from him, forcing me to breathe through my mouth.

Mr. Cosmopoulos opened the shopping bag we were swinging between us, took out a freshly washed blanket, and placed it around the man's thin shoulders, gently prying away the filthy one he had wrapped around him. "Here you go," he said, "still warm from the dryer. We'll get yours washed up nice and new. Be back with it next week. Then, as though he had not planned to do so but had changed his mind at the last minute, Mr. C. leaned down into the awful stench, and handed the man his coffee from the machine in the laundromat. "God bless you, brother," the man said.

We walked along for a while, each of us lost in our thoughts. I didn't realize until years later I was seeing the first of many victims of society's misplaced intentions, forced to leave the comfort of a warm mental hospital bed, medication, and regular meals in exchange for rights that never materialized. I could not have known this man and many like him would foreshadow a skid row that would soon spill over its boundaries, but from the way he shook his head, slowly and with great sorrow, I suspect my Mr. C. knew more about it than he would say.

Our shoes scraped along in the slush and we walked a little faster after that. The temperature was dropping and the ground was getting slick. After a while, Mr. Cosmopoulos tilted his head to a sky full of snow and said, "That's what a bum is, mister."

As PROMISED, we paid a social call on Mrs. Thelma DeVries.

Shorty walked down the track ahead of time and asked her if it was okay to come for dinner the next evening. After consulting her "schedule," which was really a grimy calendar open to May and a picture of Mount Vesuvius, she frowned at the blank pages, and said, "Well, we must do it tomorrow because as you can see, the rest of the week is simply out of the question."

When Shorty came back, he said, "She'll fit us in," and rolled his eyes.

She welcomed us like my grandmother might have.

"Luis, Shorty, and my dear Monsieur Rouge, how good of you to come. Welcome to my chez moi," said Mrs. DeVries, ushering us over the threshold of the niche she called home. She thanked Mr. Cosmopoulos for the jar of briny black olives Shorty had remembered at the last minute. "We gotta take something," he had said.

Her front door really *was* a door—battered but once beautiful oak, with delicate stained-glass panels and a crystal knob. "My treasure," she said when we entered. "It called to me from a pile of junk in front of an antique shop. A rose among the thorns, like me."

Somehow she had gotten it to stand upright long enough to attach its richly carved molding to two old bed frames fanning out from either side, upended and draped with old sheets. A piano shawl gave the impression of entering a real room. She was still wearing her turban, but this time she was dressed in something resembling a man's bathrobe tied with a piece of velvet ribbon.

"You must try one of these canapés," she said, offering us an empty paper plate with a grand flourish. "They're frightfully good."

"Just play along," Mr. Cosmopoulos whispered.

"Thank you," I said politely, and pretended to take one, thumb and forefinger together, pinky extended, the way my grandmother's friends did it.

When Mrs. DeVries offered another, I said, "Oh no, please, you must take the last one," just like Aunt Jessica when she really didn't like something. She beamed at me through a shock of limp hair that had fallen out of her turban, unable to see Shorty sneering behind her back. "Such manners you have. Just like my darling Jack," she gushed,

On one empty plate after another, she served mashed potatoes, *haricots verts*, rack of lamb with mint jelly, apple cobbler. She poured a nice, mellow port into invisible glasses and a double Gloucester with it. She was careful not to offer Shorty a drink.

We made appreciative noises and commented on her extraordinary culinary skills. When it seemed appropriate, we thanked Mrs. DeVries for a lovely dinner and bade her good night.

Mr. C. said it was kinder to pretend along with her, but I felt sorry for her all the same.

"Who is Jack?" I asked when we were safely into our own section of tunnel.

Mr. Cosmopoulos unwrapped the jaunty scarf he had wound around his neck for the occasion, and said, "Jack's her son. She was married once a long time ago. When they found her wandering around the streets telling people she was Anastasia, the daughter of the last czar of Russia, her husband took the kid away from her. He's probably older than me by now.

"Her family's got some money, old money I think, and they tried to get her to come home, but she wouldn't. They send her packages every now and then. Don't know how she gets them, but she does."

Shorty limped around looking for something to tide us over until morning.

"Still crazy, if you ask me, wearing a dish towel on her head and serving imaginary food. Better off without her, wherever he is," he sniffed. "I don't know why we didn't just stay home and eat our own olives."

I pictured Theo in a towel and a man's bathrobe and looking all over New York for me, and I wondered if she would serve imaginary tea while Claire pretended to develop pictures that were not there.

Mr. Cosmopoulos was upstairs "recycling" and I was helping Shorty straighten up.

"You know why they call me Shorty?"

"Because you have a short temper?"

"Thelma tell you that?"

I shook my head in a way that looked like a yes, but really wasn't a lie, because I was afraid he'd get mad if I said it was Mr. Cosmopoulos.

"I was a short-order cook for a while," he said. "Greek joint. Hotter than Hades in them kitchens. Would still be there, if they didn't hire that draft dodger, spouting junk about us minding our own business and leaving the Vietnamese alone to solve their own problems. Would have stayed on if he hadn't got on my nerves and made me go after him."

"With a bread knife" is all Mr. C. said when I asked him about it later.

Shorty rubbed his leg as if to remind himself that he had been right to go after the kid.

"Gimme a side of down!" he shouted suddenly. "Know what that is? That's short order talk for toast, kid. Adam and Eve on a raft, that's two eggs on toast. What's 'over easy'?"

I shook my head.

"C'mon, that's easy. Fried egg flipped over just for a second until the yolk gets cooked, but is still runny. Hard to do without breaking it. I'll bet your mother can flip eggs with her eyes closed. Boy, can she cook! I'll bet she's a real dish, too, no pun intended. Nobody makes a chicken fricassee like hers. A real underground sensation, hey kid?" He closed his eyes and smiled at his joke. Where had I heard this before?

Shorty said, "I could do with some of that right now, couldn't you?"

I could do with a lot more than Theo's cooking. A wave of loneliness swept over me. At least at Grandma's, I got to *talk* to my mother.

Shorty scrambled two eggs in a cracked dish balanced on a hot plate. He limped around the dark corner that served as his galley. I could see the anger racing through him. I gathered my courage.

"Shorty."

"Yeah?"

"Have you ever lived in Coney Island?

He brightened. "Learned to cook there. Hot dogs. A place called Nathan's. It's pretty famous, you know."

"I know," I said as calmly as I could.

THE DREAM had changed. It was different from the one that rose up from my *Peanuts* sheets at home or Uncle Roland's blue bedspread, or the mismatched flowers and stripes Aunt Molly stretched to the corners of my foldaway cot at the farm. It came up from the pavement, snaked through the steam vents, and hissed me awake in my cave under the sidewalk. It slithered through the arms of my shirt pillow and wrapped itself around me like an old friend.

Like my Cherokee great-great-great-grandfather on Grandma Doris's side, who could shape-shift into any living creature and back into human form just by thinking it, my dream father assumed many forms. He was a bundle of rags on the sidewalk, hair bleached white from the sun, eyes peeled back from the effort of searching for me, always searching for me. The face that rose to take the coffee was a mirror of my own, then it was gone.

He was a crazy old woman rubbing a callused thumb into my brow, anointing it with holy oil. "I now pronounce you Sir William of Rouge. You may rise, Sir Knight." So, too, was he the stranger in a bowler hat who came out of the crowd and offered a steadying hand. "Have you run away to lose your life or to find it?" he asked as the bicycle tore away. He looked back to see how close he had come, smiling at my quick reflexes under his black helmet.

In this dream, thunder growled in the distance, growing louder and louder, moving toward me, until finally a towering flume of water burst through the tunnel. Just as it was about to wash us away, Shorty leaped to my rescue on two good legs, as Mr. Cosmopoulos flew overhead on wings of red suspenders.

The man I saw through Uncle Peter's fence played chess with a photograph in a plaid shirt and turned himself into a shadow until Claire and her camera were safely out of the picture.

I COULD NOT KNOW it had taken everyone a few days to realize I wasn't spirited away by someone in the family. Later, I was told Theo had accused Uncle Peter of being in cahoots with my grandmother and getting me, via some kind of underground railroad, to wherever Claire was.

Grandma Hirsh accused Theo of kidnapping me, then sending me to Broken Arrow to stay with Doris and Roy because Oklahoma did not have a reciprocal agreement with New York State.

Lucy believed I had been killed and if she hadn't gotten the flu, I would still be alive. When Claire showed up one night, repentant, and worried sick about me, it took a lot of talking and begging before Theo would believe she really hadn't had any part of it. Theo wasn't convinced, but she let her sleep in my loft.

Barnaby broke his characteristic silence, cast a disgusted look at his wife and daughter, who had been threatening each other with lawsuits and disinheritance, and said: "Maybe Willy just ran away. Maybe he ran away because you're all so busy pretending what you want is for his own good, nobody bothered to ask him what *he* wants."

Taking no chances, Theo filed a missing-persons report with both the 19th and 20th Precincts, and when Claire came home, they took turns riding around the streets in police cruisers, a photo of me taped to the visor. Claire conducted her own search from behind the wheel of our yellow VW, praying my body wouldn't be found in the slimy marshes across the river in New Jersey. She swore if I were found alive, she would be the mother I needed. She would work it out with Theo. She suspected everyone. Thad, Baxter, Jessica, and Suzie were getting tired of surprise visits aimed at rousing a sleeping boy from his hiding place.

I'm not sure when I realized that even a small boy has the power to say no in a way that's impossible to ignore. Or when I understood my decision to leave rather than suffer choices made on my behalf gave me the advantage. But I did know, even then, I had to use that power before strangers decided what was best for me.

Mr. Cosmopoulos came home that night with a large shopping bag. Inside were several containers from *The Latest Dish*, sour-cream corn bread, four-alarm chili with black beans, and a crusty loaf of sourdough.

"She looks tired, mister, like she's missing you," said Mr. Cosmopoulos. "Didn't have her usual smile; she's real worried about you." I didn't ask how he managed to get these things from my mother's store, but I was grateful to him for news of her, even news of the pain I had caused. I closed my eyes and felt the hot chili in my mouth. I swallowed slowly, picturing my mother's hands stirring the big copper restaurant pot, using the scissors she wore on a ribbon to snip slender green shoots directly into the stew, seasoning the mixture with spices I could not name but identified as clearly as her signature on my report card. I felt her need in every mouthful.

The picture was taken when I was eight, before my body found its lines and gave my silver-gray eyes their present seriousness, well before my neck showed the first sign of an Adam's apple. It was the most recent picture they had because the photographer had run away and people do not record their unhappiness in the same way they photograph and frame their contentment. They do not reach for the camera when there is nothing to smile about.

Mr. Cosmopoulos handed me the inky newspaper out of which a pudgier version of myself, along with a number to call with any information as to my whereabouts.

Nobody had to say it was time for me to go home.

21

I rehearsed the voice I would use to convince my grandmother to call off the police I imagined were shining flashlights into alleys slick with fish heads and blood, combing the soiled nests of predators known for their particular interest in children. They might even be dragging the river or the Central Park lake for a bloated boy dangling under a small, undulating slick of red hair. I was sure they would not be amused to find the freckled body alive and in its mothers' apartment.

When the time came to tell them I would never go willingly, would run away again and again until my grandmother told the courts to leave us alone, my voice would not waver in the presence of that same grinning sadist who took me away from Theo.

I looked for courage past victories—when I tried out for the third-grade version of *Fantasia* and got the part of a wild mushroom in a singing forest of vegetables. How quickly I'd forgotten my embarrassment at having to wear a costume designed by the only mother who actually knew the difference between a wild morel and the pale buttons that passed for mushrooms in most of my classmates' kitchens. Carl Jacoby, the production's little orphan star, still a little puffy from where I had just recently slugged him, strode onstage to sing a solo and, struck dumb by the footlights, forgot every one of his lines. He stood in mute disgrace as our classmates snickered, snorted, then howled and I, confident that my identity was disguised, laughed so loud the whole audience could hear and became the mysterious new star of the show. Kids hooted and whistled and parents clapped for the boy they mistook for one of their own. I saw what I could do when I believed I was someone else.

In my hunger to *be* someone else, stronger, smarter, more convincing, to be anybody but a boy whose fate rested so wholly on the opinions of others, I began to see why I was so drawn to my Aunt Jessica. She, too, found her courage in costume, in the berets, feather boas, and long slides of silk that were always scattered around her. Like me, she was looking for the mushroom costume that would set her free. And now I was looking for the words she found instead, persuasive, bold, irresistible.

From the distance of flight, I saw the lesson Jess had been teaching me all my life and understood why she and my mother were best friends, why one rewrote the words, the other rearranged the pictures. "If you can imagine it, you can have it. If you can see it, it is yours."

In my last hours with Shorty and Mr. Cosmopoulos, I pictured what I so desperately wanted. It was clear and shining and so real, I believed in it entirely. I saw my mothers together and happy again.

When Mr. C. gently explained that this might not be what my mothers wanted; that they might be happier apart, I resolved to convince my grandmother and the judge that I should live with Theo and visit Claire or live with Claire and visit Theo. I would settle for being like other divorced kids who lived with one parent and got to spend weekends and holidays with the other.

Still, I imagined my mothers together again, loving each other and me as they once did. There would be summers with Harry at the farm, trips to exotic places with my uncle Bax and Aunt Jess, visits with Shorty and Mr. C. whenever I pleased. I pictured myself riding a bicycle to a new school where there was no Carl Jacoby, no rich kids, no uniforms, where I wasn't seen as a curiosity.

On my last night underground, Mr. Cosmopoulos said some things can't ever happen the same way again and some things never happen at all. Asking for them can ruin what's left. I closed my eyes and summoned all the courage I could muster, ignoring the fear coiled at the bottom of the picture. I feigned sleep, knowing Shorty would not want me to see him sitting at the edge of my mattress, smoothing the blanket around me.

THE PLAN WAS for Mr. Cosmopoulos to walk me home. "No need to meet up with the wrong people," he had said. We had talked about my going straight to the store, to Theo, but decided that was too dangerous.

The police might be watching her, in which case they'd return me to Grandma's before I got a chance to talk to her. They might arrest Mr. Cosmopoulos for kidnapping. We discussed calling first, but abandoned that idea, too. Mr. Cosmopoulos said there is advantage in surprise.

It was a Thursday, the week before a custody hearing would take place, deciding whether or not two lesbians would be allowed to care for a minor and still absent child. Mr. Cosmopoulos read it to me from the newspaper. "Mrs. Mary Hirsh, the child's socialite grandmother, believes her grandson was removed from her apartment by a group of women who drugged the housekeeper, Lucille Thomas, who usually escorted the boy to the exclusive McCall School. These women, Mrs. Hirsh believes, tricked the boy into lacing the housekeeper's coffee with an undisclosed substance."

Mr. C. frowned into the page, "Miss Thomas is quoted as saying, 'Willy wasn't himself that morning and could have been "under the influence."' Danforth Cowperthwaite III, a building resident stated he had just arrived at the main entrance after his morning run as young William was exiting the lobby. Mr. Cowperthwaite said he became suspicious when the child did not return his greeting and seemed to be struggling with an overly heavy school bag. When questioned, Mr. Cowperthwaite stated the boy had previously been extremely well behaved and conceded drugs could have been responsible for William's unusual behavior on the morning in question.

"Theo Bouvier, founder of The Latest Dish, the popular East Side eatery and catering service, is the child's natural mother. Claire Hirsh, a prominent photographer and daughter of Mary and Barnaby Hirsh, also claiming to be the boy's mother, had been missing for several months and is believed to be withholding information regarding the boy's whereabouts.

Mr. Cosmopoulos snapped the paper shut and letting it fall in a rustling pile at his feet. "People will make up anything to keep themselves from seeing what's right in front of them, won't they?"

Shorty repaired my duffel bag with masking tape and some pins donated by Mrs. DeVries, and Mr. Cosmopoulos folded my clothes in a neat stack, including a shirt of his, the one that had been wrapped around my pillow. "Make you think of us down here."

I walked to Thelma's alone. The tracks were familiar now and the dark tunnel no longer held any fear. I had gotten used to the constant rumble of traffic overhead, the scurrying of other residents, more terrified of me than I of them, and the faint *plop, plop* of water echoing in the damp walls. It was all as commonplace as the smooth hum of the elevator and the thumping bass of the stereo in the apartment above ours. In an odd way I felt more protected here than anywhere else.

"You must stay longer next time," Thelma said as she planted a kiss on both sides of my face. "I'll have a cocktail party and invite *everyone!*"

"Good-bye, Mrs. DeVries," I said, remembering what Theo taught me to say when someone invited me to their house. "Thank you for everything."

"Do write with news of Jack."

"I will."

When it was time to leave, Shorty fussed with my coat collar, pulling it up to my ears.

"Gonna snow up there," he said, giving me a nod that felt like a salute. That was all it took to slip the loose knot of my resolve not to cry. I looked at a point above his head. It had only been two weeks, but I felt safe with the little man, knew where I stood with him, even if that was directly in the path of his stormy temper.

"Get outta here," he said, and turned away.

We climbed "upstairs" for the last time. Mr. C. said it was a shame I was leaving now that I could take them two at a time. He lifted the heavy metal plate that served as our front door. "You're a regular mountain goat, mister."

Jimmy called to me from his newsstand. "Hey kid, you must have done something pretty special to deserve that."

"Deserve what?"

The wind bit off his answer.

We turned the corner and walked into our reflections in the barred window of what used to be a furniture store, the wind banging a tattered "For Sale or Lease" sign against its padlocked plate-glass door. What greeted me was a big man with wild black hair, and a boy, hands jammed in his pockets, shoulders reaching for his ears in the biting cold. The boy was taller than I remembered, or maybe just thinner, and there was a new seriousness in a face framed in copper. He carried the duffel, mended and packed to within an inch of its seams, with a new ease. Something gold shone from the front of his coat.

Shorty's Purple Heart.

"I told you he liked you," said the taller reflection.

It was bone-rattling cold, pewter sky full of snow and wheeling gusts. Mr. Cosmopoulos and I traveled uptown via his secret underground route, which I now understood was the reason he moved around the city so fast. We did this to stay warm and to avoid cops. Cabs drifted slowly against the curbs. I knew they were sometimes driven by detectives in plainclothes.

I made Mr. C. promise to visit, no matter where I ended up, no matter what happened, just like before. He said he would, but we both knew it might be impossible, for a while, anyway.

We had been walking alongside the subway tracks in an abandoned tunnel used only by repairmen when we saw light flickering eerily against the white tile of the station in the distance, heard the rumble of an oncoming train, and felt the receding safety of darkness at our backs. It was only a few short blocks to Central Park West from the subway entrance on Columbus. We agreed that Mr. Cosmopoulos would go up first.

"I'm going to Jersey after I drop you off," he said, just before we reached the platform and blended in with the crowd pressing toward the approaching train.

I nodded dumbly. I didn't want him to see how much it hurt to know he was planning his time without me, that he had already moved on, that it was easier for him than it was for me.

"Gonna visit my boy."

He was looking at me squarely now. No vacancy, no tugging on his ponytail to clear the fog that rolled in from his brain and kept him from seeing where he was going.

"Used to think he was better off without me. Figured if he thought I was too busy to see him, he'd stop looking. He wouldn't end up finding out his father is really a bum who lives hand to mouth in a tunnel with a shell-shocked wino."

"Shorty is not a wino!" I shouted, surprised at what I felt for the grumpy man with the wooden leg, remembering how he let me touch the stump one night and how it felt exactly like real skin that had been neatly folded over where there was extra. "He's on the wagon," I said.

I saw Mr. C. doing what Theo used to do, picking a fight with Claire so it would be easier to accept her leaving, and I wasn't going to let him off that easy.

"I wish you were my father."

"Yeah, I know, mister," he said. "Maybe my boy will, too."

He wrapped me in a bear hug that forced all the air out of my lungs and before I could draw an even breath, I was on the street and he was gone. Just like in the old days, when I turned away for a second and the street was empty save his words shivering in the trees.

I walked the last few blocks alone.

Andy saw me first. He abandoned his post, gold braid lifting away from his shoulders as he ran to see if I was real.

He thumped me against his thick greatcoat. "Jesus, Mary, and Joseph! I thought you were—" He didn't finish. "Oh, look at you!" He scooped up my bag and swept me off the sidewalk, into the paneled lobby of our building. With one hand on my cold cheek and the other on the intercom, he rang our apartment.

"It's a miracle, Miss! It's Willy come back!"

A popping sound, like a shriek, then a higher, angry sound, suspicion, disbelief.

"Yes. Yes. He is. He's right here. He's really here!"

Andy shouted into the mouthpiece, beamed down at me, and thanked God all at the same time. "Just now! No, he's alone. Yes! Dropped out of the sky he did, like a regular angel!"

I ducked out of Andy's grasp and bolted for the elevator.

The car moved in slow motion, approached our floor, and seemed to take an eternity to line up with the other door. I heard our apartment door flung wide, its security chain banging against the dead bolt. The slap of bare feet running. Bacon frying somewhere. My name bowled across the empty hallway. "Willy! Willy!"

"Oh my God," she cried, reaching in to grab my outstretched arm. "Willy, my baby, oh, thank God!" She was crying and I was crying, from relief, from the cold, from the shock of seeing her.

Claire.

22

W here did this come from?" Claire asked.
"I found it."

"Honey, it's extremely unusual for someone to lose a Purple Heart. People keep them forever. In fact, most people would rather starve to death than sell theirs."

Patting me down for broken bones, hugging, grinning and crying all at the same time, she'd spotted the medal glinting out from under the collar of my jacket.

"Where did you find it?"

"Under the sidewalk."

I held my breath for the next question, the one that would expose me as a liar, but I was spared for the time being. Claire was somewhere else.

I was home, but the apartment seemed different. The long corridor of photographs, the French doors with their beveled panes revealing a slice of the comfortable room beyond, soft pillows scattered everywhere, the big sofa that swallowed people whole, the pale sweep of floor where Claire and Theo kicked off their shoes and danced to Chubby Checker, black-and-white kitchen tile, red Parsons table, my loft, with its canopy of clouds, planets and stars; it was all as I remembered, but diminished somehow, and tinged with sepia as if already history.

The afternoon turned from gold to umber and this shift from night to day heightened my sense of unease. Shadows brushed the legs of chairs, crept across the rug, and inched up to the crown moldings. I wondered, *Am I really here? If not, where in the parallel universe am I?*

When Claire was satisfied I was whole and unhurt, she called Theo.

"Yes! He's here! He's fine. No! Don't tell anyone yet. Let's just have him to ourselves. No. Not even him. *Especially* not him."

Claire gave me the receiver out of which Theo's happiness overflowed. "Is that really you?"

"It's me, Mama. Come home soon."

"Put on your mom, again, okay?"

I laid my head against Claire's as if to hear Theo through her. Up close, Claire looked pinched. The latticework of tiny lines seemed to have multiplied, giving her skin the look of one of Grandma Hirsh's crackled vases. From this angle, I could read the newspaper clipping on our bulletin board. The headline over my face said, "Boy Missing in Lesbian Custody Battle." Next to it was a scrap of paper with the name of a Detective Maloney and two phone numbers, scrawled in Theo's loopy hand. It seemed odd seeing a stranger's name up on our board, knowing he was probably still looking for me at that very moment.

A cardboard box with a mailing label from the McCall School was sitting on the counter, stuffed with cards and notes and clippings. I wondered who there would willingly write to me. I imagined them in art class, biting the tops of their pencils and wondering how little they could get away with doing.

I got the feeling Claire was as dislocated as I. We waited for Theo to come home as though we couldn't begin without her. She ran her thumb around Shorty's Purple Heart.

"You know, I tried to find one of these for your mom, for putting up with me, but I couldn't. Uncle Baxter called the dealers who buy medals and military paraphernalia and they all said they'd keep an eye out for him, but not to count on one turning up, nobody ever lets these things go."

I wondered if they ever found Shorty's leg after it was blown off, if the President had come to the hospital to pin the medal on his pajamas, why the heart was purple and not red for blood, and what Theo had done to earn hers. But mostly, I wondered why Shorty had given me his.

"We thought someone had kidnapped you," Claire said. "We thought you were dead."

Claire almost never cried, preferring to make jokes to cover up her feelings, not that she fooled any of us, so when she did cry it was pretty serious. Her hands began to tremble. A red blotch moved across her face and up her neck. Tears never arrived quietly with Claire, the way they did with Theo. "A good cry is like a soaking rain," she always said, blowing her nose afterwards. "Everything is washed clean, "she'd say, punctuating her lesson with a loud and final honk.

Not Claire. Claire cried in a purple violent way. For her, it was a struggle lost. It was she who taught me it's easier to be angry than vulnerable. Because of her, I believed tears could run out and needed to be hoarded.

She didn't fight it that day. She cried in a big sloppy way, wetting both our shirts, and this was how I knew she really did love me.

"I didn't know you were gone until I visited Grandma Doris and Grandpa Roy and they told me," said Claire, wiping her eyes. "I thought you were right here with your mother the whole time. If I had known, I never would have stayed away."

I wanted her to say she had come home because she still loved Theo and wanted us to be a family again. I didn't want her back just for me, I wanted her back for us, and I wondered how long she would stay this time.

"Grandma said if I stayed with you and Mama, I'd never get married. She said I'd grow up queer. That's why I got arrested."

"Oh, Willy Wonka, you weren't arrested. You have to do something bad to be arrested, like rob a bank or hurt somebody."

"Grandma and Grandpa said we broke the law. Judge Bailey thinks so, too."

Claire jumped, eyes wide. "How do you know Judge Bailey?"

"He came over to Grandma's apartment for dinner."

She shot a disgusted look at the window as though Grandma could see it on her side of the park. "That will be your mistake, Mother dear." She said something else, too, under her breath so I couldn't hear, but did. *Bitch.*

"You didn't break the law, baby. We did. Your mama and I. But we didn't hurt anybody and, of course, you'll grow up and fall in love with somebody wonderful and get married like your uncle Baxter and uncle Peter. But if you grow up like your uncle Thad and find someone as wonderful as his Alan, that's okay too. He wasn't bad for loving your uncle Alan. Just different. Do you understand that?"

Just then, keys fumbled in the lock, the front door swung wide on its hinges and Theo was with us in a second, crying and hugging and tumbling me over like the mother bear at the zoo. Claire smiled through a face full of spots and cried some more.

When Claire told Theo she was going to break one of my ribs looking for injuries, we all laughed; then the room got quiet and we held on to one another for a long time. When we finally let go, the lights in the park had come on and the shadows had crept past us, swallowing up the room. We switched on the lamps to make sure we were all still there.

For a little while, we were *Claire, Theo, and Wee Willy, One for All and All for Three* the way we were before all the trouble. That night Claire and I watched Theo grate cheese, chop tomatoes, sauté mushrooms and flip our omelettes. I think we believed if one of us left the room, we'd all disappear. I wondered what Mr. Cosmopoulos and Shorty were eating and whether they were entertaining a special visitor named Gabe. I thought of tipsy Jimmy the Scoop at the newsstand, Leroy at the coin-op, watching for trouble in every laundry bag, Dimitri's neatly wrapped cartons of steamed rice and kung p'ao chicken on the steps out back of Fong's, and Raul's mean-looking mouser who never let me pet him, but always knew when Shorty was cooking. I thought of all the people who'd stopped by one by one first to say hello, then to say good-bye.

I was too glad to be home to miss my new friends that first night, but as Theo moved from cupboard to stove with practiced ease, Claire laid our bright plates down on the red lacquered table, and we scooped Rocky Road straight out of the half-gallon tub, I couldn't help wondering if Thelma pretended to eat when she was alone, too, and not just when she had company.

Up in my loft, I opened every drawer looking for the smell of my old life. I touched my schoolbooks, tennis racquet, pencils, paints, and old toys abandoned among the dust bunnies on the closet floor, among them the dusty G.I. Joe Uncle Baxter sneaked into my room one Christmas, ordering me not to tell anyone I had a war doll or they'd kill him. My "Peanuts" sheets were neatly folded in the big chest the window and my secret shoebox was undisturbed. In it, I found a stone from Uncle's Peter's field, a cowrie shell from our trip to Aruba, and the tooth I found dangling from my pocket the day I punched Carl in the face Only after this ritual touching and examining of things did I truly feel at home; only then did the faint parchment color that clung to the edges of the furniture finally recede.

I SLEPT between them in the big bed that night, and where I once fit neatly, I was now all arms and legs and protruding sharp angles, an ungainly anchor they held onto for dear life.

No one else knew I was home. And for a short while, our lives stood perfectly still. Claire had not left. Grandma had not taken me. I had not run away. And Mr. Cosmopoulos and Shorty were part of a dream I remembered in fragments. Only Mr. Kimsky knew better, up there in his frame on the dining room wall, locked in a chess match with a mysterious shadow. I imagined he winked at me, knowing I was the only one who knew he was a war hero; somebody who pretended he didn't like you when he really did, a man who had promised himself a hot dog at Nathan's when the game was over.

Theo got Grandma Doris and Grandpa Roy out of their bed in Broken Arrow to hear the good news and me out of mine to prove she wasn't just dreaming.

"We've got to tell Detective Maloney that Willy's home," Claire said.

"What's the harm having one more day to ourselves?" Theo asked.

"The harm is he's going to find out soon enough and it would be better if he didn't start out pissed off," Claire said. They called him. Next was Grandma Hirsh.

"No, you can't come over and see him," hissed Theo into the receiver. "I don't give a damn that you were worried. In fact, I hope you never see him again. You drove him away, you stupid old woman. You're lucky I'm letting you know he's alive."

"That's my mother you're talking to," said Claire as Theo stared at the phone she had just slammed down.

"I don't care if she's the Queen of England. She's trying to take our son away from us. *Your* son away from *you*." Theo snapped.

"I didn't mean it that way, Theo. I just thought we should be civil. Maybe she'll drop the whole thing now that he's back," Claire said in a placating tone.

But there was too much anger roiling on Theo's relief.

"Oh, really, just like that? And where have you been all this time—the moon? I've been here, Claire. Out of my mind with worry, sick with fear, while you were God knows where."

Theo's words cut deep and Claire trembled.

"I know, Theo. And I'm sorry.

Claire turned to me. "We can only hope Grandma will let you stay here, right, Mr. William Bouvier-Hirsh?"

Until that moment, it hadn't occurred to me I might have to go back.

Jessica and Baxter arrived unexpectedly.

"Doris phoned us this morning," said Uncle Bax. "Sorry we didn't ring first. I closed the store. We just wanted to be here with you. Aunt Jessica, dressed in one of the black suits she always wore to work, picked invisible lint off my sweater, and made sympathetic clucking sounds. She shot Claire a black look that said, "It's about time you got back."

The doorbell rang again.

"We thought Suzie and Thaddy should know," said Baxter, looking sheepish.

I had forgotten how much Aunt Suzie glittered in the daytime. She swept me up into a blaze of sequins and kept me in a hammerlock until the need for one of her Nat Sherman's took over and she grinned at me from the open window where Theo demanded she station herself.

"He didn't get killed on the street and I'm not going to let you murder him right in his own living room with those disgusting cigarettes," said Theo, tossing Suzie a chipped saucer to use as an ashtray. "This is the one Claire uses when she thinks I'm asleep."

Theo asked Uncle Thad if he knew any really good lawyers and he flew into action. Thad sat at our table all day, flipping through pages inked with people's names and phone numbers, stopping every now to sip the coffee Theo served him. He spoke in urgent whispers, encouraging the listener to "do everything possible." I got the feeling he was very much at home in the center of our trouble and maybe even enjoyed all the excitement a little. It had been a long time since he felt so needed.

Aunt Molly brought a pie and wore a troubled look. Uncle Peter said the traffic on the expressway was terrible and when he saw my disappointment that Harry hadn't come, he said, "maybe next time."

They too, joined the huddle, which grew with every announcement from Andy.

Theo picked her way through our crowded living room carrying bowls of chips and platters of chicken sandwiches, and refilling empty glasses, but she did so without her usual gusto. The thin skin under her eyes had a bluish cast, and her usually creamy complexion seemed waxy and slightly yellow. She looked tired, but in a way that seemed deeper and more permanent, and would take more than a few nights' sleep to fix.

I was painfully aware of the fact that I was the focus of all this, but once our friends got over their excitement at seeing me alive, they seemed to forget I was there. The talk centered on the hearing and on the chances they had of winning, which were thought to be very slim, especially in light of all the publicity, which I came to learn had been considerable and damaging in my absence. Theo's business had fallen off dramatically, and a perverse fascination with Claire's sex life had eclipsed interest in her art, according to a down-in-the-mouth Suzie.

At some point, Detective Maloney arrived and questioned me directly regarding my whereabouts.

"I was under the street," I said.

"Exactly which street were you under, son?" he asked, waiting patiently for a real answer, tapping an open notebook that was already filled with other people's answers.

"I don't know," I said. "It was dark."

"Were you alone?"

"No."

More tapping. The detective wore his coat indoors, just like in the movies.

"Who were you with?" he continued.

"My friends."

"Would you like to tell me their names?"

"If I don't tell you, will you arrest me?" I had seen enough episodes of *Columbo* to know that policemen ask you innocent questions, and then trick you into a confession before you even know what is happening.

"No, son, I won't arrest you."

"Then no."

"No, what?" said Claire from across the room.

"No, sir," I said. "I wouldn't like to tell you their names."

Theo stopped talking to Uncle Peter and exchanged a puzzled look with Claire.

"Why, honey?" she asked, moving toward me, concern squeezing her brows into commas.

Everyone waited for my answer as if they had just realized I was there. And then I said something I'd heard Aunt Jessica say once. "If I tell, it won't be a secret anymore, will it?"

No one laughed the way they did when she said it. No one even smiled. And Theo ordered me upstairs to think about being fresh to Detective Maloney. My face burned with shame. If she'd been half as loyal to Claire as I was to Shorty and Mr. C., none of this would have happened.

I banged my fist against the door to keep from crying.

"I hate you! And I hate you! And I hate lesbians!"

Theo's face crumpled. I knew I was hurting her, but I couldn't stop.

"You made Mom leave and you're going to make her leave again! I'm not telling on my friends because they'll get in trouble. And if they make me live with Grandma, I'm going to run away again!"

Claire had rushed to me, but I pushed her away.

"Why did you leave us?" I cried.

Uncle Baxter waited a few minutes, and then followed me up the stairs to my loft, leaving a gasp of adults behind me. By the time he got there, I felt better, lighter, like everyone who has ever let go and experienced the temporary exhilaration of knowing his burden has moved to another shoulder.

"You've got a pretty good reason to be mad, kiddo," he said. "But if they weren't lesbians, they'd be something else you didn't like."

I wondered what could be worse than having two mothers nobody liked and who now didn't even like each other.

"My mother and father didn't get along, either," said Uncle Bax. "They told my brothers and sisters they stayed together for us, but they weren't fooling anybody. Instead of being honest with each other and doing what was right, even if that meant separating for a while to think things through, like your mothers are trying to do, they made all of us miserable. It's not your fault, sport."

"Uncle Bax . . ."

"Right here."

"Does Grandma hate us?"

"Far from it. She really thinks she's doing what's right. And if you ask me, and nobody has, I think she's afraid that if your moms get divorced, Theo will take you away from Claire and from her. She doesn't know Theo like we do, right?"

Just then I wanted to ask Uncle Baxter the question I told myself I would never ask anybody, but I didn't. I would never ask that. I would never let anybody see how much they could hurt me with the answer. Instead, I told him a secret to see if he would keep it.

"When Mr. Cosmopoulos's father married someone his grandmother didn't like, she never spoke to him again even though they lived on the same island. She wore black and acted like he was dead. Mr. C. says she was a stoic, which he said is another word for stubborn."

"Mr. Cosmopoulos is your friend, isn't he, the man I met in Sheridan Square that day?"

I nodded.

"I thought so," he said. "I'll go tell them you're sorry, okay?"

"Okay," I said, not quite sure I was.

What I was sure of is that everyone takes you seriously when you draw a line in the sand that says, "Cross this and there will be consequences." I was beginning to see that anyone can do it, even a kid, as long as people get the idea you really mean it. I think they knew that if they made me live with Grandma, I would run away as many times as it took. They didn't push me after what I said to Detective Malone.

23

Theo had wanted a man to represent us. She said it would look better if a man stood up for a mother fighting to keep her child. Claire did not agree. She wanted an activist, someone who was passionately committed to the plight of lesbians and who was a mother herself, a feminist, preferably, who wouldn't think twice about involving the American Civil Liberties Union, or even the Supreme Court, if necessary.

Claire hovered at the edge of the command post Theo and Thad had set up at our dining room table. "Don't you mean *mothers* plural who are fighting to keep *their* child?" She said this with a quick jab aimed at Theo.

Theo did not rise to the bait.

"If a man speaks on our behalf it will be construed as acceptance. We will blatantly play on the judge's paternalistic instincts, which I'm sure he possesses in larger portion than most men, being a judge and all." Theo. "Bax says Louis Andrew is a killer."

"We need a lawyer, not a hit man," Claire said stubbornly. "Ruth knows a woman who's represented some of the people from the Stonewall riots."

"This is not a publicity case for some lesbian Ralph Nader whose only claim to fame is representing a man's right to wear pantyhose. This is our son. We want to win."

Thad looked up from his telephone book. "She's right, Claire. Much as I hate to agree, this is war. You need a nice heterosexual Connecticut lawyer with a wife and two kids, someone the judge knows for a fact is virile and middle-class. And who is as well connected as they come. With all due respect, you really don't need some storefront bleeding heart, the likes of whom said 'piece of cake' last time, as I recall."

"Who asked you, Thad?" said Claire.

CLAIRE SAID Theo was selfish and insensitive to the fact that this was a precedent-setting case; a favorable outcome could produce a new legal definition of family. Theo accused Claire of politicizing our problems, of making something very private into a public circus.

Theo fled to her kitchen, producing meals with the determination of a line worker. Her anger assumed the steady thunk of the oven, refrigerator, and pantry doors.

Claire retreated to her darkroom, where new images took shape. There were grizzled bikers and the hard bitten women who rode with them, truckers sporting Road Runner tattoos and nicotine-yellow teeth, posing in front of their rigs, mud flaps and wheels big as a man, sporting names like *Rosie* and *Lurleen* in curlicues of gold leaf. Men who washed and shaved in public restrooms and spoke of the road with the reverence of lovers

"I dunno," Claire had said when I asked her how come they let her in the men's room for the one I like best. Two men, two pairs of eyes, two white Jockey T-shirts, looking back from two mirrors, each one reflecting a face full of soap, two stainless steel razors, held as delicately as teacups, scraping the highway off sunburned necks, a radio on the shelf between them.

Claire's pictures told me more about where Claire had been than she wanted to say. One in particular—a waitress in a tight uniform winking across the counter of a diner—held the power to disturb. When Theo saw it, a tiny muscle in her cheek twitched and she stared at Claire so hard, Claire had to turn away.

We hired Alice Coombs, who'd represented Uncle Thad against the insurance company that dropped Uncle Alan when he got sick. We hired her not because Theo conceded to Claire, but because no one else would take our case.

"Honey, you can't get better than Alice—whip smart, top ten at Columbia Law. She took on Alan's landlord once, and the guy didn't know what hit him," Uncle Thad had said. "I don't know whether it's because of a defective gene, boring parents, or a childhood spent at math camp, but she has absolutely no sense of humor. Not that we need Bette Midler at a time like this."

Alice stared down a punch line the way most people look at bad food. The day she came over to take statements from Baxter and

Jessica, Thad, Suzie, and Peter, Claire slid her arm around Theo's waist as she introduced Alice to the shuffling group.

"From now on, it would be a good idea to avoid any public displays of affection," the dour lawyer had said, ignoring the offered hands, "especially where the other side might see you."

"I guess that rules out French-kissing in front of the judge," Claire said.

"Claire, for God's sake, this is no time to be funny," said Theo, but grinning anyway, grateful for a reason to smile.

Alice's waited for the nervous laughter to die down, and kept talking, giving no sign that she understood, as we all did, that my mothers were very nervous.

Alice sat in our living room and talked with each person privately. She seemed dull and brown against the room's bright colors and the vivid parade of our friends.

Suzie went first. Alice did not respond to Suzie's nervous patter, and glared when Suzie reached into her purse for one of her Nat Shermans.

"I always smoke when I'm cross-examined," Suzie said from the interior of her enormous bag, announcing the hunt for her lighter with the clatter of bracelets against leather.

"I'd prefer it if you didn't," said the unsmiling Miss Coombs, warning Suzie of private detectives, tape recorders, phone taps, and other dirty tricks from any number of professionals hired by my grandmother to report any "unsavory activities a small boy might be exposed to."

Alice pelted her with questions about her marriages and relationships, why they were so frequent and short-lived. An uncomfortable Suzie described her business dealings with Claire, and her relationship with me, and with obvious discomfort, her sexual preferences. Alice asked these things flatly, with no regard for their effect on poor Suzie.

"It would be very good for Claire and Theo to have a character witness whose own character cannot be impugned," Alice said, frowning into her notes.

"Well, I'm a character, all right," laughed Suzie.

When Aunt Jessica came out, she sighed in that way she had of dismissing people who did not interest her. "She's a hopeless frump."

Claire rolled her eyes.

"Yes, I know, Claire: What has fashion got to do with this serious problem? Please don't take this the wrong way, but she dresses like one of those awful dykes and, if she looks like that in court, we haven't got a prayer. Appearances count, whether you like it or not."

Uncle Baxter put it another way. "She's just very smart and very dull and has absolutely no charm or social skills at all. But we're hiring a lawyer, not a cheerleader.

Thad looked stung when he reappeared in the dining room. Alice had been blunt. "It would be better, given your obvious homosexuality, not to come to court." He tried to pretend it didn't hurt.

I didn't like Alice, either.

When Theo told her about the afternoon Miss Rodriguez came to the apartment to take me to Grandma's and the cop was so horrible, humiliating her, threatening her, Alice never once said, "That must have been terrible." Even when Theo got to the part that always made her cry, when the cop reached for his gun in the hall in front of our neighbors, who have gone out of their way to avoid her ever since and how afraid she was that she might never see me again, Alice just kept writing.

She'd look up every now to say, "I see . . . Yes . . . What happened then? . . . Go on," then write some more, chew the inside of her lip, as she filled up one blue tablet after another with our answers.

When she completed the interviews, none of it seemed to have anything to do with us anymore. Her words were stiff and formal—words like "rules," "writs," and "versus" this and "versus" that—and there were no pauses in which to look away from the page and draw meaning from the pictures they formed. Anytime a voice wavered slightly, an eye shined suspiciously, or a coffee cup betrayed a trembling hand, Alice would fix her gaze on her ever-present legal pad, and twist the top of her black-and-gold pen until it was over.

Alice didn't understand anything that wasn't a fact; she liked to talk about things people did, not what they felt. I asked her why nobody called the police when Jeffrey Tannenbaum's mother didn't tell his father and his new wife she had left Jeffrey home alone with the maid for a month when she went to Switzerland to have an operation on her face. And why they didn't take Henry Paste away from his dad who let him stay all by himself at the Pierre and order anything he wanted from room service in return for not telling his mother that two girls named Cindy and Irene were living in his apartment. But she just looked down at her pad.

Alice listened politely to my mothers and to our friends and to Grandma Doris and Grandpa Roy, who flew in a few days after I got ome, but I could tell she thought they were all nuts. She narrowed her eyes at Uncle Peter when he insisted the trouble was Claire's childhood and not feeling loved as much as their dead brother and when he explained that he never knew of his mother's intention to petition the court for custody until it happened.

I told her how Theo was so upset at what Carl's grandmother did that she cut her hand and had to go to the emergency room for stitches and that Claire drove all night and slept on plastic chairs in the airport when she found out I was gone. Theo closed the store so they could help Detective Maloney search for me. Grandpa Barnaby had stopped talking to Grandma while I was there because he couldn't stand what she was doing to our family. Aunt Jessica sent Roy and Doris airline tickets, so they could come to New York to fight for their grandson and "tell that woman off." But Alice said these things were irrelevant. I didn't understand how you could show how much we wanted to stay together without telling these things to the judge, but Alice wasn't the slightest bit interested in my opinion. Whenever I tried to tell her how things really were, she tapped her pen and waited for someone to explain to me that lawyers don't discuss cases with children.

The other problem was that Alice never smiled. She just drew her lips tightly against her teeth, the way some people did when they met us for the first time and pretended to like us.

* * *

CLAIRE KEPT our record albums under the stairs, near the darkroom. She loved listening to chamber music while she worked in the darkroom, which, I suppose, is why I thought judges' chambers were a series of secret rooms where important cases were discussed while someone played the cello. I soon learned chambers weren't anything special at all, or even plural for that matter. *They* were really just a singular stale-smelling office with a water-stained ceiling in a heavily trafficked corridor of the courthouse. The only music, if you can call it that, was static of a police radio coming in from somewhere on the other side of a transom. Chambers had a row of cracked Venetian blinds shielding the windows from the felons, detectives, jurors, and marshals loitering in the din outside.

On the way to this dirty peeling place, I was told the judge would listen to the arguments each side would present in court before deciding where I had to live until I was "emancipated." In the ammonia-choked hallway, I saw a bride in a tight, sequined dress and a groom in a lavender tuxedo surrounded by sullen relatives who did not look pleased with the match. And even though I knew it wasn't polite to stare, I could not pull my eyes away from a man with grizzled hair and woolen cap and a scar that rode his cheek from earlobe to nostril, carved an angry furrow across his forehead, dropped down through mutton chop sideburns, and appeared again at the edge of his bottom lip, before disappearing into the tangle of his beard.

If I looked like that, nobody would be telling me where to live, I thought as I heard the soft click of Claire's Leica behind me. She, too, saw the wedding party and the scarred man who would one day be memorialized as part of a larger work called Fighting City Hall.

"How can you be thinking about work at a time like this?" Theo asked Claire.

Claire held up Theo's finger, which wore six gold bands and a small plaster from a mishap with a paring knife.

"Look who's talking, the one who cooked all night with nobody coming to dinner."

We entered the large room, bare except for a series of bookcases painted a bilious green, its shelves buckling under the weight of thick law books emblazoned with gold-leaf spines. A dozen or so metal chairs had been arranged in haphazard rows fanning out on either side of a desk. The desk was piled high with several stacks of yellow manila folders, each one bearing bold black Magic Marker letters. One file had been separated from the rest, and set out like new pajamas on a plastic blotter in front of the judge's leather swivel chair. If I tilted my head, I could see the words, *Hirsh v. Bouvier.* A small plaque bore the name the *Honorable* Albert J. Shapiro; not the *Dishonorable* Bailey, who had come to dinner. Claire, Theo, and Alice slumped at the sight of it. When he entered the room, this judge did not smile as Judge Bailey had at my grandmother's table. This one looked at us with the kind of weary expression teachers wear when you're late for class.

Alice said Claire and Theo and I should take the seats to the left of the big desk. Grandma, accompanied by her lawyer, Chester Darlington, and that awful woman from Social Services, Miss Rodriguez, settled in the chairs to the right.

Grandma Doris was glaring at Grandma Hirsh, who was looking straight ahead pretending she didn't see. Grandpa Roy was holding Theo's hand; Uncle Peter was holding Claire's; and Suzie, Jessica, and Baxter, who had been asked to be character witnesses, took turns leaning forward to tousle my hair and tell me everything was going to be okay, which I did not believe for a minute. Alice sat in the chair closest to the judge's desk, scribbling furiously. Detective Maloney was there, too, but he stood in the back, so I couldn't tell which side he was on. When I saw him leaning against the door, squinting suspiciously at everyone in the room, I was glad Mr. Cosmopoulos hadn't come after all, even though I'd hoped he would.

In the newspaper Jimmy gave us, it said, . . . *The matter will be decided at a hearing set for March 9 . . .*

"You'd better be there, mister. You can't have people deciding things for you without speaking up for yourself." When I asked if he could come with me, Mr. C. went blank for a minute, then shook his massive head, setting the springs in his ponytail in motion. "Some things you've got to do on your own."

I knew he was right, but I was scared. Just before we left the apartment to go to court, I ran back up to my room and pinned my Purple Heart to the inside of my sweater where only I could see it, just in case Shorty was right when he told me the medal had the power to transform ordinary people into heroes.

Judge Shapiro was talking. Something about this matter being best resolved quickly, avoiding even more damage to the family than had already been done in the newspapers.

"We have a small boy here," Judge Shapiro continued, "an impressionable nine-year-old—"

"I'm almost ten," I corrected him, surprised to hear my voice lifting away from me.

"Thank you, William," said the judge in a tone that did nothing to soften the fact that he did not take kindly to interruptions, "and

I would appreciate not having to remove him from this important proceeding, which I understand he asked to attend. So I warn all of you: Anyone who disrupts the proceedings in any way, uses language or pursues any line of questioning I consider harmful to this child, can expect to be reprimanded, and held in contempt of this court, despite the informal nature of this venue. I will not tolerate offensive behavior. Is that clear?"

Alice and Mr. Darlington tilted their heads in assent.

"Well then, shall we proceed?"

Judge Shapiro looked squarely at Alice, and at Mr. Darlington, then back to Alice again the way Mom watched Theo and me play tennis, over the same half glasses Grandpa Barnaby wore to read *The Wall Street Journal*. I wondered where the jury was.

"This is not a jury trial. This is a hearing, which means I will hear all arguments for and against keeping William in the custody of his mother, Miss Theodora Bouvier, and her companion, Miss Claire Hirsh, and arguments for and against making permanent the temporary custody granted by family court and the Child Welfare Department of the City of New York to his grandmother, Mrs. Mary Hirsh, for the reasons stated in the original court order obtained by said custodian and case worker Rodriguez of that department. I will hear all relevant arguments which will be recorded for the public record."

I looked around the room for places a jury could hide.

"Of paramount importance in rendering this decision is the welfare of this child and only the welfare of this child. I will award custody based on what I believe to be in his best interests. I have chosen to hear your arguments here in chambers in order to expedite the proceedings in open court, and in the hopes that we may reach a compromise, thus sparing the family the vicarious interest the public seems to have taken in the details of this case. If anyone has a problem with this, now is the time to say so. If not, we will proceed. I remind you all that despite the venue, we are in a court of law and my decision is legally binding to all parties. Anyone who fails to comply with my decision in this matter will be held in contempt and prosecuted in accordance with New York State law. Is that clear?"

More nods.

My heart pounded so hard, I was sure everyone could hear.

Judge Shapiro glanced toward the right side of the room. "Counsel?"

Mr. Darlington remained in his chair, but squared his shoulders and raised himself up from his waist in such a way that he gave the impression of standing. There was something too easy, too confident about this posture; it resembled the languid way gunslingers yawn in the face of a shoot-out. I imagined him practicing it in his room, over and over again until it looked as unrehearsed as an actor delivering his lines.

He cleared his throat quietly, the way Grandpa Barnaby did when he was ready to make a toast. He kept his hands perfectly still, resting them on the balls of his fingers. "I think it should be clearly stated that New York State does not recognize the intimate relationship between individuals of the same sex, and in fact, considers it a crime—one not prosecuted with any vigor, but nevertheless a crime."

Mr. Darlington's voice was like all the voices I heard when Grandpa took me to his club—reasonable, silky, cultured. If not for the content of his remarks, he would have sounded kind. His voice contained no clues about what its owner really felt and fell on us like smooth stones.

"Whether we agree with Miss Bouvier or Miss Hirsh's arrangement or not is irrelevant. I, for one, like to think consulting adults have a right to their privacy, even though I consider such behavior a sin against nature. My client, Mrs. Mary Hirsh, also considers herself a modern person, and has tried to be objective, even forgiving, in spite of the fact that her daughter's way of life has broken her heart."

Claire winced at this. Alice glowered.

He waited a beat for the reaction to this to register, never moving his eyes to where we sat. "We are not here today to pass judgment on these two women, much as some of us here may think that appropriate."

Now he turned and looked directly at my mothers; he'd known Claire since the day she was born.

"Your Honor, since the law does not recognize marriage between people of the same sex, there can be no discussion of custody for both women. The only issue here today is whether or not the natural mother, Theo Bouvier, and only Theo Bouvier, is considered fit to raise her son." He paused again to let this sink in. "My client submits that Miss Bouvier is not fit, and she does so with a heavy heart because the very basis of that charge rests squarely on the fact of her own daughter's lesbian relationship with Miss Bouvier, which has created an environment unfit for the raising of children and specifically of this child." He swept an arm in my direction.

Theo pinned my hand to her lap to keep me from reacting.

"Your Honor, Mary Hirsh understands her actions will cause her daughter much pain, but in spite of that, she cannot sit idly by and watch this poor child go through life scorned by his schoolmates, and to become sexually confused himself, just to protect her daughter's life-style."

Now Peter reached for Claire.

"Mary Hirsh has already raised her children," Mr. Darlington continued, smiling sweetly at my grandmother, "and at this time of her life, she should be enjoying her leisure years. Yet she is willing to take on the responsibility of child rearing all over again out of her love for this boy who believes her to be his grandmother. She asks that young William not be remanded to foster care as the law mandates in situations like this, but that the court make an exception and allow this woman of means to provide for this child she loves so dearly. We ask you, Your Honor, to grant Mrs. Hirsh sole custody of this boy, so that she might undo the damage that may already have occurred in that"—and here he paused, searching for a word that would give everyone the impression he was sparing the room his first choice—"in that *unhealthy* home, to direct her considerable resources to provide a wholesome atmosphere in which William can develop, grow, be educated properly and take his place in decent society. This gentle woman has had the courage to remove him from a home that would deny him that basic right. We will attempt to prove to you, Your Honor, that Theo Bouvier is, indeed, an unfit mother, and that granting custody to Mary Hirsh will ensure that he suffer no future abuse."

Everyone sat deathly still. Claire swallowed hard, but I could tell from the blotches blooming on her neck that it wouldn't be long before rage lost out to tears. Just then, Grandma Doris jumped right out of her chair and said, "Claire is as much that boy's mother as Theo is, but if you want to leave out my daughter-in-law, and that's exactly what Roy and I, our family and the Good Lord consider her, then fine, leave her out. I'm the boy's natural grandmother and if anybody should have custody, it should be family. And I'll make sure he knows what that word means."

"Shut up, Mom," Theo said without any real rancor.

"You've been warned," said Judge Shapiro. "One more outburst and I will clear this room."

Alice shot Doris a look, smoothed her jacket, and stood up.

Judge Shapiro looked directly at Alice. "Miss Coombs," he said mildly, "I am sure you are as eloquent a speaker as Mr. Darlington, but I would appreciate it if you would be a little less long-winded than your opponent. Otherwise William here will no longer be a minor by the time we settle this matter."

Alice, knowing she had just been put at a disadvantage, gave him a tight smile and leaned into the challenge.

"Your Honor, on behalf of my clients, Claire Hirsh *and* Theo Bouvier, *both* mothers of William Bouvier-Hirsh, one by nature of blood and the other by virtue of love, I am here to prove they are responsible, fit, and proper guardians for their son, William, despite their sexual orientation. And, I will further prove Mary Hirsh does not have the best interests of William at heart, but rather her own need to transfer her unresolved grief for her elder son, Roland, who was killed in a tragic auto accident many years ago, and whose death she has never accepted, to this child. Any psychologist will tell you such a situation is unhealthy and not in the boy's best interest."

Alice spoke like a machine gun spraying bullets into a crowd. Judge Shapiro shifted uncomfortably in his chair, knowing it was his fault he hadn't left her any room to sugarcoat things. But I knew Alice would never have done that, even if she had all day.

"And finally," said Alice, "I will prove Mary Hirsh accepted her daughter's life-style and had even welcomed Miss Bouvier into the family. Only when there was some difficulty in the relationship between the two women, and she feared she might lose contact with her grandson, did she suddenly and maliciously take this boy from his rightful and loving home under the pretext of her concern for his sexual orientation.

"Your Honor, these good women do not deserve to have their child taken away under any circumstances and it is certainly not in the best interests of this boy to be raised by an elderly woman who cannot distinguish between her dead son and her grandson, and whose motives for this sudden about-face after almost eleven years are questionable at best."

Alice paused to aim a dead smile at me.

"I will not only prove to you that these women are fit to raise their son, and *have* raised him with love, I will further submit proof that Mrs. Hirsh is unfit for such an important enterprise."

When Alice got to the part about Grandma not being able to tell the difference between Roland and me, there was a gasp, and just before the back of Mr. Darlington's suit jacket blocked my view, I saw my grandmother's trembling hand reach for her mouth. She looked old, her haughty bravado gone. She made a move to get up, but thought better of it and allowed Mr. Darlington to ease her back down.

At this, Judge Shapiro asked if there was anything further to discuss in chambers, if there was a way this case could be resolved to the satisfaction of all parties. Alice and Darlington each said, "No, Your Honor," and we moved through a side door into a cavernous courtroom. A man called Bailiff asked us to stand while he announced, "The honorable Albert J. Shapiro," and another tapped at a machine taking down everything that was said. A juror's box stood empty and a handful of people sat in the farthest benches, watching proceedings with the detachment of strangers on a bus.

One by one, people talked about my mothers. Aunt Suzie told about how when I was small Claire would bring me to the gallery in a papoose and turn her back on each picture and ask me what I thought of it. How Claire would look at the drawings I brought home from school and critique each one with the same care she gave to her photography students. She told them I never had a baby-sitter in my life because one of my mothers was always there, and most nights we all walked home through the park together.

"Could you tell us how many times you've been married?" asked Mr. Darlington.

"Is she going to count Duane?" I whispered to Claire, who told me she had been married five times if we didn't count Duane who only lasted a week.

Claire kept her eyes on Suzie, who hesitated and said, "Six."

After that, he asked her if she'd ever had a relationship with a woman. She said yes so softly, I almost missed it.

24

Right after Aunt Suzie said being with a woman had nothing to do with her subsequent divorces and that heartache and betrayal was not exclusive to one group or another, as evidenced by these proceedings, Alice jumped up and objected to Mr. Darlington's questions.

But the damage had already been done.

Judge Shapiro tilted his head in Mr. Darlington's direction and asked him to get to the point. After giving my grandmother a triumphant smile, he said, "I have no further questions, Your Honor."

Aunt Suzie was crying when she sat back in her chair.

Judge Shapiro, looking over tortoiseshell glasses, motioned me up to his desk.

"William," he said, "will you come up here. I'd like to speak with you privately."

I hesitated, fearing he would let Mr. Darlington speak to me the way he had to Suzie, first with respectful questions and then with accusations that did little to conceal his contempt for her friendship with Claire, which he seemed to imply was criminal in some way I did not grasp. I looked to Theo and then to Claire. Claire nodded yes and Theo tugged at the back of my sweater as I scrambled up on shaky feet.

"William, I know you wanted to be here today, but I would like your permission to ask you to sit outside while we ask these people some questions. We're going to talk about some things you may not understand and which may upset you and I think it would be better if I asked Mr. Darlington to take you outside for a while."

I knew I was supposed to do what the judge said, even if it was unfair, but I thought of Shorty's Purple Heart banging next to my own and swallowed hard. "But I want to be a witness, too," I said.

Judge Shapiro leaned toward me as though we were the only people in the room. "What if I promise to call you into a special session, just you and me? Then we can talk man to man and you can answer all my questions and tell me anything you like."

"Then nobody will hear what I want to say. Just you. And I *hate* Mr. Darlington," I said, loudly enough for everyone in the room to hear.

Judge Shapiro kept smiling, but I knew he was angry. I stood my ground and allowed the low murmur of approval and laughter from our side of the room to keep my wobbly legs from folding under me. "Tell you what," he said, "when I call you back, I'll call everyone back, too, so they can hear what you have to say. How's that?"

"Okay," I said without enthusiasm.

"Okay, what?" he said.

"Okay, Your Honor."

"Good," he said, as though we had just decided a critical point of law; then louder, in his droning judge voice, to everyone: "We'll take a fifteen-minute recess during which I ask that young Mr. Hirsh be made comfortable out in the hall or in my chambers."

Theo winced. "Bouvier-Hirsh," said Alice.

"You stood up to him, didn't you?" Claire said into my ear as she walked me to the door, Theo gripped my arm the way sailors do when they help you up the gangplank.

I watched everybody gather up coats and bags. Uncle Peter jammed his tweed cap into a raincoat pocket, and looked hunted. Uncle Baxter took Aunt Jessica's hand, snapped his trenchcoat over his shoulder and gave my grandmother a hard stare.

As we approached the door to the noisy hallway, Claire pressed her camera bag into my hand. "Hang on to this for me, okay? This will be over before you know it, and we'll all go celebrate over something disgusting and gooey at Serendipity."

Theo said nothing at all, just held me. In the borrowed black skirt and blouse, which didn't suit her at all, she seemed diminished without all her bracelets whose jingling was as much a voice as any. Claire looked silly and awkward in the ruffly white blouse Alice insisted would lessen her severity. They waved me off with forced smiles and worried eyes and disappeared back into the courtroom.

I would not wait in the enemy camp, as I considered Judge Shapiro's chambers to be and as I settled on the bench in the corridor, I felt a slight shift, a tiny thrust of power coursing through me. I sensed it came from something I had said, from some ground I would not relinquish. The feeling was not altogether unfamiliar, but lighter than the one that moved through me when my mothers fought, Claire went away. It did not sink down into my stomach, but fluttered like a trapped bird in my chest, up through my throat, into my ears, to the very roots of my hair.

They took turns sitting with me after they were called to testify. Aunt Jessica, Uncle Baxter, Uncle Peter, Grandma Doris, and finally Grandpa Roy, who told me he gave the judge a piece of his mind. We drank Cokes from a machine Uncle Peter kicked because it ate his quarters and he was mad already.

As I waited for my turn to talk to the judge, I thought about how I would stare straight at Grandma without blinking and would say my moms never did the things people said they did and sometimes we laughed about who I would marry when I grew up, how I promised Claire I would go anywhere for someone I loved, even to Brooklyn, but that I would go to college first.

Without giving away their address, I'd tell Judge Shapiro about Shorty and Mr. Cosmopoulos, how they took care of each other, checked on Thelma, and were a family, too, and that I would run away forever if he made me live with Grandma and Grandpa Barnaby.

I practiced how these words would feel when I said them, so fear wouldn't make me stammer or sound like a baby. There were other people I didn't know. Aunt Suzie said the man with a stuffed tan leather schoolbag and enormous eyes behind thick glasses, who was sitting off to one side of the door to the chambers, was a shrink and he was here to say I was showing signs of gender confusion.

"What's a shrink?" I asked.

"Somebody who can shrink an hour into forty-five minutes and charge you for two," she answered with a pull on her Nat Sherman, now out of its hiding place in her handbag. "Gender confusion is when you're a boy and think you're a girl and you grow up not knowing who to marry."

"I know I'm a boy," I said.

"I know that and you know that and your mothers know that, but that snake over there is going to tell the judge that because you have two mothers, you're not sure whether to wear an athletic cup or a training bra."

I decided to ask Judge Shapiro why my grandmother should be allowed to raise me if she already raised her daughter to be a lesbian. Wasn't it her fault and not Claire's? I would look him in the eye until he answered.

But I never got the chance.

The door opened and Claire said, "Alice will call when there is a decision. Let's go home."

"But I have to be a witness," I protested, digging my heels into the dirty floor. "I have to tell Grandma I don't want to live with her. I have to tell the judge I'm going to get married."

Theo slid an arm around my heaving shoulders. "He lied, honey. He just wanted you to wait outside."

"But it's my life!" I cried.

"I know, baby," she said.

IT HAD BEGUN to snow. While we slept, thick flakes floated on brittle air and began the slow and steady work of wrapping the city in a soundless cocoon. In the icy dawn, the storm flung daggers of sleet over the soft white baffle, and by the time a frozen March sun slithered up the side of our building, the paths crisscrossing the park were a treacherous latticework of ice.

Needles of light, the peanut-brittle sound of boots, the whine of tires spinning in place, the scrape of shovels and the hollow sound of empty garbage cans penetrated the thin membrane that had rolled down over the hours waiting for Judge Shapiro's decision and snapped it open like a broken shade.

Trapped in flannel, snared by the sheets and twitching furiously, my sleeping legs had failed me as they tried to run from Judge Shapiro, who wore the gap-toothed innocence of the killer in the newspaper who tore college co-eds apart with his bare hands. Fear coiled at the foot of my bed, ready to slide back into my gut like the spicy meatballs in the Alka-Seltzer commercial.

I dreamed there were twelve people arguing in a hotel room. Alice Coombs was there, scribbling furiously on her pale blue legal pad. My grandmother's gums dripped blood. A tall man with kind eyes and rusted hair stood behind a glass wall, saying nothing. I recognized him from other dreams, but the room stretched into a tunnel and at the end of it, where he stood, was a flickering light I could not reach. A fat Spanish woman complained bitterly of the cruelty of the others. She cried out and wiped her face with a large dish towel and with each pass of the cloth, a little bit more of her face melted until all that was left were greasy streaks of makeup mixed with blood and bone. Underneath the woman's sallow skin was another face, paler and more fragile, a wash of peach coloring, a dusting of freckles rode high on delicate bones; under the heavy Spanish hair, a flash of flame, another of flax, under soulful eyes of olive black, one iris of cool gray, the other the color of moss under a cold, rushing stream.

Slowly, the dream faded. Morning tugged at the bedclothes. A feeble sun tiptoed across my bedroom floor and peeled back the skin of sleep that had grown over the waiting, until nothing was left behind but the shrill insistence of a telephone.

Somewhere in the pounding heart of our apartment, an intake of air held beyond the normal rhythm of exhalation. The tape machine clicked on. "You have reached the Bouvier-Hirsh household. We'd love to—" A hand reached out in the dark. Whose?

"Yes?"

There was no sleep in Theo's voice, only heartbreak.

"I'm sorry," said Alice Coombs. It was March 11, 1975.

Sole custody. Visitation. One of my mothers could visit at a time, but never could they see me together. Words tangled up in sheets and pumping adrenalin. Forty-eight hours. Bench warrant. Contempt. Theo mouthed these unfamiliar terms in the direction of the bed, where Claire lay huddled in the duvet. I struggled to swim up through my confusion to understanding, but couldn't.

Still warm from bed, we staggered into the kitchen, more from habit than hunger, reeling from the news, seeking comfort in one another. I climbed into the chair and stared at the granola Theo had shaken into our bowls—yellow for me, red for her, blue for Claire; too bright for this day, too cheerful. We sat at the table for a long time without speaking, running our hands over the outlines of familiar objects, shooting suspicious glances at the phone as if it, too, had defected to my grandmother's camp.

Milk bubbled in a pitcher, a spoon stood unaided in the strawberry jam, forgotten overnight, a lone banana hemorrhaged under its mottled skin and no one moved to rescue the toast from the fire taking hold deep within the toaster's coils. Smoke drifted to the ceiling and stung our eyes as the toast curled and blackened.

Forgetting this was no ordinary day, Theo had picked up Tweety Bird. She drew him out of a deep pocket in the old blue chenille robe that once seemed magical to me, with its moon rising on one shoulder, stars twinkling on the arms. She held its chipped metal body in her hand as though it were alive. Before she had a chance to wind it up and pretend life had not been unalterably changed, I swept my arm across the silver key in Tweety's back and sent him flying across the tiles. He lay on his back, a bright puddle of yellow on the black-and-white floor, and from that distance, he looked for all the world like the baby sparrows that fall out of trees and die at your feet.

"We'll appeal," Theo said finally, thrusting her chin at Claire, who was sifting through her cereal bowl for answers. "We'll appeal and appeal and appeal again."

Claire and I both knew this was Theo's way of fighting the devastation we were all feeling, but we said nothing.

"*You* appeal to the court if you want," said Claire, breaking the mournful silence that had settled over us. She pushed her uneaten breakfast away, undid the top button of her pajamas, slammed back her chair so hard it wobbled for a second on its back legs before righting itself, and jabbed a finger at Mr. Kimsky as she strode past his picture, kitchen doors banging behind her.

"I'm going to start playing as dirty as my mother. And Peter is going to help whether he damn well wants to or not."

She marched through the living room and down the hall toward their bedroom and we dumbly followed, not wanting to be out of her sight.

"I'm not running this time," she said without turning around to look at us, knowing we were right behind her. "All my life I've let her defeat me. I really believed he was everything and I was nothing. She made sure of it. Every time I detected the faintest whiff of a problem, I split, got out of there before the inevitable happened and I got left. 'You are no good,' she said. 'You are second best,' she said. 'I loved *him*,' she said. 'I am stuck with *you*,' she said, with every condescending word, every all-suffering look, every judgmental sigh, every 'I wonder where he would be now, what he would have done with his life.' She can't do this."

Claire let the anger take her wherever it would.

"I know," Theo said. "It hurts so much . . . Go ahead, let it out. It's okay."

Claire wrapped her arms around both of us, drawing us in with surprising strength. "I thought you would leave me and I couldn't bear that, losing both of you. I ran because I didn't want to be hurt again. I'm so sorry."

I pretended I was on the ceiling watching us clinging to one another, willing myself not to cry.

"Well, that's not going to happen now," Claire said, stripping clothes off hangers, slamming drawers, grabbing bright balls of cotton out of her sock basket. We watched her slide the baggy flannel pajama bottoms and pull her tee shirt over her head, exposing collarbones delicate as bird wings. Her legs were muscled from years of walking the streets searching for pictures. She pulled on her thick red sweat socks and the faded blue jeans she claimed she wore to Woodstock.

She kept talking as the soft sound of flannel hit the floor.

"I'm going to pay old Uncle Peter a visit, because it's time for my baby brother to take a side. You know, he told me a long time ago, when I was so scared you'd leave, that you were just being a mother; that our fights didn't have anything to do with me. I didn't see it then, but now I do. I see what I have to do and God help him if he doesn't get it."

"Roland is dead and gone, goddamnit, and I won't let her get away with pretending he's Willy. That's what this is about, you know, her dead son. All my life, she looked so hard for him, she never even saw me, now she's ruining my son's life." She softened for a second and said quietly to Theo, "*Our* son's life." Then, to me: "Your life, my precious darling." And, back to the closet: "And I'm not going to let her get away it. No way. I'm not running anymore."

I caught a glimpse of her bending over a drawer and counted the buttons of her spine, one, two, three, four, five, six, the last two bruised a bluish yellow. I was surprised at how fragile she really was. She seemed so strong in her clothes, so capable.

"Dakota meant nothing to me," I heard Claire say to Theo, who had stepped inside the mirrored doors. "She just reminded me of you, in a sleazy kind of way. I was scared. And angry. And horny."

"I know," Theo said, tracing Claire's cheek with a fingertip. "I know."

As Claire spoke, she touched the hard kernel of something that had been growing inside my chest for a long time, something that was calcifying into the belief that she had left us because I wasn't good enough, because she really didn't love me—love us—enough, because Theo drove her away. But that hard something softened a little in the wake of words that were too raw, too naked to be lies, and I wondered how Mr. Cosmopoulos could have known her so well without ever having met her.

The plastic sound of a bra hooking in front, like a small toy breaking, tiny breasts shifting into place. Skin against silk, silk against cotton. Theo reached up to a shelf and brought down a fluffy mohair sweater and held it out to Claire. Theo had knitted it for her before I was born, when no one could have imagined this, when things were simpler and the notion that love could be held between two knitting needles was not so ridiculous. When she slipped it over Claire's upraised arms, something passed between them that had nothing to do with me, and I was warmed by this exclusion.

"For luck," Theo said.

"Phone Peter, let him know I'm coming," called Claire from their bathroom, where we huddled in the doorway watching her slap water on her face, running a wet comb through her sleep creased hair, then just sweeping it all up into a rubber band.

"Tell him it's time to decide. No more Mr. Good Son trying to make nice. Okay?"

We stood at the front door, Theo and I still in our pajamas, robes drooping, mine dragging its sash on the floor. Claire rooted through the closet for a coat, car keys, wallet; she instinctively reached for her camera bag, then shook off this reflex and stuffed only what was necessary into her pockets.

"If I saw the Pulitzer Prize photograph today, I wouldn't have time to take it," she said, letting the satchel slump back to the floor.

"I love you so much," Theo said, pressing her nose to Claire's the way Eskimos do, zipping up her parka to the plastic toggle that dangled a tiny thermometer.

"It's cold . . ." Theo said. Then, "I could never have left you. I never will."

I waited my turn. "I love you, too, Mommy."

Claire wrapped her arms around me and tugged, trying to lift me off my feet. "You're too big for this now."

I willed myself lighter so she could pick me up the way she did when I was small, so I could breathe the sleep in her hair, the soap-and-citrus smell that always reminded me of clean clothes.

The door as it closed softly, not angrily this time, but decisive, solid, like the sound of a fighter who has found his second wind and wrestles his opponent to the mat.

THEO AND I were curiously lighthearted after that. We knew that something good had happened and that because of it, everything would change. We believed in Claire's determination to save us, and this carried us out to the snowy park, past the lake and Bethesda Fountain, and all the way over to The Latest Dish, which Theo had closed for a few days; no one would think to look for us there. We decided to make apple and cinnamon muffins; my idea of helping was to eat one from each pan I drew out of the oven, finding the appetite I had learned to suppress with my friends underground.

Someone saw us moving in the kitchen and rang the bell. Theo pointed to the "Closed" sign, but the sight of some poor soul out in that hissing ice softened her resolve and she let him in for a free muffin. We watched him eye his good fortune with that mixture of gratitude and suspicion only New Yorkers possess.

"We've got to get out of this town," Theo said. I agreed.

We didn't talk about what Claire and Uncle Peter were doing, or how he was going to help her make Grandma let me stay with them. We just knew he would, so we discussed where I would go to school when I came home for good.

"Could I go to a school where there are other lesbians?" I asked as we nibbled the crunchy parts of the muffins where they had oozed over the tins and baked crisp.

Theo nuzzled my hair with her chin because her hands were sticky.

"If you want. But we'd have to do some homework, because schools don't exactly advertise that. Other parents might not send their kids there if they thought they'd be making friends with people who had two moms or two dads. You know, there are a lot of people like Mrs.

Jacoby and your grandma who don't like us because we're not the same kind of family as theirs."

I had heard this explanation before, but it didn't help. I had even asked Grandma herself how she could love us without liking us, but all she said was that I would understand when I grew up.

"Are there kids with two dads?" I asked, much more interested in this new information.

"Sure," she said, "lots."

"Cool."

"Why is that cool?" she asked without turning away from the sink where she was soaking the batter-encrusted tins. Her arms were full of soap bubbles.

"Well, if I went to a school with people who had two dads and no moms, I could borrow one of theirs and they could borrow one of you and then everybody could have one of each when they wanted to," I reasoned, feeling a small shiver of hope take hold at the thought of a school like that.

"What a good heart you have." Theo laughed. It was a good, solid sound that felt like sun on my face. I had not heard it for so long, and didn't realize how much I had missed it. Later, it would seem like the untroubled light that bursts from the eye of a storm.

"Why don't you want to tell me where you were when you ran away from Grandma's? I was really worried." She did not look up from the sink, but let the question float in the steamy air above it.

"I don't know," I said.

"Sure you do," she answered, reaching for the sifter, which bobbed on the surface of the water.

"Because I don't want my friends to get in trouble. Because the police would think they kidnapped me and they'd get arrested. And because if the judge makes me live with Grandma, I'll go there again."

I didn't tell her why I didn't come home to her instead; I think she already knew I had blamed her for what happened. She didn't press me, even though she had a right to.

When we got too close to the things that scared us, we talked about silly things like the time Aunt Suzie fell off the pony cart at the children's zoo and the day we all posed behind cutouts of Al Capone, Frank Nitti, and Elliott Ness and sent the picture out as our Valentine's card. We giggled about the time we hid Easter eggs in poor Andy's knapsack and he sat down hard, about last summer when we were sick of Theo making everything out of blueberries, about how Claire rolled up a ball of dryer lint from her bathrobe and stuck it in the toilet so Theo would think one of us made a blue poop and switch to another fruit. We laughed about the time Theo groaned and stuck out her belly and pretended she was practically in labor so we didn't have to stand in line at St. Pat's to say good-bye to Bobby Kennedy.

We didn't pay much attention as the temperature plunged, and the afternoon moved across the small kitchen toward a dangerous night. We felt safe just knowing that Claire was back and was fixing things, so safe we spoke of things beyond the immediate future of my new school, to a house in the country, a new store for Theo, what I wanted to be when I grew up.

In the shuttered store, the news of that morning seemed far away; we both knew we had turned a corner. We were together again, really together and we weren't going to wait for other people to decide our future anymore; we were marching right out to meet it and God help anybody who got in our way.

We weren't afraid of Alice and her doomsday voice filling us with dread and dire predictions, of Judge Shapiro and his cruel decision or that horrible woman from Child Welfare. Even the telephone had lost its power to terrorize as it sang out from time to time, breaking the comfortable silence in the store. So when we heard it ringing in the apartment as we fumbled with keys and locks and mufflers, heavy, fleece-lined gloves and snow jackets, our faces flushed from our icy walk across the park, our stomachs full of warm cinnamon muffins, our hearts full of hope, our heads cleared of all but optimistic thoughts, we ran to it willingly. And once again it proved, in a split second of shock and searing pain, it still had the power to blow out the sun.

A gentle-sounding man named Antonelli, of the Suffolk County Highway Patrol, said the driver of the truck had lost control on the icy curve, jumped the guardrail, and skidded into the oncoming lane. He said the eighteen-wheeler hit our little Volkswagon head-on. He said it was over so fast, she never saw it coming. He said she could not have had time to feel pain. He said the paramedics did everything they could, but it was too late. In a voice thick with pity for the woman at the other end of a line still crackling from the fierce spring storm, he said she died instantly.

Theo's knees buckled and she slid down the wall to the floor, one painful inch at a time, her legs splayed out in front of her, the phone cord bobbing above her. Officer Antonelli pressed on, letting his words sink in, understanding the mute anguish on the other end, knowing he had to go on, wanting to stop. He carefully pronounced the name and the number of the hospital where she was taken, saying a Dr. Gwen Something would await the family's instructions. He said her things would be safe with him until the family could arrange to pick them up, knowing this was premature, but also knowing from bitter experience that he could not bear to do this twice. He had no idea it was I who had taken the phone from Theo's trembling hand.

He asked if there was something he could do. He wanted to know if she had anyone else, a husband. I hung up.

After that, I ran to the intercom and begged Andy to call the doctor and come quickly and help us because Theo's eyes had rolled back and her head had pitched forward on a neck that could no longer hold it up.

I don't remember throwing the phone out the window, just shivering in the frigid air that burst through the jagged hole it left in one of the massive panes in our living room. Nor do I remember compressing my body into a smaller version of itself, curling into Theo's lap, my ear against her heart, clutching the soft black leather of the camera bag that lay inches away from us, and waiting for Andy, who would know what to do.

I can't recollect putting the film canister in my pocket, but when I found it days later in the coat I wore to the funeral, after Theo woke up, but while she still wasn't completely there, and hiding it in my closet. What I was sure of as I am now, that Claire is still alive inside.

25

Whenever I am faced with the sorrow of others, I do not offer the prospect of a happier day, as the etiquette books suggest. Instead, I wish them, simply, the passing of time. I know, through the cruel scorch of experience, that distance is the only goal in the battle with grief, the most unspeakable of pain. I know that at some point in the slow ticking of days, its knife edge begins to dull. The face that appears out of nowhere, the memories that flood into an unsuspecting moment, no longer cut as deeply. Only time can make that happen. Not the flood of condolences written in funereal black ink. Not phone calls undertaken in tones subdued by the enormity of the loss. Not a photograph taken in good times, given back as an act of kindness that shocks the heart with tangible proof that there will be no more.

I tell people I would carry them, on my shoulders if I could, over this jagged place, so they don't have to linger on the treacherous ground between death and memory, but I know they must walk every razored inch if they are ever to arrive. The journey is different for everyone. I know it is longer for people whose bags are light, who cannot stop along the way and lose themselves in the contents, who did not have the time to gather enough to sustain them, the way it is when a child or a lover is taken too soon—or, as it was for me, when a mother hasn't really had a chance to take hold, and lives in the shadowy recollections of a small boy caught in the onslaught of becoming a man, one who remembers that his heart broke long before his voice ever did, but I do not say this part. I never say this part.

*   *   *

AFTER THE ACCIDENT, Theo and I moved to the outer edges of the Incorporated Village of Amagansett, where the tidy lawns and white picket fences of its founders gave way to wild juniper, sea grass, scrub pine, and the looming glass boxes reared up like architectural driftwood on the windswept headlands, abandoned for the winter by people who had no idea what fury could lick at their foundations in the dead season of northeasters and flood tides. People who weren't very different from the way we used to be.

Theo enrolled me in a public school with floors that smelled of ammonia and wax, hallways full of banging lockers and country boys who sneaked sidelong looks at me out from under billed caps emblazoned with exotic names like *Cauliflower League*, *Potato Association* and *Future Farmers of America*. My new classmates sniffed around for signs of summer money, and eyed my tan chinos and oxford-cloth shirts with the undisguised suspicion of people who didn't waste clothes like mine on school. After a mercifully short period of cautious circling, during which I was analyzed, discussed, and dissected like the sentences on the dusty blackboard in English class, they welcomed me into their ranks with the pull-up-a-chair matter-of-factness of a Sunday supper on the firehouse lawn.

Theo found a big, sunny space on Main Street that had housed T-shirt and bathing suit store called The Beach. In its salad days it boasted a wave machine, local beauties projected on the rear wall, and well over a ton of sand and clamshells on the floor. Theo rented it from owners desperate to recoup their bet on the future of shopping barefoot. Once we cleaned out all the sand, strained it for valuables—four American Express Cards, a small diamond ring, and two ankle bracelets—Theo began work on a bigger, sunnier version of The Latest Dish, complete with a sidewalk café that ended up earning in one summer what the little Second Avenue shop earned in a whole year of grueling eight-day weeks.

Our house was a modest cedar-shingled cottage off the beaten path, weathered and substantial in an unprepossessing way, which made it all the more appealing. It was protected by a tall hedgerow and seemed even cozier by virtue of its nightly enclosure in a shawl of mist which left a damp impression on the windows as though a large animal had pressed a wet nose to the glass. The fog always seemed to burn off in the presence of one of my mother's breakfasts.

In winter, there was very little snow, only a fine, frozen drizzle whose chill was softened by the vast, undulating Atlantic lapping at the dunes just beyond the town bridge, and the house held firm against the occasional gale that blew across the eaves. In summer, the same salt-blackened shingle that kept us warm bloomed with a tumble of roses and the fat hum of bees.

We were like people you hear about on the news, living down their pasts in small towns whose citizenry haven't the slightest idea who is in their midst. If pressed, I spoke of a father I never knew, never saying the choice to know him was always mine. Theo hinted at heartbreak in terms both tragic and vague.

Mr. Kimsky became a mystery uncle in the front hall between a Victorian hall stand, courtesy of Uncle Bax, that dangled our coats and hats and mufflers from iron antlers, and a blue porcelain jardinière unearthed in some forgotten flea market that held our umbrellas and my autographed Mickey Mantle baseball bat. Neither of us could bear to reproduce the gauntlet of photographs that had graced the other foyer. No need for warnings, instructions, introductions, explanations. In the end, they did not save us. Instead, we scattered the photographs around the house as we did Claire's ashes in the garden, so we'd never again have to meet so much of her in one place.

Later, I learned Theo saved a thimbleful of ashes for the silver locket she always wore, but I didn't know it then and I'm grateful for that. Just as Theo was spared the secrets in the shoebox I held firmly in my lap the day the movers carried our possessions and our hopes out the door. The day we left, Andy gave me a picture of a Theo so swollen she seemed to shine. She appeared to be trying to smile, hold her back, hang on to his arm, and stand up all at the same time.

"That was taken the night you were born," he said. I think he started to say "I'll always remember her," but the words caught in his throat. He just nodded, touched his cap, and pressed the snapshot into my hand.

We lingered in the empty rooms for only a moment, lost in our separate versions of this final parting. Then the shutter clicked and the tall windows that offered that vast and ever-changing view of a city forest moving from verdant to flame into which we tossed our whispered hopes and deepest prayers into its deep silence, went dark. Gone now were the distant eyes of other buildings, which looked like stars when lamps were lit adding their glow to the Milky Way indigo of the New York night, never giving us a hint of what waited for us in my grandmother's rooms on the park's eastern edge.

We closed the French doors that led to the soft center of our lives— Theo's Sunday afternoons, the scattering of homework, recipes, and contact sheets, the ease of being alone together. This was the room that held the laughter of friends, the words that stitched my mothers back together and later a broken grandfather Barnaby telling us in the measured words of his own grief that his wife would withdraw her petition for my custody and would never bother us again. How ashamed he was that he did nothing to stop her, that he let her do this terrible thing to their own child.

We stood for a moment in the kitchen that held us together in spite of ourselves, its beams empty of Theo's copper, casseroles, kettles, stock pots, sauté pans, her prized poissonère. The walls were washed clean of us. But the weight of what had happened here was still outlined on the floor, the black-and-white tile darkened by the legs of the big worktable, the familiar slap of bare feet echoing on its cold surface, still redolent of the sharp smell of the cigarettes Claire begged from Suzie and thought she was smoking in secret, lost in thoughts we'd never know, rising in a tantalizing spiral up into the loft where I learned to float my dreams on the raft of my mothers' voices. Another click of the shutter, the snap of the lock, and it all went to black.

After that, we held Claire at arm's length. Our new house was not so open to the world, not so trusting. Its deep windows let in the light in slivers, as much as we could allow, eventually taking the shape of new faces, new friends for Theo, always discreet, always hopeful, never understanding that it wasn't I who held the key that kept her locked away from them. I, too, made new friends, more than a person who was accustomed to being scorned could handle in the beginning, like too many chocolates on Christmas Day. These boys did not taunt, did not laugh, did not accuse me of having two mothers to their one. They laid their lives open to me like gutted bags of potato chips and offered their fathers like second and third helpings of everything else we ate in those years of cracking voices, muscles that did not yet know their own strength, and cheeks dotted with Clearasil.

Aunt Suzie drove out for weekends in the beginning. Once she arrived in a bright red London taxicab driven by a large Englishman who resembled Henry VIII in appetite only and who managed to tickle the corners of Theo's mouth into the first traces of a smile. He told us wonderful stories of his days as a thespian and declared at least a dozen times that Aunt Suzie was "over the moon" about him. For a short time, we were filled with a noise we hadn't known was missing until we heard it again. But Theo preferred to visit Suzie in the city, where she could manage Claire's estate and they could continue the business of a photographer who had become even more important in the requiem of praise and public outpouring that follwed her death.

I came to understand Theo's solitary trips to the city were her way of expunging the past, at first to mourn, and to sift through the evidence of that part of their life that did not include me. I imagine she looked in the places her life with Claire has begun and for the meaning it still held. I suspect Theo's solitary journey toward insight included sporadic visits to a kindly Gestalt psychotherapist named Mariah Davis. I know her very private path to healing inspired in me a healthy determination to hold back something of my own. I felt these absences at first, but after a time, I looked forward with a delicious sense of freedom to shuffling between Amagansett and the rest of my extended family in South Neck.

Uncle Peter, Aunt Molly, Harry and Charlotte, and the faithful and tail-wagging Bartie and Blisset were just a short drive across the island. In the weeks following Claire's death, Theo could not bear to see Peter, so blond, so serious, so slender, and in his own talented writerly way, so like Claire. The sight of him was for her like walking on broken glass. But one day there was a phone call, then a softening and the letting down of her guard, which finally resulted in the understanding that memories can be shared and do not choose only the worthiest to whisper their comfort. Theo began to see the one who suffers most is comforted by the sorrow of all. After that, South Neck resumed its place in our lives.

Baxter and Jessica drove out one crystalline day that hinted at cotton sweaters and corn on the cob. They promised they'd be back soon, but their lives required more rigorous planning than ours. The day-to-day glue that held us together was gone; instead, infrequent visits were filled with the past tenses of people who no longer share life, but hoard it against the next conversation.

Uncle Bax and I still had our Saturdays in the city—not as often, but all the sweeter and more sacred for it. These were times when men were men, girls were banished, and the bologna sandwich was, to Theo's feigned horror, still held in the highest esteem. We talked about sex, mostly, in between polite questions from the public, who slipped quietly among the expensive ball-and-claw feet, camelbacks, and cabriole legs of Baxter's ever-changing procession of treasures. The subject took on an illicit air we both enjoyed. Years later, this was the basis for a rude joke about my inexplicable and frequent urges to have sex in dusty antiques shops.

The years passed in term papers, baseball teams, broken bones, school, unfulfilling encounters with female flesh, and part-time jobs—a month as a willing, yet hopeless assistant at The Latest Dish; a summer spent helping Aunt Suzie catalog negatives and mount a Claire Hirsh retrospective, which required I make hourly runs for Nat Shermans and black coffee; one year, I delivered Uncle Peter's paper, proudly announcing to every customer that my uncle was the editor—and she was always there.

She was with me on every one of my awkward dates, after which Harry and I discussed breasts and thighs and other female territories in terms of beachheads won in our war against virginity. And later, in the narrow Princeton dorm where Harry and I sealed our friendship in beer and widened it, much to my surprise, to include the prodigal and repentant Carl, she was there, recording posturing of boys aching to be men.

And in the final leap of exhilaration and terror at leaving home for good, shoe box on my lap, U-Haul fishtailing, she rode with me through the Holland Tunnel to West Houston Street, where Harry and I would litter a loft with broken hearts, jugs of wine, and dirty socks and I would take the first stabs at becoming a writer, I heard the soft click of her camera. I like to think she saw us in ways we couldn't see ourselves, showing us another version of the story that could be had with a minor change of angle, a different light, a little cropping.

"SHE's BEAUTIFUL. But would you go to Brooklyn for her?" Theo said when she met Annie that first time. My mother had tiptoed up behind me on Molly and Peter's lawn and asked in perfect imitation of Claire, who would have demanded proof—subway tokens, Nathan's matches, a Klein's shopping bag, something—if she'd been there herself.

"I would go to the ends of the earth," I declared, like the lovesick fool I was. How sure I was in my ability to find that place, having not the slightest idea of what it means to go there.

"Good," said Theo, "you may have to."

As it turned out, I barely got out of Queens. It was the hottest day in the hottest June ever recorded, a few scorching days into my twenty-sixth year, the kind of suffocating morning anyone with a functioning brain would spend in an icy bathtub with a cold beer. I was driving the Jeep Uncle Peter passed along to Harry and me and stuck in a ten-mile back-up on the Long Island Expressway. I was on my way to the farm for Charlotte's wedding, a garden affair the planning for which had left all the family women, serious women, women we admired, highly competent women, women who wouldn't be caught dead at a Tupperware party, hollow-eyed and sleepless with decisions. Even Theo, who had pulled off hundreds of weddings, was torn between tulips and tea roses, white chocolate ganache and coconut angel-food cake.

In its own way, the wedding had filled the big, noisy hole Harry and I left behind when we moved into the city; if it didn't make the breaking away easier, it certainly made it less noticeable. Harry and I and even Carl, who'd inherited the apartment I never stopped believing was the scene of the crime that had set our family's fate in motion, were all pressed into service, running errands, hunting down fluffy bits of things in grimy wholesale bridal shops just off Fifth Avenue in the Thirties, staying out of the way as much as possible.

During the last frenzied weeks before the wedding, we drove out to the farm only when we could assure ourselves of a good meal and a willing hand with the laundry that was piling up on our empty apartment floor. One night, the father of the bride showed up at the loft, looking haunted and desperate for masculine company, Chinese food, and conversation that did not include the word "train."

Even the bride—who had blazed an academic trail through Bennington the likes of which put Harry and me to shame, and whose courtship with the equally accomplished, well-born and somewhat dull Orson J. Potter, had led predictably to a decision of marriage—was out of her mind with wedding mania. Overnight Charlotte dissolved into a puddle of insecurities requiring hourly reassurance that she was not too fat, not too clumsy, not too ugly. She begged anyone within earshot to tell her she would not look like a giant vanilla custard on the Big Day.

I couldn't blame her. She was a big, blond, openhearted puppy who was much more at home on a soccer field or on a tennis court than in the yards of tulle and Alençon lace threatening to swallow her whole. It was my responsibility to tell her she'd be the most beautiful bride in the world, which I did as often as I could. "Such is the price of public love," she would mutter as the circus spun out of control toward its flowery, four-handkerchief conclusion.

At one point, poor Charlotte threatened to break off the engagement rather than let the bridegroom-to-be know that his mother's antique seed-pearl headdress was too tiny for her large, intelligent brow. "How could he even consider marrying someone who looks like an elephant balancing a peanut on her head?" Aunt Molly was left to explain her daughter's strange behavior to the groom's mother, who had driven all the way down from Boston to make the presentation of this treasured family heirloom.

Not even Claire was allowed to rest in peace.

"If Claire were here to take my wedding pictures," Charlotte moaned, "she wouldn't let me look grainy fat like this pretentious fop of yours."

Jess did her best to remind Charlotte that the man was fashion's latest darling and would be there as a favor; that she ought to be grateful he even entertained the idea of shooting a wedding, much less hers. The rest of us wondered what Claire would have done for her favorite niece, what witty idea she would have come up with. We played the caption game she loved so—*Two on the Aisle, Unsuspecting Groom Falls into Charlotte's Web*, among others. I know I wasn't the only one who missed her, but I kept these thoughts to myself.

Sitting in traffic gave me time to fret about how it would go between Grandma and Theo after so many bitter and silent years. My grandmother had become frail, requiring a wheelchair and a private nurse who filled her days with injections of a foul-smelling copper compound, acupuncture, and brisk rides through the park. Mary suffered from a painful form of osteoarthritis common to overly thin women, but I believed it was the weight of her deeds slowly crushing her spine. I wondered if the nurse had a formal uniform for weddings.

"What about my grandmother," Charlotte asked one afternoon.

"You will invite her to your wedding and not worry about a thing," Theo replied with no hesitation. "There are too many regrets in this family already. I don't want to add to yours. I'm a big girl, but I love you for thinking I'm not."

She never said, but I knew what price her kindness would exact.

Barnaby's job was to keep Theo and Mary apart. Still, my mother would suffer at the sight of her. I knew I would, too.

I was just beginning to realize I'd have nothing to worry about if I couldn't figure out how to get to the next exit, then over to the Northern State Parkway via Northern Boulevard. That's when I noticed the Sting Ray convertible, '65, I guessed. It was impeccably restored—navy blue, and silver, with a silver racing stripe rolling over its low-slung body. The ragtop showed new ribs through its black canvas; the metal gleamed; I wondered if the retractable headlights still worked; I'd always loved how they opened like cat's eyes in the dark. It was impossible not to stare.

"It's my father's," said the girl behind the wheel. "I'm really the MG type."

The voice was attached to a mass of rich chestnut hair, hazel eyes that glinted gold in the harsh glare, a full mouth set in a face that could have belonged to Hepburn or Grace Kelly. Tiny beads of moisture gathered on a high forehead and on her upper lip, darkening the hair she swept back with her hand. A lesser woman would have looked clammy. On her, the dampness seemed like a fine English mist. She was wearing one of those demure linen dresses that seemed to suggest more than it actually said, and from my perspective, this one suggested a body both supple and lush as it moved around gentle curves. One brown arm lightly rested on the idling wheel, long tanned legs rode the clutch. A black straw hat with an enormous brim, the kind that reveals only the wearer's eyes, lay on the seat next to her.

As always, in the presence of such beauty—such "good bones," as Aunt Jessica would say—I became acutely aware of my size and garish coloring and wished for the millionth time I was the square-jawed, Wall Street squash player she was probably engaged to and most probably on her way to meet right now at the family estate in

Old Brookville or Southampton. At that moment, I would have sold my soul to be lean and athletic, instead of six feet four inches of freckles with dubious lineage and hair the color of an overcooked carrot. The striped pants that seemed so elegant this morning were sticking to the backs of my sweaty knees, and the gray morning coat I'd folded across the backseat looked ridiculous.

"I'm a Volkswagen bus myself," I blurted, promptly wishing I hadn't. I plunged on, attempting to distance myself from this inane opening. "Where are you heading? Or should I say, not heading?" I said, nodding at the standstill traffic around us.

"To Remsenberg. My mother's getting married." At this she paused, then leaned a little closer as though to keep the other drivers from hearing. "Again."

"Me, too," I said, holding up the morning coat and shaking it at her as though she needed proof. "My cousin Charlotte in South Neck. Her first and, I sincerely hope, last. I'm concerned about the long-term implications of protracted wedding plans. The women in the family could be irreparably damaged," I said, thinking, *Can't you do better than that? You sound like the biggest twit on the planet.*

She shifted into neutral, turned toward me, placed an elbow on the driver's door and rested her chin in an open palm. She smiled with her entire face: eyes, mouth, teeth, dimples, and brows. Even her hair seemed to shake loose the husky laugh that bubbled up from somewhere I'd like to see for myself.

"I think I'm overheating," she said, letting the implication drift between our cars.

I leaned over my empty front seat, as close to the passenger door as I could without strangling myself on the shoulder harness, and responded with what I hoped would be something between a smolder and a smile.

"That's a very good start," I said.

I'M SURE I was after something considerably more temporary than this turned out to be. I can't say I ever consciously admitted it to myself at the time, but after several heated and short-lived attempts at the mysteries of relationships, all I had come to hope for in the way of love was a few sticky months of passion. While I had every indication this would be much more exciting, my history said its conclusion would be no different. Except for my initial stammering, I was generally excellent at beginnings and, some would say, bordering on brilliant at endings. It was middles I was lousy at.

Inevitably, my girlfriends got too close, asked too many questions, expected too much. Worse, they found a way to introduce me to their parents whose hospitality contained the expectation that I would soon follow suit. In the way lovers have always done, she would tell me about her childhood in a way that begged the details of my own. This was my cue to slip quietly out of view; I'd discovered a real gift for letting the other person down easily while admitting my shortcomings in a way that left no messy scenes, no guilt, no blame but my own. I wanted to be honest, but couldn't forget the time I held nothing back and fell hard, how the girl I thought I'd marry said I'd follow in my mothers' footsteps and leave her for another man.

After that, it was easier to stay in the same place with different people.

Maybe it had something to do with the temperature or the exhaust fumes from that vast parking lot the highway had become, probably a combination of oxygen loss and tar from the road surface buckling in the heat. And maybe it had nothing to do with any of these things. I held my breath, steadied my nerves, and jumped right past the beginning into the middle.

"Want to come to a wedding?"

"Shouldn't we get to know each other a little better before we consider this important step?" she flirted right back.

"If you come to Charlotte's, I'll come to your mother's," I offered, as though this were the only reasonable choice.

"And what shall I say when I call? 'Mother dear, I'm going to be just a teensy bit late, I'm going to another wedding with a man I met in a traffic jam on the Long Island Expressway'?"

"Sounds plausible."

Now there was a noisy demand from the cars behind us to fill up the three inches that had opened up in front of our bumpers. She ignored the horns with a defiant smile, knitted luxuriant brows, and considered. "Well, this *is* number four. She'll probably do it again, and I can be on time for that."

"Four?" Could there be someone worse at middles than I?

"Four," she shrugged. "Go figure."

I nosed the Jeep into the lane in front of her. Miraculously, she followed me off the expressway and followed me down side streets lined with attached two-story houses with jalousie windows over to Northern Boulevard, down to the Grand Central Parkway, around Flushing Bay and past the shuttered gas stations on the Northern State. With each exit and entrance, I checked the rearview mirror to make sure I hadn't been dreaming.

She took the turns beautifully, downshifting into them, accelerating just before coming out of the curve, smoothing out on the straights, back up into fourth gear, tailgating, teasing. She'd come alongside and drop back again, smiling as if she knew my eyes never left her. At every bend in the road, I expected her to disappear and follow whatever direction her life had been taking that morning, but she hung on. I got the feeling that she, like the secrets that had followed me at the same discreet distance for as long as I could remember, was about to overtake me.

I don't even know her name! I tapped my right turn signal and gravel flew up into the wheel wells as I pulled the Jeep into a convenience-store parking lot and braked. She pulled in behind me. We were just outside the town of Southold, where the Northern State Parkway had long since turned into the two-lane blacktop that ran past the farms and vineyards clinging to the cliffs along the Long Island Sound.

I stretched the stiffness out of my spine and opened her door, noticing her legs were even longer unfolded, and that mine were not altogether steady. "If we're going to pretend we're old friends, I should probably know your name,"

"Anna Rose Winfield Carver Childs. Mother insisted on giving me her maiden name, her favorite husband's name, *and* my father's name in that order. Rose was my grandmother."

"But you can call me Annie. Everyone does."

Then she took my hand and shook it with a firmness that was matter-of-fact, sincere, and absolutely guileless, not girlish and tentative. Long fingers. Tapered nails with tiny moons of white. A wash of pearl at the tips. A bracelet thin as a wire around a slender wrist. Skin the color of sun. Fine blond hairs scattered along bone. She held my hand for a heartbeat longer than necessary, increasing the pressure slightly, then cupped mine with the other mine another in a gesture that promised everything, guaranteed nothing. It was the sexiest handshake ever recorded.

"William Bouvier-Hirsh," I said, reeling a little from the effect it had on me. "I prefer Will, but I'm afraid it's Willy today.

"Willy Today," she said, in mock seriousness. "That's a nice solid Native American name. Any relation to the Tomorrows? Or the Yesterdays?" She grinned, softening the first of many revelatory moments that would not be as easy as I made them look.

"My uncle's farm is just down the road. Would you like a Coke or something cold before we take the plunge into my crazy family?"

"Let's wait for champagne," she said, as though she already knew we'd have something to celebrate.

26

She didn't tell me what was wrong the morning after Charlotte's wedding when she wandered pale and troubled into the kitchen and found me leaning against the back door watching the sunrise through the screen. I didn't ask what had torn her from her bed, or which private anguish had shaken her out of her slumber, nor did I ask what dream could have raised its voice loudly enough to steal her bear's capacity for sleep, only that she dismiss these concerns to greet my own news of Annie with the reverence and wonder reserved for sons on such occasions.

She brewed a pot of strong, chicory-laced coffee, laid a tired cheek in her hand, and listened as I recounted the miracle of Annie and my night in the dunes. I told her how we leaned against a cushion of sand and found the Big Dipper, and after that, the more elusive Little. I told her how we traced the constellations; our fingers entwined, and gave credit to stiff necks, tuna sandwiches, and all those school trips to the Hayden Planetarium. I rambled on about how we lost all sense of time, our shoes, and two glasses of champagne, about Annie's whispered phone call to her mother from Aunt Molly's sewing room to apologize for not having arrived, trying to sound sincere as she explained about traffic on the Expressway and a circuitous detour. She wasn't really lying, just selectively telling the truth, promising to get there no matter how late. All of it forgotten in our moonlit dune as we told the stories of our lives in one long drink of history that did nothing to quench the need to know more, and went about the business of falling in love in the presence of skittering crabs and an ocean that slumbered before us, having heard it all before.

The rising sun warmed the memory of this night, not even two hours old, and I told Theo how I knew this would happen the minute I saw Annie in the car next to mine, how she shook my hand and called me Willy Today. How I knew she'd always be my friend, even when she became my lover.

The dark smell of the French roast seemed to revive her. "Your grandma Doris called you Willy Two Squaws. Remember?" I remembered very well.

"That's how it was with us," she said. "We talked all night, your mother and I. The Bouvier-Hirshes don't just fall in love. They talk themselves into it. Of course, in our case, food was involved. It always was. Hot dogs. We ate so many, we got sick."

"I told her about Claire," I said. "I don't know why."

"I do," she said, rising to make us omelets. That morning I saw only my question and how much was at stake in her answer; I would not remember how hard she worked at the simple act of stretching for the familiar oval pan dangling on its hook until much later.

"You told her your secrets because you wanted her to fall in love with the right version of you. If she's going to break your heart and betray your trust, it's better now," Theo said, never once crying out or ruining my happiness with what she knew.

A YEAR LATER, I sold my first story and broke all speed records driving out to the cottage, bursting with confidence and my first advance check. Grandiose dreams of Round Tables, Paris cafés and running bulls danced before me. Uncle Peter raced to Amagansett with a bottle of Dom Pérignon balanced on his lap. Again I did not comment on how thin my mother had become or ask why she placed her own portion of smoked-chicken salad on my plate and sipped the champagne instead.

"My son, the writer," she said, raising her glass to me and beaming with pride. I could see she wasn't well, but she offered nothing and I dragged out the old saw about never being too rich or too thin.

"I knew you could do it," boasted Uncle Peter, who had read every word I'd written since college, as well as the sizable collection of rejection slips I'd amassed with a certain masochistic swagger. He never once applied empty avuncular praise or missed an opportunity to show me how I could be better, no matter how close to a deadline he was himself. I wondered if he secretly wished that I was Harry, whose affinity for words extended only to pretentious chunks of Latin legalese and the "net nets" and "bottom lines" of the business slang Uncle Peter believed was the downfall of civilization.

"Why can't an executive conjugate the verb 'to speak' like everybody else? What the hell is 'interface?'" Uncle Peter's love of language was lost on the boisterous adults his children had become. Harry, with his steady stream of blondes and schemes of killings in the corporate jungle, and Charlotte, with her horses, her Labs, and a cherubic baby, called Tyler, the first of what would be her own noisy brood, had no time for lingering over ideas.

"Claire would have been so proud," Peter said.

"Just working too hard," Theo said when I finally noticed the twin smudges that appeared not to be affected by any amount of sleep. Nor did she mention any need for our concern when, after months of promises to visit and excuses for not coming, Annie and I rushed out Amagansett to tell her we'd put an end to the senseless commuting between Annie's Gramercy Park studio and the loft where I had become Harry's occasional guest who paid half the rent. She simply threw herself into the wedding plans with the selflessness of a mother and the creativity of a caterer who has just been given the assignment of a lifetime.

"I wish Doris could have been here to see you get married," Theo said that spring, when I joked about how out of her element my grandmother would have been in the old clapboard church with its ancient wisteria thick as arms, its gravestones smooth with salt and time. A striped tent transformed our garden and my mother's staff bustled even more furiously than usual in the knowledge that they were working for the boss's son, circulating their trays to guests in picture hats and summer blazers. As always, Jessica and Baxter rode the fierce currents of their lives with a grace few could carry off. Harry selected a particularly stunning blonde for the occasion and Charlotte had her hands full between Sarah, a bundle of white pique and daisies, and young Ty in short pants, deceptively angelic toddling across the lawn, dragging the ring bearer's pillow behind him.

"Not a love bead in sight," Theo said into the quiet of the last moments before the ceremony.

There was irony in the way Carl turned out to be what his family feared most, especially today, making a fool of himself over someone named Derrick. I remembered the first time I heard the word "queer," Carl's voice wavering the night he told me he was gay, fully expecting my revenge after so many years. "How could I *not* understand?" I'd said, more shocked and pleased at my easy acceptance than he.

Theo was still thinking of Doris, unable to speak of Claire.

"Being different was your grandmother's way of belonging," she said. "Roy always knew it. So did I."

Suddenly I felt ten again, able to tell her everything.

"I'm afraid of other women."

"Oh, honey, you'll be fine. I think every man is afraid he'll be unfaithful. That's what keeps things interesting."

"I don't mean me."

For as long as I could remember, I'd looked over my shoulder, first at the pretty cheerleaders in high school, then at the beautiful seniors lounging in the sorority house, teasing their younger sisters with secrets they had yet to learn. I couldn't imagine why other men didn't see fierce competition in the smug seductiveness of their ways. I couldn't imagine the object of my affection preferring my large, inhospitable body and its sweaty urgency to what was already familiar. I had never told anyone this. I lived in dread of the day Annie would meet her Claire.

"Annie likes men, sweetheart. And even better, she loves *you*," Theo said firmly, as she pulled me close and wrapped me in one last hug.

"You were married once," I mumbled, trying not to squeeze her too hard, reminding myself that I was now so much bigger than she. "What if she meets the right girl?"

"It doesn't happen that way, my darling boy. It doesn't matter who's attracted to Annie. It's Annie who has to be attracted back. And Annie is a man's woman, your woman, the woman you're marrying today. She loves you, Willy Wonka. She's not a lesbian."

"How do you know?" I wanted a solemn oath, a mother's guarantee.

She laughed. "Trust me. I just do."

IT WAS JUST before her sixtieth birthday. She and "a friend" (which was how we referred to the women with whom she occasionally spent time, and with whom she shared the part of her that still cried out for Claire), a pediatrician named Louisa who plainly adored her, were planning a week in London. Theo was looking forward to her *cook's tour* of all the new brasseries and bistros and exciting new restaurants that had sprung up in that city's restaurant renaissance.

We were all in the garden, lazy and full of one of Theo's more exceptional lunches, which even she seemed to enjoy more than usual, our torpor heightened by the delicious, sleep-inducing Merlot she had been saving for just this day. I sprawled on the grass, feeling the sun on my city face. Theo arranged herself on the English garden bench in the slightly eccentric half-lotus she'd inherited from Claire; a position she claimed was the only one that eased her stiff back. We both gazed in utter contentment at Annie, whose bare feet were tucked up under her on the dark green wicker swing, dozing against the cotton quilt Theo had gently placed under her head, a tiny mouth on each breast as our twins took their lunch in the soft afternoon.

In the presence of such a perfect moment, I left Theo's thoughts undisturbed, hoping to make her smile with my own.

"What man can say he had a mother who could explain what fatherhood is really like, being so close and yet feeling so left out?" I remembered an afternoon in the darkroom when Claire told me stories of my infancy, the shock of my infant's need for Theo, and her warnings that I, too, would be the victim of nature's preference for the mother. I felt something sharp in the vicinity of my heart at the sight of Annie nursing our new babies and thought, *Is this how it was for her?*

"I'll never forget coming home the day she tried to nurse you," said Theo laughing quietly, not wanting to disturb the dozing family. "You were both crying. I didn't know which one of you to comfort."

I wanted to blurt it right out. I wanted to say, *I'm afraid you're dying.* But this was a moment for looking back and looking ahead; not for seeing the present danger. We both knew the truth would not be told that day. We spoke of other things.

After their feeding, Annie put the twins down in the study just off the garden on the shady side of the house, where we'd hear them if they woke up. When she returned, the talk moved again to London.

"Louisa's running around like a crazy person getting gallery schedules and theater tickets, but I said, 'Lou, don't ask me which museum has which Old Master. Ask me which chef does Dover sole in the most interesting way and now we're cooking." She chattered on about the trip with such obvious relish, such anticipation, I couldn't bear to cloud her plans and this day with my growing concern. I said nothing.

ANNIE PUSHED. "She's too thin."

"She's waited all her life for someone to say that," I cracked, not wanting to acknowledge her meaning.

"I'm serious. I don't think she's well. Promise you'll talk to her, get her to go for a checkup."

I felt something familiar uncoil.

"I promise," I said.

"If you don't, I will," warned Annie, who walked right into things with a courage I often envied, and sometimes resented.

Theo told me a few weeks later, when she could avoid it no more, when she was sure it had come back. She had returned from London with Louisa, flushed and full of presents and funny stories and long, knowing silences, after she had traveled to the private part of herself that needed to be in another city in order to say good-bye, when the chemo bared the first patch of skin in her scalp, when she could escape the truth no longer. She told me on that same garden bench and I will always remember it as the sound of a curled yellow leaf crackling against metal, dry and hollow.

"I wanted to tell you, but there was no right time," she said, her voice full of sadness, eyes not meeting mine. "Your wonderful new job. Annie. The twins. You were so happy, so busy with life. I thought it was gone. There was a good chance the radiation had gotten it all. I know I should have told you sooner."

At first, she insisted on overseeing what she still modestly called the store. Under her guidance, The Latest Dish had grown to supermarket size, rambling in and out of the adjoining buildings she'd added over the years. Like good, brokenhearted friends, the staff kept their tears to themselves during her increasingly infrequent visits. Later, she stayed at home and worked on the cookbooks that gave her a certain celebrity, along with regular royalty checks. When she could no longer move freely between kitchen and study, she hired a chef to test her recipes while she directed from a comfortable chair.

Like every family before us, we denied the presence of death with a gaiety that left us gasping. Theo wound silk around her smooth head and piled scrawny arms with bracelets. She wore sweeping jewel-colored skirts, which never gave away the bones that had begun to jut beneath her clothes' deceptive fullness, and took her place in the heart of the family that had moved to Molly's kitchen from her own. Over the course of a few short months, she celebrated the children's birthdays with a extravagantly gooey cakes and homemade ice cream. She presided over a noisy cocktail party for Suzie and an elegant gathering for Baxter and Jess, whose marriage had inexplicably survived their curious habits for thirty years.

She did her best to sparkle at the family's annual Fourth of July picnic and badminton tournament. She dressed in billowing velvet and antique lace for the long, dark autumn brunches she loved best; and finally, she struggled, determined as a field marshal, to sit up without assistance at a groaning Thanksgiving table. No one who posed on the porch that day in the bright cold light of encroaching winter could shake off the feeling that this Thanksgiving would be her last, least of all the photographer, who fooled no one with his attempt to hide his grief behind Claire's old Leica.

The previous summer, Annie and I moved to a sprawling rent-stabilized apartment on Gramercy Park, which came with a key to the park, and a pretty rooftop terrace we imagined would be an outdoor playpen for the twins. My job as Assistant Arts Editor was a purposeful stride across the lower reaches of Fifth Avenue, and I could return home on some pretext or another—forgotten notes, a change of shoes, a phone number, the yen to pass on the lunchtime gossip and chili at Max's—just to make sure that I still had a family, that they had not been spirited away while I was gone. It was a home we had been slowly filling up with treasures from Baxter's "sources," out-of-the-way auctions and antique markets in small towns as far from New York as their prices. Baxter loved leading us to out-of-the-way auctions and we spent many happy hours looking for the perfect quilt or umbrella stand or bullet-glass cabinet to keep Claire's antique toys out of harm's way until the girls were big enough to handle them.

In early December, when Theo could no longer muster the strength or the bravado to come to us, we packed up and moved in with her. Annie looked after Theo and the babies and the house with the generosity of spirit and tenderness usually reserved for blood. Having convinced my new boss that technology and the opportunity to spend this precious time with my mother would not hamper my productivity; I drove the ninety miles to the city three times a week,

Relieved I didn't have to quit, a decision I was terrified of but prepared to make, we made a temporary nursery out of my old room, took the larger one adjoining it as sleeping quarters and my temporary office, and carried Theo's bed downstairs, next to the window that looked out on the garden. We piled the bed high with needlepoint cushions, Victorian shawls, soft quilts, and snowy pillows from the vast collection of antique linens Aunt Jess could not resisting adding to with every visit to her old friend. From this perch, Theo directed us in the planting of bulbs and the laying of mulch, and talked of cutting kitchen herbs come spring.

We invited everyone to Amagansett for Christmas breakfast and the opening of presents as early as possible. We asked everyone to come the night before and wear pajamas because we knew that Theo would tire quickly if she tried to dress. I shopped and Annie baked.

Christmas Eve, like intruders who do not wish to arouse the slumbering tenants, we decorated the blue spruce outside Theo's window, and filled its arms with angels and candy canes and the tiny fairy lights she loved. While she slept, we surrounded her with presents so she could wake up inside Christmas.

When she awoke the next morning, our small family was gathered around her. As usual, Suzie, in a silver dressing gown straight out of *Sunset Boulevard,* elicited one of Theo's rare smiles and took the prize for the most interesting interpretation of pajamas. Thad's flannel pajamas sported fifties rodeo cowboys, button flap and all. Peter and Molly were wrapped in Stewart plaid, and Jessica and Baxter were elegant in velvet slippers and silk foulard that could have just as easily gone out to dinner. Theo herself wore a bottle green silk nightgown and the matching kimono Annie had placed within reach the night before.

None of this halted the steady progress of pain across her features or the bodily wasting that threatened to engulf her spirit but never did. I wondered which is worse, the terrible shock of the telephone, or watching someone you love disappear. Is it better to say good-bye or to wish you had, to know there was no pain or to see there is too much?

She drifted in and out of a narcotic haze. Most of the time, she was somewhere else, her voice a running commentary on what only she could see. I imagined she stood with one foot on the earth, while the other was already firmly planted in ether; not yet ready to make the leap. Claire was there, I know, just as she was the day she left us, in her torn jeans and peach mohair sweater, encouraging Theo to take her time, to leave nothing undone, so they could take up where they left off so long ago. One morning she surprised me with the clarity of someone who wakes up after years in a coma.

"Your grandmother never saw what she had; only what she lost. Because of that, she lost everything," she said, breaking the years of silence she had kept on this subject. Her voice was tinged with regret and an understanding I never suspected was there.

I told her I used to wish Claire would turn into a man, so I'd have a father. "I used to think the accident was God's way of punishing me."

"I would have told you if you had asked," Theo said.

"If I knew who he was, then I'd have to ask him why, why he chose not to see me grow up. I guess it was easier to be left by someone you don't know."

It would serve no purpose to tell her how I had longed for this man, how much it hurt to see other boys take this luxury for granted.

Theo motioned for me to prop up the pillow, and waved away my offer of another dose of the pain killer I had been shown how to give her. I could see she wanted to be present for me. She remained still for several moments, and gathered her strength.

"She wanted to have you so badly, she would have done anything, but she couldn't. When she suggested we have a baby, I thought she was crazy at first. But I knew it wasn't a request, it was a *term*. I loved her, so I agreed—but only after we almost broke up over it and I did some soul-searching and decided I wanted you, too."

She looked beyond me at the ghosts around her. "I served her baby food for dessert, as a way of announcing my decision. Puréed apricots."

"It wasn't enough for her to be your adoptive mother, even if the court would let such an adoption take place, which was unheard of at that time. She wanted to be your real family, the next best thing to being your mother. Technically, I suppose, she was your aunt."

There was nothing in that room except Theo's voice, struggling back to me from where she was going. I wanted to speak, but didn't dare for fear of exhausting her before she finished.

"Peter and Molly hadn't moved to the farm yet. They were living in the Village, in a tiny apartment that was really too small for two people, much less three. I don't think Harry was even an idea then. Or maybe he was inspired by the idea of you."

"I went with Claire because I knew they would reject her crazy plan and I wanted to be there to pick up the pieces. Molly and I sat in a kitchen that wasn't even big enough to change your mind in while Claire asked Peter to donate his sperm. She met every one of his objections with a good reason—why you should have two sets of grandparents, two sets of aunts and uncles and cousins, what steps we could take to make sure everyone was protected, who should know and who shouldn't, right down to your legal name. She wanted to see herself in you, and she wanted you to see yourself in her. Uncle Peter was the closest she could come. In the end, he agreed. He even convinced Molly, who took a lot longer."

She closed her eyes and, after a few minutes, went on.

"We decided only Molly and I and Claire and Peter could know the truth. Peter signed a document saying he would waive all legal rights to paternity and gave Claire the authorization to adopt you, which she'd planned to do when you were older and could speak for yourself, but never . . ." In pain now, Theo shifted on the pillow. "There was no time."

"We celebrated with lunch in one of those charming little basement restaurants on Waverly Place. It's gone now."

"Why didn't he ever tell me?"

"He would have if you had asked. Any of us would have, but you didn't ask, and we respected that. While Peter was waiting, he answered your second question first by doing everything a father would do."

"'Why weren't you there?' being that question," I said, and she nodded.

"He was always there. You know, your grandmother didn't just drop the case after Claire died. Peter forced her to. He threatened he would make his secret public, seek custody as the biological father, and turn you right back over to me. He warned she'd never see you again if she pursued it. He asked her if she wanted to add a grandson to a son and a daughter who were gone forever. I know. I went with him that day. She had no choice.

"He blames himself for not threatening her sooner, before Claire had to come to him on that terrible icy day. I told him you would have forgiven him, as I have, if you knew. No one is to blame for that. Except God."

"When the twins were born, I thought it confirmed what I had always suspected.".

Theo smiled. "Baxter."

"I suppose I've always wanted it to be him," I said.

"Claire and Roland weren't identical like Jennifer and Brooke. They were fraternal twins, even though they looked so much alike. Roland was carefree, a little reckless. Claire was dark to his light. When he died she had to be coaxed to live."

"She was in the car that day, with Roland. They were on their way to a party, laughing, singing with the radio. That's why it was so hard for her, why she rarely spoke of him."

Theo mustered the last bit of energy. "I've always believed labels were overrated. Brother, sister, husband, wife, mother, son, lover, friend, uncle, father, grandmother. "He loves you very much, Willy."

IT WAS RAINING the next day, a steady sloshing unusual for January. The deep, earthy smell of it clung to the sill, promising something beyond the ice-bound cottage and the slow dying of my mother. I held her hand, nails waxen and crisscrossed with ridges, the skin papery, a sickly yellow against my own meaty pink, marked by the nicks and pings of a life that continued beyond this room, my gold wedding band loudly proclaiming all I had to live for. It was unfair that I looked so obscenely healthy in the presence of so much frailty, such bone-chilling cold.

"One afternoon," I said, "on my way back to school after lunch, I met a man named Mr. Cosmopoulos just outside the shop. He was the most interesting person I'd ever met and he called me mister, even though I was only nine. When I told him my mothers were lesbians, he said he thought I was Greek, from the island of Lesbos. He lived with his friend Shorty, who had been injured in the Korean War and who loved your cooking, which is why Mr. C. was near the store the day I met him." I paused to remember that booming voice behind me, how frightened I was, how grown-up I felt.

"After we became friends, I realized he had no money and I got you to give me the food. I always got extra for Mr. Cosmopoulos—I pretended it was for me and some new school friend you wanted to believe I had."

"Mr. Cosmopoulos wasn't really homeless the way people are now. He and Shorty lived in an abandoned tunnel under Twenty-ninth Street with a lamp and a hot plate and a secondhand cot and pillowcases made of shirts with the arms tied. They had a neighbor named Thelma who pretended she had food and invited us to a make-believe dinner, which really annoyed Shorty. That's where I went when I ran away. That's why the police couldn't find me. I was underground."

"Did he give you the Purple Heart?" she asked.

I shook my head. "No, Shorty did. He pinned it to my jacket the day I left. Mr. C. said Shorty didn't need it anymore. Shorty told him to tell me I had earned it for knowing when to run away and when to fight. Shorty wasn't good at saying good-bye either."

She closed her eyes and I waited, willing myself not to fall apart before I was finished. When I felt a light touch on my arm, I continued. "Mr. C. had a son in Hoboken who hadn't seen him in years."

"He'd walked me all the way home the day poor Andy almost fainted at the sight of me in the lobby. He said he was going to go visit him, maybe pick up where they left off. I think he figured his son might have missed him as much as I missed not knowing my father."

"I looked for him many times, but I never saw him again. I like to think he's with his son in New Jersey somewhere and that I had something to do with it."

She leaned as close to me as she could.

"I'm going to miss that good heart of yours."

THAT NIGHT she said good-bye instead of her usual good night. Annie and I found her the next morning, sleeping on her right side, her left arm extended toward the window as if she were reaching for something, as if someone had said, "come take my hand." A faint smile at the corners of her mouth said there was no pain. I touched the pale skin of her eyelids and before drawing them closed, I held the brilliant, bottomless green gaze to the place in my brain that remembers such things as the color of a mother's eyes.

She was gone. The boy who had too many mothers is now the man who has none.

I sit in Theo 's chair, where she invented the menus that would help people remember what certain moments in their lives tasted like, where she imagined combinations of foods and flavors unheard of until she suggested them. And I think of Claire. "Cropping," she reminds me; "what's left out is just as important as what's showing."

The Sunday paper is open to the obituaries and I am looking for important clues in the terse announcements. The house, still alive with her, pulses around me as I struggle to say everything and achieve nothing. I wonder why no one in this week's worth of bereaved strangers has had the pluck to tell the truth—"Dad just wasn't the same after Ma died," or "Our beloved son, Rocco, died cruelly of AIDS and left a lover who now questions the value of getting up in the morning"—instead of the utterances of family "spokespersons" and "undisclosed" causes of death and the long lists of "survived-by's" I see before me. I wonder how people can bear to use the word "survive." Isn't there something more accurate? Getting by. Still breathing. Coping.

I think of Mr. Kimsky and the shadow Claire left in, but didn't explain. I think of the words that cannot be spoken in the presence of strangers who pick up this particular edition on an abandoned subway seat or use it to wrap the good crystal for the movers, stuff in the path of a draft. Suddenly I am comforted in the precise language of a *New York Times* obituary, the euphemisms of mourning, and I, too, choose familiar phrases that do not give away what their authors really feel. No need to rake the heart with an unexpected clipping tucked into a condolence note by a distant and well-meaning friend. No need to say the words that have the power to open the wound on a day that isn't as raw as this one. No need to say what cannot be said. No use trying.

I run my hand over the patina of her desk and feel that peculiar combination of grooves worn by the way Theo worried an idea, and I think of Claire's heel marks on the stool she used in her darkroom. I think of the maimed bodies of pencils, chewed victims of my struggle with a story; of how I love to cook; of how I am funniest when I feel pain; of how I *see* into pictures. And, no matter what I've been told to the contrary, when Annie and I go to a party and she is pursued by a new friend and they punctuate their courtship with the light touching of fingers, whispered talk, secrets, plans, laughter low and secretive, and the urgent chatter of people filling in their histories up to the happy juncture of their association, I am not entirely unaware of the possibilities and still believe a woman could steal Annie away at any second.

Peter knocks quietly and approaches the desk, laying a gentle pressure on my shoulder. "It's time to go," he says. Everything I would expect from a father and far more than I would dare ask is in his eyes, sharing a place with his own sorrow. I run my finger around the cool surface of the Purple Heart in my pocket that I will place in Theo's casket, next to the tiny silver locket. Two hearts now one. I will do this for Claire as well as for me after every one else has whispered their good-byes. Peter fights his own grief for the sake of mine and I wonder how I could not have seen. He offers an arm and I accept, saying nothing of what I know.

As we walk out into a room that at first seems too sunny for this day, and into the wave of sorrow that breaks over me in the faces of our family, her friends, in my wife who loved my mother with a fierce loyalty never inspired by her own and who now beams this strength to me, I see why.

My beautiful twin girls, born together from two different eggs dropped mysteriously and simultaneously into our lives, one pale and blond, reserved, even in play, the other showing all the signs of red, already reaching for the brightest colors, look up from their game and smile.

One called Theo. The other, Claire.

"We'll be going home soon," I say, and they gurgle their fat content.

ACKNOWLEDGMENTS

I am grateful to Jane Kirkwood for her generous heart and gorgeous cover design for this special edition. Jane Krensky and Peggy Tourje continue to set the standard for what all loving families should be. Many thanks to Francesca Costanzo for her careful reading and to Michael Clancy who knows why. I salute the Mason family and the many readers who have shared their personal stories of struggle and joy; I have been enriched by all of you.

Cover design and author photograph by Jane Kirkwood

J ax **Peters Lowell** is a recipient of the Leeway Foundation Transformation Award for fiction and poetry. This, her first novel, was a Barnes & Noble *Discover Great New Writers* book. It was adapted for film by Anne Meredith, and was the inspiration for a segment of the Emmy Award winning HBO special *If These Walls Could Talk. Mothers* was cited in the William Mitchell Law Review and served as a study guide in queer studies programs. Her poems have appeared in many journals, including *POETRY EAST, The Pinch, Alimentum* and the Iowa University Journal, *An Examined Life,* and have been honored at East End Arts on Long Island. She has recently completed a memoir, *An Early Winter,* and is well known for her bestselling books on the gluten-free life. She lives in Philadelphia.

CPSIA information can be obtained at www.ICGtesting.com
Printed in the USA
BVOW01s1649010514

352279BV00001B/33/P